Hidden Rebel

Changed Heart Series #3

Michelle Janene

Hidden Rebel

Changed Heart Series #3

Michelle Janene

STRONG TOWER
PRESS

Sacramento

Strong Tower Press

Sacramento, CA USA

strongtowerpress.com

Publishers note: This is a work of fiction.

Names, characters, places and incidents are either products of the author's imagination or used factiously. All characters are fictional, and any similarity to people living or dead is entirely coincidental.

Editor: Lesley Ann McDaniel

Cover art: by D's Concepts and Designs

breaks: Lighted Sword: image # 42422439 idimair, Map Font Underworld by hmeneses

Cover: Copyright: <a href='https://www.123rf.com/profile_captblack76'>captblack76 / 123RF Stock Photo</a>

Scripture quoted or paraphrased from Geneva Bible ©1599

A God-given love of story telling - check

The cheering of family - check

The refining and polishing help of sisters - check

Readers' praise - check

Another book launched into the world.

Woo-hoo!

I am BLESSED!

KINGDOM OF
VERONIA
PLEASANT LOCH
DUSKMOOR RIVER
BRANDY RIVER
FISH RIVER
SIMMERING TIDES

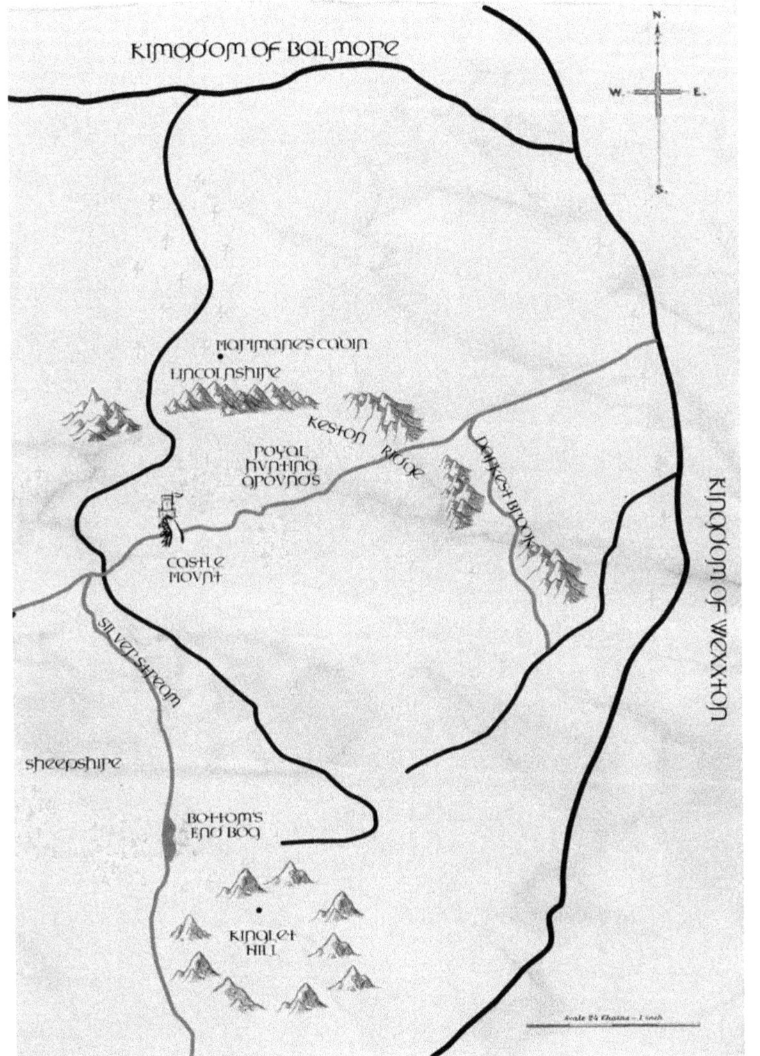

KINGDOM OF BALMORE
N.
W. E.
S.
Marimane's Cabin
Lincolnshire
Keston Ridge
Royal Hunting Grounds
Darkest Blacke
Castle Mount
Kingdom of Wexxton
Silver Stream
Sheepshire
Bottom's End Bog
Kinglet Hill
Scale 24 Chains = 1 inch

Preface

A lone warrior stumbled into the royal hunting grounds of a distant kingdom. The castle of Veronia's king peeked through the dense foliage. But the sun lay nearly spent. Best to rest now and continue in the morn. Come the first rays of light the foreign warrior would finish the distance to the prized destination, win the king's favor, and learn of the weapon to free a kingdom. On the morrow, all would be right again. On the morrow.

Chapter 1

"Please Father. You promised as soon as you returned we could go. Please, can we go today?" The early morning breeze snaking over the high curtain-walls toyed with Wyatt's curls.

Edmund sighed, crossed his arms, and tapped his foot on the paving stones as he looked at his ten-year-old son—the very image of his mother, God rest her soul. His blond curly hair shook in his excitement like a nest of wiggling worms.

"Wyatt, I know I promised to take you on a hunt when I returned —"

"Yes, Father—my first hunt. You gave me this new bow so we could go together."

Edmund sighed again. Wyatt's enthusiasm drew its energy from his very bones. His pleas started at the breaking of the fast and now continued though it was well after the midday meal. "Wyatt, son, I only arrived a few hours ago—"

"But you returned home last night. You slept well—Winslow said so. Please Father, you promised."

"I will keep my promise, son, you know I will. Must I keep it this particular day? I need to meet with Winslow and see all that has transpired in the kingdom in my absence. You are important, son, but I have our people to consider as well."

Wyatt kicked the ground in frustration. "You were gone an entire month."

"A month spent far to the west crushing marauders from the sea attacking our citizens. I must see to the needs of all my people."

"They always come before me."

"They are your people as well, Wyatt. You are prince of Veronia. You must care for them more than yourself."

"But Eric is older. He will be king next."

Edmund knelt to look at the boy eye-to-eye. "Oh Wyatt, you are my son, and a son of the king must be in the business of caring for the people no matter the crown he wears."

A tear trickled down his cheek. "But you promised. I have waited thirty-three days."

Edmund stood and grasped the back of his own neck with a firm hold and attempted to work lose the knot growing there. *Lord, help me. I can no more refuse the lad than I could his mother. How can I balance the needs of this kingdom and the hearts of my children?*

The disappointed look dragging at Wyatt's lips and the pooling tears moved Edmund to want to scale the castle itself to give him whatever he wanted. Mayhaps it was because Wyatt never knew the mother he so resembled. She died bringing him into the world. No, it was because he was the spitting image of Lady Jocelyn that tore so at his heart.

"Please Father…" Wyatt pleaded again bringing him back to the present.

He cast his eyes to the sky to judge the hour. If he took the lad now it would be over before supper. He could return to his work uninterrupted for several days.

"Majesty. An urgent matter has arrived at your gate."

Edmund turned to look on his best friend and thane, Hawkins. His broad shoulders were squared and his light colored brows pulled tightly together.

"What news?"

"Sir Charles and three knights have arrived in haste from Kirkshire. They bear news of trouble on the border with Wexxton."

Humph! Wyatt kicked the ground hard and ran off.

Edmund took a step to chase after him but turned to Hawk with a groan.

Hawk raised a brow.

"I promised the lad when I gave him the bow on his birthday last month I would take him on his first hunt."

"But we were needed in the west, and now that you have returned there are new matters to attend. It cannot always be easy being the king's son."

"No it is not, but the boy needs to learn there are more important matters than his first adventure into manhood." Edmund worked at the aching knot again. "Tell me more of what news Charles and his men bring."

They turned and crossed the inner ward to enter the small hall. "There have been raids of a sort in Kirkshire. No one has been harmed, so I have allowed the men to freshen as they requested. Winslow is seeing they are made comfortable in rooms above the great hall. They will join us before supper and tell us of all they came to report." Hawkins paused. "Ed you look tired."

A weak smile pulled at his lips. No one in all the kingdom would dare address him so informally—except this man. "I am tired, Hawk." He motioned toward the study at the far right of the room and Hawk followed with an easy swagger. "Veronia has known peace since the time of our grandfathers' fathers."

"But peace cannot last forever." They entered the study and Hawk took a chair in front of his desk.

"No, there will always be some upstart who wishes to challenge our mettle." Edmund worked at the knot in his neck again. "But must they all seek to test us at once?"

"These raiders Charles brings word of are behaving in an odd manner. He was not able to explain to me fully, but they don't appear to want a direct conflict with us."

"Then whatever do they want?"

"I can't rightly say, Ed, but you know Charles. He is seasoned by years of great wisdom and he can well discern the times to act from those where one waits to gather information."

"He is of the frame of mind to wait on this occasion."

"It would seem as such."

Hawk stood to leave. "I am sure you have much to attend before Charles comes with his report."

"Aye, until then." Edmund turned to the mound of parchments on his desk. How could such a pile form in so little a span of time? He worked at the knot.

Chapter 2

The bells for the evening meal tolled, startling Edmund from his work. He expected to meet with Charles before now. Was this urgent business or not? He straightened, rolling back his shoulders. He wondered which creaked more, his overworked body or the chair upon which he sat. Edmund stood, reaching his hands high above his head in a much-needed stretch and walked to the door.

"Charles!" Edmund took long strides across the room to greet him.

"Your Majesty." Charles bowed with a wide grin.

"Oh, has your time under Lord Radford forced you to be so formal, old friend?"

"I was trying to be a proper example to the younger men," Charles stammered as Edmund embraced him in a mighty bear hug.

After a sound thumping to his friend's back, Edmund released him. Charles bore a relaxed countenance, which further frustrated Edmund. "Please introduce me to your men, Charles, so we can get to the matter of your urgent visit."

"Aye, Majesty." Charles introduced each for Edmund to acknowledge.

When the formalities were complete, Edmund turned back to Charles. "Pray tell me the news you bring from the east, my friend."

Charles opened his mouth, but several stomachs rumbled loudly drawing everyone's attention. The knights' cheeks pinked in an unflattering way adding to their embarrassment.

"Forgive me, brave knights. You have traveled far and fast, and without a woman in my home to aid me, I have forgotten all manners. Please come, eat and share in a cup of friendship. We can talk of border matters as you take your fill." Edmund made a broad sweep of his arm inviting the men to his boards. When they were seated, several serving maids appeared from the kitchen and placed trays before them.

Edmund's and Hawk's sons soon joined Charles and his men as they partook in the sumptuous meal of roasted fowl and dark bread. Edmund tried more than once to turn the talk to the purpose of their visit, but Charles held their conversation to lighthearted banter of family and old friends.

Wyatt fidgeted at the end of high table where he picked at his food. Edmund sat in the center asking after Charles' children when feet shuffled up behind him. Wyatt's hand came to rest on his shoulder and Edmund frowned.

"The meal has yet to be cleared, my son. What is so urgent you must interrupt the conversation with my guests?"

"May we go tomorrow, Father?" the lad whined.

"Son, I have yet to learn the nature of the situation in the west—"

"But Father."

"Wy-Wy, stop whimpering!" his brother snapped from Edmund's right.

"Eric." The king scowled at his eldest.

"Your Majesty, please excuse me for being so bold, but our news will be delivered this night and may not warrant your immediate attention."

"Thank you Charles. I promised my son last month to take him on his first hunt. Then I became entangled in matters of the kingdom."

Charles nodded as an eager grin filled his face. "Oh, a good hunt sounds splendid, Sire. I would relish the opportunity to hunt in the king's forest once more. We could act as the prince's guard if you are unavailable."

Wyatt bounced like an untrained pup. "Oh, yes, Father, may I go with Sir Charles, please?"

Edmund sat torn between the freeing offer and the desire to accompany Wyatt on this grand new adventure. His eyes drifted between them. As always his decision held an unending pull between duty and family. Wyatt's final plea loosed Edmund's head in a reluctant nod.

"Thank you, Sir Charles. What time do we leave, sir?" Wyatt wiggled from foot to foot.

Charles stroked his rough, scarred chin thoughtfully, "Well, Your Highness, the best game is always brought down around dawn. I should think we might want to leave before first light."

"Yes, sir. I will be ready before the sun is awake." Wyatt spun on his heels and dashed across the room.

"Wy-Wy!" Eric snapped before Wyatt had traveled but a few strides.

Edmund watched as his younger son spun and narrowed his gaze on his brother. He knew the lad hated the childish moniker, but when Wyatt scanned the table his shoulders dropped.

"Father, may I be excused?"

"Aye."

"Thank you, Father, and Sir Charles."

"Oh, you are welcome, Highness. I look forward to our quest."

Wyatt sped from the room.

"You indulge him too much, Father."

"That is none of your concern, Eric. You must remember he is nearly half your age." Edmund fixed his son with a hard gaze and challenged him to speak again.

"You make it worse," Eric pushed.

"I have heard enough from you. Go and do a survey of the supplies we have at the ready and the horses which are fit to ride again so soon."

"I should stay and learn of the threat."

Edmund straightened his back. "You will do as you are told, boy."

Eric attempted to open his mouth.

"The securing of the kingdom is made in the details. Go and see to them as directed."

Eric bolted from his chair as if it were on fire, but Edmund knew the fire came from within. As the boy stormed from the hall, Edmund closed his eyes for a moment and prayed—not for the first time— *Lord, give him self-control.*

He turned back to the men sitting before him. They tried to hide their amusement as Edmund struggled to hide his shame. "Forgive my sons, gentlemen. They behave younger than I wish."

Charles laughed, "Don't we all, my friend?"

Edmund nodded as he stood. "Let us take our cups and move closer to the fire. We have much to discuss."

Edmund watched Hawk's son, Preston, speak quietly to his father before bowing and striding from the room.

Hawk took his seat to Edmund's right with a nod of understanding.

"He is a good friend to Eric. If anyone can cool his temper it will be Pres." Edmund said as the men followed him collecting their chairs and filling the small dark hall with their banging and scraping. They gathered nearer the central fire mead cups in hand. A sigh whispered through many of them as the large fire crackled and popped merrily.

"Now gentleman, tell of the news from Kirkshire." Edmund

settled in, relieved to at last be about business.

"Aye." Charles agreed lifting his cup in toast and taking a long draft. "Six days ago, one of the villages in Lord Radford's holding came under attack. They carried out an unusual assault, Sire. A band of near-naked men covered in black entered the village and forced the townsfolk to a central location."

A dark-haired knight spoke. "The villagers reported these fremd never spoke a word. They brandished their swords about but did no more than direct them to group together."

Charles' gaze silenced him. Edmund recognized the look as his old friend tried to temper the impulsive knight. "Aye, Sire. These odd men huddled the people together then proceeded to search each structure."

Edmund leaned forward. "What did they seek?"

"Food?" Hawk said.

"I can nay say, Sire. They took naught."

"Not a coin, or a bobble, or a crumb, animal or person was touched," another knight added before he was likewise silenced by Charles' icy stare.

"I suspect—and it is only a notion—they were hunting for someone, Sire. Naught else makes sense. Many have tried to escape Wexxton in years past, but they were always found torn to bits prior to us being able to provide aid. The few luckless souls who survived their attack live but hours, and spoke of a savage land where even the wild beasts tremble in fear."

Edmund felt that dragging information from the man was as great as sliding a giant log up the heights of a large hill. "What did these invaders do when they could not find their prey?"

"They set fire to barns and fields," the dark-haired knight blurted.

"But Majesty, the fires were small and easily contained," Charles said with a glare to the knight.

Edmund lended forward on his thighs. "What do you make of it?"

"I could not say, Sire."

"Charles, I value your wisdom and insight. Speak freely."

Charles took another deep draft and wiped his mouth on his sleeve. "Your Majesty, I believe one person, possibly more, has escaped from Wexxton. These men, or whatever they are, are hunting them but they do not wish to harm your people and thus raise your ire. They want no part of a battle with you. I further suspect this individual is coming to you."

Edmund raised his brows in surprise. "Whatever for?"

Charles shrugged. "Possibly sanctuary. Perhaps Veronia's aid."

Hawk leaned forward now. "What should we tell such a one if we should find him at our gate?"

Charles smiled. "That is wholly for the king's decision." He turned back toward Edmund. "Your Majesty, you will have to weigh the request and give it much prayer, but I can attest—should you decide to return this hunted one to Wexxton, it will be to take his last breath. The kingdom is rot with evil and terror is its constant companion."

"Thank you for your report Charles. Why did you bring the report so urgently?"

"As yet, none have been harmed, but Lord Radford learned of three more villages searched in similar fashion. He thought it prudent to send warning to the adjacent villages and report to you."

Edmund smiled as he stood to shake Charles' hand. "Thank you again, old friend. You have served me well as always." Edmund sighed, still holding fast to the man. "You have ridden long and hard. I cannot ask you to go hunting at daybreak to indulge my son's whim."

"Please, Sire. I spoke truth when I said it would be a joy to hunt in your forest. And I would be honored to have the young prince, and more so his father, accompany my men and me. It would be a good diversion after such a journey."

Still holding his hand, Edmund wrapped one arm around Charles and thumped him on the back. "You honor me, my friend. Enjoy your hunt."

"Aye, Sire."

Edmund bid the men goodnight and turned to the stairs nestled deep in the back of the hall. Climbing them to the second floor, he proceeded down the corridor to the last door on the right. He entered without knocking, startling Wyatt's aging servant.

"Welcome Majesty." He offered a stiff bow.

"Hello, Matthew. Is the lad asleep?"

"Hardly, Sire. The prince is much too excited for the morrow. I fear he won't catch a wink, I do."

Edmund smiled. "I nay could before my first hunt. I shall be but a minute, so he might at least rest."

"Father!" Wyatt shouted as the inner door opened. He bounded out of the large posted bed and raced across the room, throwing himself into his father's arms.

Edmund pulled him close and carried him back to his bed. The candlelight was low but he knew the room well. "Back under the covers with you. Then we will speak."

Wyatt crawled over the mountain of skins and covers on hands and knees as though he trudged up a hill. He stopped in mid-motion. "You have nay changed your mind?"

Edmund coaxed him to continue before sitting on the edge of his bed. "No, I have not. But I have matters to discuss. 'Tis a father's right to accompany his son on his first hunt, and it pains me to miss this import event."

The lad patted his hand, as his mother had on many occasions when affairs of state kept him from her side. "I know you want to go, Father, but our people must be safe. Truly, we shall go another day."

A deep groan roared through him. *Lord, the boy even sounds like his mother.* He pushed the ache for his lost love aside. "Yes, I will see we do so soon. Now, attend every word."

The boy straightened and gripped the covers tighter. An irrepressible smile filled his face and his eyes danced in the low light. "Aye, Father."

"I leave you in Sir Charles' care. You are to follow his instructions exactly—without argument, or complaint—at all times. Do you understand, Wyatt?"

"Aye, father. I will do everything as if you were speaking to me. And I shall bring home some tasty game for dinner." The boy squirmed causing his hair to wiggle again.

Edmund tried to suppress his growing smile. "I am serious, Wyatt. Every word."

"Aye, father, every single word." He straighten further, and his small shoulders squared as his chest puffed up." Don't worry. I shall make you proud."

"Only be safe, my son." Edmund rose, kissed the boy's head and bid him sweet dreams. He heard Wyatt laugh.

He walked to the outer door and up the back stairway to the room above his son's. His personal attendant greeted him and he passed through to his own bedchamber. He sat on the end of his bed. His head dropped low. *Father, my heart wants to join Wyatt and Charles, but there is new trouble brewing in the land.* He sighed and he yanked off a boot. "*Lord, go with them and keep them safe in Your hands, as You give me wisdom and comfort as I remain behind.*

Chapter 3

"Today we received the great honor of taking the prince on an adventure," Charles said as he and his men strolled towards Wyatt.

The boy already sat at the boards heaping great gulps of porridge and chunks of bread into his mouth in his rush to get started.

"We will miss the hunt if you choke upon your food, Highness," Charles warned.

Wyatt mumbled his eagerness but the enthusiasm became muddled and incomprehensible around the dripping porridge.

"Wyatt!" Edmund said.

His son swallowed the huge mass in his mouth. "Forgive me, sir. I do not wish to miss anything."

Charles laughed. "The sun is yet an hour in rising. We have time enough to eat in leisure, Highness."

"Yes, sir," Wyatt muttered, his eyes still locked with his father's.

Hawk joined those wandering in at the early hour. "Good morn, Majesty. Sir Charles. Everything is prepared. With your men I have conscripted four additional men-at-arms from among the king's regiment. The horses are being saddled."

Charles slapped him on the shoulder. "Thank you, Hawk, will you be joining us?"

"Alas no, my friend. I have much to attend in preparations for the possible mobilization to Kirkshire."

"Your steady bow will be missed."

"I fear no game will be brought down today," Edmund said.

Wyatt glanced up at him, his mouth agape at the ominous words.

The three men laughed and joined Wyatt at the boards. The lad turned back to his food, his feet swinging rapidly. Charles filled his plate and cup. "I expect his Highness will nay allow me to savor Margaret's cooking for one moment longer than absolutely necessary."

Edmund rested his hand on Wyatt's knee as he sat mounted outside the stable. "Remember of what we spoke."

"Aye, Father. I will follow every word." Wyatt raced ahead toward the inner gate.

"He will listen—if he can hear you—my friend," Edmund called after his son.

Chapter 4

Wyatt spurred his horse, but the closed inner gate kept him from creating any distance between him and the men charged with his care. He wasn't a baby. Today marked the beginnings of becoming a man. Everyone was moving like sap in winter. Did they not understand how important this day would be?

At last the barrier swung open. Tinsley, the healer, stood outside his house, building a fire under a huge copper kettle.

"Making a new concoction to mend the sick?" Charles called as they passed.

"Aye, sir, I make remedies by the vat in preparation for the winter illnesses."

"Success to you, healer."

"Thank you sir, and good hunting."

At the outer gate, a couple of annoying guards prevented Wyatt from flying out to his adventure. "We are going on a hunt. Let us pass." It tumbled from his lips as more of a whine than an order. Wyatt squirmed in frustration. *Please hurry*, he begged in silent protest.

Charles drew alongside. He sighed and turned to look at him. "There is an order to doing all things, Highness. Procedures give our lives structure."

"Aye, sir," he muttered.

"We will allow two of your father's men to lead us. They will serve as our protection and our guides."

"Now we follow?" Wyatt stammered, as he made ready to urge his young stallion forward.

"No, two of my men will follow next. The path from the castle is steep and winding. We must travel in pairs until we reach the valley floor. These men will be our guards on either side when we can ride four abreast, so they must go ahead of us now."

"Yes, yes. Now we go?"

"Aye, Highness," Charles said with a chuckle and directed his horse to move through the gate with him.

"Are your guests so quick to leave?"

Edmund turned from the squire he instructed to look into the shadows of the stables at the voice he grew to loath more with each day. "Does it matter whether the king's knights come or go?"

The man remained an ominous silhouette. "It matters when their travels involve the personal attention of me men."

Jocelyn's cousin grew bolder. "Then, you have no need to fret, Selvyn, as *my* men-at-arms were chosen to accompany *my* knights."

The man's broad chest led the way into the faint morning light. Hard brown eyes locked on Edmund's. The ragged scar snaking from his left ear to below his collar shimmered when he spoke. "Did I see your young son go with them?"

"Prince Wyatt is definitely none of your concern. When you insinuated yourself as the captain of the standing guard, I tolerated it out of deference for my late wife. I will nay allow you to promote yourself further. See to the proper training of *my* men, Selvyn, and mayhaps you shall remain in my good graces another day."

Selvyn's eyes narrowed and his jaw set. "Careful, Edmund, remember I lead the men with the swords within yar walls."

Wyatt fidgeted and wiggled in his saddle unable to harness his excitement. They crept from the high fortification to the wide valley floor. Charles looked off into the distance and muttered, "I fear we will bring down no game this day, Highness."

"Oh why, Sir Charles? Did we leave too late?"

"Nay, this is the best time."

"Is the season wrong?"

"There is no wrong time of year to bring down plentiful game of one kind or another."

"Is it the weather?"

"Nay, we will have a fine crisp autumn day."

"Then what is it, sir?"

Charles fought to control his amusement and hold his tone serious. "I fear over one of our company, Highness. You see, he is driving his mount to distraction, for he twitches and squirms in his saddle so his poor horse will take flight at the first snapped twig. It will be a shame, for the fleeing horse is sure to make the game go to ground."

Wyatt sat as though a great beam were thrust down his spine. "I will do better, sir, but I think I have waited my whole life for this day."

Charles' laughter took form tumbling in the cool air. "I completely understand, Highness."

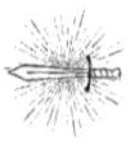

At first Wyatt thought the older knight made sport of him, but it did appear as if he understood his eagerness. Wyatt grinned.

The band of hunters rode at an infernally slow pace as they circled the castle-mount to the east. The sun broke over the far Kestron Ridge and welcomed them into the king's private hunting grounds. Only a few paces into the dense trees, the lead man stopped and held up a closed fist before pointing to a small opening where a couple of young bucks grazed.

Wyatt spotted the contented pair and flew into activity. He scrambled to seize his bow and his hand slid off it several times. It lay slung across his body as all the older men wore theirs, but when he finally seized it in his eager hand it became tangled with his quiver. Wyatt pulled and wrestled with a frantic fear—sure the deer would leave in the next breath.

Charles drew his horse closer and tried to help.

Wyatt pushed the helpful hand aside and yanked the stave over his head, but the string caught under the quiver upending it and spilled arrows all about the ground.

Wyatt's horse snorted.

The deer looked up.

Wyatt grunted in frustration.

As a cool vapor in the warm sun, the deer vanished.

One of Charles' knights dismounted and collected the wayward arrows. "Here, Your Highness. We will go further into the forest where plenty of game will be found."

"Do you think so, sir?" Wyatt hated the whine in his voice.

The knight smiled as he mounted again. "I do, Highness. And if you listen, I hear something coming our way right now."

Wyatt set an arrow, held his breath, and waited.

Chapter 5

Edmund left the stable, his hard angry steps reverberating even off the dirt of the ward. Selvyn pricked his fury and now Edmund fought for control, but he knew God had yet to appoint the time for dealing with Selvyn and his threats. His steps quickened as he neared his study. There were too many things to attend to this day to fret over Selvyn as well. He sighed and dropped into his chair, pulling the first piece of vellum from the pile to his left and placing it before him. Too much screamed for attention, but his heart remained with Wyatt.

A solid rap sounded on the sturdy oak door.

"Enter."

Eric stomped in and flung himself in a chair opposite him.

"Did you collect the information I requested?"

"That is what you *ordered* me to do, is it not?"

Edmund sat back and gazed upon his eldest son. While Wyatt embodied his late wife, Eric was his father's son. Both were dark of complexion, hair, and mood. They oft struggled with their ill tempers and lost.

Edmund took a slow calming breath. "Report."

"Thirty horses are ready to ride today. There are enough supplies still in the wagons for a week, and more could be gathered by the end of the day or along the journey. If Selvyn speaks truth, twenty-five men could be spared now, more in a week if word were sent to Lincolnshire."

"Thank you." He dismissed him with a nod.

"When do we leave?"

"I shall not be leaving for a day or more, if—"

"I *will* be going."

"As your father—and your king—*I* will decide if and when you join a war band."

Eric shot to his feet almost toppling the chair, "I am of age. Crown Prince. Knighted over a year ago. I have every right!"

Edmund rested his forearms on his desk, fingers clenched so tight they turned white, and leaned forward. His jaw locked in his fury. "You have *no* right, save that which *I* grant you. Until you contain your temper, boy, I will have you nowhere near a battlefield. You are dangerous to yourself and your men."

Eric threw the parchment containing the gathered information at his father. "You cannot cage me here forever!" The door slammed shut behind him.

"No, but I need only do so long enough to temper your fire," Edmund muttered. Threats from within and without, one son fuming at him, and one off on a grand adventure without him—all fell on him with an oppressive weight.

"Lord, my burden is too great." He worked again at the knot in his neck.

Twigs snapped to Wyatt's left. Leaves rattled to the right.

The men readied their bows for the game charging their way, but Charles moved closer to him. "Four-legged beasts do not approach," he hissed.

Tension shaded his voice making Wyatt turn to look at him. A bumpy crease between what remained of his brows formed. Wyatt swallowed hard.

"A bevy of deer, mayhaps?" one of father's men whispered.

Charles shook his head as his horse came so close to Wyatt's their legs hit. "Nay, the footfalls are too heavy. Boar?"

Battle cries burst from the trees. Swords flashed with murderous intent. Enemy warriors with covered faces bore down on them.

Arrows flew. One of Charles' men fell from his saddle.

Charles dropped his empty bow and drew his sword.

His companions' swords sang as they were drawn from their sheaths, shifting from the pursuit of game to the defense of their lives.

Wyatt screamed as his horse reared. He caught a glimpse of Charles before he lost the grip and dropped in the leaves. The horse fled. Wyatt lay motionless on the ground. He couldn't breathe. He felt as if his lungs no longer sat within his chest. His mouth opened wide and his heart thundered in his ears, but he could not capture a drop of air.

The resounding echo of crossed blades filled the forest like the frantic ringing of many church bells.

Wyatt heard his own panic echoed in Charles' bellowed orders. "Save the Prince!"

A stuttered gasp of air entered his quivering body, followed by another. Swords banged together and he raised his head to watch the frantic battle around him. Though Charles' blade came back bloody, a new enemy appeared where the last fell. Another thrust left the arm of an enemy dangling lifeless. The next swing slit a throat and showered Charles in blood.

The scene was the same anywhere he looked for Charles' men and his father's surrounded him. They fought an unending foe.

Wyatt trembled, and rose up to his elbows. Charles jerked the head of his horse around and Wyatt started to crawl backwards. More than a rod lay between the two. Charles spurred his horse toward him. Wyatt's heart thundered in his ears. Convinced that Charles's horse would trample him into the soft turf, Wyatt scurried away from him.

An enemy rider broke through the trees to Wyatt's left. His eyes locked with Wyatt's and he pumped his heels into the flanks of his charger.

Wyatt looked back toward Charles and his heart seized when he realized the newcomer would reach him first.

As if by magic, an odd figure materialized between the two charging men. He wore a white cap, and a baggy white tunic. His breeches were white as well, and tucked into his tall light leather boots. He ran toward Wyatt.

"Let the boy be!" Charles commanded above the mayhem.

The white warrior paid neither raging rider any heed as he ran straight at Wyatt who crumpled into a ball in the leaves. The foot-bound soldier reached Wyatt and yanked him to his feet. He stood with his twin short blades drawn facing away from Wyatt. Acting as his shield, the unknown defender faced the charging horse of the approaching attacker.

The number of the enemy went on without end—as though one hid behind every tree fighting like the wild beasts of nightmares. Wyatt couldn't stop shaking. Tears stung his eyes and stuttered his breaths. "Father?" he whimpered.

Charles still tried to reach him but Wyatt watched as the attacking rider dropped lifeless into the dirt, felled by the white warrior's blades. The odd knight turned back toward Wyatt gripping both his blades in one gloved hand. The knight drew a dagger from his waist, and hurled it end-over-end toward Wyatt. When he dared look up again Wyatt saw the blade—having flown over his head—lodged in the throat of a man who had charged them from behind.

Charles fought three men in rapid succession. The white warrior stood over the body of another rider he had unseated and executed him. Wyatt watched—his eyes taking in more death than his mind could comprehend.

Charles urged his men. "Be valiant, good knights."

The white warrior charged toward them—blades raised.

Charles waved him off. "Get the prince back to the castle."

The warrior pulled up short and stared at him as though Charles had slapped him across the face.

"Aye, sir. Take the boy to the castle." Charles' blood-drenched sword pointed the way.

Another wave of enemy fighters joined the fray. The white warrior turned on his heel and in a few strides swung atop a rider-less steed and charged at him. Wyatt's protector leaned far over the animal's left shoulder, his hand extended.

Wyatt's whole chest seized painfully. He became rooted to the ground.

"Your hand, boy!" the warrior ordered.

Wyatt's arm shot straight up on its own. In a half a heartbeat, he sat clinging to the warrior as they flew from the forest. He dared a glance back. The dead covered the ground nearly as thick as the leaves. Swords dripped with blood. Charles and his men continued to fight.

Wyatt clenched his eyes closed against the sight making his stomach lurch. He clung to the warrior, feeling the hardness of his muscles under the white tunic. He did not know which roared louder —the pounding of their charger's hooves or his thumping heart. Why did he come without Father? Bright light pried his eyes open. They were beyond the last of the trees. The warrior he clung to was skilled. His heart did a giddy leap at the thought. Perhaps he would stay and

Wyatt could learn the art of the sword from him.

Wyatt loosened an arm and pointed as they raced into the open. "My horse." Before Wyatt realized what the white warrior intended, he leapt to the ground and ran toward the wandering stallion. Wyatt's mount never broke stride as it sped toward home. *How did he do that?* Wyatt's admiration grew.

A few more strides and Wyatt would gain the trail leading to the safe walls of his home. As Wyatt took the first corner, he saw the white warrior pull up and slide from his stallion. He gathered the reins and held them out for one of the men coming behind.

Charles never slowed as he thundered past him. "Come with us."

As he took the next switchback turn, Wyatt saw the stranger still standing by his horse. One of Father's men stopped. The last Wyatt saw of the warrior, he was swinging back into the saddle to follow.

I want to learn to mount like that. Wyatt dreamed as he thundered through the open gate.

Chapter 6

Edmund emerged from the hall for a bit of fresh air well before midday. He worked at his tight neck. His mind jostled like the balls in a juggler's hands. Too many concerns weighed on him. It was no wonder he had completed so little today. A moment to clear his head, then he could face the mound afresh—he hoped.

After only a few steps, the pounding of hooves rattled his thoughts and his teeth.

"Father, father." Wyatt flew through the inner gate as Edmund stepped off the lowest stair. The boy's windblown hair looked a tangle of knots. His cheeks resembled ripe apples marred with mud trails streaked by tears.

Wyatt catapulted from the saddle of the unknown horse into Edmund's arms. He smiled thinking the boy returned the victorious hunter. After the barest of embraces, Wyatt dropped to his feet and exploded in a torrent of words that Edmund couldn't hear fast enough.

Wyatt's words flowed like a stream through a broken dam. "Father, we were attacked in the forest … they came from everywhere and they wore masks on their faces, and there were hundreds of them, I dropped my bow, my horse threw me and knocked me crazy, my head is still spinning, and Sir Charles and his men were fighting all around me, but I couldn't stand, the horses were coming closer and closer, and I crawled away, but a magnificent knight in a white hood came and pulled me to my feet … he used *two* swords, they flew like lightening, and cut the leg of one attacker while he charged at us on a horse, then when he bent over in pain the white knight jerked him from the saddle … the dumb man got up but the white knight kicked him high in the shoulder, Father, and spun him around, but then the white knight kicked him behind the knees so he went down and then the white knight cut the man's head clean off!" The boy inhaled a rapid gulp of air as he pantomimed the warrior's actions.

Attacked in his own forest? Edmund's mind whirled trying to decipher his son's telling and accept that Wyatt could be attacked within sight of the castle. *Were the mysterious raiders who had attacked the villagers around Kirkshire responsible? Were there others within his land who wanted to see harm come to him?* His heart pounded out the questions. Edmund became torn between drawing Wyatt into a tight embrace and ordering for the war band.

Having replenished his lungs Wyatt resumed and his wild tale held Edmund's rapt attention. "Then the white knight turned to me and threw a dagger over my head which hit another enemy right in the neck … then the white knight's swords whirled around like a windmill and he cut another to pieces, then another, and then Charles yelled at him to take me home and the white knight ran fast towards a horse and swung into the saddle—without stirrups! He charged at me with his hand over the horse's side and yelled for me to put my hand up and I did and then I sat on the horse behind the white knight and we were almost flying to the castle, but when we came out of the trees I saw my stallion—I have named him Luke, Father—and when I pointed Luke out to the white knight, he handed me the reins put his leg over the horse's neck, and slid off while we were still at a full gallop! But he didn't fall, Father, he kept running until he reached Luke and swung up in the saddle again and came after me."

Wyatt devoured air, arms swirling about him, acting every

movement.

Charles thundered through the gate, stirring up dust like a desert storm.

Wyatt abandoned his startled father and ran to greet Charles. "Charles, did you see him? Did you see the white knight?"

Charles jumped from the saddle, took two great strides, and took a knee before Edmund. "Your Majesty, I regret to report we were attacked in your forest, and two of your men are dead along with one of Lord Radford's men. I bear the blame for not recognizing the danger sooner and protecting them."

Gratitude consumed Edmund. He pulled the contrite man to his feet. "There is no blame for you, my friend."

Hawk appeared through the thinning dust and approached.

"Hawk, collect as many of the garrison as are at hand and ready your horses. You must go to the royal hunting ground, route the enemy, and collect our dead," Edmund said.

Hawk didn't wait for an explanation. He turned, shouted orders at the stable hands, and charged out the gate.

Turning to Charles, Edmund laid a comforting hand on his shoulder. "You returned with a large number of our men and my son. I will be eternally grateful to you for his life, Charles."

"Thank the Lord, for we were greatly outnumbered, and could not have been saved by our own hand."

Wyatt bounced up and down, grabbing Edmund's arm. "There he is, Father. There is the white knight who saved me."

Edmund glanced up at the last two riders coming through the gate. The oddly-dressed fellow wore a near-complete covering of unbleached linen—now heavily covered in vivid red splatter. Only his young face could be seen. His eyes darted about the collection of men until they met Wyatt's, and the boy raced to his side.

Wyatt nearly pulled the man from the saddle and dragged him to stand before Edmund. "Father, this is the white knight. White knight, this is my father, King Edmund."

The man dropped to his knees, "Your Majesty, I thank God Most High, for He alone saved your son this day."

"As I hear it, He chose your hand to wield the swords and bring about such a rescue."

"He is God almighty, and He is capable of using even one such as I."

Edmund reached for the man's forearm and pulled the knight to his feet. He looked lean but Edmund could feel well-toned muscles through the rough tunic. He kept his eyes cast to the ground as Edmund addressed him. "What is your name, friend, so we might honor you for your kindness and your bold service?"

"I require no such honor, Majesty, it belongs to God and God alone."

"Nevertheless, I will honor you for being His willing servant."

"Truly, there is no such need, Your Majesty. I am but a foreigner in your land. I have lost my companions and must return to search for them."

"Good knight, do you refuse to give me your name?"

"Ari, Majesty."

"Welcome Ari, warrior of the Most High, and defender of the defenseless. What brings you to Veronia?"

"A matter of grave concern for my people."

Edmund's eyes moved to Charles and they both nodded in understanding. "You hale from Wexxton?"

Now the knight looked up, eyes wide in surprise. Unable to form words on his tongue yet his head bobbed once.

"I received reports only yesterday of blackened warriors searching my shires on our shared border."

The knight crumpled to the ground again, his face covering the toes of Edmund's boots. "Oh Majesty, forgive us please, we never meant to bring harm to your people. We believed we escaped the horde undetected. We have come seeking only knowledge with which to carry back to Wexxton. I am so sorry. Please forgive us. We will leave at once."

Edmund bent and, taking the knight by the upper arms, hauled him to his feet again. "Peace brother, there is no call for such distress. The horde, as you say, has harmed no one."

Again Ari's hazel eyes stood out in his thin oval face, "Truly?"

"Aye, no harm has been done. I spoke with the villagers myself before bringing King Edmund the report," Charles said.

"Praise You, Lord," Ari said lifting his face to the heavens. He turned again to Edmund. "I am grateful beyond all measure for this news, Your Majesty. Now I must find my companions and return before the horde does harm to any of your people."

As Ari pulled from his grasp, Edmund noted the blood covering his hand. "You are injured."

"It is but a minor cut, Majesty." Ari turned further and his stomach bellowed in complaint.

"Hold, sir." Edmund raised his chin to the guards at the inner gate and they secured it.

Ari turned once more toward him. His shoulders sagged and his chest rose and fell in a deep sigh.

Edmund did not wish the knight to believe he was being held prisoner so he spoke with a gentle calm. "Sir Ari, you have traveled far to receive the aid of Veronia. You have saved my son. You are wounded and obviously hungry. I will see you fed, mended, and hear of your need before you take your leave. Now, please come and make yourself to home. You are welcome."

"Please, Majesty, allow me to leave before I bring trouble upon your kingdom."

"Not until these matters are seen to, good knight."

Ari's shoulders and head slumped further and a large expanse of air escaped from his lungs. "Sire, please."

"I will hear no more." Edmund swept his hand toward the hall. "Come, Ari, my friend."

With slow steps, the knight followed.

Chapter 7

Winslow hurried from the kitchen and raced across the ward. The castle stirred with the report of the attack on Charles and his men while they hunted with young Wyatt. Winslow sighed as his joints protested each step into the hall. As the king's steward, things were supposed to be calmer when his lord sat in residence. But Winslow had seen enough years to know things did not always proceed as they ought.

The small hall echoed with the excitable chatter as the few warriors who had remained behind pried information from those who had returned safely. Several tried to coax Ari into conversation, but he stood far removed looking like a caged creature about to become their next meal.

Winslow saw Ari turn as he passed and the crimson stain on the upper arm of Ari's tunic reminded Winslow that Tinsley needed to tend the fellow. He would see to it next.

He rapped on the study door and entered when the king beckoned.

Wyatt sat atop Edmund's desk as his father examined him. Edmund glanced up from his survey, relieved. "Aye, Winslow?"

"Sir Hawkins and his men have left to fulfill your orders."

Edmund sighed. "I should have gone with them."

"You needed to be with your son, Sire." Winslow's gaze dropped to the boy. "Are you well, Your Highness?"

"Oh, aye!" Wyatt said. "The White Knight, Sir Ari, saved me. You should have seen him, Winslow. His swords flew like magic—"

"Enough, Wyatt." Edmund seized his son's hands as he recreated the motion of Ari's blades in flight. "The Good Lord forbids us from seeking the dark arts and our new friend, thus far, appears to be an earnest follower of our God. He would therefore not use magic."

"Aye, father, but he has skill."

"Charles and those with him are in agreement with the young master, Majesty. Your hall is already filling with talk of what the warrior did and their desires to see more of his abilities."

"How does Ari fair?"

"Trapped, Sire."

Edmund nodded. "Is there anything further?"

"I have requested Margaret begin the dinner early Sire, and she is already well under way. You should be able to eat within the hour. I also made the chamber maids aware of our new guest and they are preparing a room upstairs for Sir Ari."

"Can he stay next to me?" Wyatt pleaded.

"Son, you must leave this man be. He has done enough."

The boy opened his mouth to argue, but Winslow interrupted.

"I am heading to Sir Tinsley next. He will need time to collect his medical satchel and all he requires for the treatment of the knight's wound. Ari may be finished with his meal before there is proper time for the tending."

"Thank you, Winslow. As always you have seen to every detail. I believe this castle would cease to function without your faithful service."

Winslow bowed his head. "Thank you, Sire."

He left the king and started back across the hall. Again Ari turned as he approached, this time stepping into his path.

The warrior's gaze bore into him like arrows shot from a bow.

Winslow slowed and turned to step around the young man.

Ari moved with the stealth of a predator into his path preventing Winslow from continuing. Winslow said naught and made another attempt.

Ari spoke. His voice resonated in the small space and all turned. "The king wishes to see me?"

Delivered as a question, but said with conviction, the intensity of the words raised the hairs on Winslow's neck.

Ari's eyes pleaded with him. "May I enter his study or will you escort me?"

His bearing willed Winslow to turn and walk back to the king's door. Winslow knocked again and Ari stepped to the threshold with bold confidence before being announced.

"You wished to speak with me, Your Majesty?" Ari stood in the king's doorway, for all to hear, back straight and head level.

Winslow watched as Edmund looked past the warrior at him with a raised brow. Edmund waved the men in and dismissed Wyatt to wash before the meal.

Winslow closed the door and watched as Ari dropped to his knees on the hard stone floor, hands in his lap and head bent low.

Edmund stood to see him.

A great moan rent from the crumpled warrior. "Please, Majesty, you must allow me to leave. Keeping me here will only cause you trouble—great trouble I fear. You have been more than hospitable in your offer to feed me and tend my wound, but I wish no harm to come to you or your people."

Edmund came around his desk, rested back against it, and crossed his arms and his ankles. "As we have told you, good knight, no harm has come to my people. You are safe here."

"Aye Sire, but you are not."

"You will have to explain yourself, sir. Surely the king is safe in his own home?" Edmund fought to keep the bit out of his words.

Ari's shoulder's dropped even further, and Winslow feared he would soon be prostrate.

But Ari did not continue to cower. He pulled off his gloves and Winslow caught a glimpse of flesh as a small hand worked at the top buttons of the high-collared tunic. The hand moved to loosen the buckle of his hood, and long graceful fingers of the man's right hand bearing two gold bands lingered on the crown of his head. Ari sighed and removed the covering releasing a cascade of long straight hair the color of copper ore in the mid-day sun.

"A woman!" The words tumbled from Winslow before he could stop them.

Edmund's arms dropped to his sides and his jaw swung slack.

"Aye. I am a warrior, *and* a woman therefore, for your sake, Majesty, I must be allowed to leave." Her voice, softer and of a higher pitch, washed over Winslow like a gentle breeze.

Edmund stood riveted for several moments before leaning forward and bringing the woman to her feet.

As she stood, Winslow caught her face framed by her rich red hair and marveled at her beauty. The mistaken youth of her features was in fact the fine-cut features of a handsome woman, leaving Winslow to wonder how he could not have seen it before.

Edmund's words broke into Winslow's thoughts. "I would not allow you to leave when I thought you a man. I think you need to explain your situation from the beginning before I will even contemplate sending you back out to face your fate now." He motioned for her to sit in the chair behind her.

She plopped into the seat with a heavy sigh.

Edmund turned the other chair to face her. "Please, my lady, tell me what has brought about these events?"

Ari sat wringing her gloves and hood in her hands and Winslow marveled at the power they wielded. Her strength convinced him that if she willed it so, she could rend the items in two.

"Wexxton is a land beset," she said, staring at her hands. "Many years ago the Black Knight came and, seeing our people divided and squabbling amongst ourselves, made himself to home. He turned the young and the old to his evil will by filling them with a blackness of soul, which oozes out into their flesh.

"When he arrived, near half of Wexxton worshiped the Lord God Almighty. But as more and more of the lost joined him, and many holy warriors fell in battle, our numbers plummeted. In the last generation so many of our men were killed, the women were required to take up arms to defend our land and families. Now we begin training at ages younger than your son, and there is no end to the battles—save death."

Edmund rested his forearms on his knees. "What did you hope to find here?"

"There are but few of us left, Your Majesty. It has been foretold one last great battle is yet to come. It will be a battle in which my people will find ultimate victory or face utter destruction. We know Veronia fought the Black Knight many generations past with a mighty weapon of God."

"You and your companions hoped to seek this weapon?"

"Aye, Sire. We prayed you would share this good news with your distant brothers and sisters, so we too might free ourselves of this evil. If you could but tell me of the weapon you used to defeat the Black Knight and his horde, I could be on my way within the hour."

Edmund straightened, "And if I refused you this weapon did you intend to take it by force?"

Ari bolted to her feet. "Sire, no! Heaven forbid—oh, God forbid—

we do such a thing." She looked to the heavens for confirmation from God Himself. "We came only to ask, and prayed you would be agreeable. We know our future is held in God's hands alone. We—we couldn't. Sire, please don't think so poorly of us because of me."

Edmund extended a hand of peace and Winslow watched as a bemused smile parted his lips. "Peace, dear sister. I did not mean to cast aspersions on your motives."

Ari slipped back to her seat, still holding the king's gaze.

"If you do not mean to attack me for this weapon, than how can your presence bring me harm?"

Ari stared at him for a time and her brows drew together. Her head tipped to the side, "Sire, if you keep me here, your people are bound to learn the truth of me. This leaves you with but two options; either you were too foolish to uncover my deception yourself or you hid the truth from your people. Both situations will cause you to lose the respect of those you govern. It is a fact of history, once a ruler loses the trust and esteem of his subjects the end is near. I will not be party to ending your rule, Your Majesty. I have seen the people of your land and they are healthy and happy, generous and kind. You are a good leader and your kingdom needs you. I but need information. Please, you must see it is best for me to leave?"

Edmund bowed his head, remaining silent for several moments. Winslow knew his king would not act on a matter of such import without first praying for guidance. After a time, stillness came over him. When he raised his head—peace was awash over his countenance.

"You are to remain."

"Sire—"

"Warrior of the Most High, it is the will of God for you to remain. You will be safe here, and it will allow time to find this weapon you seek."

"You do not know of it?"

"Nay, I have heard stories of the long ago battle, and a miraculous victory won. But I do not know how. Do not fret though, I am sure it was recorded in the annals of the kings. I should be able to find the item you need in a short time. Until such is found and the good Lord give you leave to depart from here, you shall be my honored guest."

She sighed with a small jerked nod and sat back in her chair. "What will you do?"

"I will keep your secret. Both Winslow and I will shield you here, until God Himself reveals this weapon and His purpose for your stay, my lady."

"And when your people learn the truth?"

Edmund smiled at her. "The Lord will make a way. He has been with you thus far and you have arrived safe at my door. We will trust Him to see you through until the end."

Ari bowed her head in resignation. "Aye—trust and pray."

She collected her hair at the nape of her neck and twisted its length with a wince. She proceeded to replace the cap on her head and buckled it again as Edmund stood and examined her arm.

"This wound is deep. It will require sewing."

Ari pulled from his grasp as she fastened the top two buttons of her tunic and slipped into her heavy gloves. "It is a trifling matter, Sire. Send some ointment and I will see to it."

"The royal physician, Tinsley, will be along following the meal to see to your proper care."

She stood looking into his eyes again. "And how will you explain me to your good healer, Sire?"

"Trust us, my lady," Winslow said, finding his voice again. "I already have in mind a way to both see you treated and hide your secret."

"Fine, my life—and your own I fear—is in your hands, good sirs. I hope you do not come to regret your actions this day."

"It is God's will," Edmund said.

"Well, before we continue this pretense I feel I should tell you, those who attacked your men did not lay in wait for them. I arrived in your forest at dusk the eve before last and found it devoid of men. This very morning I first heard the hunters approaching. I turned to leave but came near face to face with the attackers as they entered your forest in heated pursuit."

"Thank you. I will inform my thane. This is even more troubling than I first considered. If they were not there prior to my men, they knew of them going and followed after."

"I will also tell you they were not of the horde, for these men have not yet lost all of their souls. Furthermore, they sought the life of the prince. Take great care, Your Majesty. Someone is seeking you harm and they aim to use your family to exact it."

Ari's stomach rumbled again.

"Let us see you fed, dear lady. We can speak of these matters later." Edmund raised his chin to Winslow who grasped the latch.

Winslow paused and turned to her before he opened it. "May I be so bold as to ask, is your name truly Ari?"

"It is Aria, sir, but Ari would serve us best now."

He released the latch, leaving the door closed and extended his hand to her. "Welcome to Veronia, Lady Aria. You are among friends here. Any need, you have but come to me."

"Thank you, sir. You have both been more than kind."

They left the study and Winslow felt every gaze fall on them. He cast a glance to Edmund who wore a deep frown and Lady Aria who stared at the floor. At the time the truth of the female warrior would be revealed, those present would think back on this day. They would remember hearing Aria summoned to a private meeting with the king, and recall it lasted almost an hour. When Edmund and Aria emerged no one looked happy. It would appease a few, Winslow thought with a sigh.

Chapter 8

Aria neared the tables, her mind a tumult. She had arrived safely at the door of the very man to whom she was sent, though separated from Ri and the others. She was drawn impulsively to a battle—for her training would never permit her to remain idle in such a circumstance. God allowed her to aid in saving the prince, endearing her to the king before they ever met. God's hand clearly covered her.

Aria took a moment to again survey her surroundings. With the matter of her prolonged sojourn settled, she now not only looked, but also saw the odd arrangement of the king's hall. A rather small space for a great hall of the high king of the combined kingdoms of Balmore and Veronia. Less than a hundred could be fed comfortably. *Surely King Edmund has more nobles and knights than could be seated here.* A neglected dais sat off against a far wall with a single high-backed chair. *King Edmund does not have much of a throne.*

The few tables before her were set in a pattern reminiscent of a squared-horseshoe.

"Sir Ari, sit with me."

She sighed. Her actions also enamored her to the young prince. He bounced up and down at her approach.

The lad bolted from his seat at the corner of the front board and flew toward her. Wyatt seized her hand with the strength of a man twice his size and pulled her along. "You can sit next to me, sir Ari. We can talk until the food comes and then eat together."

Aria dared a glance at the king walking to her left, but his eyes were distant as if he considered the weight of his agreement. 'I will keep your secret,' he'd said. She prayed he would not come to hate her for his making such a foolish promise.

Edmund passed behind her to take his seat at the head table beside Wyatt, who sat at the end on his left.

He was an odd one—this king. He gave her the way and passed behind—showing he did not demand authority. He did not sit alone on the high dais, though he had one. He preferred the company of his men and his son.

Without the king's intervention, Ari allowed herself to be dragged to sit on the other side of the corner from Wyatt. Her saving grace was the boy's excitement, which filled his mouth with his own words affording her no time to answer any of the queries he fired at her.

A tall, dark-haired, man approached and sat to Edmund's right. The scowling young mane was cut from the same mold as the king— clearly an elder son. Yet he sat in the center of the table to the king's right. The place traditionally saved for the most honored member present. Edmund did not behave like any king she'd ever met.

A blond man of the same age as the older prince sat beside him leaving one chair empty at the far end of the board.

As Wyatt chattered on, Ari noted the two pairs of boards running perpendicular to the king's table. The inner benches filled with young men of a myriad of ages in a rainbow of colored tunics. Clearly squires. Ari watched the few men present turn and call to different ones of them. The squires did not sit behind their masters, but anywhere along the bench on the same side. Next to join them were a small host of simply-dressed people of all ages. They sat at the same boards, opposite the squires, and talked freely with them.

Good heavens, the castle workers and servants eat with the squires. Truly is an odd land.

Serving maids exited from the door at the opposite end of the hall from Edmund's study and waited in a line near the wall.

Edmund stood and everyone rose to their feet, causing the benches and chairs to scrape over the stones, bunching the straw in neat mounds at the legs. "Friends let us thank our Provider."

Every head bowed.

"Most gracious Father, I come before You today in humble gratitude. You spared the life of my son and my friends this day, and we know Your hand alone saved them. We ask Your favor on those lost this day. Welcome Your faithful men into Your arms, Father. They served You well and in doing so were the best among us. We know their sacrifice will never be in vain for naught done in Your name is ever lost. Comfort us and strengthen us for the days to come. As You did for David when he cried out to You, 'Keep us, O Lord, from the hands of the wicked: preserve me from the cruel man, which purposes to cause my steppes to slide'. Bless our new friend Ari, Lord, for this faithful one is dear to us. Watch over him as he tarries here, and grant the desires of Ari's heart, as You granted mine this day. We thank you for the bounty of Your land and the strength it provides. You are ever good to Your people and we praise Your name, Most High. Amen."

"Amen," everyone echoed and returned to their seats as the tables where laid.

Ari marveled as even once the meal came, Wyatt's continued babbling never slowed. His words often muddled around his dark bread and savory mutton, but she paid them little heed, continuing her assessment of her surroundings. The cramped room resembled a cave with its smoke-covered windowless walls. The fire pit looked as though it was meant to be central but the back wall lay too close to it.

Edmund ate little and returned to his study before all of his men collected at the boards.

Ari reached to fill her cup again only to have Wyatt snatch the pitcher of ale and begin to pour it for her. "Here let me, sir." In his excitement, he splashed half a cup's worth over her hand, soaking her glove.

Ari sighed and shook off the soggy appendage behind her.

"Oh," Wyatt groaned as the pitcher landed with a thud on the boards. "Forgive me, sir I—"

"'Tis but a little ale, Highness." She drank slowly as Wyatt sat beside her his lower lip projecting out far beyond his small chin.

The meal continued more sedate until the distinguished white-haired man, who served as the king's steward, approached. "I hope your meal was to your liking, sir."

"Aye, the best I can remember sharing."

"If you are finished, a room has been prepared for you upstairs. You may rest and refresh yourself."

Ari stood as the man bowed with a sweep of his arm. Before she could turn to follow him, Wyatt again seized her hand and pulled her toward the stairs at the rear of the hall.

"I'll show him the way, sir Winslow," Wyatt said.

Only a few remained in the hall, and they stood watching, smiling intently like silly children. Their eagerness spoke of their hopes of meeting and talking with her. With the choices before her she picked up her pace and followed the boy up the stairs and hoped he would permit her some time alone to think, and pray.

Wyatt released her hand at the top of the stairs and dashed to the second door from the far end on the west side. He threw the door open and leapt up with a whoop of enthusiasm. "You have the room next to mine. Is it not grand, sir? We can tap on the walls and talk to one another. We can share secrets and you can teach me how to fight like you." Wyatt took a wide stance and his arms whirled about him as his imaginary blades cut down phantom enemies.

Ari's stomach churned as the thought of sharing secrets plucked every nerve like a bard strumming his lute. This boy would be her undoing. She closed her eyes struggling to still her racing thoughts, and hoped her stomach would settle before she wretched on the king's fine tiles.

"Wait here Sir Ari, I want to show you something."

Ari heard a door slam. She was alone. Her feet hit the first step in the next breath. Her heart pounded out a native rhythm. Lungs burned for a deep breath. She took huge strides across the empty hall and burst out the doors as if the devil himself was in pursuit. She leapt off the steps and became rooted in the earth of the ward. Leaning forward she braced her trembling body with her hands on her knees and fought for a calming breath.

The sharp scent of hay from the stable tickled her nose. An angry cry of a crow high on the wall mocked her, leaving her unexpectedly rattled. A seasoned warrior—having participated in near one hundred battles—and here she stood terrified of a ten-year-old child.

Reason returned to her and her tight muscles relaxed. She straightened and caught sight of Winslow coming through the inner gate. 'Come to me should you need anything,' he'd said. *Thank you, Lord. You have again provided for my every need.*

She took long firm strides and hurried as quickly as she thought dignified toward the man. "Sir Winslow, you must help me."

"I am at your service, sir Ari," he said with a bow.

"I have been given a chamber next to the young prince, sir." Winslow nodded.

"His Highness is quite smitten with me and hopes we can stay up long nights and share all our secrets."

The wise man grew straight and his smiled slid into a deep frown. "That will not do, will it, sir?" His eyes scanned the small ward and its sparse structures. When his gaze fell on the building behind her, his shoulders dropped with a relieved sigh. "This way, sir."

She followed with easy steps.

"This is the king's great hall," Winslow told her as they entered. "King Edmund only uses it when his lords are in residence and for holiday gatherings of his people."

A proper hall filled with long boards stretched before her. A high dais lay at the far end. They turned immediately inside the door and Ari followed him up a narrow curved stone stairway. At the top, they proceeded down a long corridor past many doors until they reached the door at the end where the passage turned to continue along the back wall.

Winslow opened the door and motioned her inside ahead of him. "Sir Charles and his men have the two rooms at the front corner of the opposite side. They will be leaving in the morning with their fallen man, so you should not be bothered here, sir."

The good-sized outer room contained a divan, with a low table before it, a high narrow chair beside a small desk with a lamp on it sat near the window. Ari moved to the opening and pushed out the shutters to look down on the roof of a low building attached to the hall.

"The kitchens and bakery, sir," Winslow said as he passed her to open the inner door.

Before she moved to follow him, her eyes raised to the inner wall only a few paces beyond the kitchens. The shadow of a figure disappeared behind a tall merlon. Someone had hidden on the battlements over the inner gate when she arrived earlier, and she felt the unseen presence still spying on her. A chill ran down her spine.

She pulled the shutters closed, walked past the hearth and joined Winslow in the inner chamber.

A tall wardrobe stood at the foot of the curtained bed across from her, and a small hearth sat nestled beyond in the corner of the room. Further to the right another door opened to the bathing chamber where a large wooden tub stood flanked by a table with a basin and pitcher and a small cupboard full of towels.

"Will this serve your needs, sir?"

Ari let out a long sigh, "Oh aye, sir. This is splendid. Thank you."

"I am pleased I could be of service, sir."

"Please, don't stand on formality. Ari is sufficient."

"Only if you do so in kind."

"Thank you again, Winslow. I feel better already."

Winslow smiled, adding a couple of new wrinkles to those already gracing his face. "And mayhaps a bath might be in order as well."

Ari felt her lips part as a bubble of laughter tumbled between them. "Are you saying I stink, Winslow?"

Winslow looked as though she'd slapped him. His mouth gaped open, he inhaled sharply, and a jumble of muttered words tried to form on his lips.

"Oh peace, brother, I do stink. A bath is a rare delight I would welcome with all the excitement of the young prince."

A sigh of relief relaxed his shoulders. "Then it shall be provided you, Ari."

She followed him back into the sitting room and for the first time she noticed he carried something in his hands. He raised the item now, offering it to her. She took the bundle of cloth and unfolded it to find a short-sleeved tunic and a clean pair of breeches.

"I thought these would be more suitable for the healer's visit. If you would like I can give your garments to the seamstress after they are laundered and she can fashion you several sets. You may be with us a spell."

"Thank you, Winslow. You are exceedingly thoughtful. A far greater boon would be for you to convince your king to allow me to leave."

"You heard him, Ari. God told him you are to stay."

She flopped on the divan, her hands hanging limply between her knees. "Aye, and I heard God's directions clearly myself. But …"

"But what?"

"I am a warrior, and a great battle is coming to my land. It is not my custom to sit about in luxury when my people are in danger."

Winslow stepped forward and knelt before her. "God is sovereign over all things. You were brought here for a reason and in His time He will reveal it to you."

Again she felt the tug on her spirit as God used yet another human voice to speak His words to her. "Aye, and His timing is perfect."

Drawing up to his full height, Winslow smiled at her. "Indeed." He turned to the door. "Now if you would change, I will collect the physician and return shortly, for your arm is bleeding again."

Ari hitched her shoulder and glanced through the tear at the wound. It did indeed require suturing.

Chapter 9

Hawk returned as Edmund sat picking at his food. He left the meal unfinished and joined Hawk in his study.

Edmund took his seat. "What did you find?"

"Our three fallen, but naught more."

"Charles assured me that a greater number of the enemy fell."

"Their bodies were removed before we arrived. We found naught of them, Ed." Hawk sat back.

Edmund reached for his neck. "Then it is as Ari said."

"Ari?" Hawk leaned forward, a brow rose.

"The warrior who saved Wyatt," Edmund struggled over his words. He'd promised to keep the woman's secret, but Hawk knew him too well. "He is one of those who escaped Wexxton seeking my aid. Ari spoke of arriving in the royal forest last eve and saw no one until the hunting party entered this morn. The assassins followed after."

"What aren't you saying?"

"If these rogues followed my son—who they clearly targeted—and they collected their dead, we can only assume these were Veronian—men we know, or knew." With a slow sigh, he allowed his hands to drop to the desk as he sat fully in his high-backed chair.

"You trust this fellow?"

"Ari has been abundantly forthcoming in all matters." Edmund knew Hawk would not let the matter drop. Could he be so quick to betray Aria's confidence and still hope to retain her trust?

"Something still bothers you about him."

"I have promised to keep a confidence."

Hawk straightened. "Even from me, Ed? How am I to protect you and our kingdom if you maintain secrets from me?"

"This will not affect the kingdom."

"He is a foreign warrior, arrived on the day of a personal attack on your son, and sought the king's aide. How can this not affect you and the kingdom?"

Edmund groaned. "I have promised."

"I will keep your vow as well." Hawk countered quickly.

Edmund worked at the knot. He sighed.

"Ed? Your reluctance affirms that I must know the truth of the matter. I will not leave the man alone until I learn what he has done to so quickly sway my closest friend to hold secrets from me."

"The warrior is a woman," he groaned. "And I swore to conceal her identity. She asked only to leave."

Hawk flopped back in his chair as if struck. "A woman?"

"Aye, a woman, Hawk. She comes seeking the weapon used by our great grandfathers to defeat the Black Knight. Things in Wexxton are so desperate they require their women to fight alongside the men on the battlefield. Aria says she has trained from a younger age than Wyatt and fought in her first battle before she reached Eric's age."

"Who cares for the children?"

"Those left unfit to return to the battlefield."

Hawk rubbed his chin and his brows drew together. "This is going to be difficult. The men want to see his—her—skill, and some have voiced an interest in sparring with the accomplished warrior."

"She voiced the same concern and begged me to allow her to leave. I am not inclined to send anyone from my gates, and her being a woman complicates matters. I prayed about it and God has been clear —she is to remain."

"If He has ordained it, He will provide the way."

Edmund nodded. "Will there be anything else?"

"No. God's peace, Ed"

"Thank you, brother. I sore need it."

Chapter 10

After gently rapping on Ari's door, and receiving a groggy admittance, Winslow led Tinsley into the room. "Sir Ari, I have brought the physician to see to your wound."

Ari sat with her legs stretched along the divan and her head resting on its tall arm. Her eyes were lazy slits. She nodded and slid the woven blanket from her left shoulder.

Tinsley pulled a chair close to the divan, straightened the spectacles on his narrow nose and squinted at the injury. He slid his hand under her elbow, lifting it, and drew the lamp near.

Ari turned to Winslow with a crooked smirk and tight brows.

"Tinsley is the king's private physician, sir."

"This wound is deep," Tinsley whined, the high-pitched squeak of his voice caused Ari to cringe. Winslow had long since learned not to wince at the man's grating nasal tone, but it still left his nerves raw. "It will require suturing. It has continued to bleed which will aid in warding off the rot."

He released her arm and started to set out his supplies in a jerking, fussing manner.

Ari laid her head back, closing her eyes again.

Tinsley thrust the lamp into Winslow's hand. "Hold the light here," he ordered.

As Tinsley threaded the needle, Winslow marveled as the light fell on her arm. The cut of her muscles resembled any other knight's in its tone though devolved of thick hair. Tinsley rose from his seat drawing Winslow's attention away from Ari. He disappeared with shuffling steps. *He walks as though he is older than I, yet he is over half my age.* He returned from the inner chambers with a towel and placed it under her arm.

"And me the wine, Winslow," Tinsley said pointing to a pitcher on a small table near the divan.

Her muscles drew taunt and hard when the scarlet liquid splashed over the open gash. She made no other movement.

Tinsley offered the bottle to her. "Take a draft to deaden the pain, good knight."

She pushed the bottle away with her right hand. "Do your work, healer."

"Will be painful."

"Of that I am well aware. Be done with it."

Tinsley's nose lifted into the air. "Very well."

Winslow smiled, for Ari never noted the offense her dismissing tone created as her eyes closed once more. When the needle bit deep into her sore flesh, the rise of her chest stopped and her body tensed. But she made no further response or sound. Winslow shook his head in wonder. Many a knight cried out in pain at such treatments. What must she have suffered in her young life to warrant such steeled composure?

The stitching completed, Tinsley washed the wound again and slathered it with a sticky ointment. He pulled a length of cloth from his satchel. "This ointment needs to be reapplied twice a day and the wound redressed."

"Leave the supplies and I shall see to it." Ari yawned.

"I will come by in the morning—"

"There is no need," Ari stated as she sat up and threw her legs over the side to face him. "I would be a poor guest if I occupied the royal physician for such a trivial matter. It is easily seen to, sir." She put out her gloved hand to accept the items.

"Very well," Tinsley huffed and dropped the jar and cloth into her palm.

"I thank you for your administrations, healer. You do fine work."

The man now placated, his chest puffed out and his lips parted in an arrogant smile. "'Tis the least one can do for the hero who saved the prince."

Winslow saw Ari frown. She did not favor accolades. He waited for the healer to leave before turning to her again. "How do you feel?"

"Sore and tired."

"I will ask the kitchen to prepare a tray for your supper, and inform the king you will be dining in your chambers tonight."

Ari afforded him a sweet smile. "You are ever thoughtful, my friend. I would welcome a quiet night next to the fire."

He inclined his head and left.

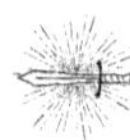

Ari dozed again after the healer left. She woke at the soft knock on her door. "Enter," she called out. She sat up and stretched as Winslow entered with her tray and a young boy in tow.

He placed the tray of tempting meats, cheeses, and bread on the low table before her and retrieved the pitcher from the child. "Here is the meal I promised, sir."

She nodded, pulled a hunk from a dark loaf and dunked it in the meat juices.

"I also thought it wise for you to have a young attendant to see to your needs, and help with your acclamation to our kingdom." Winslow waved his hand toward the child trembling next to him.

Ari frowned as her gaze fell on the lad. His blond hair hacked short, he wore an ill-fitting tunic and breeches. His blue eyes were as large as saucers and his head trembled with a nervous twitch as he stared at her.

"This is Lindsay, sir. She is an orphan, as her mother died recently of the fever. Our parishes try to find homes for our needy children in the community, but when such is not possible they are brought into service of the castle. Lindsay arrived this morning."

She smiled, realizing what he had done for her. "And I assume she was sorely infested with fleas to be so shorn."

Winslow's face filled with wrinkles as a great grin parted his lips. "Oh aye, sir."

"And there were no kirtles her size, for you to dress her like a lad."

"It is the truth of the matter."

The poor child trembled all the more.

"Forgive Sir Winslow and me, Lindsay. We have been indulging in a bit of sport at your expense. Sir Winslow has seen to my care since I arrived in the king's home this morning as well. He knows I will need a companion and friend while I sojourn here."

Ari removed her gloves and unbuckling her hood, then slipped it off.

"Ya're a girl!" Lindsay said.

"Those were my exact words, when she told the king earlier," Winslow said, patting the child on the shoulder.

Ari sighed, "My name is Aria. This will not be easy Lindsay, for we have to pretend to be boys without letting anyone know the truth. Do you wish to play this game with us? I will not fault you if you wish to serve your king elsewhere."

Lindsay brightened with a huge smile, which consumed her whole face. "It'd be a grand adventure, Lady Aria. I'll serve ya well."

"I thank you for your kindness, Lindsay." Ari considered her for a moment. "I am called Ari when I am disguised so, and I have known warriors named Lin, so we shall call you that."

Lindsay stood tall, shoulders back, and head held high. She extended her hand. "Hello, Ari, I'm Lin. I'm pleased to meet ya."

Ari bit the inside of her cheek to stifle a laugh as she took the child's hand. "A pleasure, Lin. How old are you, lad?"

Lindsay giggled. "Eight summers," she announced with pride.

"Well, he is young, but should serve you as a fine page," Winslow mused. "But under the circumstances it may work to your advantage."

Ari nodded as she pulled her hair up and secured her hood again. "Thank you for your thoughtfulness, Winslow."

"It is my pleasure, sir. I will collect a few servants and begin bringing in the water for your bath."

Ari noticed Lindsay as she cocked her head at Winslow. She motioned for the child to join her on the divan and offered her some bread. As Winslow left, Ari explained. "It is far easier if we always refer to one another as boys. We will not be prone to slip when we are with the others if we always speak in the same manner."

Lindsay giggled again, "Aye, sir."

Ari bobbed of her chin. "And young pages, never giggle, lad."

Lindsay tried to make her lips straight as she sat a little taller. But a small chuckle escaped. "I'll do better, sir."

She patted the child on the knee with a sigh, closing her eyes in prayer. *Lord, what have I done? I am not in Wexxton. This child need not grow up so soon as I did.* She glanced at the girl. She sat engulfed in peace—her manner slow and thoughtful. She poured them each a cup with the skill of one far beyond her years. *Please protect this young one and help her also to never regret her choice this day.*

Chapter 11

Ari and Lin ate in comfortable silence as a parade of young servants brought up buckets of steaming water and filled her tub. As they returned to the kitchen for more, a new face appeared in her doorway.

Lin ran to greet the newcomer, a tall imposing man with a deep scowl. "Good evenin', sir. May I announces ya?"

The man's displeasure increased as he looked over Lindsay. "Sir Hawkins, the king's thane."

Ari's stomach rolled and dropped deep into her innards. "Let the man in, Lin. Finish your meal," Ari told the young girl as she slapped the seat beside her.

"I came to discuss the attack." His features were sharp and his gaze keen. He well deserved the name Hawk, for she felt like a mouse in his shadow. He grabbed the chair Tinsley had used, jerked it a respectable distance away, and threw his full weight into it.

His eyes bore into her face and brushed every inch of her body. He knew the truth, and it angered her. "Did you indeed come seeking knowledge or only to gawk at the spectacle?"

The heavy stubble covering his cheeks made it hard to gauge the set of his jaw, but the grinding of his teeth said everything. "Do not blame His Majesty. I have known him from his first day, and he is closer to me than a brother. He could not hide your secret—not from me. How distasteful of you to make the king take such a vow."

"I made no demand on King Edmund other than that he allow me to leave," she retorted. "I will be gone this instant if you can but convince His Majesty to permit it!"

"I would hear the truth from you first," he said, leaning forward with his elbows braced on his sturdy thighs. "All of it," he said raising his chin toward Lindsay.

The troop of servants returned.

Hawkins stood and filled a cup from her pitcher.

Ari sighed.

The servants left and Hawkins closed the door behind them.

She removed her hood and watched his eyes go wide. "Winslow thought she would be an aide to me," she said gesturing to Lindsay. "What else do you wish to know, sir?" She bit the inside of her cheek in an attempt to control her temper.

He sat again, staring hard at the girl. His tone softened as he spoke. "Tell me of the battle. The king says you believed the men followed the prince."

Ari replaced her hood as she recounted the events of the battle. She provided every detail and described the men she could recall.

"Is there anything more you noticed?" he said, sitting back and drawing from his cup once more.

"I felt evil gazing on me as I entered the inner gate and again from the wall when Winslow moved me to this room." She pointed toward the window. "The threat may come from within your walls."

"I have suspected as much. Thank you for your candor, sir." A slim smile softened his features. He stood and opened the door as the servants returned. "Is there anything else you require?"

"I am unaccustomed to sitting still, as there is little opportunity in Wexxton for idleness. I can't imagine I will be doing much fighting or even training while I am here. I would appreciate something to occupy my inactive hours."

"Did you have something specific in mind?"

"I noticed many books in the king's study." She offered a sly smile.

Hawk nodded as he leaned against the doorframe. "We have a scholar for a king. Do you favor any specific titles?"

"The king spoke of annals from the past?"

"Those are for the king's eyes only. Even I do not read those. Something else mayhaps?"

She sighed. "Pick any of your favorites. I will relish the opportunity to lose myself in a grand tale."

"Come young page, let us go get your master some reading material." He turned back to Ari. "I welcome you to Veronia, Sir Ari. I am at your service should you be in need of anything." He inclined his head as he left. Lin's light steps trotted behind him.

Some time later the young girl returned, her arms laden with a great stack of volumes from the king's library. She tried to set them on the table but they tipped and tumbled to the floor. "I've never seen so many books, sir. Are ya gonna to read them all?"

"We can read them together, my friend," Ari said, moving past her to the inner chambers. Ari pulled off her short-sleeved tunic, revealing the padded vest beneath.

"What's that?" Lin asked, retrieving the discarded garment and folding it.

"It is armor, lad. Two layers of heavy horse hair padding with a thin sheet of steel within." Ari reached under her arm to pull the laces loose and jerked in pain. "Help me with this."

Lin worked both sides, pulling the laces loose.

"Lin, grab the bottom and pull." Ari pulled against her on the front separating the two panels from her flesh. "Now push it up." Working together, they wiggled the heavy garment over her head and it crashed to the floor. Ari stood and moved to the bathing chamber while Lin scrambled to collect the wayward item.

"Is yar armor supposed to be so difficult to remove?"

"Nay, I can usually do it myself, but the wound in my arm has become stiff and aching."

Lin gasped as she entered the chamber.

Ari stepped into the water slowly and slid under the surface. "What is the matter, child?"

"Ya're...ya're all curvy."

Ari chuckled as she slid into the warmth and leaned back with a sigh. "We already established we are both girls, Lin."

"But ya don't look nothing like a girl in yar clothes."

"Is that not the point of a disguise, to conceal the truth?"

Lin stooped and collected the discarded breeches. She handed Ari the soapwort root. Lin reached out with the item but her eyes stared under the water at her thigh. "Did it hurt?"

Ari dipped under the water to wet her hair. When she surfaced she took the root and worked it into a lather. "Aye, it was extremely painful," Ari murmured of the wound, which left behind an ugly scar on her thigh.

Lin stood staring at her.

"You want to hear this tale?"

Lin gave a slow nod, eyes opened wide.

"Many years ago, during the third year of battles for me, I charged one of the horde on horseback, my horse stumbled in a hole and I missed blocking the strike. The creature laid open my leg. I fought on until weakness overtook me and I dropped from the saddle."

"Weren't ya scared," Lin whispered.

"I was angry for being so foolish, and frustrated at being

bedridden for months on end. The healers thought they would have to take my leg, but God healed me. I regained my strength and returned to the battlefield." She slid back under the water and rinsed her hair.

"Do ya like fighting?" Lin asked when she surfaced.

"No one likes going into battle, child. It is a necessary evil, a thing which must be done to save my family." Ari searched the water for an item she had dropped in earlier. She located the flimsy article and scrubbed it with the root.

"That's a strange thing," Lin said, rubbing Ari's hair with a towel.

"It is another form of armor."

"That?"

Ari laughed. "It is an ancient fabric made far off in the distant home of the rising sun. It is called silk and woven so tightly an arrow has trouble piercing it."

"Arrows, swords. It sounds scary."

"Which is why we spend every day training, Lin. Evil must be confronted or it will run amuck." Ari stood and stepped from the tub.

Lin's lips parted in a shy smile.

"What is it, now?"

"Ya're very curvy, sir," she giggled.

Ari rubbed her fuzzy head. "All right, child, let us get ourselves to bed. Set this near the fire to dry. I think the nightrails Winslow found for us are in the top dresser drawer."

Lin scurried off and Ari dried herself. She sighed. Oh, it felt good to be clean. She donned the night garment Lin had brought and went into the bedchamber. Lin knelt near the fire and added a log.

"You know how to tend a fire?"

"Momma taught me," she said with her puffed chest.

"Very well, your first official duty is to see our that fires are well tended." Ari moved to the outer chamber. She snatched up the servant's pallet and carried it back into the bedchamber. She laid it on the floor near the fire and arranged the blanket she'd used earlier over it. Next she reached into the curtained bed and pulled off a pillow.

She stepped back and surveyed her efforts, "What say you, Lin. Will this serve you well?"

"Oh yes, sir. 'Tis even better than where Momma and I slept every night. Thank ya, sir."

"I must thank you, Lin, for your willingness to walk this road with me."

Lin's bright smile filled her precious face. "Come, sir. Sit by the fire and I will brush yar hair."

Ari relaxed under the tender ministrations of her young friend and after having Lin change the bandage on her arm, they slipped into their beds for a good night's sleep.

Chapter 12

Ari slipped from bed like a whisper in an effort not to disturb the young Lin, but she found the fire stoked hot and Lin dressed in the outer chamber.

"You are up early, young page."

Lin stood tall, raising her chin. "Yes, sir. Momma always said the best work is done at the break of day."

"Your mother was a wise woman."

"Yes, sir," she whispered as sadness touched her voice. She brightened in the next moment though. "Sir Winslow brought these."

Lin handed her a stack of folded fabric. A new long-sleeved tunic for her and cloaks for both of them. Ari smiled. "Well, I think it best to redress this wound and prepare for our day. The king will be expecting us at his boards today."

Lin collected the ointment and clean cloth, then brought them to Ari where she sat in the chair. "Does it hurt this mornin'?"

Ari shrugged. "Not as bad as some."

Lin completed her task with quick efficiency and helped Ari into her armor.

While Lin brushed out Ari's long hair, Ari helped Lin prepare for the day. "This is your first day as a boy, Lin. I want you to watch the other young pages, notice the way they walk and talk. Watch where they stand and sit so you will know what is proper. You are quite young and many will forgive you for any errors in your behavior."

Ari paused to twist her hair and don her cap. "I, however, will be watched with a more critical gaze. A warrior is expected to act in a certain manner. Any notable deviation from this and I will draw suspicion and even closer scrutiny. I will need you to warn me if such an occasion arises."

"I'll look out for ya, sir."

Ari forced a smile, as trepidation again captured her heart. *I am asking much of this young one. It is unfair, but Lord, You have provided for Lindsay to be here with me.* "We will look after each other."

Ari stood and moved back to the inner chamber, then looked under the bed and opened the drawers.

"What-cha ya looking for?"

"A safe place to hide our womanly items."

"Will this work?"

Ari looked up at the small chest in the bottom of the wardrobe. "Aye, this should serve us well." Ari took the box and set it on the floor. She removed the key from the unfastened lock and opened it with a faint creak. She folded their nightrails, then placed them inside. "Grab my brush."

The girl returned a moment later and dropped the item inside. "Why's there a locked chest in here?"

Ari shut the lid and squeezed the lock closed. "When the king's nobles visit, they bring priceless jewelry with them. They can secure the pieces in here when they are not wearing them."

Lin's eyes grew big. "Are there lots of thieves in the king's castle?"

"I imagine not," Ari chuckled. "Especially as it sits up so high on this great rock, but it gives the nobles peace of mind." She pushed the chest under the bed and did the same with Lin's pallet.

"Now our identities are safely hidden. Let us be off to break the fast, young page."

Lin beamed and raced to open the outer door for her.

Ari paused and glanced at her blades as they lay sheathed on a tall table near the shuttered window in the inner chamber. She never went anywhere unarmed. She felt off balance without their dependable weight secured around her waist. Their cold rigid presence gone from her thighs left her feeling less than dressed.

"Sir?"

"I imagine I ought to leave them here."

"I don't know much about castles, but no blades—other than eatin' daggers—are allowed in the king's hall."

Ari nodded and walked through the open door. She entered the small hall and every head turned to stare. Her heart pounded out a ruckus beat. She couldn't catch her breath and she struggled to put one foot in front of the other. Lin brushed her ever so gently as she ran past, toward a group of young men at an outer table. The sensation managed to propel her uncooperative legs forward. She glanced at Lin and saw her throw a glance over her small shoulder.

Thank you, Lord. The dear child helped me without anyone seeing more than an eager young page.

Ari gathered her jumbled nerves as one scoops up scattered garments—quick and un-bothered. Her brisk steps carried her toward the back of the nearest table. Steadying herself, she dipped her head in acknowledgment of raised cups.

"Sir Ari!" a voice plucked her tense nerves. Wyatt raced to her, grabbed her gloved hand, and pulled her forward to sit with him once more.

Her palm grew damp inside the leather.

"I went in my room and when I came out you were gone. I

knocked on your door but you never answered. I wanted to show you my bow."

Ari sighed. "I asked Sir Winslow to find other accommodations for me."

"You are not staying next to me, anymore? Why?" Wyatt's lower lip slid out in a pout.

"I am a simple warrior, Your Highness. A room in the castle is far grander than I am used to occupying. I am more comfortable where I am now."

"I will show you my bow after we eat and we can—"

"Wyatt," the king's heavy steps echoed in her ears. "Leave the man be."

Her eyes rose to meet Edmund's. From the tone in his voice she expected him to be steeled with anger, but his eyes were soft. "Good morning, Sire," she greeted him with a formal bow.

"I trust you slept well, Sir Ari."

"Your hospitality has been too generous, Sire."

"Consider this your home, until God calls you elsewhere, good knight," Edmund inclined his head and moved to the center seat today. The older prince still sat to his right and the blond youth on the end. As Hawk took the seat between Edmund and Wyatt, Ari saw the resemblance with the blond young man—obviously Hawk's son. Ari scanned the tables, noting that almost no one sat where they had the previous night. No ranking ordered those seated at the tables. You either sat at the high table or the knights', or squires', or servants', but within those tables no one held any greater honor than another.

Ari attempted to move further down the table.

"No sir, you have to sit with me so we can talk." Wyatt pulled her again and she sat with another heavy sigh. "Tell me about fighting, sir. I want to know everything you know. Will you teach me?"

Ari speared a flank of venison on her dagger and flipped it onto her plate. She cut off a portion and stuffed it into her mouth before she could reply. She thought she might gag on the lump—*perhaps choking to death would be preferable to the infatuation of this boy.*

Wyatt nibbled at the strips of deer on his plate and stared longingly at her.

"My skill is unremarkable. I would relish the opportunity to set aside my blades in this peaceful land, Highness."

"Then I will take you on a tour of the castle."

She put more food in her mouth.

"Sir, is there anything you require?"

She smiled at Winslow. She stood and stepped away from Wyatt. "Do you have a wax tablet and a reed?"

Winslow raised his brows.

"I thought spending the morning within our chamber teaching Lin his letters would be preferable to a private escort by the young prince."

Winslow's gaze shifted to the lad. "Indeed, sir. I will bring the items at once." He turned to the prince. "Wyatt, Brother Peter is waiting in your chambers."

"Winslow, do I have to go? How is Latin ever going to help me?"

"You know your father's wishes, Highness."

Wyatt kicked the leg of the table. "I hate Latin."

Ari tried to send him on his way. "The greatest scholars recorded their wisdom in Latin, Your Highness."

"You know Latin, Sir Ari?"

"Sapientia quod scientia es instituo dictis."

Wyatt cocked his head at her. "Wisdom and… Wisdom and… "

"Knowledge," Ari offered.

"Wisdom and knowledge are found in ... words," Wyatt groaned as he said the final translation.

"You would benefit from more time with Brother Peter, Highness," Winslow said.

"May I give you the tour tomorrow, Sir Ari?"

"The knight is here on business of great import, Highness. Mayhaps when these matters are attended to, Sir Ari will have time to spend with you."

Wyatt's pleading captured her heart as his brows knit together and his lip popped out again.

"Let us see what the days ahead bring, Your Highness," Ari said with halting reluctance. "I promise not to go out without your guidance."

The boy's demeanor erupted as if black powder had exploded inside him. "Thank you, sir." He ran off and Ari sighed.

"You may regret such a promising, sir." Winslow turned to walk from the hall beside her.

"Oh aye," she groaned.

Ari returned to her quarters with her faithful shadow, Lin.

"What'd Sir Winslow give ya?" she asked, pointing to the items Ari carried wrapped in a bit of hide.

Ari patted the place next to her on the divan. "This is a wax tablet."

"What's it for?"

"I am going to make good use of our many hours trapped within these dark walls and teach you to read."

Lin's eyes grew to the size of goose eggs in her small face.

"Did your mother teach you your letters?"

Lin shook her head and the light from the flickering lamp sparkled on the ends of her hair.

"Do you wish to learn?"

Lin's mouth sagged open as she managed a slow awe-filled nod.

"Good. It is proper for every young page to learn to read. In many places the lady of the manor or even the queen sees to these matters, but …"

"But ya're the lady of our manor," Lin whispered with a devilish grin.

The corner of Ari's mouth rose. "Well, I have never taken the opportunity to be much of a lady, but I suppose it will be the best we can manage. Come, let us begin."

They worked until the midday meal, then joined the others in the hall. Ari returned to her chambers following the meal in her continued attempt to keep her distance from Edmund's men and his young son. She selected a book from the stack borrowed from the king and read aloud as Lin fluttered about the chamber straightening and cleaning.

Each day followed the next in the same reclusive manner. Ari spent as little time with those in the hall as she deemed polite and retreated to her chambers to teach Lin and search the grand tales of Veronia for any hint of the elusive weapon she sought. Within the first hours this inactive routine grated on her and stretched her nerves as tight as gut on a bard's lute. As day followed day, Ari became restless and agitated. *This is intolerable, Lord.*

"Is somethin' the matter, sir?" Lin asked after Ari stumbled over the same passage the third day of her confinement.

Ari flopped the book closed with an exasperated thump. "I hate idle hours. I train or fight nearly every day. I rarely indulge in even one whole hour of reading, so you would think it would be a blessing to be in a land of peace. But I don't know how to be at peace! The infatuated prince and the admiring warriors make the king's hall a cage in a Gypsy traveling show. I feel on display for their entertainment. And while this,"—her arm waved out indicating their room—"is far finer than the battle tent I live in much of the year, it feels like a cave. It must remain shuttered to keep out prying eyes, and thus barring the light and fresh air. It is unbearable."

She tossed the book onto the table with a thud. "And nowhere can I find any mention of the weapon my people have so long believed is here. How could we have been so wrong—or worse—how could Veronia have failed to record such a valuable treasure?

Ari stood and paced across the room and back, her angry steps smacking the floor. "I need to know what has become of my companions. I can't sit here taking pleasure in mindless Veronian history or a heroes tale when my country men are fighting for the right to exist and my men are hunted by the horde!"

In her next pass, she flung open the door and stormed out of the room. She heard Lin's hurried steps tapping behind her as she fled through the corridor and down the stairs. She burst from the building and scanned the ward around her. Lin closed the distance between them as Ari turned to the right and raced past the kitchens toward the tower beyond.

Ari entered the base of the structure and saw the internal stairs she hoped to find. She climbing them two at a time, then emerged at the top onto the battlements of the outer wall.

She inhaled a lungful of the breeze tumbling between the merlons and rested her hands on the crenel directly in front of her. She closed her eyes and allowed the sweet air to fill her lungs and her frantic breathing slowed. The wind caressed what little of her face lay exposed under her hood, and her spirit calmed. Warm sun rested on her back and relaxed her tight muscles.

Lin's soft footfalls joined her as the girl's breaths puffed. "Sir?"

Ari turned to look at her. A shadow drew her attention to the lower battlement of the inner wall. She rose to her full height and looked closer but saw no further movement. A nervous shiver ran up her spine as though some creature scaled her backbone.

Lin stepped beside her and dropped to Ari's feet with her back resting against the outer wall. She sat collecting her breath.

Ari scanned the battlements for any of the king's men. The few guards at their posts took no notice of her. Her eyes turned to the ward below. She could see the back of the great hall and the shuttered chambers above it. Here the outer wall rose much higher than the inner wall, which ran perpendicular to it. From the height of the battlement one could not easily see into her bedchamber for it lay three paces below where she stood.

Lin came to stand beside her. "Yar room?"

"Aye, and I am thinking we could crack those shutters. No one could see us from here."

"Will it make ya feel better?"

"It will help."

Ari remained standing atop the battlements and turned to look out over the land. She leaned against the wall and bowed her head. *Lord Almighty, be with Ri and our men. Protect them and guide them here. Thank you for Your provisions and going before me.* She sighed trying to find the words she needed. *Lord, I am strained and unsettled in this peaceful land You have clearly blessed. I need Your peace and Your direction. What would You have me do here?*

No answer came and she groaned.

"Sir?"

"I hate being still," Ari muttered in disgust. She turned back to the tower, descended the stairs and returned to her room.

Chapter 13

The next morning, the king stepped forward to greet Ari before Wyatt could pull her to her seat. "Good morning, sir Ari. How are you faring in your time with us?"

"I regret to tell you, I am becoming quite restless, Sire. How has the search of the annals progressed?"

"Well, perhaps I bring a little good news. I have told Wyatt he may escort you on a tour of our home. As to this weapon, I have yet to learn anything other than what I already knew. God fought for our people and delivered us with a miracle of … light."

Ari frowned. "Light?"

"Aye, but I am still searching." Edmund leaned forward and his voice dropped to a whisper. "But the tour. I thought you would prefer one eager lad over the great quantity of other requests I have also received to train or spar with you from near the entire garrison."

Her head lowered, her heart stuttered an odd beat, as she felt the heat of her regretful ingratitude fill her cheeks. "Thank you, Majesty, for your consideration. I welcome the tour."

She moved to her seat and ate with the energy of some great behemoth of a beast. Wyatt chattered beside her, fidgeting and squirming as if vermin filled his breeches, unable to sit still. One of the last to finish eating, she stood with movements slowed by a troubled heart. "Lin, we are to be given a tour. Follow."

"He doesn't need to come," Wyatt groaned.

"It is the page's duty to attend his master."

"I can see to anything you need."

"You are a prince and not a page in training to be a squire and later a knight of the realm, Highness. Lin's service teaches him all he needs to know to move up in the ranks. You cannot deny him advancement to meet your selfish desires, young lord. Lin deserves to earn the advantages you received by being born son of the king."

Wyatt's lower lip drooped at Ari's harsh chastisement. "Aye, sir."

"Forgive my bluntness Highness, I am accustomed to speaking my mind among men."

Wyatt stood a little taller and his lips turned in a small grin.

"I came seeking the favor of a foreign king, but I am no ambassador. I would enjoy an adventure outside the inner ward, if you are still amenable, Highness."

Wyatt brightened in the next heartbeat and bounded toward the door. "Come, sir." The three adventurers exited the hall and crossed the ward. Wyatt passed the stables. "We will end here. Let's start in the armory."

Ari followed the young prince's eager steps with long strides, and the soft crunch of Lin's footfalls hastened behind them. The clanging from the smith's hammer sang a welcoming melody as they rounded the corner beyond the inner gate. The hiss of the bellows bid her enter. Her heart danced with joy at the familiar surroundings so far from home.

Wyatt greeted the smith and introduced her.

"Welcome, Sir Ari. I understand you are quite skilled with the blade." The leather apron crinkled, as the slender man bent in a deep bow revealing the pink crown of his head. His hair appeared thin for one who looked to be no more than twenty-five. He stood tall once more and his long narrow face filled with a smile framing a missing front tooth.

"Sir Ari uses two blades." Wyatt's arms flew through the air mimicking her.

"Two?"

"Aye, I use twin knight's blades which are similar in length to the ancient Roman gladius."

The smith nodded and pulled a few of his shorter blades from their holders on the walls. Ari tested a few from the selection. The feel of their weight in her hands soothed her restless heart like a healer's balm. She tested the balance and admired the hone of the edge. Ari stepped back and practiced a few smaller swings in the tight space. Her heart sang a joyous melody. "You are a craftsman, sir. These are excellent."

Wyatt grabbed another of the smaller blades and using two hands he brought it up to collide with hers.

Ari placed her palm on the flat of his blade and pushed it down. Her hand ran along its length and she took the hilt in her other hand. "Not today, Highness. We have the whole castle to explore." She handed the weapons back to the smithy.

Wyatt groaned. "Can you teach me?"

"I would not take the honor from your father. It is a father's joy to train up his sons."

"If Father says 'tis all right, would you?"

"I will pray on the matter *if* your father gives consent." She inclined her head to the smith and turned to leave.

Lin stood in the doorway with her head cocked to one side.

"Does something puzzle you, Lin?"

"Ya looked happy with the swords, sir. I thought ya said wars were a dreadful thin'?"

"War is horror itself, but I am a soldier. The feel of the blades in my hands is well known. The mastering of the weapons has been my daily pursuit since I was of your age, and I found comfort in the familiarity so far from my home."

Lin nodded and stepped aside to allow them to pass.

Wyatt rushed ahead leading to the next building to hug the outer wall as Ari glanced around. Not a great many dwellings stood within King Edmund's walls. The rock on which his home perched allowed for an extensive view of the surrounding valley, but not much room to live.

"Does something trouble you, sir?"

Ari turned to Wyatt. "I was noticing the size of the bailey."

"We don't have room for many people to live up here. They reside in the town at the bottom of the mount. What are castles like where you come from?"

"If you move your lower town inside this bailey and place it all on a wide rolling hill it would look similar to King Maddix's home in Wexxton."

"Do many live there?"

Ari sighed with a heaviness, which resembled a groan. "Not as many as once did in generations past. The battles ahead may see the end of us."

Wyatt stopped and turned to speak, but Lin's small voice filled her ears first. "That's awful. Why don't ya move here?"

"Wexxton is our home, as Veronia is yours. It is now beset with evil, but we pray God will deliver us." A strange scent tickled her nose and she again raised her eyes toward the next building. As they approached, several dogs stood. Their tails wagged as they barked a ruckus greeting. Ari gasped and stepped back colliding with Lin. Their feet entangled and both were only a misplaced step from falling.

Wyatt laughed as he stroked the shaggy heads. "They are tame, Sir

Ari. These are some of Father's hunting dogs."

Ari tried to swallow her heart back in place. But it would not move.

Lin scampered past her to pet one of the smaller dogs as it loped from the building. "They're nice, sir. Don't ya wanna pet one?"

Ari shook her head. She fought to bring air into her lungs. Panic twisted her stomach into knots.

"Haven't you ever seen a dog before?" Wyatt chuckled.

She nodded. Both children gazed at her with tight brows and cocked heads. "There are such beasts in Wexxton, but they are wild. We do not live with animals among us, other than horses. It is too easy for the evil one to enspell them. He bends them to his will and they fight for him biting and clawing to fill my people with his wicked poison."

The children stood slack-jawed.

She swallowed, her parched tongue scraping across her jagged lips. "Is there perhaps something more we could see, Highness?"

"The hawkers are next." His face contorted as one corner of his lip rose. "Are you afraid of birds too, sir?"

A mere innocent query of a child, yet it cut like a long sword at her warrior's heart. She would not allow herself to fear the creatures. She, however, knew better than to trust beasts or tolerate their presence. The child did not understand the danger. She attempted to shake the uneasiness gripping her, but she shuddered instead. *Give me a blade and I would cut these vile beasts down. Confound this child!*

"We can move to the healer's house?" Wyatt said.

Ari straightened, forcing calm to her word. "The healer's house would be welcomed." She turned aside as Wyatt shrugged and moved beside her. She tried to calm her spirit and suppress her rage, but a falcon's cry staggered her next steps. She fought the urge to run for the safety of the nearest tower. She tossed her head and shook free of the unwelcome feelings.

If Wyatt noticed, he did not speak of it. "The royal physician, Tinsley, lives here. He has treatment rooms in the bottom and he lives upstairs.

As Wyatt explained, Tinsley stepped from the structure. "Good day, sir," Wyatt called.

"Aye, and the same to you, Highness," Tinsley squeaked with a small bow. "Sir Ari, have you come to have your arm tended?"

"No, sir, Lin has seen to the regular dressing. It heals well."

Lin stepped close without speaking, causing Ari to glance at her.

"We're low on supplies, sir," Lin whispered.

"We could use some more bandages and ointment, if you have them at hand, Healer."

Tinsley frowned. "Of course I have them prepared. Come, page, and fetch for your master."

The wiry man disappeared.

Ari scowled at having again offended him.

"Father says he thinks too much of himself," Wyatt moaned under his breath.

Ari motioned Lin to follow the healer. "Gather what is needed and return it to our chamber. Join us again when your task is complete."

Lin scampered off and Wyatt moved along the buildings nestling against the outer wall proclaiming each occupant by name. Ari reined in a snort. Did the child believe she would commit to memory every inhabitant of the castle? Or did he believe she knew them already, for he talked of Thomas adding, 'you know, the baker,' as though she should have known him.

Passing between structures, Wyatt turned to her. "Why do you cover yourself so, sir? Were you burned like Sir Charles?"

Ari scanned the buildings ahead. "How was Sir Charles injured?"

"Years before I was born, Father says Sir Charles patrolled the area around Dellshire to the west. He used to be captain of the garrison." Wyatt pointed to the three-story building beyond the outer gate some distance to their right. "Selvyn, Momma's cousin, came to Sir Charles and reported a house on fire with people still inside. Sir Charles ran past the flames and saved everyone. But as he made his escape through the hole he had hacked in the back wall, the burning thatch of the roof fell on him. The husband pulled Sir Charles out but burns covered his body. Father sent him to Kirkshire to heal." Wyatt rolled his eyes. "But he fell in love with Lord Radford's daughter." His nose crinkled. "He stayed there and became Lord Radford's captain and Selvyn became Father's."

He stopped. "What do you hide under all this fabric, sir? You are covered from head to feet."

"It is a common manner of attire in Wexxton, Highness," she sighed. She turned to the final structure on the south wall before the outer gate which faced west, and continued forward.

"Greetings, Dell," Wyatt called to the man sitting on a rough-hewn bench in front of the small stone building. "This is Sir Ari. He comes from Wexxton."

The man, bent over a length of leather, scarcely moved his head. His gaze did not rise to hers but shifted from his work to her feet. His large round head—which reminded her of a melon—drew nearer to them. He set his tools and skin on the bench and knelt before her. He examined the inner and outer stitching of her boots, running his thick fingers over them. His hand moved to the back of her heel and she felt the pressure as he pulled her foot toward him. Shifting her weight, she allowed him to raise her foot and examine the sole.

"Interestin'."

Ari looked to Wyatt for an explanation as she teetered on one foot. "Dell is the cobbler. He likes shoes." Wyatt shrugged.

"These have an unusual configuration. The sole is unbendin', with ridges across it. It appears to be thick as well." He reached his fat fingers toward her laces.

Ari freed herself and placed her foot on the ground once more. "We have little time to waste replacing our shoes every season. We use less desirable, thicker leather for the soles to make them last longer. They are carved with simple patterns for better footing on the changing ground of the battle field and they are padded with softer leather on the inside to allow for comfort."

"But they are so tall." He now lifted his head, revealing a shaggy mustache dangling over his lips.

Ari bent back the corner near the laces below her knee. "The leather here is thick as well. One never knows when they will be called to battle. The less armor to don the better."

Dell touched the material, rubbing it between his thumb and forefinger. "So they serve as greaves?"

"Aye, they have served me well." She pointed out a gash in one and several nicks in both.

Dell rose abruptly, causing her to step back to avoid his head colliding with her chin. "I have a proposition for you, sir?"

Ari felt her brows rise high.

"It would give me great pleasure to fashion you a pair of my finest footwear—in any style of your choosin', if you will allow me to have your old boots."

She continued to stare at him, an odd merriment bubbling in her.

"I would like to make a closer examination of them and even take them apart to see how they were assembled. I could learn a great deal from my eastern brothers."

Her shoulders rose high about her ears in befuddlement. "If it would assist you, I will be honored to give you my boots." She stifled a chuckle.

Dell whooped a momentary cheer and motioned her toward his humble shop. Waving her to sit on the bench, he disappeared within. He reemerged with a small scrap of parchment and a length of charcoal from the fire. He placed it on the ground at her feet. "Please remove your fine boot, sir, and I will measure your foot."

Ari hesitated for a moment wiggling her toes. Good, she'd wore her heavy wool stockings today. Once she unlaced the cord, Dell pulled it from her foot. "You wish to use parchment for your pattern?"

Dell grinned. "It is an advantage of also preparing all the parchment for the king. As I cut the tanned and cured bits into manageable pieces for his use in books and scrolls, I often have an irregular bit left for me own use."

She placed her foot on the scrap and he traced the outline. "Yar feet are much smaller than I would have reckoned by the size of yar boots and solidity of yar frame."

"A family trait," she mumbled.

"Are yar feet the same size?"

She looked at him confused.

"Ya would be surprised at how many men—due to injury or malformation—have two different foot shapes."

"No, my feet are the same. Do you need me to show you?"

He shook his head and brushed his tools aside to join her on the bench. "Tell me your requirements for the new boots.

He sat so near. She bent and busied herself with donning and re-lacing her boot. She relished the slow process in her thick gloves. She described her wishes and he asked for clarification until he understood.

"I will have them ready in a couple of weeks. I have acquired new skins which I will cure to your specifications."

She rose and stepped from him. "I look forward to enjoying the work of your hands."

He bowed. "I look forward to havin' your boots."

Dell waved as they turned, passing the outer gate and Lin rejoined them. Ari marveled at the pleasantness of the morning and the soothing effect it offered her soul—other than the animals. She felt her nerves work free from their restless knots, and she took a deep breath of the crisp autumn air. No trees could be seen over the tall walls of the castle perched so far above the valley floor, but she closed her eyes for a few steps, recalling the bright reds and gold of King Edmund's royal hunting ground.

She sojourned in the place where she might find the secret to save her people. For now they would be repairing and forging new weapons for the coming season of trouble. Things would be quiet for a time as those, who survived for another year, gathered about the fires and took their comfort in conversation instead of battle strategy. If she could find this elusive weapon and her men soon, she could join her father around those warm flames before the snow grew too deep.

A cold chill raced up Ari's spine. The hairs on the nape of her neck stood to attention. The Spirit within her alerted her to danger. Her eyes snapped open. The garrison stood before her—tall and imposing. The cold stones made her shiver. A bulky man stomped out the open door. Heads of passing servants and men-at-arms training nearby turned. On one side, narrow gazes of suspicion cut into her. On another, wide-eyed looks of wonder greeted her with near uncontainable fervor. Her heart trembled at both the anger and the eagerness. The stout man moved to block her path. Every nerve flared to full alert.

Chapter 14

Ari approached the man blocking her path with slow steady steps. She held his gaze unwavering. This short man posed no threat to her. She noted his ragged scar and her heart thrilled at the thought of adding to his trophies.

He stood with arms crossed, feet shoulder-width apart.

She did not stop until she stood toe-to-toe with the man, and stretched to her full height, forcing him to look up to meet her gaze. Squaring her shoulders, she brushed her forearms against her hips and remembered she stood naked before an enemy. Her blades lay sheathed on the table near her bed.

She blinked.

"I do not need nor do I wish ya here, confusin' me men with yar foul warrior skills." His lip curled as if he'd eaten something rancid.

"Who said I would be so willing to offer my secrets to those I may soon face on a battlefield?"

His chin jutted out. "Ya're a spy."

"Selvyn, this is Sir Ari. He saved me and is now Father's guest." Wyatt's words bubbled between them, annoying her.

"Selvyn—it's the name of the Greek god of the trees. An odd name to give one born in a kingdom protected by God Most High. Why would your parents want to invoke the name of a false god?" She shrugged and offered an off-handed thought. "Hal would suit you better. It means 'captain of the guard.'"

"This is not my kingdom." His chest puffed up. "I am Balmorian."

"But we are all the same kingdom since Momma married Father."

"Watch yar mouth, boy." Selvyn's gaze shifted to Wyatt.

"You are addressing the son of your liege, *Sel-vyn*." Ari drew out his name, disgusted by the taste of it.

His eyes narrowed on her again. His crossed arms dug deeper into his firm broad chest, muscles bulging. "My allegiances are nay concern of yars, stranger."

"Selvyn, Ari is Father's guest."

"Be warned, boy, yar protector may not always be at yar side."

A breath caught in her throat. Shivers like ice water raced down her spine. She stepped back from Selvyn. She gave him ground.

"Ya'd be wise ta leave."

"I begged King Edmund to allow me to leave. He will not release me. Perchance you would have more sway with him." She gagged on the soft-spoken words.

"Sir Ari is my friend and he will stay—"

She thrust her gloved hand into Wyatt's chest and pushed him behind her. "Stop meddling in the affairs of your elders, Highness." She felt his stuttered breaths at her rebuke, and knew—if she turned to look on him—tears would be pooling in his eyes.

Selvyn's eyes widened and danced with satisfaction. His chin raised and he tossed a knowing glance to the neck-less mountain of a man coming to stand next to him.

The look exchanged between them forced Ari back another step— and Wyatt with her. She gauged the distance from Selvyn to be at the outside of a thrust broadsword. Again she regretted her lack of weaponry. She made a hasty scan of the surrounding yard, judging who may be foe and who may serve as friend. Her heart pounded.

"Is there a problem, gentlemen?" King Edmund approached with quick footfalls.

She did not look at him, keeping her eyes trained on the threat before her. "Not at all, Your Majesty. Sir Selvyn spoke to the merits of my prolonged stay." She tasted bile with her honeyed words.

"As you are my guest, I see not why it would concern my captain."

Wyatt trembled and sniffled before he dashed back the way they came a few moments and a lifetime ago.

Now she turned her gaze to the king. "I am finished with my excursion," she quipped and turned on her heel to her left. She entered the tower serving as the frame for the outer gate. Pounding up the stairs, she could hear Lin's rapid scurrying as it filled the enclosed space.

The sound of her footfalls thundering across the battlement drowned out all thought until she reached the inner wall and a tender hand took her arm pulling her to a stop.

"Ari, wait."

She whirled and slapped the offensive appendage away. "Do you coddle all your warriors with such tenderness, Majesty?" she hissed. She stepped from him and her eyes searched for witnesses.

Edmund rocked back on his rear foot with a boyish grin. "Not to my recollection."

She huffed her distain and turned to look down on the inner ward.

"Tell me what happened." His soothing words grated on her raw nerves.

"It is as I feared it would be, Sire! My presence is bringing trouble on your home." She turned to glare at him but her words were softened by regret. "Your Majesty, I did naught less than imply I am here to spy on you and your men for a war Wexxton will soon wage on Veronia. Forgive me Majesty."

She turned away from him, shame heating her cheeks. "If you could but find the weapon we need, I could be on my way this hour."

"It is not yet time for you to leave."

Frustration boiled over in her again. "You are avoiding a proper search for this fabled weapon to keep me here," she ground out. She whirled on him with a wagging finger. "I do not know to what purpose you detain me, Sire, but God has a destiny for me, and no one will keep me from it."

Edmund pushed her finger aside, and spoke with an annoying calm assurance. "Good knight, it is the Lord Almighty Himself who impedes your forward step."

She pulled away with a heavy sigh. "Aye Majesty. Forgive me— yet again."

"Think no more of the matter."

Hawk approached and they turned toward him. "I have spoken with many of the men as you requested, Majesty. They are divided on their thoughts of our visiting knight. Opinions range from dangerous enemy, to future captain of the guard."

Ari sneered.

"Of one thing they can all agree. Sel instigated the confrontation. Ari stood his ground as unmoving as Sel until Ari stepped away. No one is quite sure what made him shift."

They turned to her.

"The Spirit—at last—overcame my hot-temper."

Edmund's brows rose.

"I am a guest in your home, Majesty. I am loath to speak a disparaging word against your men—I do not know them."

"I will have a talk with my captain." Edmund turned away.

"Take care, Majesty," she warned.

His head snapped around to hold her in a hard gaze. "Now I will insist you tell why you would give such a warning."

She shifted her weight between her feet.

Hawk drew near and spoke in hushed tones. "Speak the plain truth —without fear. We know the manner of the man."

"Why would you tolerate such evil in your walls?"

"What makes you believe him evil?"

She spoke in earnest. "The Spirit makes it as plain as the hilt of my swords. He has no respect for you, Sire, and I believe he threatened your son."

Hawk nodded his agreement. "A few of the men said the same." He turned back to Ari again. "Many of the men have yet to see the blackness of his heart. They esteem him as an accomplished warrior and a trusted teacher."

Edmund sighed. "Until such a time as God opens their eyes, I must bear the burden of his hatred."

Ari acknowledged her understanding. "With one in such a prominent position, care must be taken in his removal."

"As I said I will speak to him. He *will not* trouble you further."

As Edmund left, Ari kept Hawk from leaving. "Sir, I have a boon if it is not too much of a burden."

"I am at your service, friend."

"I have hurt the Young Prince. My words were callous and harsh and I know he left in tears. I regret the pain I have caused him. Would you see if perchance there is some way to make amends? The lad reveres me so."

"One should exalt none above the Lord God."

Ari managed a weary smile. "You see the full depth of my concern, sir."

"I will speak to him at the first opportunity.

"Thank you. You have lightened my worry."

He inclined his head and moved toward the nearest stairs.

Ari looked up and saw Lin standing nearby, eyes the size of saucers. "Come, page. We are late to your lessons," she said without emotion.

The child's face split in a wide grin and she raced ahead to the tower nearest their chamber. Ari met Lin as she held open the door into the ward. Lin's infectious smile caused the corners of her own mouth to turn in response. *Father, what are You doing to me? These joyful, vulnerable, innocent children are going to be my undoing as a warrior.*

"Sel I would speak with you," Edmund ordered through the open barrack's door.

Selvyn appeared and leaned against the doorframe his arms again crossed over his black heart. He made a quick scan of the men about. "Majesty? Ya have need?"

"I would hear your account of the encounter with my honored guest."

"He, himself, said he came as a spy."

"Sir Ari met your challenge."

"Majesty," Selvyn mocked. "The man's own ill intensions colored me innocent words."

"Your words are anything but innocent, Sel."

The man shrugged.

Edmund raised his voice to collect a few more ears. "I find it strange this man you claim as a spy takes full responsibility for his words spoken in haste and again seeks my favor to leave at once, while my captain refuses any culpability."

"I bear no guilt."

"Granted, but you did provoke the confrontation—as many will attest." Edmund's arms swept wide to include those standing within earshot.

Selvyn stood, arms dropping, a scowl cutting his face. "Perchance not as many as ya might think." He turned toward the men in the sparring corral. "See to yar drills!" He turned his back to Edmund, then disappeared into the garrison and slammed the door.

Chapter 15

"Sir, why did the captain stand in yar way?" Lin closed the door behind Ari as they entered their chambers.

"He saw me as a threat to his power."

"I don't understand." Lin put her hands on her hips and looked hard at Ari as she sat in the chair. "I ain't never seen him. He don't come to the hall to eat with us, and I ain't never seen him in the inner wall. How could he be threatened?"

"Those loyal to the king have seen while others have only heard of my ability to fight. Though far from the most skilled in my kingdom, my fighting style must differ in some marked way to Veronian fighting. They want to learn from me. Selvyn instructs in the art of warfare here, but he must fear I come to replace him."

"But ya haven't even practiced since ya came and ya done said ya didn't wish to be trainin' with the king's men. Who ya gonna to teach?"

"It is the way of men, Lin. Throughout your life you will encounter many who fret so over their own value they will see every newcomer as a threat to their position and their worth. These can be the most dangerous sort, for they will see every word and action as a personal attack. Such men—if cornered—are capable of great violence as they seek to hold to what they perceive as theirs alone."

"He's naught but a fool," Lin concluded with a stomp of her foot. "Ya wanna go home and help yar family. Ya don't even want to stay here with us." Sadness colored her words.

'You don't want to stay here with us…' The truth of the statement resonated within Ari like the peel of the steeple bell, yet it also filled her with a foreign longing. She stood and yanked a new book from the pile, upsetting the ones above it. They banged to the floor, further frustrating her.

Lin hurried to collect them.

"Practice your letters," Ari instructed as she removed her gloves and replaced the books on the table.

Lin stood still, hands clasped tight before her. "I'm sorry. I upset ya, sir."

Ari flipped her hand at the perceptive girl. "You did naught, child. As I have said I am restless within these walls. Do not take offense at my brusque manner. It could never be caused by anything you say or do, Lin. It is a flaw in my own character."

Lin's arms dropped to her sides and a sweet smile graced her face. "Before lessons, I must fetch more wood? No servants have come. Little but embers are left." She rubbed her arms.

Ari smiled despite herself. Only eight and the child possessed the awareness to see the folly of stupid men and the knowledge to keep the hearth continually warm. She was also observant enough to notice the need for more wood. Something Ari herself failed to recognize. "Of course, faithful page. See to your duties and we shall attend your lessons in warmth."

Lin started to curtsy and her cheeks pinked as she hid a giggle behind her delicate fingers. She switched to a formal bow and dashed from the room.

Ari's smile grew.

The remainder of the day proceeded without notable event in their near complete isolation. Wyatt didn't even acknowledge her at supper.

Ari took the opportunity to dine further down the boards, yet her heart stuttered with guilt so she could not enjoy her meal even there. Several of the men engaged her in conversation, their favorite topic being her confrontation with Selvyn. She voiced her regret more than once to which they answered with their praise of her actions.

Lord, act quickly, or I will have Your whole kingdom turned on its end.

Chapter 16

The next morning, following the breaking of the fast, Wyatt approached Ari with soft steps and his gaze fixed to the floor. "Sir?"

"Good day, Your Highness. I wish to—"

"Please forgive me, sir."

"Highness, it is I who must apologize. Again my words were too harsh—"

"Was my fault, sir. I need to stop interrupting people when they are talking."

Ari bit her lower lip to contain her laughter. "'Twould be a good discipline for us all, Highness."

"Sir Hawk also says I have put you before God. I don't know how I did so but I know it is not something one should do." He raised his face, head cocked to the side and brows tight together. "If one doesn't know how he has done a thing, how is he supposed to stop doing it?"

"I think if you treat me like any of your father's men-at-arms, and naught special, God will retrain the throne of your heart, Highness."

"But you are special, Sir Ari. You saved my life. No one else has ever done so before."

"God spared your life, Highness. Almighty God used many people —not me alone—to see you returned safe to your home. I could not have done it on my own and three men sacrificed their lives for yours. We must pray for their families."

Wyatt nodded his head, but remained silent. The corner of his lips pinched tight together.

"Lessons, Wyatt," Edmund called.

Wyatt left without his usual exuberance.

"Perhaps we might find a time in the coming days to finish my tour, Highness."

His head snapped around with a joyful smile. "Oh aye, sir. We still have half the castle to see yet."

Ari bowed. "Until later, Highness."

"He pouts when he don't get his way," Lin whispered as they exited the hall.

Again Ari tried to resist the laughter tickling her insides with little mercy. "He is your elder—"

"Only by two years, sir."

"And he is the king's son."

Lin sighed. "So we must tolerate his behavior?"

"We must never gossip and always be a good and proper example."

Lin nodded as she held open their chamber door. "Aye, sir. I shall do my best."

After morning lessons and the midday meal, Ari loathed to return to the confines of her prison. She went on the battlements and looked over the valley to the north of the castle. She could see the royal hunting grounds a little way to the east. *How different matters would be if I had stayed with Ri. He ordered us to continue south, but I wished to go west. If I had left a day prior or later, would Wyatt have been saved?* She chided herself for her own arrogance. *Of course he would be safe. For God willed it so, but He used my involvement in Wyatt's rescue to bind the king to me.* She sighed and leaned back against a merlon looking down into the castle grounds. *Lord, this intolerable inactivity is making me crazed. Please reveal this weapon to us or show me what I am to do here—and make haste.*

Stillness answered her desperate plea and she stomped along the battlements in frustration. Looking down on the bailey, she noted Selvyn coming out of a small thatched building beyond the barracks with the large neck-less warrior beside him. She learned this morning that his name was Godric. Serving as one of Selvyn's closest men, they were seldom seen apart. His name also carried a distasteful meaning—strong god. Ari bristled at the sight of them and continued along the wall.

She watched Edmund's men train as she passed above on the battlements. *There are not so many differences between our styles. Why are the men in such an uproar?* She skirted a guard above the outer gate.

He smiled with a nod of greeting.

She stopped at a crenel facing south and looked out at the huge valley before her. It continued to the horizon unbroken except by one great forest and the occasional low hill. Everything lay blanketed in rich golds, reds and evergreen hues. God's blessing spread everywhere her eye scanned, stirring the longing afresh. *I ask this for Wexxton, Father. Will You yet bless our land once more?* With thoughts of her home, the ache in her heart grew unbearable and she turned to look on the bailey.

Ari groaned and rested her forearms on the inner crenel.

"Sir? Does somethin' trouble ya?"

Ari turned toward her faithful shadow with surprise. Lin completed her duties with such stealth there were many times Ari forgot she remained so near. "Tomorrow is the Lord's Day."

"Aye?" Lin prodded.

"I belong in God's house on the holy day. I never fail to attend anytime I am able, and there His holy house sits." Ari pointed to the large structure occupying the majority of the bailey's center area.

Lin tipped her head. "I'm sure King Edmund'll welcome ya."

"I cannot enter God's house like this," she groaned waving her hand in front of her to draw Lin's gaze to her clothes. Ari turned her back on the chapel and slid down the rough stones to sit on the battlements, her head in her hands. "I am required to sit with the women, but I cannot as I am now and God's Word makes it plain, *The woman shall not wear that which perteineth unto the man.* I cannot dishonor my God more. Have I not brought Him enough shame already?"

"Sir?"

Ari raised her head to look as the girl bounced from foot-to-foot. A sweet smile with no trace of fear of discomfort graced her face. *Oh what have I done? I have dishonored my God's commands, and I have conspired to bring this innocent into my depravity. Lord, do not hold my sin against her. I alone am to blame.*

Lin continued to wiggle. "Sir?"

Figuring the child had an urgent need to relieve herself, she waved her off. "Go Lin. I will meet you in our chambers."

She dashed off without another thought, as Ari turned her face to the heavens. *My God—Precious Father—do not forsake me. Forgive me for breaking Your commandments. Show me how I may do what You require. I wish naught more than to be Your faithful servant. Help me, Lord God.*

Silence.

Her head dropped back against the cold stones behind her. Her eyes closed in despair.

Silence.

She pushed to her feet. She would need to speak with the king before she acted with a recklessness, which would allow her sin to affect others.

She approached the last tower on the south wall and noticed a space beyond its base almost completely enclosed by the back of the stables, the east rock of the castle mount, and the garden wall. She sped down the tower stepping out into the empty space. A narrow opening lay between the garden wall and the stables. With the entrance from the ward about two paces wide, the open space beyond lay well hidden from prying eyes. She spun around with slow purpose, gauging the area contained within the high walls. The space stretched several rods deep and at least a rod wider in the other direction. It was larger than King Edmund's sparring corral and far more private. Perhaps one day she could hide away here and train.

Chapter 17

Ari stepped from the secret place and out into the busy ward. She glanced back again to judge the ability to see into the space before proceeding across the ward to her chambers. She had traveled but a few steps when shouts drew her attention toward the inner gate.

"Sir Ari, Sir Ari?" Lin bounded toward her with near Wyatt's energy and excitement.

Ari noticed the turned heads and she frowned as Lin reached her and grabbed her hand. Ari pulled away. "Young page, you are turning heads with your childish exuberance."

Lin stood still and as tall as her small frame would allow. She bowed low. "Sir Ari," she said with more calm. "There's somethin' important I must show ya. Would ya please follow me?" She leaned close with an infectious smile. "Ya must come, sir. 'Tis most wonderful."

Ari sighed and gave Lin a nod. She followed the young girl as she skipped every third or fourth step out into the bailey. They turned toward the right and moved to the center structure. Ari stopped at the bottom step, which led up to the chapel doors carved with ornate scenes for the life of Christ.

"Please, sir," Lin whispered from the top step.

Ari shook her head and trembled.

Lin stepped down and took her hand. "'Twill be all right. I promise."

Ari's feet moved forward unbidden as Lin tugged on her arm. The coolness within raised gooseflesh all over her body. Lin released her and Ari thought she would flee but the rattling of a lock in the dim light kept her feet rooted in the narthex.

The lock banged open in the empty space echoing through the small nave. Ari's head turned to the creaking door as Lin put her shoulder to it.

"Sir Winslow says he'll put oil to this so it don't make such a ruckus." Lin pulled the door closed behind them and locked it once more.

The corridor devoid of light sent a shiver through her. Ari felt Lin brush past her, and she whispered. "There're stairs, Aria. Take care."

The shock of Lin calling her by name for the first time jolted her into movement. She reached out for the wall to her left and felt its chill through her glove. Next she slid her right foot forward until it bumped the first step and raised her foot placing it on the surface. The step was narrower than her foot and from Lin's footfalls above her head she knew the stairs rose in a tight spiral. She climbed with halting tentative steps until her eyes were drawn to the faint light glowing above. She climbed double the distance of the stairs in the great hall and emerged in a small gallery above the nave. The small dark space held three short pews—two on the left and one on the right —and looked down on the high altar, which sat forward of the choir. Most altars were hidden in the east end—thinking on it now Ari realized she entered the chapel from the east. King Edmund's ancestors set God's house like the ancient Tabernacle, which always faced east. The thought made her smile.

"Aria?" Lin whispered from the middle of the closest pew.

Ari sat on the end of the short bench and Lin slid close.

"Sir Winslow said we can come here anytime. He says we need'nt fear 'cause it's always dark and there's only one key." Brass glinted in a ray of light from the stained glass window opposite them as it lay on Lin's upraised palm. "Ya can remove yar hood here and meet God as yarself. And we're over the women's side," Lin leaned against the railing and pointed.

Ari removed her gloves and pulled the covering from her head. Looking at Lin, she could not tell her hair color even as close as they sat. No one from below would be able see their presence at all. Ari rested back in the pew. *Will this please You, Father?*

A distant door creaked. "Psalms 112. Praise ye the Lord. Blessed is the man that feareth the Lord, and delighteth greatly in His commandments. His seed shall be mighty upon earth: the generation of the righteous shall be blessed. Riches and treasures shall be in his house, and his righteousness endureth forever. Unto the righteous ariseth light in darkness: he is merciful and full of compassion and righteous. A good man is merciful and lendeth, and will measure his affairs by judgment. Surely he shall never be moved: but the righteous shall be had in everlasting remembrance. He will not be afraid of evil tidings: for his heart is fixed, and believeth in the Lord. His heart is established: therefore he will not fear…" The passing voice faded into the distance as the priest traveled through the choir into the rooms beyond.

The peace filling Ari consumed her fear. How odd to think God would view her as righteous when she behaved as she did, but the Spirit within her confirmed the sacred words as directed at her.

"Does this make ya feel better?"

Lin's tender query pulled her from her worship, but she smiled at the child. She raked her fingers through Lin's short hair. "Oh precious child, you are God's hand of blessing on me."

Lin's eyes grew wide and Ari could see light glisten in the

moisture growing in them.

"Lin, what is it?"

The girl didn't say anything for several minutes. A tear sparkled as it slid down her cheek. She swallowed hard. "Momma used to say that."

"Then you are twice the blessing, Lin."

Lin's arms reached out and encircled Ari's neck tugging, on her unbound hair.

Ari felt at a loss as to what to do. She trained younger children but none of them ever hugged her. Her arms came around the crying child, and an agonizing ache pierced Ari's heart so she couldn't breathe.

"…He maketh the barren woman to dwell with a family, and a joyful mother of children. Praise ye the Lord. Psalm 114 When Israel went out of Egypt…" the priest said, continuing his recitation of the Psalms as he went about his work below.

Ari startled at the words. This verse did not bring her peace as the one before. She pulled from Lin's grasp. "Perhaps we should go for now. The bell for supper should toll soon."

Lin brushed away a tear with the back of her small hand. "Here's the key."

Ari reached up and pulled the cord holding the key for their chest from her neck. She worked the knot free, added the new key and retied it. She took the cord and looped it over Lin's neck. "You keep our secrets and our treasures safe, my friend."

"Me?"

"You are ever responsible. I trust you," Ari said as she wound her hair and replaced her disguise, but she couldn't look at the child. Her presence unsettled Ari. "Do you know what time service begins?"

"Sir Winslow says if we arrive prior to first light, we should go unseen for everyone else will arrive before the breaking of the fast."

Ari stood and moved toward the stairs. "We should take a loaf of bread from supper to our chambers. It is not fitting for our stomachs to grumble in God's house."

"I'll remember," Lin promised as she wound down the stairs and unlocked the door.

Ari stepped out into the afternoon light, bright compared with the dark chapel. Selvyn walked a pace away, heading toward the thatched building. Ari recognized it now as an alehouse. Selvyn and his followers must prefer to take their meal there.

He turned and his gaze narrowed. "Still here?"

"As long as the Lord deems my presence necessary."

"Then I shall pray hard tomorrow to be rid of you." He disappeared, leaving Godric glaring at her as she turned toward the ward. She felt the heat of his stare on her neck until she passed well beyond the inner gate.

Chapter 18

Ari and Lin made their way to the secret gallery long before anyone ventured into the sanctuary below. Ari removed her hood and gloves and knelt at the railing. Lin sat in the rear pew allowing Ari time to seek God.

Lord, it has been long since You spoke to me. Please, do You not still have a word for me? What am I to do here? Why do I remain? She knelt still and silent.

Bang! The doors of the chapel opened.

Ari's head snapped up and her right hand went to her waist by instinct.

Reverent footfalls whispered down the aisle. They were no longer alone. The faithful slid into the pews below.

Ari sighed and returned to sit beside Lindsay. Unable to see below, Ari could hear the shuffling of feet, the brush of fabric, and the creak of wood filled the space. After a time, the room stilled as if they were again alone.

Incense flirted with her nose.

The high priest peeked into view as he stepped near the altar. His full vestments made him look like an expectant queen.

Judge not, that ye be not judged.

Ari shuddered as the thought tumbled in her mind. *Forgive me.*

The priest raised his large hands to the heavens and his voice rang out, filling the nave like the deep, rich peels of a gigantic bell. "As

David said, so say we all. 'Plead thou my cause, O Lord, with them that strive with me: fight thou against them, that fight against me. Lay hand upon the shield and buckler, and stand up for mine help. Bring out also the spear and stop the way against them, that persecute me: say unto my soul, I am thy salvation. Let them be confounded and put to shame, that seek after my soul: let them be turned back, and brought to confusion, that imagine mine hurt. Let them be as chaff before the wind, and let the Angel of the Lord scatter them. Let their way be dark and slippery: and let the Angel of the Lord persecute them. For without cause they have hid the pit and their net for me: without cause have they dug a pit for my soul. Let destruction come upon him unawares, and let his net, that he hath laid proudly, take him: let him fall into the same destruction. Then my soul shall be joyful in the Lord: it shall rejoice in His salvation.'"

The Spirit reverberated within her chest, causing her breaths to come in stuttered gasps. *This is the cry of my heart, Father.*

"A-men," the priest concluded with a pleading that her soul echoed.

"A-men!" the congregation answered as one.

"Oh a-men and a-men. May it be so Lord," Ari whispered in the high gallery.

"Let us give voice to our praise."

The choir of holy men—though small in number—rose to their feet. The faithful below must have done likewise for pews creaked and rustling stirred the air. The familiar song—*Come, Creative Spirit* propelled from the seats below to lift the beams over Ari's head. As though she heard them for the first time, they captured her soul.

> *...Fill our hearts with love enduring;*
> *In our bodies strength implanting,*
> *Faith and firmness ever granting.*

Far the foe to grace repelling,
Give us endless peace indwelling;
Thou, as leader deign to guide us,
That no evil may betide us ...

Other hymns—some new, yet many familiar—floated up from below, but Ari's mind lingered in a heavy fog. The old fight stirred her warrior heart. She knew there would be endless peace in her Father's hands. She must trust Him to keep evil from befalling them. She rested, as her act of obedience. The protection and the fight remained God's alone. Yet being still near drove her mad.

The pain of the internal battle dropped her to the pew. The last strains of the final hymn evaporated like morning dew. Her elbows rested on her knee and her hands cradled her aching head.

Over the din within the voice of the young assistant priest, she had heard reciting from Psalms the previous day, took time to penetrate her thoughts.

"Finally, my brethren, be strong in the Lord, and in the power of His might. Put on the whole armor of God, that ye may be able to stand against the assaults of the devil. For we wrestle not against flesh and blood, but against principalities, against powers, and against the worldly governors, the princes of the darkness of this world, against spiritual wickedness, which are in the high places. For this cause take unto you the whole armor of God, that ye may be able to resist in the evil day, and having finished all things, stand fast. The Word of the Lord. Ephesians chapter six."

"The Word of the Lord," the congregation echoed.

The elder priest came forward to stand in front of the altar and scanned the faithful before him with a slow turn of his tonsured head. One hand held the other over his wide girth. His gaze rose. Did he see her hidden in the dark gallery? Ari jumped when his authority voice rang out.

"Train and prepare!"

Ari's heart seized in her chest.

"Train and prepare, my people. The Lord teaches, 'Take heed therefore that ye walk circumspectly, not as fools, but as wise, redeeming ye season: for the days are evil.' We are admonished repeatedly to prepare, to don our armor and fight evil in all its forms. I tell you again men and women of Almighty God: train and prepare. Blessed be the Lord my strength, which teacheth mine hands to fight, and my fingers to battle. He is my goodness and my fortress, my tower and my deliverer, my shield, and in Him I trust, which subdueth my people under me."

Breath refused to be drawn into Ari's stone lungs. *God never contradicts Himself,* she admonished. *Lord, am I to train as Your warrior for the coming battle or am I to trust You to vanquish my enemy? Please. I seek only to be Your obedient servant.*

Her heart stumbled in her ears. Her lungs burned as though they held a raging fire.

Lord what do you require?

"'For I do not trust in my bow, neither can my sword save me. But Thou hast saved us from our adversaries, and hast put them to confusion that hate us.' I tell you, God will defeat our enemy. He may use us by the power of His mighty right hand. We are only to be obedient. Train and prepare—and trust in the Lord."

Like being dunked in a mountain stream, clarity dawned. Air flooded her lungs until she sputtered and coughed. Her jumbled thoughts stood at attention awaiting the Master's inspection.

All glory in the victory belongs to You. I will prepare for battle. Thank You, Father.

Ari again found herself on her knees. Silence blanketed her. Lin sat on the seat as before.

The child smiled, her shoulders relaxed, and fingers laced in her lap. "Ya're pleased ya came."

Ari's brow rose.

"You look like the people Momma always said hear the voice of God. I hope I hear Him someday."

The bell tolled.

Ari donned her disguise. "God wants to talk to you, Lindsay. He wants to talk to all His children. We must learn to listen."

"What's God sound like?"

Ari stared at the stained glass window. "God has many different voices. Sometimes He has the voice of the reader of His Word. Sometimes He has the voice of a friend, or a parent. But most often He has no voice at all. Words, ideas, truths come to your heart and it makes your spirit do somersaults."

"I'll pay closer attention."

"We should go to break the fast," Ari stood.

Lin laughed. "Those bells are for the midday meal. Ya talked to God a long time."

"I am slow to learn and it takes God an extra measure till I comprehend His direction."

Lin stopped halfway down the stairs, causing Ari to almost collide with her in the dim light. "But ya listen. Isn't of more import to learn and understand than to think ya know and move in error?"

"Child, God has given you the wisdom of Solomon."

Ari squinted against the glare of the bright sunlight. New peace overwhelmed her. With slow and calm steps she entered the ward as Edmund and Hawk stepped from the stables. The two men drew alongside her and fell into the rhythmic stride of her steps.

Edmund smiled. "You should have been in service this morning,

Sir Ari. It was quite moving. Father James admonished us—"

"To train and prepare."

Edmund and Hawk stopped in mid stride. Edmund's gaze shifted from her to Hawk and back again. A foolish grin grew across his clean-shaven face, the softness of it contrasting with the cut of his square jaw. "You have found my great-grandmother's gallery."

Before she could apologize, Edmund started walking. "Splendid." His deep rich laugh warmed her. "Come to my study after meal. We have matters to discuss." He inclined his head as he moved past her.

Chapter 19

Lin moved to follow into Edmund's study. "No, page. You must remain without."

Lin sighed, but she moved to an empty bench against the wall.

"You need not stay. 'Tis a beautiful day—the Lord's Day. Go enjoy your day of rest."

"I'll wait." Lin crossed her legs and placed an elbow on one knee. Her chin dropped into her hand with a deep sigh.

Ari shrugged, entered the room, and took the far seat. Hawk sat to her left. Edmund secured the door and moved behind the great desk.

"I am pleased you found a way to attend service. The matter crossed my thoughts late last eve, but it vanished before I addressed it with Winslow. The queen's gallery shall serve you well until such a time as you can take your rightful place."

"It is also an excellent place to hide," Hawk added with a soft chuckle.

"Oh aye. It is on account of the two of us a door and lock were installed. We used it in an effort to hide from our tutor." Edmund smiled, leaned back, and gazed upon her.

She struggled to breathe under his scrutiny. Her gaze lowered. "Little Lin sought Winslow after I voiced my desire to attend. He knew the perfect solution."

"The man is a gem." He laid his forearms on his desk and leaned forward. "Our good priest is of a mind we should join your coming battle."

"Sire!" Ari's head shot up and she became captured once more in his heated stare. "I could nay ask you—"

"Aye, you did not ask."

She pulled from his gaze. "Sire—"

"Listen but a moment, friend. Hear my thoughts."

She nodded but avoided looking at him.

"Veronia failed to vanquish this evil which is now plundering your land. I have read the accounts of my father's father's father. The battle he fought routed the enemy army but the Black Knight escaped. They pursued him but only as far as your border. We rid our land of him but thought naught of the welfare of our neighbors. It is to our shame your countrymen now suffer so."

Ari only allowed her gaze to climb to his square jaw, but he put his hand up to stop her.

"And as Father James said, evil must always be opposed by the righteous. I will not stand by again and see your people fall without raising a sword with you." Edmund sat back. "I cannot at this time promise my war host. I shall present the situation to my lords at the Christ Mass. I only pledge my sword, and that of my thane."

Hawk's head inclined. "I know many will follow their king's example and join us."

"There are many unlanded knights within my kingdom who itch for a good battle. My troublesome captain and the many tourneys bare witness."

"Sire," Ari smiled as she dared raise her eyes to his well-formed lips and jutting cheekbones. "I have an offer, if you are agreeable. Wexxton, though once rich and productive, is a wasteland as God has withdrawn His hand of blessing as the evil spreads. If we are victorious God's blessing will return. But we no longer have the numbers to hold all of it. Thus my offer. Tell your unlanded knights, if they join us, when God grants victory, King Maddix will offer each a fief of his own for his reward."

Edmund's mouth hung agape. "Truly, you believe your king would make such a generous offer to foreign knights?"

"If they are God-fearing and upright, King Maddix will welcome them with open arms and great joy, granting them land so his kingdom will again be fruitful and filled with holy men."

"You can speak for this King Maddix?" Hawk asked.

"Aye, he sent us to King Edmund to secure the weapon and we were granted leave to offer compensation for such favor. This would be a fitting payment for an offer to join us on the battlefield."

"It is a great reward indeed. I shall present it to the lords and they will convey it to their men. Many will join you with such a promise." Edmund sighed. "As for the weapon you seek, I have found mention of it in the annals of the kings. It is called the 'Light of God' but I have no idea what it is or where it now resides. I will continue my search, though it appears so common as to indicate every man knew of it and how to wield it. It was so common my ancestors didn't see the need to explain it. They believed it would always be a part of our arsenal."

"And being it is known by my people as well, it must have been widely used by your ancestors." Ari concluded, fighting to keep ire from tainting her words.

"We will continue the search as we will prepare for the battlefield."

"Your Majesty, in regard to such preparation, there is an area behind the stables I wish to seek your favor to——."

Thud!

Ari fell silent at a thump against Edmund's outer wall and the sounds of a scuffle outside.

Chapter 20

Ari followed Hawk out of the king's study.

Lin lay entangled with Wyatt on the floor.

"Lin!"

The girl released the prince and rolled away from him. Her eyes met Ari's for only a moment before she rose to sit on her knees, head low. "Forgive me, sir, I—I only tried ta prevent—wasn't my place …"

"Your page would not allow me to enter my father's study." Wyatt stood and brushed the rushes and dust from his fine garments.

"Sir Ari said we must remain without while a meetin' was held with King Edmund." Lin snapped at him like a fearsome river monster.

"He is my father and I am allowed—"

"Wyatt!" Edmund now stood in the doorway, arms crossed. "You know well I do not indulge your every intrusion into my private study. It is a realm where matters of great import are addressed."

"But the page need not attack me for it."

"Lin, in his faithful duty to both his master and his king, risked suffering wrath from both of us in an attempt to save you from punishment."

Wyatt sniffled. "But Father …"

"Wyatt, you know protocol and my wishes. Lin gave you warning."

Wyatt offered a sheepish nod.

"Then the struggle was of your own making and nay the fault of the worthy page."

The sniffling grew louder.

"Apologize!"

"Your Majesty, I truly regret layin' hands on Prince Wyatt. Your Highness, I apologize for fightin' with ya. I swear 'twill never happen again. I await punishment, Sire." Lin's words were honest and calm. She did not fear her king.

Wyatt remained silent.

"Wyatt, Prince of Veronia, a faithful page—one you deem your lesser—has offered his contrition to both me and you. He accepts both the responsibility for his actions, and the consequences, which are to follow. Yet you, son, remain silent. I am ashamed of your behavior."

"Father?" Tears flowed like twin waterfalls. "I am sorry I disturbed your meeting. I am sorry, Father."

"And what of Lin. Will you offer him no remorse? You wronged him in refusing his wise council."

"Sorry, Lin." Wyatt whispered.

Edmund growled. "I did not hear!"

"Forgive me, Lin, for not listening to you."

"Very well. As punishment, both of you will serve the stable master each afternoon for the week in whatever fashion he sees fit.

Lin gave a quick answer. "Aye, Your Majesty. I'll serve my penance willin'ly and without complaint."

"Father …" Wyatt whined.

"Fie, Wyatt! You would do well to follow Lin's example and stop competing with the lad." Edmund turned from his whimpering son and slammed the door to his study.

Hawk turned to Ari with a bemused smirk. "I think our meeting has concluded."

"It is for the best. I feel I must speak with my page, for his impetuousness."

Wyatt fled toward the back stairs.

Hawk leaned close to her. "You have to admit, your page is as stalwart as her master. Wyatt is two years her senior and many pounds her better, but she held her own. I see no marks on her like I saw on Wyatt."

Ari frowned. "And how much more shame will the soft-hearted prince suffer when the truth of my page is revealed?"

"It is time Prince Wyatt grew tougher skin. His only shame is thinking so little of others. He will now be forced to train better, for there is no fault in losing to a better opponent, no matter who *she* may be."

Ari nodded. "Come Lin. We shall talk."

Lin fell into step behind her.

"By my sword, child, what were you thinking?" Ari demanded as Lin secured their chamber door.

"I told him not to enter. The king met with ya in private. He wouldn't listen."

"Why did you presume to instruct a member of the royal family?"

"I merely told him the truth as he reached for the door."

"And how is it I came to find you brawling with him on the floor?"

"He said, 'I am the king's son. I can go where I please. Ya're only a page and not allowed.' He is such a child."

"Lin." Ari hid her lips, stifling the laughter of Lin's near perfect imitation of the prince.

"I know I'm nay supposed to talk ill of those in authority. But sir, he acts as if he's king and I am a bug under his boot." She plopped on the divan. "I came over and told him again he mustn't enter. He pushed me and reached for the door. I grabbed his wrist. He shoved me against the wall and we fell. I didn't intend to roll about with him, sir."

"Being we have already discussed this issue of your disrespect for Prince Wyatt, I will require you to serve an additional week in the stables."

"Aye, sir." Lin's eyes remained on the floor.

Ari moved to the divan and considered her. "However, seeing as you conducted yourself with honor and wisdom before your king, it shall only be two additional days. Well done, Lin."

Lin's face rose with a soft smile.

"But I do not wish you to put yourself in such a position again." Ari warned.

"No, sir."

Chapter 21

The following morning, many were not present at the high table or the long boards for the breaking of the fast. Wyatt sat alone at the end of the table picking at his food.

"Is there trouble, Winslow?"

"Nay, Ari. King Edmund and many went to hunt before first light. I regret he did not include you."

"As a foreign knight, he need not entertain me."

"I think he favors you more than as a mere knight."

Ari waved off, not wanting to contemplate his meaning. "'Tis of little import. Might you know when he shall return?"

"With easy game, they often arrive by midday. Do you require something?"

Ari shook her head. "Nay, Winslow. 'Twas a small matter of no urgency. I shall see to it upon his return."

"Fie!" Ari slammed the book resting on her lap closed with a bang.

"Sir?" Lin looked up from her wax tablet. "Are ya upset, sir? I've nay heard ya stumble over words before."

Ari stood and paced the few strides between the divan and the window and back again. "I cannot concentrate. Father James' words are pounding out an unrelenting rhythm in the head. Like a deranged minstrel with a tabor, it beats without end 'Train and prepare! Train and prepare! Train and prepare!' I can nay take it!"

Struggling to slow her breathing, she stormed into the inner chamber, snatched up her blades, and stomped across the outer room toward the door.

"Whatcha doing?" Lin said as Ari grabbed her cloak and raced down the hall.

"I must train and prepare or I will lose my very mind!"

Lin caught up at the bottom of the stairs. Ari paused to don her cloak and conceal her blades within its folds.

Her steps slow and calm to avoid unwanted attention—though few marked her passing—she slipped into the hidden space. The coolness of the shadow-filled enclosure welcomed her. She tossed aside the cloak. Lin retrieved it, brushed it off, and folded it into her lap. She perched on the steps of the vacant tower, concern marring her gentle features.

"You need not stay."

Lin would not be moved.

Ari secured the belt around her waist and tied the chape below each knee. She marveled at the comfort the weight of her blades afforded her. Eyes closed, she drank in their familiar presence. Her hands came to rest on the square pommels and the cool kiss of the smooth metal—even through her gloves—acted as a balm on her restless spirit.

Shuffling steps alerted her to another. "What's he doing?" Wyatt muttered to Lin.

"Training."

Ari kept her eyes closed and suppressed a rebuke of Lin's disgusted tone. She shook off the irritation and listened. She slowed her breathing and focused her mind. Soon the competing heartbeats of the children and the whisper of the wind tickled her senses. A horse neighed. Her well-trained senses hum to attention and her heart thrilled.

Ari took several firm steps forward, listening to them echo off the back of the stable. When she recognized the tenor of their reverberation, she reached out her hand and laid it on the wall.

"Why are his eyes shut?"

"I don't know the training habits of a Wexxton knight." Lin scooted away from Wyatt, closer to the wall.

Ari turned to her right and walked toward the garden wall. Heavy vines of climbing roses and wisteria swallowed her steps but the smell of a few late blossoms helped her gauge her distance. A bee buzzed above her, she reached out for the wall.

She turned and marched across her new territory to the south wall. And she did the same with the east rock face. Confident in her surroundings after her sightless survey, she moved back to the center and stood still—eyes remaining closed—and listened. Shuffled steps moved along the stable wall toward the children and stopped without a word.

Train and prepare!

Ari startled as the words thundered in her mind. She forgot the newcomer and moved her hands across her body to the leather grips of her blades. She drew them with slow purpose, enjoying their ringing praise of freedom. She spun her wrists, taking pleasure in the weight in her hands.

Train and prepare!

She bent at the waist, her blades inches above the ground.

Whispers distracted her. "Father's knights do not move so."

Lin sighed.

"How can such a position help on the battlefield?"

"I don't know. Hush, and perchance we'll learn somethin'!"

Ari still stood bent in half, blades hovering above the dirt, but she raised her left foot to hover high over her head. As she seesawed to right herself, she crossed her blades and drew them apart in a smooth slice of air while three kicks flew from her raised leg until it joined the one planted in the dust. She moved with familiar ease into the well-practiced dance of her training. She spun and thrust, ducked and parried through each of the forms she'd learned while still a child.

Her mind settled, breathing steadied, and her heart calmed. She bathed in God's good pleasure of her obedience and efforts.

She repeated the forms. As she neared the end of the second set, a presence approached. She stilled and judged the intruder without opening her eyes.

The stranger stopped a half a pace from her.

Eyes closed, blades outstretched in each hand, she brought them down the challenger's sides without touching him. The resistance of the wind on her blades told her the breadth of the man. She rocked forward on the ball of her right foot, felt the man's breath on her cheek and knew his height. Rocking back, she caught his scent.

She knew who stood before her. Her heart skipped. Many feet shuffled. A myriad of voices whispered. An audience gathered. Her heart stuttered again.

Ari took two firm steps back. Her blades came to rest crossed behind her.

Train and prepare!

Lord, please. Is there no other way?

Silence.

Ari felt the Spirit stir. She waited. She would not strike first.

Chapter 22

A sword hissed from its sheath and Ari knew its length.

She remained still—eyes shut—yet seeing every movement as though they were wide open.

The sword cut through the air from high above.

Ari squared her shoulders and waited.

The man huffed. The sword arched down toward her and whispered through the air.

Lin gasped.

Ari's blades rose above her, crossed, and trapped the opponent's descending sword in their deep V. She pivoted on her right foot, wrenching the blade from his hand. It clanked to the ground a pace away. Ari stood shoulder-to-shoulder with the man, him facing one way and her the other. As he continued his forward motion, she brought up her left elbow and drove it between his shoulder blades. Were she in battle, she would have driven her blade into him.

The man huffed. He stumbled, scraping the ground in an effort to keep his footing. He dropped to one knee with a thud.

The crowd—and indeed a great many now gathered about them— murmured with excitement.

The long sword screamed as it scraped the ground, once again in its master's hand.

She heard the approaching footfalls. Facing him, both blades caught his wide swing and pushed his arm to continue the motion until she forced his sword arm across his chest.

He fought for balance.

She twisted his torso and drove her foot down behind his knee.

He dropped again with a grunt. Before he regained his feet, his sword lashed out.

She pivoted away, completing her full turn, and drove his sword back over his right shoulder until he groaned in pain. The long sword clanked once more in the hard packed dirt.

Ari again took two steps away and crossed her blades behind her. Eyes still closed.

The crowd grew.

This must stop.

He bellowed a war cry and charged.

Her blades pin-wheeled. She blocked his erratic swings first with one blade and then the other. Repeatedly their weapons clashed. The ringing of steel against steel overwhelmed the small sparring area as it echoed off each solid surface. Ari crossed her blades capturing his sword, spun, and wrenched it from his hands for a second time.

Blessed silence. Ari inhaled a lung-full of autumn air, relaxing taunt nerves. She fought her every warrior instinct. *Do not attack. Only defend. Do not bring trouble on good King Edmund by besting this man. Let him be seen the victor. Lord, help me.*

His blade flew again.

The rhythmic clanging jarred her nerves and overwhelmed her senses.

The edge of his sword found her left arm and bit deep.

She drove the pommel of her right blade into his sword arm and turned away from him. "Fie Godric!"

The crowd gasped as one great beast.

Her eyes opened to examine her arm. Blood already soaked the bandage Lin had placed there earlier. Her heart thundered an angry cadence. She whirled on Selvyn's man but only saw the crowd. Her breath caught. *Lord, the whole castle has gathered. What have I done?*

She dragged a slow draft into her aching lungs and stepped from him. She relaxed her shoulders and again allowed her blades to cross behind her. She swallowed hard as her gaze met from the enormous man. His hatred burned. She swallowed, forcing her jaw to unlock. "Thank you, Sir Godric. You have revealed a weakness." She hitched her oozing shoulder. "I will endeavor to correct this shortcoming." She tasted bile. She could not force one more conceding word through her teeth without retching. Inclining her head, she remained still.

Godric smiled at the crimson stream on his blade's edge. His leer grew and he brought the blade to his mouth. He licked her blood.

Ari grimaced.

Those gathered gasped.

A deep guttural laugh rumbled from him. His tongue traced his thin lips and his sword point leveled on her. A heartbeat later he charged.

Ari's blades came up and pushed his sword high above them. She seized handfuls of his tunic along with her hilts, and fell back pulling him down on top of her.

Hands out to brace himself, he yet struggled to remain up right. But his forward striking momentum in combination with her pull proved too much. He fell toward her.

Ari lifted her feet and planted them on his hips as his full weight lowered on her. She thrust up while continuing to pull on his tunic.

Godric flipped over her, landing hard on his back with a *humph.*

Ari planted her feet, arched her back, and popped upright. She turned and watched the large man lumber to his feet, huffing for the breath she had driven from his lungs.

He raced at her again.

She slapped his blades away, spun and smashed her pommel into his back as he staggered past.

He stumbled forward, but recovered in the next step and came at her yet again.

They went blow-for-blow, thrust-for-thrust in rapid succession. Neither gave ground. The strikes were so quick the echoes melted together into one continuous toll.

Ari knew she could gain no ground against the man twice her size. The next time his blade swung at her middle, she arched back allowing the blade to pass over her untouched. She planted her blades on the ground and did a handstand as her feet kicked him in the jaw and she back-flipped away from him.

Godric staggered back two steps. He rubbed away blood as his gazed leveled on her again.

This time when he charged, she whirled like a matador and slammed her foot into his rump.

Godric's face plowed into the dust. Curse words exploded as he sputtered and spit the grime from his mouth.

Ari backed away. *Don't get up.*

He charged toward her again.

She ran at him and dove under his blade like she entered a refreshing deep pool. She landed at his feet and rolled into a ball.

He stumbled and leapt over her.

She somersaulted under him, came to her feet behind him back-to-back and kicked out like a mule.

Godric lay flat once more.

Don't get up! Don't get up! she pleaded in silent desperation.

He gained his feet, whirled, and roared. Like a mortar launched from a trebuchet, he hurtled toward her.

Ari turned and fled.

The crowd gasped.

Godric cheered at seeing the wall looming before her.

Ari never slowed. She planted one foot on the wall. And another. She rose over him until she back-flipped, coming down behind him. She kicked out with both feet, driving him into the wall.

The sickening crack of his head colliding with the unmoving stone filled the air.

Ari crossed her arms, laying the flat of her blades against her shoulders and twisted, still moving through the air. She landed on her sore left arm and rolled three times before planting her foot and spinning upright again.

Godric crumpled and groaned.

She backed to the center once more.

He struggled to stand.

Stay down. Please, stay down.

Lin's gasped breaths tugged at Ari's heart.

Godric sat on one knee and placed the other foot in the dirt.

Stay down you fool! Have you no sense? I can nay allow you to kill me. Stay down!

He pushed up to his feet, then staggered forward one step and back two. He landed hard against the wall and allowed its strength to steady him. He rubbed his head and shook to clear it. He narrowed his gaze on her and started forward, his steps slow and unsteady.

Ari waited.

Godric bellowed unintelligible animalistic sounds.

Her left blade came up and knocked his sword out of the way. She added her right, smashing the pommel into his jaw.

His neck twisted and he stumbled back.

Her right foot landed in the center of his chest.

Another step away.

She circled him and kicked behind his knees.

He dropped with a groan.

She whirled, kicked into his right shoulder spinning him around until he landed flat on his back with a huff. Ari stomped on his right wrist, to keep him from raising his sword, and dropped to her knee in the middle of his chest.

Air rushed past his teeth, washing her with a foul odor.

Sun glinted on the blades spinning in her hands. She brought up her arms as the sword tips pointed down at him.

Godric's eyes widened.

Every person drew in a breath pulling the air from within the walls like a great swirling wind.

Ari thrust down.

The crowd held their breath.

Godric closed his eyes.

Chapter 23

The tips of Ari's blades drove deep into the dirt on either side of the limited distance between Godric's jaw and his hulking shoulders. She crossed the hilts until the well-honed edges nipped at his skin. When he took in a startled breath, they drew a thin line of blood from either side of his neck.

She held his gaze, anger bubbling up in her until she shuddered under its power. "Sire?" she called out. "What would you have me do with this one of yours?"

The air filled with muttering. People shuffled about.

Edmund approached in a growing chorus of 'Your Majesty'. Soon his well-polished boots came into view near Godric's head. Another pair joined them.

Hawk reached down and relieved her opponent of his weapon.

"Godric, you have acted without honor. You gave the challenge when Sir Ari sought only to practice in private. He defended every strike without pressing the attack. When you drew blood, Sir Ari gave you the victory, though in truth your performance did not warrant it. You pursued this guest of mine with murderous intent. Yet, Sir Ari gave you opportunity to end it without disgrace time after time. Had Sir Ari not been far more skilled, he would be dead. And had this good knight not possessed the temperament of Job, *you* would now be dead.

"Godric, I strip you of the title of knight of the realm. I grant you the life Sir Ari has spared, and banish you from my kingdom. Should you ever see my face again it will be the last thing you ever see."

Ari pushed off Godric and yanked her blades from the ground, drawing another drop of blood.

Godric huffed and breathed deep as her weight lifted.

"Get out!" Edmund growled.

The shamed man rolled to his side and worked to his feet. He stood to his full height and pushed back his shoulders, looking at those gathered. He turned his hateful gaze to Edmund and a snarl curled his lip.

Edmund's hand came to rest on his sword. "Go while you still have leave."

Godric lumbered into the ward.

The crowd whooped in excitement causing Ari to jump. They moved as some undulating creature closing around her. She stepped nearer Hawk.

"Hold." Edmund called out above the din. He raised a quieting hand. "My good people, I know your heartfelt desire to congratulate the victor and beg him for the opportunity to spar."

Ari's heart seized and jumped to her throat. She worried her lip while the crowd teamed like a single living, breathing beast.

"As your king, I claim the right of being first."

They groaned.

"There will be days ahead when you will have opportunity aplenty to speak with the skilled warrior. For now I wish to offer my praise in private."

Their great sigh hit Ari like a blast of summer heat. Yet, they turned and wandered off with animated talk and mimicking her movements.

Lord, what have I done?

"I must remember to apologize to Wyatt," Edmund said.

Ari turned her bewildered gaze toward him.

His face split in an enormous grin. "You are amazingly skilled with the swords, sir. It does appear near magic."

When the crowd dispersed, small steps raced toward her. Lin smashed into her leg with such force, Ari reached out for Hawk's arm to keep from falling. Lin seized her leg with a grip that made her toes tingle.

"Father, did you see? Did you see?"

"Oh aye, Wyatt. You spoke truth when you described Sir Ari's skill."

Wyatt jumped up and down, arms flying about with his imaginary blades. "Can he teach me the sword, Father? Can he?"

Edmund moved toward the ward, wrapping his arm around Wyatt's shoulder. "Mayhaps when he is done training me, son."

Hawk moved to follow and Ari struggled to pry Lin from her leg so she could join them.

Lin whimpered and clung to her as Ari limped forward, dragging the child.

Hawk and Edmund waited for her a few feet away and allowed her to walk between them. As they neared the opening to the ward, the Spirit within her awakened, covering her skin in gooseflesh. She stopped and reached out both hands staying the men. She still carried one blade since Lin would not release her enough to sheath it, and its presence caused Edmund on her right to pull up short.

She closed her eyes and the Spirit stirred all her senses.

Evil loomed beyond the wall.

She moved her sword to the left hand and reached for her other blade. The hiss of another sword being drawn made her eyes pop open.

Edmund left his son and moved forward.

"The stable, Sire. The danger is near the stable," she whispered, unable to move to assist him as Lin tightened her grip.

Hawk followed, sword drawn.

Wyatt looked between her and his father. He took several tentative steps to follow.

Ari dropped her swords in the dirt, grasped each of Lin's forearms and thrust her away. "Child, whatever is the matter with you?"

Lin erupted in a fountain of tears.

Ari knelt before her.

"What has come over you?"

Lin's arms slid around her neck and she sobbed. "I don't wish ya to die too."

Ari sighed. She took Lin's wrists and pulled her from her neck. "Lin, hear me. Do you believe God speaks to me?"

Lin nodded through hiccupped breaths.

"Do you believe He always keeps His promises?"

Again the child agreed.

"Lin, I tell you true, God has promised I will fight in the final battle with the Black Knight."

Lin stared, trying to take a single steady breath.

"If I am to fight in the final battle, can I die in Veronia?"

"No," Lin whimpered.

"Aye, naught can happen to me until the final battle, or God will be a liar. Lin, God is never a liar."

An exchange of angry words drew Ari's attention. She snatched up her blades and sped through the opening. Beyond the wall, Edmund pulled his blood drenched sword from Godric's stammering body.

"I gave you life, and this is how you repay me?"

Godric muttered something Ari could not hear and breathed his last.

Edmund wiped his sword on the dead man's shirt as Lin buried her face in Ari's thigh.

"I will see he is disposed of, Majesty," Hawk said, sheathing his own blade.

Edmund's gaze lifted to Ari's. A strange mixture of anger and regret pooled in his green eyes. He turned to his son. "Wyatt, go fetch Tinsley for our friend. Bring him to my study."

Movement on the wall above drew Ari's attention as Wyatt raced off. Selvyn loomed above the inner gate. A glint of sunlight sparkled on the tear running down his cheek. Selvyn's gaze shifted from Godric to her, and finally to the king. He smashed his fist against the top of the wall.

"Ari." Her glance lowered to Edmund.

He raised his arm in a wave for her to join him.

When she looked back to the wall, Selvyn could not be seen.

Edmund and Ari—Lin still clutching at her—walked through the hall in silence.

Chapter 24

Lin would not be left outside the study this time. Ari sat in a chair, Lin on the floor with her head against Ari's knee.

Edmund left the door open and moved to his seat. A great foolish grin filled his face. "You are a wonder."

"I am unremarkable among my own people, Sire." She avoided his intense gaze.

"Well, you are now of notable renown in Veronia, for after such a display I will be hard pressed to keep my men from pursuing you."

Ari groaned. "Forgive me, Sire …"

"I nay blame them their awe. You possess superior skill."

Something in his words or in his tone pricked Ari's ire. *Did he doubt me a true warrior when he learned I am woman? If Godric is any example, I could take down this entire castle …*

The Spirit within jolted her as if He had struck her with lightening. *Pride goeth before destruction, and a high mind before the fall.*

When her attention swung from herself to Edmund, she found him in the middle of a litany of crushing praise.

"… with incredible speed, and flexibility. You used your feet as a weapon more than I have in my entire life. The skill you have with dual blades far outmatched anything Godric challenged with brute force."

"You defended yourself with impressive skill—even with your

eyes closed." Hawk slid behind her chair and sat to her right with an admiring nod.

Wyatt bounded in behind him. "Why *did* you fight with your eyes closed, sir?"

"Because warriors are danger-seeking fools!" The healer dropped his wares on the king's desk and jerked up her elbow. He straightened his spectacles and peeked through the hole in her shirt at the bleeding wound.

"Sir Ari is nay a fool, Sir Tinsley," Wyatt chided.

"Forgive me, Highness, but on this day I behaved the fool. I should never have gone into the space behind the stables without King Edmund's approval. I have bested one of his honored men, and it resulted in the man's death. His blood is on my hands, for I bear the blame for my rash actions."

Ari's arm dropped without warning and she winced.

Fabric rent as Tinsley tore the sleeve free from the tunic at the cut and pushed the loose fabric down her arm.

Ari looked to Edmund for help but he stood for a better look.

Tinsley unwound the cloth over the old cut. As it tore from the wound, she bit her lip to stifle a yelp. She closed her eyes as Lin tightened her grip on her calf. She preferred to spend her painful moments with a healer reciting Scripture and praising God for continued life. There were too many distractions in this room to focus on anything but the pain.

"Is it deep, Tinsley?" Edmund said.

Hawk made an effort to gain her attention. "Sir Ari, I too am curious as to why you fought so long with your eyes closed."

Ari glanced at Hawk. She made to answer but choked on a gulp of air as Tinsley probed the injury.

"Much of the bandage is now imbedded in the wound," Tinsley

squeaked, raising the hairs on Ari's neck. "Unless the bandage is removed, the wound will fester, and rot will claim the whole arm, if nay the life."

Lin gripped harder yet and Ari lost all feeling in her toes.

Tinsley pulled tiny metal tongs from his satchel and, gripping her arm from below, he used his thumb and forefinger to pull the gash open.

Ari sucked air between her teeth. *I appear to be less than a warrior now. Is this the way God intended to bring my haughty spirit low?*

Edmund retrieved a tankard from the table. He filled it and offered it to her.

Pain and the healer's grasp kept her from claiming it. Hawk passed her the drink. She took it in a shaking hand and swallowed a deep draft of the sweet wine, hoping it would make quick work of deadening her pain.

"I thought you too tough for spirits," Tinsley quipped. His tiny taloned instrument bore into her sore flesh and she failed to stifle a yelp.

"Ari?" Edmund's tender concern incited her.

Ari's anger flared. "Majesty, could this nay be seen to in my chamber?"

Tinsley went after another bit.

"Fie, man! You have the touch of a lion taking down a kill." Ari said with a snap.

Tinsley huffed, snatched her cup and dumped the remaining contents over her wound.

Air hissed through her teeth again as the wine seared her flesh.

"Perchance if a more cooperative patient sat before me." Tinsley raked a clean cloth over the injury as Ari fought the urge to draw a blade and relieve the man of his head. "This wound reopened the old injury but it looks to have fallen in the same path as the previous cut."

Ari now looked deep into the king's green eyes. "Same depth. Same angle. Same cut. Same weapon."

Chapter 25

"Such an identical injury is nay possible," Tinsley scoffed.

Edmund leaned back against his desk. "'Tis possible if 'tis made by the same man."

Ari offered Edmund a quick nod in agreement.

Hawk stood and moved to Edmund. As they conversed in hushed tones, Ari retreated into her thoughts and Tinsley sutured.

Tinsley left. Ari sighed. Wave of relief washed over her until she opened her eyes to see both men and Wyatt staring at her.

"Did it hurt over much, sir?" the lad asked.

"In truth I would suffer a hundred such injuries before I would welcome a healer's needle. The blade cuts quick and is done. The knitting back together lingers as a persistent torture."

Lin quaked against her leg.

Hawk sat again as Edmund refilled her tankard. He offered it to her with a deep scowl. "You truly believe Godric numbered among those who attacked Wyatt and my men?"

"Father, why would—"

"Wyatt, you will be silent and repeat not a word you hear spoken here or you will leave this moment." Edmund stretched up in his chair to consider Lindsay seated at Ari's feet.

"Neither lad will say a word of what is spoken here, if my life matters a wit to either," Ari said with confidence.

Wyatt moved to sit on the floor on Ari's left. His crossed his arms and set his jaw. "I will never speak of this."

"Aye, Majesty. I am quite convinced of Godric's involvement in the terrible events of my first day. Though it had been but a brief encounter on the battlefield, I recognized his style and stance—and the familiar bite of his blade."

Edmund and Hawk exchanged glances. "He grows more bold," Hawk warned.

Wyatt leaned forward to see the thane better. "Who is so bold?"

Ari nodded. "He is more dangerous now. Godric mattered to him. I saw him over the inner gate, Majesty."

"Who is more dangerous? Who did you see, Sir Ari?" Wyatt said.

Edmund's forearms rested the desk. "He saw with his own eyes that I ran Godric through and not you."

Wyatt smashed his fists into the floor. "Who saw?"

"Selvyn. You simpleton!" Lin said.

"Lin!"

Hawk cleared his throat and wet his lips to hide his laughter.

"Forgive me," Lin trembled.

It felt as if the children's exchange vanquished the tension from the room. As each one of the adults released the air trapped in their lungs and leaned back into their chairs, they exchanged knowing glances until their smiles turned to snickers and the snickers into outright laughter. They regained their composure and remained silent for several moments.

Edmund's glance shifted back to Ari and a smile spread across his face. "So good knight, are you able to tell us now why you fight with your eyes closed?"

"It is part of our training. The horde, who fights for the Black Knight, is oft times accompanied by a malevolent fog. There have been many battles when I have relied on every sense God gave me, save my sight. Many have mastered this fine art, but most fail. Today it only cost me a small cut. It has been far worse."

"I found it extraordinary." Hawk's admirations caused beads of sweat to form along her hairline.

Edmund leaned forward again. "So extraordinary indeed. I wish you to train me."

Ari's gaze flew to Edmund's "Sire!"

"It is the logical course, sir. You have fought this horde and I have never seen them. I will need training if I hope to survive." Edmund said.

Hawk nodded. "I will join His Majesty."

"May I join too, Father? May I, please?"

"Majesty please, consider—" Ari attempted to dissuade them.

Edmund's raised palm stopped her protest. "I have done naught but consider since I saw you marking off your area without your sight."

Ari's head dropped. "You were there from the beginning?"

"We saw every swing, kick and thrust," Hawk leaned forward, forearms on his thighs. "I would be honored to train under such a skilled warrior. There is no shame in losing to one more skilled, and a wise man would seek to become more capable from such a one."

"What about me, Father?"

"Wyatt, later. You still have lessons to learn from Brother Peter. When Hawk and I are well prepared for the coming battle, we will discuss your training."

Wyatt's arms crossed with a huff and a protruding lower lip.

"What say you, Sir Ari? Will you train us?"

"Sire, do you truly think this wise?"

Edmund nodded with a grin. "Oh aye, it is the wisest course. We must 'train and prepare.'"

Ari sighed. "Aye Sire."

Edmund's hands smashed together in a thunderous clap. Lin startled, her head jerking off Ari's knee as she gasped. She gripped Ari tighter and trembled. "Splendid! We can begin early on the morrow. I commend your choice of sparring areas. We shall meet there."

"Aye." Hawk and Ari spoke as one.

Chapter 26

Lin hovered close as a pesky leech the remainder of the day. In one of the rare moments Lin did not cling to her, Ari stumbled upon the child praying as she built the fire in the inner chamber.

"God, I never knew me father for Ya took him afore me birth. And Ya took Momma away too. Please don't take Aria away. I'll do anythin' Ya ask. Please stop bein' mad at me and taking away everyone I love."

Ari reeled back into the outer chamber as though struck with a jousting lance and staggered to the divan where she dropped. Hot tears choked. *Oh, Lord ...* She found no words. Lin's tiny pain-filled voice cut her deeper than any blade. *Father, You know my destiny—and therefore what is ahead for this precious child. Show me how I might spare her this pain again. Should I send her away?*

As Ari prayed, small arms encircled her neck. Lin knelt beside her on the divan and buried her face in Ari's hair. "Promise ya'll nay die."

"Oh, Lindsay." Ari stroked her cropped hair. "Child, we all die, some young and some not till old age."

"Promise I can stay with ya till ya get old."

Ari looked the girl in the eyes. She rested a hand on her soaked cheek. "Lindsay, you know I must return to my home and fight for my people."

"Take me with ya."

She felt as if Lindsay's plea tore her heart from her chest and laid it open in her small hands. "Lindsay," she moaned. "God has a call on my life, one which you cannot share."

Fresh tears covered Lindsay's face, splashing over Ari's hand.

"He also has a plan for you, child. His word tells us, '*For I know the thoughts, that I have thought towards you, saith the Lord, even the thoughts of peace, and not of trouble, to give you an end, and your hope.*' God has a beautiful calling on you, Lindsay. He has gifted you with wisdom beyond your years. He never gives a gift we will nay use. You will be a blessing to a strong man of God someday and raise beautiful children."

"I don't want a husband or children. I want ya." Lindsay pushed Ari's hand away and threw herself into Ari's arms sobbing until she fell asleep.

Ari carried her to her mat and covered her before going to her own bed. She spent much of the night in prayer before sleep claimed her.

Lin built the fire, dressed Ari's wound and helped her with her armor as though the previous day had never occurred.

"Are you well this morning, my friend?"

"Oh aye, sir." Her words were untroubled but her voice remained quiet and her familiar smile remained hidden as the sun behind a great cloud.

Ari reached for her blades and the girl gasped and shuddered. Ari sighed. A hardened warrior, she cared nay what any thought of her. Yet the fear her actions elicited from this precious child pulled her willful heart into a deep mire of regret and these unwelcome emotions would not allow her to hurt Lindsay further. She left the blades and stalked out of the hall.

Following the meal, Edmund and Hawk approached her.

"I regret to inform you there will be no training, Sire," she said.

"Have you changed your mind, Sir Ari?" The disappointment shading Edmund's words surprised her.

"No Sire, but it appears my actions yesterday did more than make my faithful page forget her penance with the stable master. I have somehow wounded the lad, and the mere movement to pick up my blades made him tremble in fear. I cannot explain, Sire, for I nay understand it myself, but I will do the child no more harm. I cannot."

Hawk smiled. "There is time, sir. For now we shall pray God will help Lin."

Edmund nodded. "Aye, God is forever faithful." A wry smile turned his mouth. "And I will make sure Wyatt joins him this afternoon. I fear he did not forget his duty yesterday as much as he ignored it."

They parted and Ari retuned to her chamber to work with Lin on her lessons. She proved to be such a quick study, Ari believed she would be reading on her own before the Christ Mass.

Chapter 27

Lin entered the stable and bowed to the dark-skinned man who served as stable master. "I'm here for me penance, sir. What'd ya require?"

"I am no nobles man that you shoulds address me as sir, boy. Me name is Olin."

Lin bowed again, "Forgive me sir, but are ya not still me elder and the man who'll oversee me work? Should I nay always address a superior with respect?"

Olin rubbed his fat chin between his dirty thumb and bent forefinger. "Well, I gives you the point, lad. I reckons in suchs light, I mights be thought of as sir, but I'm still preferrin' you calls me, Olin. I ams a simple man. I see nay good reasons for making more of a matter than oughts be."

"If ya wish it so, I'll call ya Olin, sir."

Olin smiled, revealing his few remaining blackened teeth. "I likes you, lad."

"Thank ya. I like ya too. What's me task?"

Olin pointed to a small, square, wheeled cart in the middle of the long aisle between one column of stalls. "Grabs a shovel and mucks out the last of the stalls on that there side of this row. When the cart is as fulls as you can manage takes it out to the wagon next to the inner gate and the squires wills help you dump it."

"Aye, Olin sir." Lin snatched up a shovel and scooped up the sticky feces in the first of her assigned stables. It stunk and slurped as she stuck her shovel in it. A sucking noise followed as she lifted it to plop in the cart and emitted more stench. Lin wrinkled her nose and her eyes watered, but she dared not complain.

The prince sauntered in about a half an hour later. "I am here, Olin, as ordered. What is my punishment?"

"Highness, as yous are late comin', your mate has use of the cart for the mucking. You will rake these heres stables on the right into piles and when the lad is done finished with that there cart, yous mayen have use of it to put your piles into."

The pampered boy put his hands on his hips and stomped his foot. He waited until Olin stepped away before he turned and approached Lin. His chin jutted into the air. "Olin says I am to use this cart. You can have it back when I am good and done with it."

Lin let him push it away to the front of the building and his assigned stalls. She did not want to waste her time or increase her punishment in the stinky stables, so she snapped her teeth shut and looked for a bucket. She found a large one a few stalls further down. It reached to her thighs but it would work. She picked it up and returned to her work.

As she struggled out to the wagon with the first load, Olin watched her pass. He stood in the doorway staring at Wyatt with his arms crossed when she returned.

Though she didn't have the cart she made quick work of her mucking, finishing all her stalls before Wyatt completed half of his. *He wastes so much time wiping his brow and whining.*

"Olin sir, do ya wish me to put down fresh straw?"

"Mighty fines, lad." He pointed to the huge stack near the door.

Lindsay grabbed up an armful and made her way to the back of the stables. Flop! She landed on her belly, her crossed arms saving her chin from slamming into the dirt. Wyatt tucked-in his foot and returned to his work. Lindsay stood without even looking at him. She delivered her load. When she collected her next armload, she made sure she could see over it and gave the prince a wide berth.

"I have finished. I need a bath," Wyatt said.

"The stalls needs straw Highness and the horses coulds use a good brushing."

Wyatt groaned.

Lin, having finished laying her straw, grabbed a brush and moved to the first horse.

Her arm was jerked behind her and her brush flew across the stable, startling several horses. The space filled with their whinnies. "He is my father's charger and you are not to touch him."

Lin bowed, retrieved the brush and moved to the next stall.

Wyatt ran against her—arms straight out in front of him—and knocked her flat on her back. "Jack is my horse! Never touch him!"

Jack snorted and pawed the ground.

Lin stood, walked around Wyatt, and collected the straw for his stalls.

Wyatt brushed Jack as Lin finished putting the bedding in all his stalls.

She next went to the well and cleaned the bucket she had used. Olin greeted her when she returned.

"A job wells done, wells done, lad." Olin patted her on the shoulder. "You are free to prepares yourself for suppers."

Wyatt turned to leave.

"Highness, yous still has the brushing to complete. Sees to it."

Lin heard him stomp his foot and huff as she left. She passed the king on her way back to Ari's chamber.

Chapter 28

Ari smiled when Lin entered the chamber. "Welcome. A bath has been drawn and clean clothes are on the stool."

"A bath, sir?"

"Aye. Do you wish to smell like the stables at boards?"

"Nay sir, but I've never bathed before."

Ari smiled with the mischievous grin she always wore when they shared girl-secrets. "Oh, well you are in for a treat, my friend. One which you will want to repeat often. I warrant the first thing you ask of your husband as he builds you a home, is to make sure to have a room and tub for a proper bath."

Lindsay doubted such a prediction, but she ventured into the bathing chamber and stared at the huge basin. It waited half-filled with steaming water. She released the breath she held and pulled off her filthy tunic.

"Wrap your soiled clothes in the burlap on the floor to keep down the stench, and leave them in the corner to wear again tomorrow afternoon. We won't trouble the servants to launder them until your time in the stable is complete," Ari called from the outer chamber.

Lin did as instructed and climbed into the tub. The water burned at first but as she became used to it, she liked its warmth. She felt light, and watched with wonder as she relaxed and her arms came to the surface and floated there. She swayed her arms and paddled her legs, feeling the caress of the water over her skin.

"I told you." Ari leaned against the doorframe with *the grin* again.

"Do you want me to wash your hair?"

"Yes, please." Lindsay turned away. Momma used to wash her hair in a small tub beside their door. The water was always cold, but she liked Momma's fingers rubbing her head. "I have little left but it has been long since it was washed."

Ari snatched up the soapwort and knelt. "I am sorry Winslow did this."

"It's all right. Momma cut her hair short once, but it grew back. Mine will too."

Ari's hands were not like Momma's. They were hard and strong and at first Lindsay wanted to pull away. But Ari's hands slowed and she worked more.

"Am I hurting you?"

"Nay. It feels nice, like Momma."

Ari's hands stopped working, and she cleared her throat. She remained still with her hands on Lindsay's head for several moments, before they were snatched away. "Best rinse. The supper bell will toll soon."

Before she could respond, Ari left the room. *Why do I keep upsettin' her so? She acts so tough—swin's those hideous blades, but she falls apart when I say somethin' nice or when Wyatt or the king says anythin' nice. God, do the people in Wexxton nay talk with kindness to one another?* Lin sighed, and dumped handfuls of water over her head before climbing out.

King Edmund stood with his arms crossed at the bottom of the steps outside his small hall. Lin moved to go around him.

"Good eve, Majesty," Ari said formally as they both bowed.

"I would have a word with your page."

Lindsay's heart did an odd flip.

Ari waved her forward. Ari bowed again. "Aye, Sire."

Lindsay bowed too but kept her head low waiting.

"Tell me of your work today."

His words were firm but not angry and Lindsay's shoulders relaxed. "I arrived after midday, and mucked a few stalls and laid fresh straw, Yar Majesty."

"No problem arose while you worked?"

"Nay, Majesty. Have I done somethin' wrong?"

"Olin spoke of your difficultly with my son."

Lindsay did not move and clamped her lips tight.

King Edmund dropped to his knees. The high king of all of Veronia and Balmore knelt before her. She felt like stone, she couldn't move. He raised her chin to look in her eyes and cradled her hands in his. "Speak freely, without fear, Lin. I must know the truth."

"I nay fear what ya'll do to me, Majesty. Ya are a good king and always kind." She dared a glance at Ari who stood a little straighter and her chin rose. "I've been taught not to talk ill of me betters, Sire."

King Edmund smiled. "You are a precious child. Oh, would that you were my blood, I could stand proud before my men. But God has chosen to stretch my character with an ill-tempered elder son and an ill-mannered younger son. Please, tell me Lin, is it true Wyatt arrived late and made your work more difficult?"

She pursed her lips and nodded once.

"Did he yell at you, order you about and push you down?"

Again she nodded without a word.

"I beg your apology, Lin. You showed the restraint of your master in not knocking him on his spoiled bum. Your penance is paid in full, Wyatt will serve out the remainder of both of your times."

"But Majesty—"

King Edmund smiled, "Do not argue with your king, child. You have done right time and time again. You stand clean of conscious before God and your humble king. Thank you, Lin." He rose and waved them into the hall.

Ari patted her shoulder. "God Himself is proud of you this day, Lin. You ever walk upright before God and men."

Chapter 29

Wyatt glared at Lin all through the evening meal and again at first meal the next morning. Lin tried to ignore him but the heat of his stares made the small hairs on the back of her bare neck stand on end. His visible hatred haunted her as she attempted to concentrate on her lessons.

"Are you hale, Lin?"

There must be something I can do to make the prince stop being mad at me. Something, which will make him forgive me.

"Lin?"

I could ask the king ... Mayhaps Ari could ...

"Lin!"

Lin turned to look at Ari. "Sir?"

"Lin, are you to right?"

She nodded.

Ari's brows scrunched. "Something troubles you. Your copy work lies half done, you stumbled over passages, then stood to see to the dusting, but you have no rag."

Lin looked about.

"Truly, are you hale, my friend?"

"I got lost thinkin'."

"I find, when I am adrift in thought, the battlements and fresh air are excellent for clearing the head."

"May I try, sir?"

Ari nodded with her silly grin, and Lin felt the corners of her mouth turn in response. Her steps were slow at first then she dashed up the north tower and raced around the entire battlements. Her chest heaved and her legs ached. She dropped and sat crossed-legged, elbows on her knees, and head in her hands.

The wall stared back at her as unmovable as Prince Wyatt. "Hello, God. Aria says Ya talk to her. She also says Ya want to talk to me too. I'd very much like to hear Ya. I don't wish to cause Prince Wyatt any trouble, and I don't like knowin' he hates me so. What should I do?"

Lin waited. She strained to listen for God's voice. The wind blew. Horses nickered. Squires laughed. The ping of the armorer's hammer tapped in the distance. Birds chirped and bugs clicked. But God remained silent. Lin sighed. The bell tolled the gathering for the next meal and Lin lumbered down the stairs, disheartened.

As she ate with Wyatt's stare burning a hole in her neck, a thought came to her. She raced ahead of Aria back to their chambers and flew into the bathing room long before Aria arrived. She came out and stood before Aria in her soiled clothes.

Aria sat with her head propped on the tall end of the divan. A brow rose as Lin paused in front of her.

"May I be dismissed, sir?"

Aria's head cocked to the side. A smile turned to one corner of her plump red lips—it still amazed her to think everyone believed she could be a man. "It looks as though God has supplied you with an answer to your predicament. Be about your appointed mission, page. And God's speed."

Lin staggered out the door. *Did this idea come from God? Did He speak to me and I didn't know it?* She shook her head clear as she pushed out of the great hall and into the ward. She watched as Wyatt plodded out the small hall and crossed to the stables ahead of her. His head and shoulders hung as though he were hundreds of years old all bent by age. She watched him heave a great sigh as he entered and took up the shovel Olin offered him.

Lin skipped in after him, "Good day to you Olin, sir."

"Well Lin, what evers brings yous here this day?"

She reached for a shovel leaning up against the wall behind him. "I have work to do." She walked down the aisle to where Wyatt labored and stuck her shovel into the muck then plopped it into the cart and turned for more without a word.

"What are you doing?" Wyatt's words pitched high as his voice struggled between shock and anger.

"I'm helpin' ya. I got ya in this mess, and though King Edmund feels I've paid for me sins, I know ya don't."

Wyatt kicked the straw bunched at his feet and cleared his throat. He stared at his boots. "The fault is not all yours. I fought with you as much as you fought with me."

Lin kept scooping the filth.

"In truth, Lin, you took more than you gave."

"'Tis all right, Yar Highness. I'll work with ya and we'll finish in no time."

Wyatt dumped a single shovelful and stopped again. "Why are you being nice to me?"

Lin stopped to consider him. *Why did she want to help him?* "I don't think ya have many friends." Lin startled at her own words. She raised a hand to cover her wayward lips. "Forgive me, Highness. I don't know why said such." Heat filled her cheeks. She forced her shovel into the dung hoping Wyatt wouldn't notice.

"Because it is the truth."

She dared raise her gaze to meet his. He looked like one of the pups the hunter cared for.

"I'm sorry, Highness."

"'Tis nay your fault no one my age lives in the castle. Eric has Pres, and father has Hawk. I guess I hoped Sir Ari would be my friend." Wyatt sighed and shoveled another heap. "But he has you." The accusation felt like a slap to her face.

"Your Highness, ya are jealous—of me! I'm an orphaned peasant. Ya are the son of the high king."

"But you spend all your time with him." Wyatt's pitch rose to a desperate whine.

"Yar Highness, we sit locked in our room readin'. Sir Ari is teaching me letters. 'Tis as dull as yar lessons, I wager—more so perhaps for I struggle with the simplest of me own language with no thought of Latin, or philosophy, mathematics, or the grand thin's ya learn."

"You make learning sound like an adventure."

"'Tis a grand adventure for one from a low state. 'Tis foolish to envy one such as I, Highness."

Wyatt raised his eyes to her again.

Lin groaned. "Forgive me, I have gone and insulted ya again. I'd be better served to be struck mute." She clamped her lips shut and turned back to her task.

Wyatt laughed. "You sure do think over much."

Lin nodded. She moved several shovelfuls in rapid succession.

"You had better stop, Lin. It will take both of us, as it is, to move the cart to the waiting squires." He smiled at her as she glanced at the over-burdened cart.

She felt a smile tug at her lips. "I think so much, I oft don't pay attentions to what I'm doin'."

They leaned their shovels against the stall and moved to the handle of the cart. Standing shoulder-to-shoulder, they tipped the heavy cart and slid back in the loose straw as they tried to push. Wyatt started to laugh first and Lin soon joined him.

"Mayhaps if we give it one great shove at the same time it'll move, Highness."

"Once we get it to move a little it will be easier."

"I was thinkin' so too. Ready?"

"On the count of three. One. Two. Three."

They both shoved. The cart lurched forward. Their feet slipped again and fell flat on their bellies. They lay there in fits of giggles unable to get to their feet.

"What mischiefs are you twos up to backs here?"

Lin looked up at Olin, her breaths coming in hiccups. She turned to Wyatt. He still laughed so hard tears trickled, and she burst out laughing again.

Olin shook his head at them and pushed the overfull cart outside. They composed themselves enough to climb to their feet by the time he returned.

"Thank you Olin, sir," Lin stammered as she fought to suppress her giggles.

The two worked side-by-side until Olin dismissed them to clean for supper.

"Thank you for helping me. I am grateful, for I did naught to earn your kindness."

"Well, we do naught to earn God's kindness. I guess I'd some to spare this day," she said with a shrug.

"It was more than kind." Wyatt bit his lower lip.

Lin tipped her head at him. "Is there something more, Highness?"

"Two things in truth."

"Ask and I'll do what I can to help."

"First, will you call me Wyatt? If we are to be friends we should treat one another in kind."

Lin smiled. "Thank ya. I'd be honored to call ya me friend, Wyatt. The first proved easy enough. What's yar second boon?"

"My tutor has gone away on family matters and will not return for a week more. May I study with ya and Sir Ari?"

"I don't see a reason why not, but I'll ask Sir Ari, for the chambers are his and not mine to offer."

"Thank you, Lin." Wyatt turned to enter the hall. "Oh Lin, would you sit at the place near me for supper."

"Do ya think yar father would allow a common page to sit in such a place of honor?"

"Father and Eric sit with their friends. He will allow me to sit with mine."

Lin nodded and raced off to clean and change.

Chapter 30

Ari ventured out of her quiet chamber and watched the two children laugh as they worked together. The sight was endearing, but her thoughts were perplexed. Why should it stir her heart so to see the two young people getting on? They meant naught to her, strangers in a strange land. She would be leaving soon.

Ari stumbled and braced her hands on her knees as she fought to recover from the physical blow the thought of leaving inflicted on her. *Lord, You have called me to battle. I cannot be trapped here by unwanted emotions.* She straightened, forced air into her stone lungs, and the blood out of her cold heart, as she thrust her foot forward.

"The Lord reprove thee, O Satan!" She said for all on the walls to here. She lowered her voice as she continued. "You, or any you place in my path will not take me off my course. 'Direct my steps in Thy word, and let no iniquity have dominion over me.' I call on the name of the Lord. 'Thou wilt guide me by Thy counsel, and afterward receive me to glory.'" Ari determined not to be entangled further with the children and stomped out her resolve around the battlements.

"Sir Ari!" Lin burst into the chamber with such exuberance, that if her thundering steps down the hall hadn't alerted her, Ari would have sprang to her feet to do battle.

"By all that is holy, child! What is the meaning of bursting into my chambers so?"

The radiant smile vanished from Lin's precious face. "Forgive me, sir." Her words trembled and Ari's hard heart seized.

Ari tried to shake off the regret. *I cannot let her weave any deeper into my heart.* Her stiff neck formed a fearsome knot in its unbending determination. She attempted to lean back as though relaxed. "You are at the end of a successful mission, now go and bathe."

A shadow of Lin's smile returned. "Oh aye, sir. Wyatt thanked me for helpin' him."

"Wyatt?" Ari raised a curious brow.

Lin giggled. "He wants to be friends like King Edmund and Sir Hawk, and Prince Eric and Sir Preston. He asked me to call him by his Christian name. He also wishes me to sit near him at supper." Excitement caused her to shift from foot to foot, as her smile grew with each word.

"The water awaits."

"Thank ya, sir." The grin dimmed again as she turned toward the inner chamber.

Thank you. Such a simple turn of words, yet they were said with such love, Ari felt her heart constrict tighter. *It is good Lindsay has found such a welcoming home here, Lord. I bless Your holy name for making a place for her. The king and now his son are fond of her. They will see to her care once I am gone.* Again the thought of not seeing Lindsay into womanhood doubled her in agonizing pain.

"Sir?"

Ari fought for a steadying breath and forced herself up to look at the child peeking out from the inner door. A bare shoulder revealed that she had removed her clothes already.

"Are ya to right?" Lin said.

Ari waved her hand for Lin to proceed as she struggled to capture any breath in her lungs.

"Wyatt asked for a favor, sir. His tutor is away and he wishes to study with us after first meal. Will ya agree to havin' him here?"

She sputtered and coughed. *Lord, what are You doing to me? I seek only to be Your warrior and You place these children in my path to keep me from it. Am I a nursemaid? Nay! Nor am I their mother.*

"'Tis all right, sir. This is your refuge. I'll tell Wyatt mayhaps we can study somewhere else."

The disappointment in Lin's small voice fell on Ari as though the castle's great iron gate broke free and landed on her. She turned but Lin no longer stood in the doorway. *She asks so little.*

Ari pushed to her feet but remained motionless, waiting to see if her trembling legs would support her. *I understand You not at all, Lord. But it would appear You will not allow me to refuse the child.* She walked into the bathing room and watched as Lin splashed and played in the water. Her heart fluttered at the simple joy. "You may tell his Highness he is welcome here." Granting the simple boon freed her lungs as the cutting of a constrictive corset.

Lin spun, splashing water over the side of the tub. "Truly, sir? Ya don't mind?" The joy radiating from her face filled the room brighter than the sun.

Ari could do naught but acquiesce. "Your friends are always welcome in our chambers, Lin."

"Thank ya, sir."

Ari could not bear to remain in the girl's elated presence for fear she would promise to forget her destiny and stay with her always. "Hurry and finish, the bell will toll soon." She turned and sped from the room.

Chapter 31

Wyatt came each of the next three days. He sat on the floor at one end of the low table before the divan and Lin sat the opposite end. Lin learned quickly under Ari's tutelage but now with Wyatt assisting her, she flew beyond all expectations. While Ari focused on the basics of written language, Wyatt shared mathematics, philosophy, and even a few Latin phrases.

Ari sat in the small, straight-backed chair at the desk, for she could not figure a way to recline in a masculine fashion on the divan. The children were seated behind her talking of Socrates when a heavy knock sounded on the door. Ari stood and waved Lin to remain as she opened the door herself.

"Ari, I am looking for my—"

She pulled the door fully open allowing King Edmund to see Wyatt.

"—son?" His gaze turned to her and his brows touched in the great furrow created between them.

"Prince Wyatt asked to study here until his tutor returns," she said.

"Forgive my son's intrusion."

"Lin made the request and it has done him good to study with your learned son, Sire. Think naught of it."

Lin stood and bowed deep at the waist. "I hope it's all right with you, Sire. I'm only a peasant and nay worthy of such grand knowledge. Forgive me for reaching beyond me station."

Wyatt shot to his feet. "All our people should be well educated, Father!" His fists flew to his hips as he stood in noble defense of his friend.

Edmund smiled and raised his hands in surrender. "Peace, both of you. I place a great value in learning and I esteem all who seek knowledge—and those skilled enough to teach."

Wyatt's shoulders pushed back and he straightened.

"Thank you, Majesty," Lin whispered with another bow.

"Thank Sir Ari for opening his chambers to you. It is more than gracious. Perchance when Brother Peter returns we might seek his agreement to instruct you both."

Wyatt bounded up and down, and Lin covered her face with her hands.

"Thank you, Father!"

"Oh Majesty, thank ya indeed." Tears pooled in Lin's eyes and dripped to the floor as she bowed again.

"You are too generous, Sire," Ari added with a smile. *Why does it please my heart so to see good things befall this child?*

"Perchance you would care to show your gratitude by coming to your sparring area?" Edmund coaxed with a mischievous grin.

Ari turned as Lin gasped and watched her tremble in fear. "I fear not this day, Sire, but pray soon."

Edmund nodded and turned to leave. "I almost forgot the reason I searched for Wyatt." He turned back to face his son. "Olin says Lin has been with you every day this week as you worked."

"Lin came to help me."

"I chose to work, Majesty."

"Lin has been kind to me even when I was mean. He is my friend, Father."

"I envy you, Son. Such a faithful and kind friend is rare. God has blessed you with a fellow of exemplary character as your companion. Never tread on your friendship thoughtlessly."

"Nay Father—never."

Edmund smiled at the children, winked at Ari, and left.

He does remember Lin is a girl?

Chapter 32

The Lord's Day dawned as the sun turned the smattering of clouds a vibrant pink. Ari and Lin slipped into the hidden gallery and waited for the others to arrive. Ari bowed her head in prayer, but her thoughts were undisciplined and wandered to and fro at their own whim.

The hymns drew her back for a time, but as the priest read from the Scriptures she soon became lost again.

"Hear, O Israel: ye are come this day unto battle against your enemies: let not your hearts faint, neither fear, nor panic, nor be adread of them."

Afraid? Ari tossed her head. Fear is not something that plagued her. She had seen others in the moments before battle—male and female—first battles and old veterans—succumb so to the fear of the enemy till they could not sit in their saddle. Others had fled the field as she thundered ahead.

Ari sat back against the pew and sighed. She so lacked fear, others hurtled into battle with her to their own doom. She listed such thoughtlessness of others as one of her many failings.

The priest's words filtered into her consciousness once more. "Ye shall not fear them: for the Lord your God, He shall fight for you." He repeated the words from the Pentateuch and continued. "My good people, fear is of the devil. He alone causes our hearts to quake, for Scripture confirms again and again we are not to fear but to trust in the Lord."

I do trust in You, oh my God. You alone are the source of my strength and the victory for my people will be found in You alone.

Ari caught snatches of the sermon but could not focus her attention on the whole. As the others went forward to partake of communion her heart longed to leap over the railing and join the faithful below. She waited. The benediction followed and those in the lower pews filed out unseen.

Ari sighed and reached back to twist her hair. Lin remained silent beside her. She buckled her hood and turned to the child.

Lin sat with her head low, and Ari thought her asleep for a moment but her shoulders heaved and shuddered. Even in the dim light the wet stain of her salty tears on her lap could be seen.

Ari reached out a hand to lay it on Lin's back and the child recoiled from her. "Lindsay whatever is the matter?"

She sniffled and hiccupped her breaths, unable to control her tears enough to speak.

"Naught can be as bad as all these tears."

"I could cause yar death."

"What!" Ari could not have been more shocked if Lin had reached out and slapped her. "What would make you think such a thing? I am a warrior and will die in battle. How could you possibly cause a war?"

"I've kept ya from trainin'. Ya heard God tell ya to prepare. Ya obeyed and train for one day, but I was afraid for ya—I don't wish ya to die. Ya'll nay pick up yar blades for it makes me quake. Ya are disobeyin' God to please me." Lin turned to her now, eyes red and puffy, cheeks drenched in tears. "I've allowed the evil one, to make me afraid and ya haven't trained 'cause of it. Aria, if ya don't train, ya'll not be prepared and ya'll be killed. I'll have killed ya as if I picked up a dreadful sword meself."

Ari tried again to lay a comforting hand on her shoulder. "The battle season is still some time off. I will be prepared when it arrives."

Lin pulled from her again. "Ya call out in yar sleep, Aria."

"Whatever do I say?"

"Train and prepare, train and prepare, over and over and over again."

"I am sorry, Lindsay—"

"'Tis what ya must do! Ya must be prepared so ya'll not die."

Ari sighed and closed her eyes, searching for the right words. She fixed her gaze on the trembling girl once more. "Even if I train every waking moment from now till the day of battle, there is no guaranty I will survive the next great confrontation with the enemy, my friend. God alone knows the number of my days."

"I'll not stand in yar way a moment longer. Ya'll train tomorrow." Lin gave an angry swipe at her wet cheeks and stood.

"Lindsay—"

The girl spun on her with such force Lin came close to falling. She wagged a finger at Ari as she stood and slipped into her gloves. "Ya'll train! Everyday! Ya'll be prepared!"

"Aye, Lindsay."

Lindsay stomped across the ward ahead of her and marched into the meal. To Ari's amazement, Lin approached King Edmund, gave him a quick bow, and stated in slow sharp words, "Sir Ari will be trainin' on the morrow. Ya may join him if ya desire—but he'll train regardless." Lin spun and dropped to the bench near Wyatt.

Edmund spoke as Ari came along side him. "I understand we are to train on the morrow?"

Ari offered a concerned smile. "I can only guess that the Good Lord used Father James' words to convict the child's heart. He was quite beside himself at the conclusion of the sermon. He now fears keeping me from training is more likely to cause my death than my refraining from it."

"We have all experienced God's correction. It can be a difficult thing to move in obedience, but Lin's heart is willing and God will honor such effort."

"Aye, Sire."

Chapter 33

The next morning, Ari finished lacing her armor under her right arm as Lin approached and thrust her blades at her.

"Could I perchance finish dressing before I take them?"

Lin blinked before a shy smile slid across her lips. "Of course, sir. I wanted to assure ya didn't leave them this morn."

"Blades are not allowed in the hall, page. 'Tis a place of fellowship not contention. We will return after the breaking of the fast and collect them."

"Some knights leave theirs on the unused benches near the door. I'll place them there." She left the chamber with stoic determination.

"Lin? Could you help me with my other laces before you see to the placing of the blades?" Ari called after her.

Lin returned, dropped the weapons in Ari's lap, and lifted Ari's left arm to rest it on her shoulder. She made quick work of the task, pulled a blue tunic from the drawer and helped Ari into it. She snatched up the blades again and stomped out of the room.

Ari found her holding open the outer doors, and she finished with her hood and gloves and they made their way to the hall.

Following the meal, they moved to the space behind the stables and Lin again thrust her blades at her. As Ari strapped the belt around her waist, Edmund strolled in, grinning broadly. Hawk arrived moments later as Ari finished. He handed each of them a waster. Ari took the heavy wooden sword in her hand, feeling its weight.

Designed for training warriors to use the long sword, it swung awkwardly in her hand. Even with two hands, Ari found the weight and length awkward. She handed it back to Hawk.

"I prefer my own blades."

"These would be safer for training," Hawk offered.

"Do you not trust me to take care, sir?"

Edmund laughed. "You never laid a blade on Godric, though he deserved it and you had ample opportunity. I believe you—above all —can be trusted." He elbowed Hawk who offered quiet agreement.

She drew each of her blades, tossed them a small distance in the air with a flip so they landed in her hands with the hilts pointing toward the men. She offered her weapons to them for inspection.

Edmund rested the blade on his finger below the hilt. "Excellent balance. I would have thought the large squared pommel and guard would have weighted the handle far more than the blade."

"The blade is thicker, adding the needed counterweight and making the sword stronger."

Hawk compared the waster to her weapon. "The reach is shorter but it feels more comfortable in my hand. It would account for your speed in combat."

Ari took back her swords and sheathed them. "Many—*like me*— prefer the two smaller blades to the one longer heavier broadsword. They serve us well."

Both men nodded their understanding.

"Well, sir, Majesty, I think it best to begin by observing you spar. I am confident our styles are not as different as everyone claims. Once I know your skill, 'twill be easy to add the few talents I may offer."

"Agreed," they said as one.

Ari moved off a pace, crossed her ankles, and slid effortlessly to the ground where she sat crossed-legged, watching them.

Chapter 34

King Edmund and his thane, Hawk, ran through their forms and did mock battle as Ari took mental note of things she did not need to teach them, and determined a course for their training.

They gave one last strike at one another. The wooden shafts of their wasters thudded and filled the air with their hollow *thack*. The men grunted and shoved each other. They staggered back a step and bent over their would-be weapons which held them up like the canes of the old and lame. Their chests heaved in the great effort of capturing a full breath.

Ari pushed to her feet with minimal effort. "As I expected, you know all I know, Majesty, sir. Our tactics vary by a degree, but it is of little note."

Edmund straightened and stepped nearer yet. A boyish grin on his face, his intense gaze filled her with disquiet. "Show us these tactics."

The playful request sent unwelcome waves of warmth washing over her skin. She shook her head to clear it of the emotions threatening to surface. "You attack with brute force."

Hawk laughed. "Is not one's aim to overpower his enemy?"

"Sire, sir, the horde are not so overpowered. They draw their strength from the evil of their master, which infests them. They can fight even when gravely wounded and long beyond the stamina of the average soldier."

"How ever do you maintain the fight?" Edmund slipped closer

still, his words becoming a tender whisper.

She could feel the hot puffs of his breath caressing her cheek, and she stepped back. "We use their own efforts against them."

"I do not understand," Hawk said.

"Let me demonstrate, Majesty, sir."

Edmund stepped forward, waster raised ready to do battle. The pull of his eager gaze made her insides tremble. She turned to Hawk for an escape. "Sir, I will show you and you can work with His Majesty."

"Fie," Edmund groaned. He tried to draw her attention back. "Sir Ari, if you are going to spend all our time addressing us with such formality, we will accomplish little each day. Call us by our Christian names. It will save time."

She would not look at him. "I could never dishonor the gracious king who has opened his home and offered to stand with us in battle."

Edmund sighed heavily. "There would be no dishonor if I have requested it."

"Would seem practical while we train." Hawk smirked.

Ari tossed the thought around as a juggler would his torches. "Very well. Here, within these walls, we shall speak as equals."

"Splendid!" Edmund mirrored Wyatt's excitement. "Now, Ari, will you show us these tactics?" He moved to step between her and Hawk.

She ignored him, avoided his stare, and tapped Hawk's waster with her blade tip. Stepping almost into Edmund in her determination to remain out of the influence of his stares, her eyes caught on those gathered in the opening to the ward. Her blade dropped to her side and she refused to move.

"I will send them on their way," Edmund said with deep frustration.

The crowd dispersed for a short time but reformed a few steps further outside their training area, their necks straining to see Ari's instruction.

"Now Sir—Hawk, attack." She waved him forward with her left hand while her blade rested relaxed in her right.

Hawk's practice sword rose level with her chest and he lunged.

She rocked back on her right heel, used the flat of her blade to sweep his arm up high over their heads and rocked forward onto her left toes, planting her empty left fist in his ribs. Though not a harsh blow, the pressure would tell him that if she held her other blade, he would be dead.

She stepped back and coaxed another attack. She switched her blade to her left hand as he lunged in the same manner as before. Shifting her weight forward to her toes, she pushed the blade far off to his right and planted her right fist in his stomach. Another deathblow.

Again, she waved him forward.

He brought his waster up high and swung it down like a guillotine.

With her blade back in her right hand she shifted back, brought her weapon down on top of his and forced it to the ground.

Hawk stumbled as she set him off balance, and her free hand slid across the back of his neck.

He came again, swinging wide, and found himself struggling once more for a sure footing as his blade arm crossed over his body and her fist again thumped his ribs.

Hawk took two steps from her, huffing. "I can nay make contact."

Ari smiled. "And look how winded you are. I have never moved my feet. I shift my weight from the forward foot to the rear and back again. Yet I have delivered a deathblow to your every attack."

"Show me how you do it," Hawk said.

Ari demonstrated her actions as he attacked her with slow drawn-out movements. Next she attacked in the same manner to allow him time to react to her. They practiced one counterattack several times before a heavy sigh drew their attention to Edmund.

"Hawk, allow Edmund to attack you. Let us see what you have mastered."

Her heart fluttered as Edmund grinned like a child at the mere passing of his name over her lips. She turned to Hawk and watched them spar for a time. "Good. Now Edmund your turn to practice this counterpoint."

They switched roles and Ari monitored their progress.

"Fie! You can nay be indulging in such treachery!" A voice interrupted them

Chapter 35

Edmund and Hawk stopped and turned to Eric. The prince stood with arms crossed and a deep scowl.

"Eric, explain yourself," his father said.

"You want me to explain myself? You are taking instruction from a foreign knight while he sits back looking for your every weakness. You stand there with useless wasters, while he brandishes his deadly blades. You have lost all thought of your safety and I must explain myself?"

"What makes you think that King Edmund has any such weakness, and has placed his life so carelessly into my hands?" Ari countered.

"I will not be spoken to so by an alien come to mooch of my naive father."

"Eric!" Edmund thrust past her and stormed toward his son. "You think me such a simpleton, and announce it here, in the open, among our people? If you think so little of me you need not live under my roof any longer."

"You would take the count of this outsider, over your own blood?"

"Ari has demonstrated the character of one who deserves honor and respect—I have yet to see the same of you, Eric."

"Ari." The word dragged across Eric's lips and dripped with disgust and accusation. "Are you so close in such a brief span of time?"

"My relationship with Ari does not concern you!"

"Relationship? What relationship can a king have with a foreign knight? What relationship should a king have with an outsider?"

"Get out of my presence!"

"With pleasure!" Eric spun on his heel, staggered a step as he attempted to avoid his friend Preston, and stomped from the sparring ground.

The church bells tolled, as Edmund stood clench-fisted and rigid across his shoulders.

Ari moved beside him as she sheathed her blade and worked to unfasten her belt. She held out her blades and Lin ran to collect them. "Take them to our chambers before you go to midday."

"Aye, sir." Lin ran off as the crowd melted away.

Hawk joined them on Edmund's other side.

"Forgive my son," Edmund groaned.

"He should know the truth."

"If he hates you now, know it would be tenfold if he knew."

"I will defer to your judgment."

"Shall we head to our meal?" Hawk offered with an air of hope.

"I have lost my appetite. I go to the chapel to pray!" Edmund tossed the waster and stomped off without looking back.

"Sir Ari," Hawk waved for her to proceed.

She nodded and moved toward the hall.

"All things work together for the best unto them that love God, even to them that are called of His purpose." Hawk quoted. "God will work out everything in His time."

"Aye, but there will be much to endure until such a day."

Hawk smiled. "Yet much can be endured with good friends."

A smile tugged at her lips.

"Thank you for the training today. I found it beneficial."

Ari bowed as they neared the tables. "I am pleased I could be of service, sir."

Edmund and Hawk met Ari each morning after the first meal to train together. The air developed a bite and the leaves in the valley erupted into a bright display before dropping to the ground. Ari was content, for a time.

Chapter 36

Edmund approached Ari as she entered this morn to enjoy breaking the fast. His familiar heated gaze lay shrouded in concern. His brows made deep ruts in his forehead and his eyes would not hold hers as they flitted about like a bird in a cage. Her stomach lurched.

"Sir Ari, I would speak with you," his tone was low and his words slow as though burdened.

"What has happened?"

"Please, come with me." He motioned her back toward the door.

She walked beside him, yet still he would not look at her or speak. She stepped to the dirt of the ward and heard the door behind them open and close.

Edmund turned and knelt before Lindsay as she made to follow. "Not this time, faithful page. This is nay a matter I wish you to see."

Lindsay looked to Ari.

"Return to your meal. I will join in a short time." Now Lin looked as worried as Edmund. Her lower lip disappeared between her teeth as she turned with the speed of an advancing sundial back toward the hall.

Edmund waited for her to disappear within before he led Ari to their sparring area. He held out his hand to stop her from entering. He cleared his throat, but he still would not look at her. "My people arrived late last eve. I fear they have brought you terrible news, Ari."

She steeled her nerves. "Show me."

They stepped inside and Ari saw the prone form of a body covered by course cloth lying against the back of the stables. Her heart seized and she could not breathe.

Edmund knelt at the head and gripped the edge of the fabric but did not remove it. He looked to her. His great brows drew together and concern filled his eyes.

She nodded for him to proceed.

He pulled back the cloth and revealed the face.

Ari dropped to her knees with a moan. "Oh, Dunham."

"'Tis as I feared. He traveled with you?"

"He served as my personal guard." She swallowed hard, trying to keep back the tears. "He was charged with my safety. I prayed he stayed with the others when I parted." Her head dropped and her voice shook. "Forgive me, Dunham. You deserved better." Her head turned to the sky and her hands rose. "Lord, please welcome your servant home. He loved You above all and he remained faithful to me always." Her hands dropped to her lap and her eyes slammed closed to prevent a flood of tears from escaping. Yet one lone drop evaded capture and slid unbidden down her cheek. "Tell him I am sorry, Father," she whispered.

Tiny arms encircled her neck and she startled. Lin embraced her as tears flowed down her face, dampening Ari's neck.

Edmund covered Dunham's face again and came to gather up Lindsay in his arms. "I asked you not to come, child." His words were tender as he turned her away from the body.

Ari heard Lindsay whisper, "She needs us, Sire."

Ari swiped away another unwanted tear. "The horde did not take him." She stated the words to focus her mind on something other than her pain and need.

"No. The people who found him live in a small shire two days' journey from here. They said his horse lay nearby with several festering viper bites to its forelegs. It appears his horse threw him. Dunham suffered a broken neck, according to Tinsley."

"So he did not suffer?"

"Nay, death came quick."

Ari nodded but could not speak for the pain clutching her in its unrelenting grasp. She did not believe she could hurt more if she lay impaled on an enemy sword.

"We will leave you alone." He paused and when he spoke again his words dripped with compassion. "'Tis not our custom to bury anyone in holy ground who our priests cannot attest to their salvation in Christ. If you can swear Dunham demonstrated such an allegiance with his Lord, I believe I may be able to sway Father James to concede to a proper burial."

"I do so swear, and attest to his salvation in Christ." Ari shook her head in disbelief as her eyes remained fixed on the covered body of her friend. "In a time of peace, he would have been a holy brother or perhaps a priest himself. His fate was dictated by the war ravaging our land. As are all our lives." She tried again in vain to hold back her tears.

"We will leave you and I will begin to gather those needed to prepare Dunham for his final rest."

"I do not know how your men mourn, Sire."

Lin sat straddling his hips as he cradled her tight to his chest. One arm held her fast about the waist and the other held her head to his shoulder so she could not see. Ari suffered from a sudden and unexpected desire to be so cradled in his arms. She needed to be held and comforted. The longing became so strong she rose to her feet.

"Mourn as you need, Ari. No one will disturb you. I alone will return when all is ready." Stepping toward the opening, he looked about and placed Lindsay on the ground. He took her hand so she would not return, and spoke over his shoulder. "May God comfort you."

They disappeared and Ari trembled from a loss now doubled. She dropped beside Dunham's body once more and gave herself over to the tears, which soon turned to great gut-wrenching sobs.

Chapter 37

A tender, warm hand brushed her shoulder, startling Ari. Her tears long since spent and dried, she looked up at Edmund.

"All has been prepared. You may return to your chambers and my people will prepare Durham."

She pushed to her feet, still struggling with the longing to feel his strong arms around her. "I will not leave him again."

Edmund nodded. "Of course." He stepped from her to the opening and beckoned others to enter. He returned to her side and drew her back so the newcomers could place a long board from the hall near the body. Hawk and two others lifted Dunham onto the table with care as women surrounded him and sat buckets of water on the ground.

Ari watched as the women took great care in removing his torn and dirty clothing before washing his entire body.

"You say they found him two days' journey from here?" Ari asked.

"Aye, two days south, in Hamshire."

"So they found him soon after death?"

"They said his body still held some warmth in it."

Ari sighed. "God wished him to have a proper burial, for no time passed for the wild beasts or decay to take him."

"This is the argument I gave Father James."

"He agreed?"

"Aye." Edmund's elbow brushed hers and he directed her gaze

toward the opening. "He has come to bless Dunham."

The women finished washing him and the priest prayed over her friend. Next, they wrapped his body in wide strips of cloth and bound it with several thongs of leather. Finally the men who earlier carried the table and who had stood as sentinels in an outer ring round the women stepped forward and placed Dunham in a small wagon in the ward.

Ari moved to follow and Edmund kept pace. Lindsay stepped to her other side with Wyatt as she exited the inner area.

Father James moved to the front of the procession, and a group of warriors from the garrison followed in his wake. Hawk led the horse pulling the funeral cart and Edmund, Ari, Lindsay, and Wyatt walked behind. As they passed into the bailey and toward the gate all the castle's occupants joined the procession.

"We have no burial grounds on the mount. We will accompany Dunham to his final rest in the tradition of our fallen heroes."

"Thank you, Majesty." Tears threatened again, but those gathered broke into song as the gate opened. The hymn of praise taken from Psalms and put to music lifted her spirit and she almost missed seeing Selvyn glaring, crossed-armed, from the garrison doorway.

"Several men I trust are staying behind to keep an eye on him."

She nodded and gave herself to the hymn and the other laments which followed as they snaked down from the precipice into the town and to the cemetery behind the large church.

A hole lay ready to accept Dunham's body. The men lowered him in as Father James motioned for her to step forward and whispered. "'Tis our custom for those who know the deceased to take a handful of earth, speak on their experience with the departed, and sprinkle it over the body. Tradition says three handfuls are required to honor the Father, the Son, and the Holy Ghost who will accept his spirit."

Ari nodded her understanding. She took a deep breath and collected her first handful from the mound beside the open grave. She gazed down at Dunham's wrapped body lying in the dark hole below and cleared her throat of tears. This was not the time for crying. She must tell of his life. Later she could return to her room and again cry until her eyes would make no more tears.

"Dunham of Melville in Wexxton followed after God with his whole heart. He loved God's Holy Word and whether on the battlefield or at home, he always carried it with him. The Scriptures are no small trifle to load in your sack, but he would not be parted from them. I long since lost count of the times his reading comforted me both before and after battle. Even as I have sojourned here in his absence, still his sure voice comforts me with God's Word."

She scattered the dirt along his body and looked to the heavens. "Well done good servant and faithful… enter into thy Master's joy."

She bent and picked up another handful. "Dunham of Melville in Wexxton was my friend. Assigned to watch over me from my youth, he ever sought to be my servant, but he became so much more. A faithful trainer and sure confidant, the kind of friend who would call you to account for your ill behavior as easily as praise you for conducting yourself true and honorable."

She looked out at those gathered and swallowed a tear. "I am quite sure his tongue gave me a sound lashing for running off as he searched in earnest to assure my welfare." She scattered the dirt. "Forgive me, dear friend. You, as always, have been faithful to one who failed you so many times. I will miss you above all others. 'Go in peace: that which we have sworn both of us in the Name of the Lord, saying, The Lord be between me and thee, and between my seed and between thy seed, let it stand forever.'"

Ari was slow to pick up the final handful of earth. Its coolness seeped through her glove, and she fought against her own cold heart. She cleared her throat once—twice—thrice, took a deep breath and continued in a voice leveled and controlled.

"Dunham of Melville in Wexxton, though a priest at heart, was a mighty warrior for his God. He fought by my side as my sure right hand in times of trouble. He fought for the glory of God and the freedom of our people. Never did his blade rise in hate or anger. Never did it fly, that his heart did not grieve for the soul lost."

She spread the last of the soil over her friend. "You did not see it in this life, my friend, but know, 'He maketh wars to cease unto the ends of the world: He breaketh the bow and cutteth the spear, and burneth the chariots with fire.' Your days of warring are done. We have but one more. Rest now in the Father's arms."

Ari stepped back from the grave and stood stoic and silent, her hands clasped behind her back as the priest gave the blessing.

"Dunham of Melville in Wexxton is here reported and attested to be a believer in the one true God, a faithful friend, and a fearsome warrior for his God. I regret I never knew the man in this life but look forward to meeting him in glory. He now waits with his Savior in the beauty of heaven for those who will follow in God's time. Let us follow Dunham's example. Let us never neglect the sharing of the Word in fellowship one to another. Let us be a trusted and needed servant to our friends. And let us fight not in anger or malice of heart but for truth and right and for the glory of God. 'In the sweat of thy face shalt thou eat bread, till thou return to the earth: for out of it wast thou taken, because thou art dust, and to dust shalt thou return.'"

Father James took up a fistful of dirt and tossed it into the grave.

Edmund stepped forward next and took up a handful as he looked out to his people. "Dunham of Melville in Wexxton lies here unknown to us, but he served as Ari's protector. I will take up his place and serve in his stead until such a time as we are parted in death." He too threw in the bit of earth.

Edmund moved to her right, as first Wyatt, followed by Lindsay, and then each man gathered came forward and repeated their king's words. "I too will serve in Dunham's stead as Sir Ari's protector."

One after another, they came and swore to watch over her in Dunham's place. Ten, twenty—she lost count of their number. When they finished, the grave lay nearly full. She looked at them and could do little more than bow, slow and deep. Her voice cracked and betrayed her. "You have honored my friend and me beyond all measure this day. May God return to you tenfold the kindness you have shown this day."

"Amen," Father James sang out and as one they turned and re-formed the procession as before. They sang hymns of praise to God up the mountain. Many dispersed into the bailey and a few more once they entered the ward.

Ari stood still in the silence left in their absence. Her mind trapped in a fog of regret and sorrow, she could not think what to do next, or where she ought to go.

Edmund's hand rested on her shoulder and the desire stirred in her again. If she stepped forward now, would he encircle her in his embrace as he had Lindsay?

Pounding hooves thundered through the inner gate and pulled them apart.

"Father, we heard the singing as we exited the hunting ground. What has happened?" Eric leapt from his charger and threw the reins to a nearby squire.

"The body of one of Sir Ari's companions was brought to me in the wee hours of the night. Father James has overseen the burial."

Eric's hard gaze slid to her and narrowed. "You allowed him to be buried in holy ground?"

"Father James believed in his salvation as attested to by Ari."

"And what if he lied?"

"God can deal with an unwanted body in consecrated ground and the one who bore witness with equal holy justice."

Eric huffed his displeasure and turned to pull the buck from the third horse tethered to Preston's saddle.

Preston stepped down. "May God give you comfort from this loss," he said with a bow.

Ari nodded and Edmund turned her toward her chamber. "Rest now Ari. Mourn, as your heart requires. No demands or expectations will be placed upon you. If you have need, send Lin. God's peace be upon you." He entered his hall.

Lin stood looking up at her, tears welling in her small eyes. "Come, sir, let's retire to the privacy of yar chambers."

Ari's feet felt as though great weights were bound to them. She trudged forward and struggled up the stairs before she fell into her chamber and slumped to her knees on the floor, leaving little room for Lin to secure the door without hitting her.

"Come, Aria. I'll help ya out of yar armor and ya can rest." Lin tugged and cajoled until she got Ari to her feet. She led her to the bed where she parted the curtains and drew back the covers. Ari dropped down and allowed Lin to remove first her boots followed by her tunic and armor. It crashed to the floor with a thud and Ari buried her face in her pillow. Sobs tore through her body like hot blades and she cried until sleep claimed her.

Chapter 38

Lin fretted as Ari remained locked in her chamber for several days.

"How fare's our knight, Lin?" King Edmund crouched and asked on the fourth morning. Lin stood outside the kitchen waiting to gather Ari's meal.

"He'll nay speak and only eats when pestered beyond all tolerance."

He caressed her cheek. "Is there anything I might do?"

Lin shook her head and worried her lip. "I keep prayin'."

"As do I." Edmund patted her on the head.

When Ari did emerge into the grey autumn light, the fearsome drive of a warrior consumed her.

Edmund worried and spent much of his free time in prayer. Ari ate little at his boards and talked less. The one thing she did do was train, and this she did to excess.

Every free moment between meals, she trained in the hidden space as long as the light allowed. Edmund could not keep pace with her insatiable fervor, but he joined her even if only to stand watch. Hawk took his turn as well, but Lin never left Ari's side.

Edmund and Hawk attempted to spar with her but Ari's fierceness caused them to falter.

Edmund narrowly missed being struck. "Ari! I know not what demons assail you, but be assured, we are friends."

Ari's blades came to rest at her sides and she stared at him as if he had grown another head. "I prepare for battle."

"Aye, I am aware of your pressing need, but I am not your enemy."

"Aye?" Her head tipped to the side.

Hawk attempted to aid her understanding of their concern. "You fight with steel and we have but wasters."

"You own blades. I see no reason why you choose not to use them."

"We are not in a battle at this moment. There is no need for unnecessary risk which could cause a serious injury. We would be unable to train, and diminish our effectiveness on the battlefield, or— the heavens forbid—kill us before the battle lines are even drawn." Edmund stepped toward her, his hand outstretched in an offering of peace.

Ari snatched it, jerked him forward a step, spun on the ball of her right foot, and now standing shoulder to shoulder with him, drove her elbow into his back, forcing him forward another step with a grunt. In the blink of an eye, Edmund went from offering her friendship to staggering under her mock attack.

"If I wished to do you harm, I could without thought." She glared with distain. "If I hold back in training, I will not be prepared for battle. Dunham sacrificed his life to ensure I would be present to fight." The tip of her blade rose and pointed at him like the wagging finger of a disapproving parent. "I will not dishonor his memory by coddling you in my training. You need not join me, but you choose to come each day. If not to train, why show your face?"

Edmund held up his hands in surrender. "I come to train—same as you. But Ari, Dunham's death is not your fault."

Ari's other blade sliced the air as she stepped toward him. It came to rest a flick from his throat. "He was charged with my care. I left without him. He came to find me to fulfill his sacred duty. And he died in the trying. If I am not to blame—then who is?"

"'Twas an accident—"

Now her first blade flashed before Hawk's nose, silencing him. "Which would not have happened had I done as instructed."

Edmund swallowed and placed the palm of his hand on the flat of her blade. He pushed it out of the way as he stepped toward her. He whispered in hopes of soothing her agitated spirit. "All life—yours, mine, Lin's, Dunham's—is cradled in the Almighty's hands. 'One of them shall not fall on the ground without your Father knowing.' Naught can happen to us without the Father's consent, 'in whose hand is the soul of every living thing, and the breath of all mankind.' Forgive yourself, Ari."

A slow breath whistled through her teeth. She trembled. Tears pooled in her beautiful dark eyes. "I cannot." Her swords dropped to her sides and her breath came in uneven gasps.

Edmund longed to draw her into his arms and comfort her, but with so many gathered to watch—against his wishes—he could not endanger revealing her. "Perhaps Father James could help." He placed a tender hand on her arm.

Ari jerked away, her blade flashing between them again. "Only one thing will help me now—seeing the Black Knight impaled on my blade before I die and join Dunham. It is the least I can do for him." She whirled and left their sparring area like a violent twisting wind racing across the valley.

Edmund sighed and tossed down his wooden weapon.

Hawk joined him. "She bears a blame not meant for her to carry."

"She hates feeling for anyone."

Both men turned and stared as Lin spoke.

"Dunham crept into her heart and now she hates him for the pain he has caused. But she loathes herself more for the hating." Lin finished and ran after her master.

"Lin?" Edmund called

Already several steps away she turned but a fraction. "Sir Ari talks in his sleep."

Chapter 39

They met for another week and Ari softened by degree each day. Edmund trusted that God would right her in due time.

"We cannot spar for the remainder of the week," Edmund announced as they prepared to finish on a cloudless morning.

"Why ever not?" Ari huffed.

"The harvest festivals have arrived and I must attend the details."

Ari and Hawk both opened their mouths in protest but Edmund raised his hand to stay them.

"You may not train without me. I will not be left out of the fun and camaraderie in my own home. Four days is but a trifle and will not harm our preparations. Rest now, but I expect both of you to join me in celebrating each eve." He did not wait their agreement.

Edmund loved the harvest celebrations. He oversaw every detail, from the decorating and preparation of the great hall to the menu each night. He strolled toward the large structure and resisted the childish urge to skip.

Winslow drew alongside of him and matched his steps as they proceeded together. "The items you requested have arrived, Majesty."

Edmund slapped his back. "Good, good. Let us see to their arrangement."

They entered to find evergreen boughs heaped in a pile on one table. Strips of bright red, orange, and yellow satin lay in neat piles across another. Long narrow strips of linen in like colors lay in a pile down the length of one long board. Buckets of apples, pears, and cauliflower still nestled in its leaves sat on the fresh rushes. Tin plates and cups were stacked high on another table closer to the kitchen.

"'Tis marvelous! God has richly blessed us again." Edmund could not suppress his smile. "Have the invitations been received?"

"Aye, Majesty. There will be three groups as last year. Sir Hawkins and I worked hard to divide the town so everyone could share in the festivities."

"Do you remember when we started this?"

Winslow chuckled. "Oh aye. I thought you were mad. The idea of bringing the entire town into the castle for a meal confounded me."

"The town was small at first. We were able to include everyone in one night. Over the years we added a second night to accommodate them all. And now we are at three nights."

"If the townsfolk continue to multiply, we may need to add a fourth next year."

Edmund again pounded his steward's back. "Would that nay be splendid?"

"How long will you allow it to grow, Sire? Everything you serve at your boards comes from your own fields. If you give it all away at the beginning of the long winter what will you and the others living in the castle eat?"

"Oh Winslow," Edmund *tsked*. "Ye of little faith, my friend. God is forever faithful. Do you nay think He will provide for us when we honor those who support us?"

Winslow inclined his head. "Forgive me, Majesty. God will indeed provide. He will bless you for blessing your people."

A handful of servants entered and Edmund turned his attention to them. "Hello, my friends."

"Your Majesty," they said as one and gave observance. Attending to each detail, he instructed them as to the many tasks needed to be completed.

Edmund spent the entire day moving from one group of workers to another. His heart overflowed with so much joy, he thought it would burst. But he felt this way every year.

He slept well and the following morn he woke early to place the final touches in preparation for the first night of the feasts.

The torches were driven into the hard rock of the ward and bailey at intervals. They would form a lit pathway for his guests from the outer gate to the hall doors where he would greet them. His smile only grew as he entered the chapel.

Kneeling before the altar, he bowed silently for several minutes before giving voice to his petition. "My Father, Jesus the Son, and the Holy Comforter, I come to You with a humble request. Your children come to my home these next eves. May all be welcome here. May none feel lesser for his station or occupation. May all sit as equals under Your love. May You alone receive all glory, and none look to me as their provider or protector. May I only be Your servant this night— and always, Lord."

Edmund remained for a time, reveling in his Father's good pleasure, before he returned to his tasks.

Chapter 40

Dusk settled on the land and Edmund stood atop the battlements over the outer gate, Hawk at his side. The procession of his first night's guest snaked up the mount. Knights escorted the villagers as they wove along the twisting path like some ancient sacred pilgrimage. He smiled. They did not come to bow to some useless idol but to fellowship in the love of God. Edmund's heart thrilled.

"Your first guests will enter the gates in moments," Hawk said. "Do you plan to greet them?"

"Aye, 'tis the best part. To shake each hand and bid them welcome. 'Tis my greatest blessing all year."

Hawk shook his head and smiled. "You are an odd one, Ed. Any other king would demand tribute with an iron fist. You welcome the nearest town into your home and feed them of your own stores. What would your father say?"

Edmund laughed. "By my sword, son, but it has taken you enough time to master the idea of being a servant to your people."

"Aye, and a faithful servant to your God as well. These people love you so, they would follow you to the ends of the earth and beyond."

Now Edmund turned with a serious thought. "Do you think they will join us in fighting with Wexxton, Hawk?"

Hawk's smile filled his face in the waning light. "You have but ask and they will start to sharpen their blades on the morrow—with or without the promise of land for the knights. If you ask, the farmers will pick up their sickles and march beside you."

Edmund sighed with contentment.

Hawk laughed as he pointed below them. "You better go. The lead guard is stepping through the gate."

Edmund began to move. "Did you inform Ari where to sit?"

Hawk waved him to continue, "Aye, I told him, but he has been brooding these last few days. Do not expect him to comply."

For over an hour Edmund greeted each of his guests as they entered and found their seats. Beautiful people one and all with darling children. He loved each and every one of them and he received their love as well. His heart sang praises to God in his overwhelming joy.

When he followed the last one inside, his eyes caught on the figure sitting at the table nearest the doors with the others from the castle—Ari. He groaned within. She sat in the dimly lit rear of his hall with her back to his raised dais. Her shoulders slumped and head hung low. The burden she carried was visible.

Edmund proceeded toward his seat on the dais. The position he had reserved for her at the front remained empty and his heart ached. Hawk shrugged. *Lord, comfort her and rid her of her unwarranted guilt.* Edmund turned to his people and opened the evening.

"My dear friends, I bid you welcome. Let us thank the Lord for all He has done."

Everyone stood and bowed their heads.

"Gracious Father, Provider and Protector, we honor You this night for all You have done, and every blessing You have bestowed. Thank you, Lord. May our fellowship be an offering of praise. Amen."

"Amen."

"Eat and enjoy." Edmund took his seat and spent more time joyfully watching his people than eating himself. But long before the night ended, Ari slipped away.

"I will speak with him on the morrow," Hawk said.

The second night unfolded as the first. Sweet villagers welcomed, Ari skulked in the last row with her back to him, and she again retired before the night concluded. *Lord, is there naught to be done?*

King Edmund approached with arms held tight against his stomach. He did not welcome Ari in friendship, as was his habit. No smile graced his face. Worry drew his brows together, and as he neared, he opened his arms to her. They were drenched in blood.

"Edmund! Edmund!" Ari gasped for breath as she bolted up in bed and gratefully tore from the horrible images.

Lin parted the curtains, flooding her dark retreat with the flickering fire. "Aria?"

Ari squinted in the unwelcome light. "Forgive me for disturbing your sleep, my friend. An unpleasant dream, naught more."

"Ya've been troubled from the day they buried Dunham. I worry over ya."

She chafed at the child's concern. "I am fine, child. Do not waste your time over me."

"But I love ya, Aria," the child whimpered.

"Stop it!" Ari flung back the covers, almost hitting Lindsay, and fled from the bed.

"But, Aria—"

"Stop! I order you to stop this moment. You know full well I cannot stay with you. God has called me to something of far greater import than your silly attachment to me."

"I could go with ya."

"I will nay allow you to watch me die in battle!" Ari flung open the inner door and stormed into the outer room. The fire here long since dead, a chill bite through her thin nightrail.

"What if ya don't die?" Lindsay persisted.

Ari raked her bare fingers through her tangled hair, desperate for an escape from the child. "I will."

"Ya don't know—"

Aria grabbed Lindsay by the shoulders and shook her. "I will. I know. God has foretold my destiny. I will die in the final battle with the Black Night. 'Tis ordained by God." She pushed the child away, shoved both hands into her hair and held her aching head.

"Do you see now, child, why I do not wish you to be attached to me? This has been a mistake. I never should have allowed you here."

Lindsay burst into tears and fled back to her pallet by the fire.

Ari groaned. After listening too long to the child's sobs, she snatched up her clothes and cloak. She dressed in the outer chamber and fled.

She paused as she approached the inner gate. She wore no armor to hide her figure and her hood rested beside her bed with her gloves. She pulled the cowl down over her eyes and wrapped the cloak tight about her, hiding her hands inside its folds. The guards greeted her as she stepped through the small door into the bailey.

She made her way to the chapel and lay prostrate before the altar. Whispered movement behind her danced in the stillness. Lindsay knelt a pace behind her in the aisle. Ari sighed and returned to her prayers.

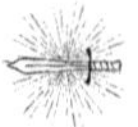

Edmund entered the great hall for the final night of the festival. Ari did not sit at the back table. As he approached the front, he spotted her. She sat in the place he had reserved for her each night—though on the opposite side of the table so her back was to his high seat. She sat straight and shoulders squared. She scanned those gathered but did not look at him. As he climbed to the dais to open the evening, he too looked out over his subjects. They looked as happy and festive as each of the previous nights.

He glanced down at her before praying. Ari sat watchful not bowing her head for prayer as she remained an alert sentry. Edmund finished and swept a glance over the hall. His stomach knotted. He felt it now too. Something foul stirred.

Chapter 41

The food circulated about the tables. Guests chatted amiably. Edmund scrutinized Ari. She scanned the room as she waved away a food tray with a curt hand.

The plates filled.

"Long live the king."

Edmund raised his cup in gratitude.

Ari moved.

She grabbed her tin plate, then sent it spinning into the air. Like a frantic wagon wheel it spun upward, its bottom faced the dais and empty surface shown out on those gathered.

Edmund sat mesmerized by the whirling disk until it came to its zenith level with Eric's face. It hovered for a fraction of a heartbeat, and took one turn in descent.

A hurtled dagger impaled the plate through the center.

It wobbled in the air, and crashed to the ground.

Before it landed, Ari snatched the plate of the man dining across from her, dumped its contents and spun it into the air as the first. Another dagger drove through it, sparing Edmund's younger son.

The assassin came into view as the second plate thudded onto the dais and oscillated as it rolled along the length of the platform before dropping to the floor. The darkly-clad man stood for a moment glaring at Ari as she rose to her feet. Even from where Edmund sat behind her, she looked foreboding.

Eric vaulted over the high table and down to the floor.

Ari shouted and reached to stop him.

The villain fled, knocking down any who dared venture into his path.

Eric tore from Ari's grasp and gave chase.

Ari followed close on Eric's heels.

By the time Edmund and Hawk caught up to them a pace outside the doors, Ari stood blocking Eric's chase.

"Get out of my way, you filthy traitor, or I will have you thrown in the dungeon for conspiracy."

"Your Highness, I gave the man no aid. But I cannot allow you to run off into the night after him. 'Tis too dangerous."

"Get out of my way!" Eric tried to push past her but she shoved him back.

Eric threw a punch.

Crack! He connected with Ari's jaw and spun her around.

"Ari!" Edmund called out in horror. "Sir Ari, are you all right?"

Eric snorted like a charging bull. "Do not dare to ever touch me again!"

Ari rubbed her jaw with a gloved hand. A huge smile lit her face as she licked a drop of blood from the corner of her mouth. And she laughed. "Well done, Highness. Well done indeed. You managed to do something the king and his thane have failed to do in better than a month of training. You made contact."

Edmund took another step toward her. "Are you sure you are unharmed?"

"Father! Honestly, why do you favor this traitor so?"

"Ari is no traitor! He saved your life this night."

"Yet he will not allow the assassin to be brought to justice."

"This plan has been well thought out, Your Highness. No doubt if they failed he would lie in wait for whoever chased after him. God did not spare your life once tonight only to have you blunder after the knave to your death."

"Sir Ari gives sound advice, son."

"Of course, you would think so. Your new favorite son can do no wrong. Has it not occurred to you, Father? Your illustrious guest could have himself planned each attack so he might be your savior and win your favor."

"Eric—?"

"There is but one Savior, Your Highness, and I can assure you it is not me."

"Prove it and get out of my way! Let me hunt this evildoer down and question him before he is drawn and quartered."

"Vengeance is mine: I will repay, saith the Lord." Ari continued to block his path. Hands in surrender she would not touch him, but neither would she allow him to pass.

"Son, listen to sound council."

"Not from him! Never from him!"

Eric charged and ended up on his back at her feet in the same moment. "Oh Your Highness, forgive me. Our feet became tangled. I never meant … I am so sorry." She reached a gloved hand to help him up.

Edmund expected his hotheaded son to slap it away and start ranting at her.

Eric surprised him when he took the offered appendage and stunned Edmund further as he yanked Ari down on top of him only to plant his feet in her hips and flip her over his head as she had done to Godric weeks prior. Ari landed with a thud on her back as Eric popped to his feet.

Now free of her interference, he did not run after the attacker but turned and crossed his arms awaiting her sharp rebuke.

Ari lay on her back, her mouth open, her knees pulled toward her chest and she trembled.

Edmund feared she suffered serious injury and now reeled in pain.

But as she got to her feet air returned to her lungs and she erupted into laughter. "Highness, thank you."

Eric stared at her.

"I have not had such fun since I left home. 'Tis clear, I am a far better instructor from afar than when one crosses blades with me." She turned a hard gaze on Edmund, which caused him to shudder. Tension filled her next words. "I would relish the chance to train with someone who does not coddle me so."

Eric's arms dropped at his sides and his mouth hung agape.

"I speak the honest truth. You have challenged me far more than any I have met in Veronia, Your Highness." She bowed low before him in deep sincerity. "It may do us both good to work together."

Eric gave a slow nod and moved back toward the hall. "Mayhaps," he stammered, a grin touching his lips.

Ari watched him go as Edmund and Hawk came to stand in front of her. "Are you quite sure you are hale, Ari?" Edmund asked with tenderness.

She swiped away the hand he offered and the torchlight reflecting in her eyes only added to her anger.

"How dare you! You have done me no service. Your kindness has been no boon at all." Her harsh words carried both anger and hurt. "I am to walk onto a battlefield—the final battle for the sake of my people and my home, and you have led me to believe I am ready. Yet all the while you have held back—gone easy—and treated me as far less of a warrior than I am. By my sword, I will not train another day with you! I will be prepared for the sake of my people if I must train with Selvyn and his menacing band."

"Ari, we never meant—"

"I will not hear another word from your lying tongue. You know the truth and you have no respect for me. I am finished with you." She disappeared.

Edmund turned to Hawk with a sigh, as those gawking at them slipped back inside. "Nay did I treat him any different."

"It is unlikely you will be able to convince Ari of such, Ed." Hawk forced a smile to his lips. "Come enjoy the last night of the feasts. We will investigate this attack and try to make amends in the morn. A new day may bring cooler heads."

Ari did not return to the meal.

Chapter 42

Eric approached Ari the next morn. She stalked across the ward, having not eaten the previous night nor did she break the fast. Edmund feared her anger caused her to avoid him.

She bowed low and greeted him with a slim smile. "Good day, Your Highness. 'Tis a fine morn."

Edmund marveled at his son's reply. "Far better than I deserve."

Her brow rose.

"You have nay heard the report?"

"I only now left my chambers to train. What has happened?"

"At first light the guards discovered the body of the assassin. He fled the castle in such haste he fell from the path. His body lay broken halfway down the side."

"God has repaid."

"And you saved my life twice last eve." Eric bowed.

Ari shook her head. "God spared you for His own good purpose. I but stood in your path until reason returned."

"If not for you, I would have chased after him and fallen to my death as well. I have treated you with distain and hatred since the moment you entered our gates. Yet you have honored me, treated me with respect I do not deserve, and saved my worthless life. Thank you."

Ari bowed. "Thank the Lord alone, please. I am but His servant."

Eric offered his hand in friendship. "I thank you for your service to our mighty God."

She grasped his forearm and smiled.

Eric held her. "I wish to accept your offer to train together."

Again Edmund watched as Ari's brow rose. "Would you now?"

He nodded.

"I shall challenge you since you have already proved your skill."

Eric grinned. "I would expect naught less." He released her. "I have one further boon if you are agreeable?"

"I am at your service to do anything within my power, Highness."

"I need to calm my ill temper. Lord knows my father and others have done their level best to put out the flame raging within, but it will not be quenched. Through all, you kept your head last night. I need to master such restraint."

Her arms crossed and she considered him. "Quieting a fiery temper is not a lesson easily learned, Highness."

"Well I know. Will you try?"

"It will be unpleasant."

"Understood."

"We have but forged a friendship and this will cause you to hate me again."

"I will nay hold against you anything you do in these efforts."

"Truly?"

Eric groaned with exasperation. "Aye."

Ari stepped forward and, with the speed of a flying whip, slapped him across the face.

Edmund choked as a bubble of laughter lodged in his throat.

Eric's fist rose to strike, but Ari snatched his wrist and held it fast. "Highness?"

He growled.

"What is your first thought?"

"To rip your bloody head off!"

"Take a slow deep breath. Now, what is the next thought?"

Air whistled through his locked jaws. "I not a second prior gave you permission to do such."

"And another slower, deeper breath. Now what thought come?"

He pulled from her and took a step back. "I cannot hurt you for doing the very thing which I asked. I choose to leave your head upon your shoulders—for now."

Ari smiled and bowed. "Thank you, Highness. Lesson one is complete."

"And how many might I expect?"

She shrugged. "Depends entirely on the hardness of thy head, Highness."

Eric sighed, "A great many indeed then."

Ari stepped to his side. "Shall we proceed to our morning training—with the sword—Highness?"

He nodded and as Ari took a step past him she tossed up her heel behind her and kicked him in the rump.

Eric's fists clenched at his sides and he snarled, low and menacing.

"Breathe, Highness. Breathe."

Edmund followed a few steps behind as Preston joined Eric and Ari. She inclined her head to the newcomer's request to spar with them. The two young men stepped with great eagerness into Ari's training ground, but she paused.

Spinning with the speed of a striking viper, she drew her blades, and held them before the center of Edmund's and Hawk's chests. "Did I not make myself quite clear last eve, I will nay be training with you again. I will be prepared for the battle to come, and you have assured me you are incapable of assisting with the task. I, therefore, have no further need of you."

A thousand thoughts assailed Edmund, rendering his tongue useless.

"Do you require further lodging?" Hawk asked in a firm whisper.

Ari's blades lowered by a degree. "I have spent many a night beneath God's roof. It could be done again if you wish to be rid of me. And such would at last fulfill my request to leave. As no weapon for our salvation can be found, so you say, there remains no reason for me to tarry further."

"Winter is upon us. The noblemen of Veronia and Balmore will begin arriving any day. I will present your need to them at the high council as I promised, before the Christ Mass is celebrated. You will remain." Though not an order, Edmund's heart remained set. He did not wish her to leave, not now—mayhaps not at all. "I will leave you to your training, friend. May it be more to your liking."

Before Edmund entered the hall, the ringing of blades stirred a longing he feared would devour him.

Chapter 43

Ari thrilled at the challenge of the two young men. She did little instructing as they set about crossing honed steel blades at once. The fierceness and danger worked as a balm to her angry, guilt-ridden spirit. This mock combat served as a medicine far more potent than any in a healer's bag.

The three met every morning as she had with Edmund and Hawk. She did not miss the king's hot glances or his obvious indulgence of her. The thought of the king and his thane going easy on her for being a woman stirred the fire in her belly until it doubled her in pain. But something else stirred in her as well. Something quite unwelcome, and she refused to acknowledge it. She pushed the unwanted emotion deep within and attacked with a fierceness the that younger men matched.

The smashing of blades with Eric and Preston drowned out the guilt of leaving Dunham to die searching for her, the frustration of not finding a weapon to take back to her people, and the growing attachments to these people. Especially the king. Desiring to be held in his arms was unthinkable. She could afford no ties to anyone. Not these strangers, if not her own people.

The metal clashed again, and reverberated down her arms. Here she could escape even her own thoughts. If only she could stay crossing blades every moment of every day.

Returning to her chambers with her devoted page and sequestered in the quiet of her curtained bed, every unwelcome distraction crashed back in on her. Each person, every misstep, all her failures overwhelmed like a rogue wave, and left her in tears.

Soon the weather fouled like her mood, sending her and her new students for drier training grounds. They spent the wet days in an empty room of the tower enclosed within her sparring walls. Here they trained on mastering control of their inner nemeses. On the rare fair days, they worked with swords until her muscles ached and sweat soaked the silk garment beneath her heavy armor.

She longed to be free of her hood and gloves and feel the crisp air on her hot skin. Yet despite her inner turmoil, she often laughed as the prince and the thane's son stretched her skill and her determination, and thanked them for their time together.

But Edmund re-entered her warrior's ring. A wild wind of emotions erupted in her at the sight of the smiling green eyed king. The repugnant longing surfaced with such force it felt as though she were punched in the gut. Yet at the same time her heart thrilled at the return of a dear friend. Both feelings whirling within her pricked her ire and she snapped at him.

"Do you require something, Sire?"

His smile cooled. "We wish to join you once more."

Ari opened her mouth to protest but Hawk produced two wasters and offered them to her. They were the length and style of her steel blades.

She sighed and sheathed her weapons before she took up the practice swords. She tested their weight, reach, and balance.

Edmund's smile grew once more at her appraisal of them. "Perhaps with these we might fight with more confidence."

Edmund handed Eric and Preston wasters as he took another from

Hawk. He brandished it at her with a hopeful grin.

Ari struggled to rein in the swirling feelings. She swiped at him and the hallow thud of their contact echoed.

Edmund did not wait for another offer and came at her with his full force. Ari spun out of his way only to find Hawk there to meet one of her mock weapons. She blocked Hawk and ducked Edmund's next swing.

Ari broke free from their full attack and took up a stance ready for what they would bring next. They did not hold back. It made her smile, her heart thrilled for the challenge. Soon she took on all four competitors at once. She countered and drove one back, whirled, blocked two, and kicked the third. They circled around her and she tucked and rolled out of their path, springing up with two flying wooden blades and a well-placed foot where they least expected her.

But the men were becoming wise to her ways. She felt the whack of Eric's waster on her right arm above the elbow, followed a moment later by another from Hawk's weapon to her left thigh. She ducked under Preston's swing only to be poked in the ribs by Edmund.

Then it happened.

As they tightened their ring around her, she back-flipped, kicking out at them and driving them back.

Her left hand landed on the ground first.

Snap!

She yelped in pain, and crumpled to the ground in a heap.

Tears stung her eyes.

"Ari!"

She swallowed her pain, and her anger at Edmund's panicked cry.

"Father! What is the matter with you? You have seen any number of injured warriors before. Why do you treat him as such a child?"

Ari righted herself and sat cradling her hand to her chest.

Edmund knelt, concern marring his features. "Ari, what happened?"

She pushed to her feet and shook off his concern. "A trifling matter. A couple of broken fingers—they mend with little trouble. Naught to fear." She brushed past Edmund toward the others.

"I don't understand, sir?" Preston asked.

Ari flipped the waster that was still in her right hand toward him, grip first. "It is a matter of the hilts. I forgot I fought using the wood and not my own blades."

Preston held the wooden sword, and the others gathered around him as she drew her blade and flipped it toward them in the same fashion. "As you can see, my blade has a large square pommel and hilt surrounding the grip." She took hold of the grip and laid the sword on the ground. "When I perform such acrobatic moves on the battlefield these oversized features allow me to retain hold of my weapons while protecting my fingers." She wiggled the digits of her right hand in the space created between the grip and the dust below. She stood again and replaced her weapon on her hip.

"Forgive me, Ari. I never meant—"

She held up her uninjured hand. "As I said, Sire, 'tis a trifle. Lin will have these wrapped in short order and they will be long-since healed before the battle." She bowed and returned to her chambers.

Chapter 44

Lin helped remove Ari's blades and hood and pushed her hair from her face. Now Ari sat on the divan and cradled her throbbing hand.

"What can I do?" Lin whispered and worried her lip.

"The glove must be removed and the fingers set and wrapped," Ari released a long heavy sigh. She did not relish the thought of the pain still awaiting her. Anger bubbled in her for accepting the useless wooden sticks. *They are naught more than children's toys. You are such a fool. You never should have allowed Edmund back in the sparring area. Now you must suffer near two months of healing and time lost in training with both blades.*

She used her teeth and removed her right glove.

The door burst open and Ari sprang to her feet.

Edmund slipped through and secured the door behind himself.

"Majesty, what in heaven's name are you doing?"

"Assisting you."

"I do not require—"

He ignored her and placed several items on the table. "Lin, go to the kitchen and tell Margaret the king requires two egg whites in a bowl."

Lin took two steps toward the door. "Lin wait. Majesty—"

"Lin, do as I say at once."

The child darted from the room and slammed the door.

Edmund placed the chair so it sat a hand-width from touching the divan where she stood. He moved in front of it and seized her left wrist. As he sat, he pulled her down again on the long seat. Her left knee brushed his right and her stomach fluttered like a flock of birds were loosed.

She tried to pull away from him.

He held her fast. "Be still—woman," he added the last with a stiff whisper. "I will see to the tending of your fingers, and I will hear no complaint."

"I have no need of your assistance."

"It is because of me you are injured. I will see you hale."

She struggled against him. "You did not intend me harm. 'Twas an accident. More my fault for the stunt, than yours for the offer of the wasters." She gave another hard yank of her arm, trying to free herself. "Sire, you do not belong here. What would Eric say? What will your people say when they learn the truth? Please—"

He pulled against her until she came within a breath of his nose. "Stop fighting me and let me see to your needs and then you can be rid of my hateful presence."

The hurt tainting his words and clouding his eyes lodged any further protest in her throat. She could not look at him any longer and she stopped fighting. "I do not hate you, Sire," she whispered.

"No, you merely wish not to lay eyes upon me, or speak a single word to me."

She tried to swallow the regret choking her. "Sire ..."

"I meant you no disrespect, Aria. You are a mighty warrior—and you have a great weight pressing upon you. I wished no harm to come to you so you could fulfill the destiny God has called you to. You are more skilled than any warrior I have ever known and it would be unthinkable to cause you injury and keep you from such a noble purpose. I never thought less of you for being a *woman*." Again he whispered the word. "I feared my own clumsiness would cause you harm." His words were calm and low, burdened with regret.

She opened her mouth to speak but cried out as he removed her glove.

"Forgive me, Aria."

Their eyes met and his stare held her with an embrace as secure as his hand held her wrist. His gaze bore into her, searching for some forgiveness, some softening of her spirit. Again she tried to speak but his other hand brushed over her exposed skin. The sensation sent flaming waves up her arm and across her shoulders. Flashes like lightening shot to her head, addling her brain. A raging fire engulfed her core and raced to her toes until she thought her boots would melt.

His hand ran over the base of hers, searching for injury and adding another wave of heat. He moved to the thumb, the tips of his fingers exploring its every curve. Next he examined the first finger and moved to the second.

She winced and air whistled through her teeth.

Edmund's gaze met hers again. "I regret anything I have done to make you believe I thought less of you, Aria." His hand encircled the broken finger. "I have never thought more highly of anyone, save my own blood and Hawk."

Ari yelped as he jerked hard and set the finger to right again. She swallowed and closed her eyes to hold back the tears—more from his words than the setting of the bone. "I am an ill-tempered fool, Your Majesty."

His hand moved to the marrying finger. New waves of heat surged through her body and stole her breath.

"I did not intend to provoke you."

She looked at him again and he set the finger. She bit down on her lip to keep from crying out again and tasted blood.

He moved to the littlest finger, and finding no injury there, released her wrist and brushed away a tear from her cheek. "I never wished to cause you pain."

She straightened and blinked back the remaining unshed tears. "You have done naught to me, Sire, except welcome and shelter me. I am the one in the wrong. You have nay deserved the manner in which I have treated you of late."

Lin returned and her gaze shifted several times between Ari and Edmund, bewilderment coloring her features. "The eggs ya requested, Yar Majesty." She set them on the table and knelt beside Ari. "What do ya use eggs for, Sire?"

Edmund's face brightened as he glanced at her. "Well, page, to set a small bone like the finger, you need a small stick." He picked one up from the table to show her. "You place it along the length of the broken bone once it is reset." He placed it under Ari's second finger. "Next you take a small strip of cloth, dip it in the egg whites, and wrap the finger from the tip to the base." He covered the finger as he continued to explain. "The sticky clear egg will soon dry and become hard to make sure the finger does not bend or slip from the straightening stick."

Edmund waved Lin to come closer. "Come and see how the cloth is best wrapped and secured. You will need to do this for Sir Ari for the next several weeks." He glanced at Ari and his smile lessened. "You should keep it wrapped until the time the Christ Mass approaches, only changing the bandages when they are dirty or wet." Edmund moved to the other broken finger and demonstrated again.

"I will take good care of Ari, Sire."

Edmund put his hand on her small back and kissed the top of her head, and the unwanted longing pricked Ari again.

He rose and looked at Ari. He drew a dagger from the back of his waist and handed it to her. "You sacrificed your own dagger months ago in the saving of my son. Please accept this replacement as a small token of my gratitude." He moved to the door. "Be well, Ari."

She stood. "Thank you, Majesty. You have treated me with the utmost kindness even when I have behaved reprehensibly. Please, forgive me."

He inclined his head with a grin, glanced through the crack in the door, and slipped out.

Ari dropped back to the divan and laid her throbbing fingers over her pounding heart.

Chapter 45

When Ari looked up from her book, stirred by her growling stomach, Lin could not be found. She fumbled with her hair, hampered by her two stiff fingers, and replaced her hood with difficulty as Lin slipped through the door.

"I did not hear you leave."

Lin bowed with a foolish grin. "I think you drifted off. I told ya I would be running an errand but ya didn't respond." With her master of reading, and her time with Wyatt, Lin was beginning to lose some of her common speech. The girl grinned and presented Ari with the item in her hand, a well-warn glove.

"What is this?"

"You can't fit yar glove over yar injured fingers. I asked Sir Winslow for something. He gave me this. 'Tis larger than yar hand and you can cut away anything that will injure further."

Ari could not suppress a smirk. "You are a brilliant child, Lin."

Lin's chin rose.

Ari picked up the dagger Edmund had given her again. The small weapon, twice the length of her hand with a well-honed double-edged blade, was the work of a skilled craftsman. A small ball of silver formed the pommel, securing three twisted bands of metal. One dark, like the king's hair, another looked to be copper with a bright red hue, the third—like bronze—though it shown like gold.

"'Tis pretty."

"Aye, Lin. The finest work. 'Tis too grand a gift for such an ungrateful guest."

"The king wished to show his gratitude. The swordsmith made it to King Edmund's specific directions."

Ari looked at her.

"Wyatt told me. We went to the armory one day and watched him work. The smith grumbled." Lin shrugged. "He said something about being forced to wait for hematite. 'Tis the black metal."

"I have never heard of it before."

Lin smiled and her shoulders pushed back. "'Tis something new and found near some iron deposits, but they don't know why 'tis formed in some areas and nay others."

Ari nodded, rubbing her thumb along a hematite band.

"The red metal looks like yar hair."

"I thought the black looked like the king's hair." Ari chuckled. "What do you think the bronze looks like?"

"'Tis gold. The color of God's hair. A strand of your hair, the king's and God's all wound together." Her chin rose, back straight, as though she'd just solved the mystery of the universe.

Ari's head shot up and she nearly dropped the weapon. "What? Were you told the strands symbolize this?"

Lin scrunched up her shoulders again. "Nay, 'twas a picture in me head. I don't think the king put any meaning to them." Lin turned to prevent Ari's search of her face. "Should we go to midday, sir? Ya haven't eaten since yesterday. You must be hungry." She waited at the door as Ari cut away the two middle fingers from the new glove. She took care as she pulled it over her injured hand and wiggled into her own right glove using her teeth.

But she left the dagger on the table, unable to shake the thought of her and the king wound together with God.

Chapter 46

The rain turned relentless. Ari did not meet with any of the men or train. Instead she hid in her chambers for several days.

"I go to the chapel, Lin."

Lin popped to her feet and moved to the door. "Something trouble you, sir?" She carefully formed each word.

"I know not, but I feel I must go."

Lin nodded and held the door open.

They climbed the stairs and Ari knelt. Her head barely bowed before the main door opened and heavy steps echoed down the aisle.

Edmund slipped to his knees below the raised dais. Soft whispers floated to her but she could not make out the words. She could nay remain and trespass on the king's petitions. She moved to rise, when God filled her mind with a vision. Her heart stopped as she saw King Edmund cut down where he knelt.

Ari rose and leaned far over the balcony to see who might be lurking below. She saw no one, but a whispered approach skipped across her skin.

"Sire, danger!"

Edmund sprang like a startled buck. His eyes looked to her.

She pulled the dagger. "Protect yourself." She tossed it down hilt first.

Edmund snatched the weapon from the air and turned to the man she still couldn't see.

She raced down the stairs.

Lin stood at the door she'd unlocked but held closed.

"Stay hidden," Ari ordered as she burst out and charged into the nave.

Clanging of metal echoed as she approached the man from behind.

The king's curses were drowned out by her warrior cry as she charged the man's back.

Cornered between the two warriors, the attacker fled across the front of the sanctuary and ran along the far side.

"Follow him. I will cut him off before he reaches the door," Edmund said.

The assassin bolted between two rows and sprang up on the pews. Leaping across the backs, from one to the next, he reached the entrance to the church before Edmund and burst out into the sun.

Edmund followed a heartbeat later and Ari in the following moment. Edmund stood growling in the bailey at the sight of his assailant dead on the end of Selvyn's blade. "What have you done? I wanted him alive. He could have held the answers to the attacks within my home." Edmund stepped closer, raising the dragger at Selvyn.

The Spirit of God stirred within Ari again and she moved beside Edmund. Her eyes remained on the captain as he removed his sword, allowing the body to drop before he raised it toward Edmund. "He but performed his sacred duty as a faithful servant of his king."

Both men's hard eyes whipped around to hold her. Their mouths hung slack but they uttered not a word.

"Selvyn is the captain of the garrison guard. It is his duty to see to the safety of the people sheltered within these walls. Selvyn failed to keep out this one, and he in turn tried to kill you, Majesty. Sir Selvyn knew if he did not dispatch the villain with quick efficiency, he could be the one on the end of a blade."

Both remained mute and staring.

"Aye, Sire," Selvyn sneered at last. "Duty forced me to see he did not escape to try again." The words were muttered as Selvyn narrowed his puzzled gaze on her.

"You were as duty bound to take him alive and hold him for interrogation," Edmund grumbled, shooting her a sideways glare.

"I heard the commotion within the holy walls of the church, and came to lend my aid when the man burst out. He all but impaled himself on my blade."

"Do you recognize him?" Ari asked.

Both men shook their heads.

"He is not from the town at the foot of my mountain. His pale complexion may indicate he comes from the northern reaches of my kingdom in Balmore."

"Or more likely he comes from a foreign enemy, for all King Edmund's people love him so." Selvyn's mocking tone further stirred her fear.

"Will you see to the disposal of the body? I am sure King Edmund has greater matters to attend," Ari offered, dismissing him.

Selvyn nodded and Edmund turned toward the inner gate.

Ari fell in step beside him and nodded at Lin, who stood with her head poking out of the chapel door. She followed.

They made it as far as the center of the ward before Edmund pulled up short, crossed his arms, and glared. "Explain yourself! Is Eric correct? Do you work for my enemy?"

Ari shook her head. "Nay, Sire. God warned me. I saw Selvyn raising his sword. His men surrounded him and you held but a small dagger. I thought only to save you, Sire."

Edmund's arms dropped. He looked to the weapon still in his

hand.

"'Tis no match for the reach of a long sword in the hands of a dangerous man."

"Indeed," he whispered. He handed back the blade. "Thank you, Ari. Now you have saved my life."

"God spared you, Majesty."

Chapter 47

The morn following the attack, as the rain beat the land, Eric approached Ari at the morning meal. "How fare your fingers?"

"Well, Highness. The throbbing calms and I trust God to restore them to their full usefulness soon."

"God is ever faithful," he said with an incline of his head. "I hoped we might work on our other training this morn."

Ari nodded as Preston and Lin joined them. They raced in the heavy rain and entered the large empty chamber in the vacant tower. They shook off their damp cloaks, stirring the layers of dust marred only by their previous visits. Today their breaths hung visible.

Preston shuddered, rubbing his arms. "I will go fetch wood."

Lin followed him, leaving Ari and Eric alone, which stirred her unease.

"Thank you for the training, Sir Ari." His words were guarded.

"But something troubles you?"

"Something indeed does trouble me." He did not choose to say more as Preston and Lin returned laden with supplies for the fire. It did not take the skilled page long to have the flames leaping high.

"Come near the warmth and we will begin," Ari said. "In order to avoid lashing thoughtlessly, one must be aware of his surroundings. Sit still and tell me what you hear."

Eric groaned and tried to relax. "Rain."

"Besides the rain. What else?"

He squeezed his eyes closed and tipped his head from side to side and turned it about. "The popping of the fire within and the sheets of rain without are all I can hear." He groaned in exasperation.

Preston chuckled. "There must be more or Sir Ari would not have asked."

Eric exploded whirling on his friend sitting beside him. "What do you hear then! Tell me true, do you hear more than fire and rain?"

Preston leaned away from him and shook his head, his laughter silenced.

"I hear a rat running in the room above, a shutter bangs in the wind upstairs, and a cricket chirps in the corner." Every eye turned to Lin sitting with a book in her lap and her back against the wall at the end of the hearth.

Ari forgot her broken fingers and clapped her hands together in excitement. She winced at the pain shot down their length but it could not suppress her pleasure. "Well done, page! Well done indeed."

"Ari is making a fine knight out of you, Lin." Preston offered with pride. "Soon you will be rescuing your own fair maiden like the knights of your stories."

Lin offered him a twisted smile. Ari knew she dreamed of being the fair one rescued.

Eric popped to his feet. "Why does it matter if I can hear a wretched cricket or a disease infested rat? How will this help me on a battlefield? I see no purpose in this."

"It is the quieting of your mind you seek. If you are controlled by rage you will miss the draw of a blade and be run through. You will miss the sound of distant hooves and lead your men into an ambush. You will—"

"And what have you missed because you did not quiet your mind? Have you never lost men in battle due to your own errors? Can you detect danger when anger assails you? Are you the unbeatable famed warrior who does no wrong? I say nay! You have done much wrong here—you have done my father a grievous wrong. In your quiet mind have you failed to hear the whispers against him? Do you not know he is despised for his unholy attachment to you? Have you not heard the whispers of repentance, excommunication, and damnation called out over his head?"

Ari reached both hands over her right shoulder and clamped the flat of Preston's blade between her palms before he could deliver a mock blow. "Aye! I can spot danger even while the anger boils." She yanked the weapon from his hands and let it drop to the floor between Eric and her with a deafening clang.

"I have failed more times than my feeble heart can bear to recall, Prince. I cover my hands to hide the blood which stains them so dark they appear black." Tears welled in her eyes and choked her words. "So many have died because of my foolishness and temper. They have chased after me into battle only to be cut down, walked head-long into ambush unaware as I brooded, and followed orders given without thought to their deaths. I wish to spare you the weight of guilt I carry. You will be a far better leader than I ever hoped to be if you will but learn from my mistakes.

"As for your father, do you think so little of him to believe these vicious lies? King Edmund is above reproach in his conduct and in his fervor in following all the commands of the Lord Most High. He is not capable of the depravity of which you accuse him. How can you, above all those here, not trust him?"

He pulled away and turned from her, his hand working the muscle at the base of his neck, the picture of his father. "I do not want to believe. I know him to be more like the Christ than any, but ..."

"But what?"

He turned to look at her again. "I cannot deny what I have born witness to with my own eyes. He favors you unlike any other. It causes knots in my middle I cannot ignore."

"You must discuss these matters with the king. He alone can explain himself. There is much you do not know, and therefore cannot see the truth of the matter."

"Tell me."

"It is not my place as a guest in his home to go against the king's expressed wishes. Go to him as his son. Tell him what you have heard rumbling in his walls. Mayhaps he will confide the truth in you." Ari drew her cloak tight about herself and hurried from the tower.

Chapter 48

Ari watched later as Eric met his father near the study door when Edmund left to join supper. Eric's hands flew about him in animated ranting, though no words could be discerned from the distant boards and the talking around her. Edmund stole a glance toward her and shook his head. Eric stepped in his path, refusing to allow his father to proceed. More inaudible words were exchanged and Edmund seized his son's upper arm. Ari could see clearly as the word 'No' was formed on the kings taunt lips. He pushed Eric aside and moved to his seat. Edmund again refused to confide in his son and as both men sat staring at her—Edmund with sympathy and Eric with disdain—Ari determined to avoid them both.

Noblemen soon started arriving from the far north, before the snows blocked the high passes. They took up residence in the rooms above the great hall near Ari's. Edmund pleaded with her to move within the castle to better protect her, but she feared it would only add fuel to the gossipmongers' fire.

With so many newcomers about and the roaming of their many servants and knights, she did little training. She chose instead to lend a hand wherever needed in preparation for the arrival of the remaining nobility. She helped scatter new rushes, and furnish empty rooms in the palace and above the great hall. Every space would be filled when all arrived. Long boards and benches filled the halls so one could not walk between them without brushing against his fellow man.

The excited reunions of friends, son's under conscription at other lord's home, and daughters married off to distant villages, filled the rooms and the open spaces. The frivolity and gaiety rang all around her, but Ari's heart remained troubled. Something stirred her fear, as the last of the noble families arrived. She sought opportunities to visit the chapel and seek God, but found it filled with worshipers at every hour of the day. From the battlements to the bailey, ward and halls, she could nay find solitude. Even her rooms were no solace with so many roaming the halls and speaking loudly in the adjoining chambers. No quiet remained to hear from God of the stalking danger.

Chapter 49

Lin spent little time with Ari. As Ari worked to help prepare the castle, she sent Lin off to her to own tasks. Now Lin returned to their rooms alone to clean and change into new clothes for the first night of dining with all the gathered nobility in the great hall below.

She swung open the door to find three men in the outer chamber. Lin whirled to flee back down the corridor.

She was seized around the waist and lifted off the ground, her mouth covered to muffle her screams.

The door slammed as the brute carried her to the man in the middle of the room. Selvyn.

This man always made her skin squirm. Lin quaked and kicked. She bit the hand holding her.

Her abductor cursed.

"Let me go!"

They laughed.

Lin thought of Ari—she was strong and braver—and that she would be returning soon. Lin had to get free and warn Ari. She took a deep breath and summoned all her weak courage. She tried to sound like Ari as she growled, "Selvyn, let me go right now."

The stocky leader wagged a finger at her. "I am a knight. Cousin to the king of Balmore. And when I kill Edmund, the future king of both Balmore and Veronia. You will address me with more respect, boy."

"Sir, I know this child." The blond man to his left stammered.

"Brayden, why do I care if you know the lad? He is insignificant. Good for little more than bait."

The blond pinched Lin's chin between his dirty rough thumb and forefinger, then turned her head to examine her face.

Lin shuddered and jerked from his grasp. She knew him too. He had broken into their hut late one night and hurt Momma. Her stomach rolled and she thought she might vomit.

"This is no lad, sir. She is the daughter of a woman I knew in Lincolnshire."

"A girl?" Selvyn's hard stare washed over her. He stepped closer and his hand reached between her legs. She kicked him in the chest though it had little effect. "You are correct, a girl."

Lin quaked as Selvyn's gaze narrowed on her again. "Tell me true, what has your wretched master done to you?"

"Ari has never hurt me."

"Sir, there is no pallet out here for the lad," the man holding her said, turning her about in his efforts to look around the room.

Another dark-skinned man moved into the inner chamber and reappeared a moment later. "There is naught within other than the knight's curtained bed."

"He sleeps with her." Selvyn's hateful grin grew. "What will the king say when he learns his favorite companion has taken this innocent child to his bed under his own roof? What will his lords say?"

His eyes never left her face. "Lin—or is it Lindsay mayhaps?" His words were sweet but she felt the danger in them and trembled in the firm grasp of the man holding her. "Lindsay, you may speak freely. We are your saviors. We have freed you from this unthinkable abuse. The vile man who defiled you will pay for his crimes as will the king who harbored him."

Lindsay squirmed against her captor. "I swear, by God on high, and the Christ His Son, Sir Ari has never laid a hand on me! Let me go, for God alone is my Savior."

Selvyn shook his head with a frown. "Poor simple child. She calls up an oath of the king's God and thinks the warrior loves her and will not betray him, even now." He waved her away. "Put her in the corner. We will keep her to control the depraved wretch. She will soon see what a loathsome creature he is."

The man holding her dropped her where her pallet should have been. He turned his back and walked away.

Lindsay bolted for the door at a full run.

"Stop her!" Selvyn ordered.

She dodged one man leaping onto the divan from the seat to the high end. She jumped over the reaching arms.

A hand snatched her arm before she could land on the floor and threw her back onto the seat. The hand released her only to smash into her face.

Pain exploded in her entire head. Lindsay covered her face with her arms to protect against another blow and hot tears stung her eyes.

Someone grabbed by her hair, and pulled her to her feet. "You have mettle, girl, but you are no match for my men. Quiet yourself and no further harm will come to you this day." Selvyn turned to the man holding her fast. "Brayden, bind her and put her over there. And by my sword, watch her this time. The wild warrior has put all manner of foolish notions in the girl's head." He released a menacing laugh. "The girl child now fancies herself a warrior."

Brayden dropped her on the floor and bound her wrists until she cried out. He laughed and licked his lips. "Mayhaps he is not the fool I took him for," he whispered. "Mayhaps he found the daughter as pleasurable as I the mother."

Lindsay held one fist in the other and struck him in the chin.

He backhanded her again and stepped away. "You surely have your mother's fire, girl."

Bitter tears tore from Lindsay as she buried her face in her knees. *Lord, do not let Aria return. Please, Father. I will die in her place if You would but allow me. Do not let her come back to face these men.*

Chapter 50

Ari reached her hands over her head and stretched the tight muscles in her back after moving the last divan. She turned to the knight at the far end. "At last our tasks are complete for this day."

"Aye, sir, we best hurry to prepare for the festivities. It would not do for the king's honored guest to arrive late."

Ari offered him a weary nod and moved across the ward toward her chambers. The inner ward lay eerily quiet when so many were in residence. She looked about, noting the few scurrying servants. *Danger is near Lord, I feel its power. What am I to do?*

No answer came, but a whisper tickled her ears. Was that Lin's cry carried on the breeze? She moved to climb the stairs to her room. She wound around half a rotation—out of sight of both the base of the stairs and the landing above—a blade tip touched her throat.

The narrow stairwell left no room for a battle. Her attacker stood several steps above her, out of her reach in the cramped space, and she wore no blades, even her dagger lay in her chambers. She considered she might retreat and descend the stairs.

Before she could, the pock-faced man with blackened teeth snarled at her. "If you value the life of the sweet girl you've corrupted, you'll come with me."

Ari steadied herself, fighting for the air. *Father, please. I can face any torture, any pain, even the pain of death. Please, Father, do not allow them to harm Lindsay.*

"Move. Now."

With shaking legs, she placed a trembling foot on the next step. She inched upward at the tip of his wagging blade. She gained the landing where the wider corridor allowed more room to fight him.

He kept out of her reach, walking backwards ahead of her. "Don't attempt escape or try to save the girl. If I do not enter first they'll slit her throat." He laughed.

Ari stepped through her door. A blow slammed her middle and hands forced her to her knees. She ignored the pain and scanned the room for Lindsay. She sat near the inner door, hands bound and face red.

"You beat small children, a feat low even for the likes of you, Sel," she growled. "If you wished to have words with me I would have come to you. There is no need to cower behind an innocent child."

A fist smashed into her face. Bolts of light to dance before her eyes.

"Ari," Lindsay cried out.

"You have not left the girl innocent. Forcing one so young to your bed, and you have the guts to call me low. You have convinced her of your love. Listen how she cries for you. You have ruined her. She will only be fit for the brothel after this."

Ari pushed to her feet, knocked the man who hit her aside and stormed toward Selvyn. "You lay one hand on her and I will sever it from your body."

Something large smashed across her back, driving her to the floor again. Splinters showered down around her as she fought for air on her hands and knees.

"Ari!" Lindsay stood and charged toward her. "Stop it! Stop it!"

Selvyn's blade hissed from its home and lay under Lindsay's chin. "Silence, girl!"

Lindsay quaked on the blade's point and tried to quiet her stuttered breaths.

Now Selvyn narrowed his gaze on Ari. "Make any further attempts and I will cut her in a thousand pieces as you watch. I assure you, it will be slow and as painful as possible."

"Lindsay, quiet yourself. Worry not over me. You know the truth."

Selvyn laughed. "What truth would that be?"

"Go to the other room, Lindsay," Ari pleaded.

"Sit, and do not move again!" Selvyn ordered.

Ari nodded for her to comply and Lindsay walked backwards until she ran into the wall with a thud and slid down it, tears tumbling.

A fist smashed into Ari's face once more and when she looked up again Lindsay sat with her eyes hidden behind her knees and her fingers laced so tight together they were white.

"Bring him." Selvyn said, "Bind his arms behind him."

They grabbed the back of her collar, then dragged Ari to kneel before Selvyn as he stood brooding near the divan. He sheathed his sword and reached for her dagger. "This is far too fine a weapon for the likes of you. Where'd you steal it?"

Ari remained silent. *Lord, I am Yours alone. In You do I trust.*

"Ari is no thief. The king gave it as a reward for saving Prince Wyatt," Lindsay mumbled through her tears.

"I shall take it as my reward, for exposing you for a loathsome despot." He glanced at the men standing on either side. "Shall we see how hideous this man is that he must take children to his bed?"

Those gathered gave their quick approval.

The dagger slid along her cheek and as it twisted to cut through the strap of her hood, it bit into the flesh of her jaw. Several drops of blood oozed down her neck. The one who brought her to the room grabbed the top of the hood, and a handful of her hair, and yanked it free. Her red locks cascaded about her face and she tossed her head to keep her eyes on Selvyn.

"She's a woman too," the blond said.

Selvyn considered her. "A woman indeed."

"Do you think the king knows?" one asked.

Selvyn smiled. "It matters not. I have secured him in my trap either way. Either he is a dolt and never knew the warrior he harbored to be a savage woman, or he knew and trained with her as his equal."

He tossed the dagger on the desk behind him, and tore open the top of her tunic. "Put her on the divan and hold her." He started to unlace his breeches. "I aim to show this wench the one thing all women are good for."

Two of the men threw Ari on her back as Selvyn approached her.

Lindsay screamed and charged at the blond who readied himself to follow his master's assault. The girl smashed into his leg beating against him with her bound fists.

"Throw her in the other room, before her wails draw the attention of nosey neighbors."

With the two men near her shoulders holding her secure, the blond picked up Lindsay. Selvyn turned to watch him dispose of the disruption, and Ari brought her knees up to her chest. She inhaled a deep breath and drove both feet into Selvyn's groin before he could avoid her.

He gasped, dropped to his knees, and moaned.

Ari pulled her feet up over her head kicked out at the men holding her and flipped over the divan as they released her.

They lashed out at her.

She slid under the protection of the low furniture as far as she could. She brought her knees to her chest and lowered her head to almost touch them. Much like a tortoise in its shell, she left little more than her armor-covered back and her bound arms exposed to their violent kicks.

From under the divan, she saw Selvyn stagger to his feet and felt the cushion press into her shoulder as he sat upon it. "Leave her," he gasped.

Thank you, Lord.

"There will be time a plenty to have our fun with the wench." He still wheezed each word. "We will let every man who finds her warrior ways an affront, have a turn at her."

Ari shuddered.

"Throw her in the other room with the girl. We must see to the final preparations for the night's festivity."

God filled Ari's mind with a vision of a sword battle within the king's hall.

"Tonight, I shall have my vengeance on the arrogant Edmund. And tomorrow will see a new king on the throne."

The two men who moments before held her for Selvyn, now pulled her from under the divan and jerked her to her feet. A fist smashed into her face before they dragged her to the inner door and threw her inside. She landed on her shoulder and remained still.

Chapter 51

When air returned to Aria's lungs, her stunned mind once again became aware of the pain wracking her body and the gentle sobs of Lindsay nearby. She pushed up with a groan and great difficulty.

Lindsay walked on her knees and looped her bound arms over Aria's neck and buried her face against Aria's skin. "I'm sorry, Aria. I didn't move fast enough. I couldn't warn ya."

"Hush your tears, Lindsay. I am unharmed. Let me go, child. We have work to do."

Lindsay choked down her tears and released her, to stare with wide, red eyes before her small hands reach for Aria's ropes.

"Nay, my friend, the knots are too tight and I must ask something greater of you." She took another breath and turned her back towards the girl. "See if you can pull the top of my gloves from the ropes."

After a few tugs the leather slid free and she felt a slim amount of freedom in her constraints. She lay on her back and gritted her teeth against the pain as she slid her hands—with Lindsay's help—under her hips and pulled her feet through so her hands were in front of her.

"Take my wrist and pull against me as hard as you can."

Lindsay gripped her left wrist between the glove and the rope. She leaned back as she braced herself against Aria's strength.

Aria pulled against her. Tears pooled as she gritted her teeth. "Now twist it towards me." Aria moved against the rotation and the arm fell back into its socket with a pop that echoed through the still room. She cried out in pain and bit her lip to silence her tears as she sank once more to the floor. Her head dropped back against the bed as the pain consumed her.

After a few moments, she reached out and untied Lindsay. Brushing the child's bruised face with a gentle hand, she cradled the girl's small chin. "Do you trust me, Lindsay?"

She nodded.

"I need you to be braver than you have ever been before. You must warn the king."

Lindsay nodded again.

Aria rose and moved to the window beside her bed. With caution she pushed it open, scanning the battlements high above and the ground far below. "Thank you again, Lord." She turned to Lindsay and knelt before her. "No one lurks above and God has prepared the way for you below."

Lindsay gulped.

"Lindsay," Aria brushed her face again, summoning her own courage. "Come see." She took the girl to the window and pointed to the huge mound of old rushes heaped below their window. "I must drop you into that pile. It is large and you will not be injured. Do you believe me?"

She stood on the tips of her toes to see the hay and nodded yet again.

"As you fall you must relax. Bend your knees. Any limb held stiff and straight may break. Do you understand?"

A wide-eyed nod answered.

"When you land, do not try to stop yourself. Allow your body to roll until it comes to rest of its own." Aria gripped both her hands. "You can do this, Lindsay. You are the king's only hope, for when you are able, you must run and find King Edmund, or Sir Hawkins, or even Sir Winslow. No one else. It must be one of these men whom we know we can trust. You must tell whomever you find there are swords hidden in the king's hall."

Aria helped Lindsay to sit on the windowsill facing her.

"Swords are not allowed in the hall," the girl mumbled.

Aria smiled at the simple innocence of the precious child. "Indeed they are not and if you do not warn the king they will be used to kill him and take his crown this night."

Lindsay nodded again and grabbed hold of Aria's arm. "Will ya be all right?"

Aria pulled from her grasp and held her chin. "Understand this, Lindsay—the king and his kingdom must be saved tonight. It matters not what happens to me. You must not try to save me. You must save the king above all. Remember God's promise to me and do this. Am I clear?"

"Yes, my lady," a fresh tear slid down her cheek.

"God has been faithful, and we know His promises. We must trust Him."

She swallowed her tears and nodded.

Aria helped her turn around on the sill. She took hold of Lindsay's wrist with her strong arm while she used her injured arm to wrap around Lindsay's waist for more support, "Are you ready?"

"Aye."

"Remember to remain relaxed, like a cloth dolly."

Lindsay nodded. "I'll nay fail ya."

"Do not fail the king, Lindsay, and you will do more than I dare ask of you."

Aria drew Lindsay's arm over her head and she slid off the sill to dangle in the air. Aria winced in pain but pressed her hips against the window casing and leaned out as far and low as she dared without falling headlong after the child. Aria centered her over the heap of rushes below and released her.

Aria held her breath as the child fell—though it seemed to take an hour to reach the ground rather than mere seconds. She landed in the soft hay, rolled once, twice, and sprang to her feet. In one swift instant, she popped up and started running around the kitchens toward the ward and help beyond.

Aria closed the shutters, and sighed as she slid to the floor below them. "Go with her, Father. Protect her and bring success to her mission. Please Lord, let no more harm come to her."

She rested her head back against the wall and waited.

Chapter 52

Lindsay felt the air rush past her as she fell. She pulled her arms and legs close as Aria had told her and landed on the pile of rushes. It reminded her of jumping on Aria's bed. Before she realized it, she raced toward the ward. She sprinted around the corner and ran headlong into Sir Hawkins. The impact knocked her to the ground.

"Fie, child. Where are you going in such an all-fire hurry?" He reached out a hand to help her up.

Lindsay stood and burst into tears.

Sir Hawkins knelt in the dust. "Whatever is the matter? Are you hurt, Lin." His hand brushed the sore place on her face.

She pushed his hand aside and glanced around. She leaned in close and whispered. "We have been discovered, sir."

Sir Hawkins' hands took hold of her shoulders. "Who has discovered? Where is your master?"

She swallowed. "Selvyn and three of his men. They were waitin' in Aria's chamber when I returned. They hit her when she came in and cut her hood away. Sir, Selvyn ripped her tunic and tried—he was gonna—"

"Where are they now?"

"The lady is held in her inner chamber. I don't know how many still remain without."

Sir Hawkins stood and took her by the hand, but after one step she would go no further. "What is the matter? We must go and save your master."

Lindsay shook her head. "She made me promise I'd tell ya."

"Tell me what?"

Lindsay did not want to answer. She wanted to rescue Aria.

He took a knee before her once more. "Deliver your message, page. It is your sacred duty to your king."

Tears ran down her face. "There are swords hidden in the great hall. Selvyn plans to kill King Edmund and take his kingdom."

Sir Hawkins shot to his feet. He looked around the empty ward, back at Lindsay, and to the heavens. "Forgive me, Aria. Lord, protect her," his whispered. "Come, Lindsay."

She cried as she followed him into the hall.

Sir Hawkins scanned the empty room.

"What about Aria?"

He released her hand and moved to the nearest long board reaching below it but finding naught. He bent down and looked under the tables. He moved to the next.

"We have to help—"

He pried a sword free from under the table with an angry grunt and smashed it down on the tabletop as he stood. "We are helping. God will protect Ari. You must believe."

The kitchen door swung open and Sir Winslow stepped into the room.

Sir Hawkins snatched up the blade again and drew it on him. He sighed and lowered the weapon at the sight of a friend and not a foe. "Winslow, glad I am to see you!" He used the sword to point down the aisle to Lindsay. "They have been discovered. Can you care for her? I must remove the rest of these from the hall before any of the guests arrive."

Winslow stammered as he stumbled toward Lindsay. "Who has

dared hide arms in the hall?"

Sir Hawkins moved to the next table and yanked another blade free as Winslow looked down at Lindsay trembling before him.

"Selvyn hopes to kill King Edmund," she whimpered.

"Come, child. Let us see to your needs and allow Sir Hawk to make the room safe."

They had taken but a single step out of the hall when Lindsay pulled from him. "What of Aria? We must not leave her with them."

Winslow stepped beside her and stroked her short hair. "We cannot do for her now. We know not who fights for us and who is against. All will be revealed soon, and God will see Aria safe. Come, Lindsay. We will go and prepare you and pray for her."

Lindsay cried as Winslow led her to a room in the back of the small hall. He motioned for her to sit on the stool outside as he knocked.

He pushed it open. "Fanny dear, how are you this eve?"

"Frantic, Winslow. Why is it these noble women wait until the night they need a gown to request repairs or alterations. I am but one old woman. How can I meet so many needs in one night?"

"Your skill is renowned and your services are in demand. It is an honor to be so respected."

Lindsay heard the woman she could not see humph her doubt to Winslow's praise. "Fanny, do you have the items I requested you set aside some time ago?"

"Aye, there in the top drawer. Please collect them thyself, for I have to run this gown to the good Lady Radford."

Lindsay watched as a fat woman waddled from the room and disappeared around the corner to climb the stairs at the back of the castle.

"Lindsay, please come." Winslow held up a soft pink kirtle in one hand and a white wimple in the other. "Come, put these on. If Selvyn expects to find a girl disguised as a boy we will hide you as a girl in the kitchens." He handed her the items and stepped from the room then closed the door.

She hurried to do as he bid. It felt odd to be in a dress again. The breeze wafting up her skirt made her shiver. She opened the door and found Winslow sitting on the stool. He waved her over with a smile and tied the wimple below her chin.

"You are quite pretty, Lindsay." He stood and offered her his hand. "Let us see what help Margaret needs."

They returned to the kitchen through the outer door on the far side of the building and Margaret, the cook, assigned Lindsay several tasks to occupy her until Selvyn sprang whatever trap he planned. She prayed with every step as she swiped more than one tear from her cheek.

Chapter 53

Locked in the inner chamber, Aria did not sit bemoaning her fate for long. She shook off her fear over Lindsay and pushed to her feet. She needed to find her blades and cut her bindings. If she were free when Selvyn and his men came for her, she might have a chance to overpower them and prevent whatever he had planned. She yanked the wrapping from her injured fingers and worked the stiff digits with slow care as she moved about the room.

She made a quick search of the bedchamber and the attached bathing room but found naught at all to free herself. *Stop fluttering about like a frantic child,* she scolded herself. *Sel obviously secured the room before you arrived. Your own hand will not free you. Focus on the real matter before you, woman! The king is in danger. You know not whether Lindsay delivered your missive. Prepare yourself.* She closed her eyes and took a slow breath, forcing her mind to clear. *What will they do when they return? They will expect to take both of us... I need to find a way to explain Lindsay's absence.*

Aria dropped to her knees and, using her bound hands, positioned things under the bed. Once the few pieces were positioned to her liking, Aria pushed back the curtains of her bed and rested her hips against the high mattress. *I must find a way to save the king.* She tossed her head in frustration and bit her lip to stifle an exasperated scream erupting from deep within her. Why did the thought of a sword hovering over Edmund's heart, make hers flutter so? Only one clear course of action remained. *I will not be used as a pawn to hurt him. Do you hear me, Lord? I will not be his undoing.* She trembled and her defiant head dropped to her chest. "Please, Father, protect him, and the land he loves."

The outer door opened and closed.

"Get them. The time has come to reveal our prizes." Selvyn's order was clear through the closed door of her inner chamber.

The door creaked open and a blade tip entered first. The man from the stairwell followed close behind. "Well, my lovely, 'tis time for you to be useful."

Aria stood.

The blond stepped into the room now to join them, his sword also drawn. "Where is the sniveling girl?"

Aria remained silent and waited for the two men's gazes to shift. She pivoted her heel by a degree and pushed Lindsay's pallet, which lay hidden under the bed. It in turn shifted against the chest.

"What's taking so long?" Selvyn bellowed.

The first man stepped to the front of the bed, out of reach of Aria's foot and with his backside high in the air looked under the fabric hanging off the mattress to the floor. "The girl is hiding somewhere under the bed, sir. I cannot see her, but I heard her." He sat up and turned to his master. "How do you wish me to get her?"

"The girl-child is of no import." Selvyn's hard gaze narrowed on Aria. "We have all we need here to wrestle the throne from Edmund's cold, dead hands."

"I will not allow you to use me to hurt King Edmund," Aria announced as she lunged toward the blond man's blade.

Selvyn pulled the weapon out of her path, preventing her from impaling herself. He laughed at her efforts. "Oh, I have plans which require you to remain breathing—screaming preferably." He ran the back of his hand down her cheek along her neck and he dragged his hand over her chest.

She jerked from him in disgust.

His fist smashed into her face, bringing flashes of light and needles of pain. "All in good time. First I take the crown, then I will take you—as oft as I like."

Her stomach twisting in knots, she pivoted on her foot and tried to kick him in the head.

The blond pushed her back against the bed with a shout.

Selvyn turned from the room with a sinister laugh. "Bind her feet, cover her with a cloak and carry her to her fate."

The blond man's massive hand pressed against her chest and held her down on the bed while the other man wrapped a rope around her feet.

As the holding hand slid lower on her body she squirmed and popped to her feet. She fought for balance as she glared at him.

"Soon wench," he hissed.

"I will die first."

"Makes little difference to me."

They threw her cloak over her shoulders and secured it at her neck. The blond swept back her hair and raised the cowl over her head.

The men sheathed their blades and grabbed hold of her forearms lifting her off the ground.

She bit on her cheek and tears pooled in her eyes at the pain shooting through her shoulder. They dropped her in front of Selvyn and he sneered as he pulled the cloak around her to cover her hands and yanked the cowl further down over her face. "We do not wish to spoil the surprise before 'tis time. Come."

Aria set her arms rigid to lessen her pain as they lifted her once more.

They carried her through the door and along the hall. A momentary discussion ensued when they came to the stairs, for they could not continue on three abreast down the winding staircase. Soon one man stood behind her with his hands in her armpits, another grabbed her feet and led the way down. The pull on her shoulder from a new direction as they wound down brought new bolts of pain.

At the bottom, she stood again and the men returned their grasp to her elbows.

A new voice greeted them. "The last of the guests have been seated and the priest has started the prayer, sir."

"We will wait until the king is done with his greeting," Selvyn mocked. "Let it serve as his farewell."

Aria thought of bellowing out a warning but a gloved hand covered her mouth. She sighed against it. *Lord, this is not my fate. I trust Your will for my life.* She swallowed as her heart struggled. *I trust You with Lindsay's life and King Edmund's. You are sovereign, God, and I say with Abraham, 'Be it far from Thee doing this thing, to slay the righteous with the wicked: and that the righteous should be even as the wicked, be it far from Thee. Shall not the Judge of all the world do right?' Our lives are in Your hands, Father.*

Aria waited now. A peace settled on her as she listened to the quick breaths of the men about her. She could almost hear the thumping of their hearts. Father James' prayer must have ended for those assembled echoed an "Amen". The hands on her arms tensed.

"Wait," Selvyn sighed.

The heartbeats quickened.

"To God be the glory," Aria said in a bold breath against the glove.

A fist thumped into her back. "Silence."

Chapter 54

"Now!"

They moved forward at a quick gait down the center aisle. Aria could see naught but her swinging feet though she heard the gasped murmurs. "Hold Ed. I would speak to those gathered here."

A chair scraped against the floorboards of the dais.

"Father—" Eric cried in a panic as the sounds of a short struggle tickled her ears.

A hard thud sounded as when Eric leapt over the table the night the assassin came to attack him.

"Lady Aria," Edmund's cry was close and frantic. He jumped down in front of her. He shoved her guards away, threw back her cowl and revealed her face.

Those gathered gasped.

Aria saw Eric drop back to his seat as he exclaimed, "Lady? Oh thank the Lord Almighty!"

"Lady Aria, are you well? Are you harmed?"

"I am—well, Majesty," she struggled to find her voice with Edmund's face so close to her own.

His thumb brushed her bruised cheek and down to the cut on her jaw. Fire flashed in his eyes so bright she felt the heat of its flames on her face.

"So you knew she was a woman?" Selvyn called loud for all to hear.

Edmund spun on him and Aria reached out her bound hands to keep from falling. His hand reached into the back of his tunic and he pulled out something then pressed it into her hands. The cool steel of a dagger identical to hers lay in her gloves. Keeping it well hidden behind Edmund's broad shoulders, she went to work cutting herself free and stayed alert.

"Sel, what do you hope to accomplish?" Edmund growled.

The fury in his voice caused the hair on Aria's neck to stand.

"I want all to know the truth of course. Is not truth the virtue we are to hold to above all, Ed?" Selvyn's pitch dropped as he continued his challenge. "So you knew from the beginning the truth of this vile creature?"

"I am your king. I will not be spoken to so—"

"Aye," a voice called out from near the back of the hall. "King Edmund knew he—rather—knew the warrior he welcomed to be a woman."

Aria looked up at Sir Charles, the king's friend whom she met when she rescued Wyatt on her first day. She returned to her ropes.

"Aye," another man from the same day sitting on the opposite side of the room stood now. "I heard with my own ears, the summoning of the warrior to the king's private study moments after her arrival."

Another knight stood and continued. "They talked for near an hour before both emerged and neither looked pleased."

"The king knew to whom he offered safe haven," Charles concluded and they all sat.

As she struggled with the awkward position of her hands as she cut at the rope, she noted that Edmund's trusted men were scattered about the hall. Her heart thrilled. Lindsay had delivered her message. They were not caught unaware. *Thank You, Lord.*

"So Ed, knowing the truth of her you allowed and encouraged her to train your men?" Selvyn laughed.

"Stand if you ever received training from the Lady Aria's own hand!" Edmund growled.

Hawk, Eric and Preston stood on the high dais.

"King Edmund would not allow the Lady to train with us," one voice called out.

Another rallied, "Aye, King Edmund did not even wish us to stand in the entrance way and watch as they trained."

"He promised to show us later what new skills he learned from the visiting warrior."

Selvyn snarled. "How could you allow a foreign, heathen women to so corrupt you and your kingdom, Ed?"

The hall remained quiet for several heartbeats. "She is a godly woman."

In her shock of the bold pronouncement Aria's hands jerked and the bindings around her wrists snapped. She searched the room and watched as Father James rose to his feet. His hands were clasped before him and his face remained grim.

"Sir Winslow requested the keys to Queen Mariamne's gallery near the time of the Lady's arrival. I have heard the door creak open early every Lord's Day since. God Himself further compelled me to leave the Holy Sacraments on the altar. It was for her to partake of Holy Communion before she left. I have seen the warrior bowed in prayer on numerous occasions. She is a follower of the one true God." Father James slipped back to his bench.

All eyes turned back to Selvyn, and Aria moved to cutting the rope around her ankles.

"I charge you with murder, Ed. The blood of both my boys is on your hands."

A rumble rushed through those gathered.

Edmund waited for the noise to die down. "Sons? Since when have you sons? I know not of them."

"Marlow was my blood—"

A sharp guffaw sounded from a table nearby. "Marlow was a stubborn fool!"

"The idiot charged headlong into battle without staying in formation."

"Ever a danger to himself and those fighting next to him, he sought naught but his own glory and refuged to take orders."

Charles stood again. "I remember well the day he died. After twice charging ahead and breaking the line, I lashed him to a tree. He should have remained far from harm."

"But someone, unknown to us, cut him free." Hawk now took up the tale. "He charged down the embankment from the camp and straight onto an enemy's blade."

"The fool's blood is on his own head," the first man concluded and the room filled with grunted agreement.

"There is no denying the blood of my youngest is on your hands, Ed. Godric was my son."

Again the retelling of events bounced from man to man around the room as Aria freed herself and slipped the blade back to Edmund.

"The man came uninvited into the concealed area where Ari— Lady Aria sought to train alone. He challenged her," Preston started.

"She made no attack against him."

"But he could not get past her defenses."

Edmund nodded. "She sought to train, but he harbored murder in his heart."

"The Lady Warrior gave him opportunity to take the victory offered—though not earned—and leave, but he would not relent," another continued.

"Even when given the opportunity for a death blow she spared him. And Edmund granted him his life as well. But he lay in wait and struck out against his king first," Hawk concluded.

"A great fool, raised two sons as equal fools," one final knight offered and the room filled with a tense laughter.

"I demand the throne that is rightfully mine!"

Aria put her back against the dais and hopped up on it, wincing at the renewed pain. She rose to her feet and stood at its center, above Selvyn and Edmund, as they glared at one another. "Good men and women of Veronia and Balmore, heed my words." She threw off the cloak and twisted her long hair into a lose knot as she continued. "I came here as a stranger and your kind-hearted king sheltered me for my sake alone. All of Wexxton knows God protects your land and covers you with His mighty hand. Few fight for the honor and glory of God in my land and women, like me, are obliged to pick up the swords of our dead fathers, brothers, and husbands in defense of our children. It is a way of life we cannot escape, save death. I came seeking an ancient weapon to end our fighting and save my people. Your king has been gracious and aided me in this search. Now, good men and women, you are presented here with a choice. You, this day, must decide who will rule over you.

"I give you first King Edmund, the descendant of five rulers of Veronia and husband to the heir of Balmore. He is a servant to his people and cares for them above himself. He welcomes the least among them into his home and feeds them of his own bounty. He places no undue burden on his people and loves God above all.

"In kind you have Selvyn, the distant cousin of the late Balmorian king, who did not deem him worthy of the crown he now demands. He has plotted evil against the rightful king, beginning with amassing a band of barbarians to attack Prince Wyatt on his first hunt."

Gasps rippled through the people gathered before her.

"Next an assassin came into this hall during the king's harvest celebration and tried to kill both Prince Wyatt and the Crown Prince, Eric. Finding he could not strike a blow at King Edmund's heart—and too much the coward to confront him as a man—another assassin tried to kill the king himself as he knelt in prayer before the altar."

Angry shouts now filled the hall and fists pounded on the tabletops, but Aria continued.

"Now you come to this day. Selvyn and his band of miscreants lay in wait for me in my chamber. They beat the young child who has been faithful to care for me since my arrival to bend me to their will. And when he learned I was a woman they did this!" Aria brushed her sore face and flipped at the torn fabric of her tunic, and a roar went up around the room.

"This is the man who wants to be your king. He believes it is his right to rule and not a God-given honor. He hoped to use me to turn you against King Edmund but you have heard all around this hall those who stand with him. King Edmund has no need to defend himself. His actions have spoken. And if Selvyn could not convince you with me, or his accusations, he planned to force you at the tips of the swords he hid within these walls!"

Over the roar of the room Aria called out again. "Decide this day Veronia and Balmore. Who will be your king? As for me I fight with King Edmund!"

Fists pounded tables in a staccato rhythm. "Ed-mund! Ed-mund! Ed-mund!"

In the cacophony, Aria almost failed to hear her name called. She turned to Hawk behind her as he loosed a long sword. She snatched it from the air and the pain in her shoulder erupted once more. She turned and dropped it into Edmund's hands, as Selvyn lunged at him.

Chapter 55

Bedlam exploded within the king's hall.

Edmund crossed blades with Selvyn and the clang of their swords rang out like a pealing bell in the church tower.

Aria kicked the blond in the jaw from her position standing above him on the dais, preventing an attack on Edmund from behind until the others could arrive.

Eric, Hawk, and Preston rushed forward and met Selvyn's armed men, who had brought Aria into the hall.

Those loyal to the king went after any who reached for a hidden sword. When no promised weapons were found, eating awls and feasting knives flashed in their place. Edmund's knights carried naught but their daggers as well.

Women screamed and pulled their children close to the walls.

Aria leapt to the nearest table. She kicked one conspirator and distracted another, giving Edmund's man the opportunity to bury his dagger in a wretch's chest. Aria leapt to another long board and another—her sights set on the guard at the doors blocking escape.

Another of Edmund's knights tossed her a dagger of a fallen enemy and pointed behind her.

She turned her attention to one man so vile as to hold his small blade at the throat of a noblewoman's young son. He stood a table away with his back to her.

"Aria!"

She leapt to the table, knelt behind him, raised his coif and sank her blade down his spine.

The man slumped to the floor and the child ran into his mother's arms.

"Aria!"

She raised her head to search for the owner of the high-pitched call.

"Aria!"

She smiled. Lindsay stood in the niche under the stairwell. Draped in pink with a wimple on her head, the girl stood with Aria's blades clutched to her chest. Though they were short weapons, they ran from her chin to hover inches above her feet. Aria bounded from table to table, in quick succession. She dropped to the floor and took hold of the crossed grips in her right hand.

Lindsay nodded and turned her face to the side so Aria could draw them without harm.

"Follow me," Aria called over the din as she dropped one blade into her weakened left hand and moved toward the door. She sprang into view from around the entrance of the stairs and confronted the man at the doors. They crossed blades with a clank.

Taller and broader than her, the dark-haired brute lunged forward, throwing all his weight and strength at her.

Aria spun out of his way, blocked his swing, and spun back around to slice him across the throat. His blood drenched her as he dropped to the rushes.

"Open the doors, Lindsay. Lead these frightened people to safety."

Aria bent and pulled the body out of the way as the cold winter air raised gooseflesh on her sweat-covered skin.

"Charles!" she called out to the knight across the aisle. She threw him the fallen guard's sword and climbed atop another table.

"Mothers of Veronia, and Balmore!" she bellowed. "Grab your bairns and follow my friend Lindsay into the safety of the ward!"

Edmund's men cleared the aisles to allow the escape toward the back of the room, but assured none who fought with Selvyn would join them.

Aria moved down the length of one long board to free a woman trapped by a menacing thug. Standing above him on a table, she slid her blades over his shoulders, crossed them and drew back. Blood splattered the wall as his would-be victim darted under his falling sword arm.

A hot pain seared her left hip and she jerked her sore left blade-arm back, hacking her attacker's hand from his arm and was jarred by the bone strike. She turned and ran the man through as he writhed in pain. She glanced up but too many men were still compacted at the front of the expansive chamber for her to know who still stood and who lay fallen. She bounded across several tables only to stop and cross blades with a man who held a long sword.

As she leapt over his swing, the reverberating clang of metal filled the air. She thrust her right blade down behind the collarbone of the man before her and dispatched him before turning to see another in the blind spot to her left. He stood swaying on his feet, and blinked with slow unseeing eyes as his blade hovered in the air near her. She killed him before he recovered and as he dropped, a lady in an elegant gown came into view. She stood behind him with a serving tray raised high over her fine white hair, which lay drawn up into a bejeweled snood.

Aria looked at her for several moments. The lady's gaze rose from the lifeless form at her feet to meet Aria's, and she gave a small incline of her head. Aria did likewise and leapt down as two loyal knights pushed several of Selvyn's sympathizers toward them.

Aria knocked one in the back of the head with the pommel of her blade. Another on her left turned to confront her and she knocked him in the jaw. As he staggered back, another on her right reached for her throat. She broke his hold, kicking him to his compatriots. The first man lunged at her again.

"M'lady!" she called as she kicked, spinning him into the tray-wielding noblewoman. Aria turned back to the one on her right as he moved toward her again, ran him through, turned and dispatched the man who had been spun back toward her by the lady's blow with the heavy tray.

Quiet descended on the hall with the same haste as the had din erupted. No one spoke. Panting breaths gave the hall a feel of the inside a monstrous beast.

Aria scanned the room. Her heart refused to beat. Her lungs burned.

Two knights with their backs to her stepped aside.

Hawk came into view as he used his forearm to swipe blood from his face.

Wyatt ran forward from his place on the back of the dais.

Aria's stomached twisted into an unyielding knot.

Hawk stepped over a body to his left and moved toward a long board.

Eric and Preston staggered back two steps and parted.

Aria closed her eyes, sure her knees were about to collapse. *Lord, please.* She dared open them to see Edmund standing, his sword point on the ground to steady himself, blood smattered over his fine doublet.

Their eyes met and he smiled. Though weary, he did smile.

Air filled her lungs and her heart roared to life. She placed both blades in her right hand and moved forward. She held his gaze as the distance between them shrank.

"Lady Aria," Eric stepped into her vision and brought her up short.

The spell broke and she came to herself again. "Your Highness." She started to bow, thought better of it, and curtsied low.

He took her left blood-soaked hand and kissed it. "Thank you for the training, my lady."

It took a moment for words to form on her startled tongue. "You are not angry with me?"

His infectious smile pulled the corners of her own mouth upward. "I can, with all honesty, say I am so overjoyed to know you are a woman, I would not hold it against you if you possessed three arms and snakes coming out of your head—though I am much relieved neither is true."

Hurried steps swished through the rushes behind her and someone seized her about the thigh. Lindsay clung to her and would not lessen her grip, preventing Ari from moving.

Eric knelt. "And this must be our faithful page, Lin? Or is it Lindsay?"

The same girl who held her blades, ran errands, and bested the grown prince at mental challenges in the tower only a few weeks before became a shy girl in her pink kirtle. She turned her face into Aria's leg and squelched a quiet giggle. Aria felt her nod her head as she moved her body more behind Aria as if to hide.

Still on one knee, Eric bowed at the waist. "It is a pleasure to meet you proper, Mistress Lindsay."

She giggled again and slid further behind Aria.

Eric rose to his feet as Preston and Wyatt came forward.

"My lady, I am grateful for your training in the last weeks and your aid this day. Both have served us well," Preston said with a deep bow.

Wyatt looked at her with his head cocked to one side. "A girl. You are truly a girl."

"She is a lady, Wyatt." Edmund stepped forward, draping his arm over his young son's shoulders.

"My lady," Wyatt said with a bow.

"Are you quite sure you are unharmed, Lady Aria?" Edmund's gaze threatened to trap her once more.

She dropped her gaze and pulled Lindsay a little closer. "Very well, Your Majesty." She scanned the hall and noted the dead strewn about. Regret filled her. She might thrill at the mock battles of training, or even rejoice to cut down one of the evil-enspelled horde. But these were men—Edmund's men. Their deaths were necessary to save the innocent but she took no pleasure in the killing.

She turned back to the king, though she avoided his direct stare. "I lament Selvyn discovered me and used me to harm you, Sire. Will your lords forgive you?"

"Forgive him! They are singing his praises." They all turned to see Charles strolling toward them with a boisterous grin. "I have been outside with them as they attended to the welfare of their families, and they are quite relieved you still sit upon the throne. They understand too well the fate they would have suffered under that wretch's ruthless hands." He turned to her now with a bow. "They even speak with favor of you, my lady."

Aria released a deep sigh. "Thank You, Lord most high."

"Amen," the men around her echoed.

"Lady Aria, you are bleeding," Hawk said.

She glanced down to where he pointed and noted the blood staining the hip of her breeches. She shook it off. "A minor scratch, sir."

"I will fetch Tinsley," Wyatt raced off before anyone could stop him.

"Let us see you to your chambers, my lady."

Aria raised her hand to stay Edmund's approach. "Sire, you have guests to attend to, and your men need to clean the hall of this riff-raff. The food has not been spoiled and with some quick work your supper may continue."

Edmund's mouth opened but Lindsay spoke first. "I'll see the lady to her chamber, Sire. I promise to take good care of her."

Edmund glanced at those around them. "I do not know if any will return to my hall."

"Clean it, invite them back and dine with joy. God's hand has saved your kingdom this night. Celebrate His faithfulness and prove to your people that Sel will never be given another thought."

"Lady Aria, gives wise counsel, Father. We cannot allow this man to change a thing about this night. The supper has been but a little delayed. What will the people eat if we send them back to their chambers and what will they be prone to discuss in such privacy?"

"Very well. Gather those needed to see to these matters. Lindsay, when you have seen to your Mistress's needs come and collect a tray for your supper."

"Aye, Your Majesty." Lindsay loosed her tight grip and they moved toward the stairs.

Aria took no note of her injuries until she lifted her leg to climb the stairs. By the time she reached the upper landing, the heat of the battle had dissipated and left her whole body aching from its many injuries. Lindsay helped her recline on the divan. They did not wait long before a knock sounded and Tinsley entered.

"Forgive me for pulling you away from your other patients this night, Healer."

He giggled like a small girl as he stood staring at her. "You have naught to fear, none of the king's people were injured to a degree they have much need of me." He continued to stand and giggle. "I see now why you have been so reluctant to accept my ministrations." Another giggle followed high and shrill. "You could not risk me learning your secret."

"Lindsay, get Sir Tinsley the chair."

"It has been broken to bits, m'lady."

"Well, however did such a thing happen?" Tinsley said.

"One of Selvyn's men broke it over my back when I tried to attack him."

This jolted the physician to actions. "Oh my, there may be a great many injuries I must examine. Child, is there not a chair within the other chamber?"

Lindsay fetched it and Tinsley sat beside her to begin his work.

He slid down the edge of her breeches and revealed the gash. "'Tis not too deep but will require suturing." He pulled things from his satchel and sent Lindsay for a towel.

Lindsay left while the healer stitched and returned with their dinner.

Tinsley covered the wound with ointment and instructed Lindsay with her care. "Now let us see to your other injuries."

"I am well, Healer," Aria groaned.

"Her shoulder suffered an injury," Lindsay offered as she mumbled around a hunk of dark bread.

Aria glared at her. "'Tis reset, sir."

Tinsley stood and motioned her to sit up.

She winced as she moved.

Tinsley's hands ran across her shoulder blades. "You wear armor?"

"Aye and it has protected me well. You need not—"

"I will perform a full examination before I leave," he crossed his arms and tapped his foot. "Remove the armor or must I remove it for you?"

His squeaky insistence grated on her weary nerves. "Sir, I am a woman …"

"And I am a physician. I will examine your injures before I leave."

She sighed and turned her back to him. "Lindsay, assist me, please." The ruined tunic slid over her head until Lindsay took it by her fingertips and threw it into the fire. The smell of it filled the room, causing Aria to cough. The unwanted convulsions wrenched whimpers of pain from Aria's clenched jaws.

"Such things should be done out of doors, child," Tinsley scolded and moved to crack open the shutters.

Next, Lindsay unlaced the armor and slid it over her head and carried it to the other chamber. But Aria refused to remove the silk undergarment.

Tinsley's skilled hands brushed her left shoulder. He explored the joint and raised her arm to rotate it with slow care. Air whistled through her teeth.

"The joint is seated properly but'tis strained. Will pain you for several days. Rest it and keep it still. No battles, my lady."

She nodded and sighed again at his giggle.

He lifted the garment, running his hand over her back. "Many bruises are beginning to show their color and deeper ones at your hips?"

"Aye, in my struggle with Selvyn and his men, I ended up here on the floor with my back exposed to their many fearsome kicks."

Lindsay gasped.

"Oh do not fret so, Lindsay. The armor served me well."

"'Tis true the strength of your armor saved you serious injury, but you still suffered a few cracked ribs. 'Tis why breathing pains you. These will take the longest to heal. Three or four weeks."

Tinsley lowered her shirt and Lindsay helped her into a clean tunic.

As she turned back around he handed her a vial. "It is a mixture of rocket, Solomon's seal and a dose of poppy."

She shook her head. "I will take no opiates, Healer."

He groaned and leaned forward till his forearms rested on his thighs. He pushed the earthenware container into her hand, closing her fingers around it. "It will do you no harm, my lady. I merely suggest a couple of drops before bed to ease the pain and allow sleep. Take it or nay, but if pain banishes sleep it will slow your healing."

She nodded and Tinsley left. She nibbled at the meats and cheeses on the tray but soon requested Lindsay help her prepare for bed. After the movement of undressing and donning her nightrail she did take a couple of drops of the medicine before moving to the bed. She slept through the night and much of the next day as well.

Chapter 56

When Aria did rouse, Lindsay brought food to her bed. "I should get up."

"'Tis already late in the afternoon, m'lady. Why not rest one more night and join the festivities tomorrow?"

Aria rested her head back against the stack of pillows. A few more hours would make no difference to the king or his guests, but time spent resting could serve her well. She agreed, ate a little, took another dose of medicine, and slept through another night.

When she arose in the morning, Lindsay handed her a beautiful deep blue, satin gown. She held it up to see the adorned long flowing sleeves and full skirt. Gold ribbon encircled the waist, wrists, and hem. Pearls sewn with gold thread formed diamond patterns over the bodice. "Where did this come from?"

"Sir Winslow asked Fanny to make them not long after we arrived." Lindsay curtsied in her kirtle.

"It is too fine a garment—"

"Nay, m'lady, 'twas made for yo. You can nay go about in a man's tunic and breeches now."

Aria sighed. The child spoke the truth. She saw no other option, and soon stood examining her reflection in the long looking glass. "This will not do." Aria straightened and the garment slipped off one shoulder. In her attempt to catch it, the other shoulder fell as well. Even when resting correctly upon her shoulders, the neckline scooped low, exposing far too much. Holding the sloppy gown tight to her sides with her upper arms, she brushed her naked collarbone with her hand. "I can nay be seen like this, Lindsay."

"Excuse me, m'lady." Lindsay didn't explain as she dashed full speed through the outer room and out the door.

Aria shook her head. "The girl still behaves the eager page. I will have to see to her re-education if any are to think her worthy to serve as a lady-in-waiting." Aria sat before the fire and waited.

After a time, the outer door opened and Lindsay directed someone inside. "Lady Aria?" the girl yelled from the other room—another thing she ought not do. "I have brought Fanny to help."

Aria held tight to the gown and moved to the outer chamber.

A short, round woman stood near the door with a satchel in her hand. A frown pulled her many wrinkles down, making her face look as though it was about to slip off. "I understand thee are not pleased with mine work, m'lady," she croaked.

"Oh nay, madam. Your work is lovely and far too fine a garment for such a rough woman."

"Thy girl spake of a problem."

"Aye, a small problem of the fit only—not of the impeccable skill of the sewer."

Fanny crinkled up her face as her eyes squinted, adding wrinkles to wrinkles. She waddled forward and dropped her bag on the low table she passed. As she came near, Aria relaxed the hold on the garment and it started to slip from her shoulders. "Oh, heavens!" Fanny explained as her eyes opened so wide Aria could see their dim brown contents.

Fanny *tsked* her consternation, took Aria by the arm, and pulled her to the middle of the room. She searched through her bag and brought out a ball of cloth filled with a great quantity of pins. "Child, come ye, and hold this for ol' Fanny." She handed the ball to Lindsay and appraised the gown again. "Well, if thou turns heads dressed as a man, think the attention thou would garner when thy gown dropped about thy waist." She chuckled softly. "We can nay have all the men in the kingdom so flustered. 'Twould be unseemly, do thee not agree?"

Aria swallowed the lump in her throat. "Aye, madam, most unbecoming."

Fanny gathered a handful of cloth on both sides of her waist and pulled the bodice tight over her bosom. "Ol' Fanny is nay oft so wrong in judging the size of a form. When Sir Winslow requested this garment he said thou wished to take a gift home to thee sister. And he spake thee were much of the same build."

"Lady Aria wears armor to hide her curves."

"Aye, thus would account for mine mistake." Starting at Aria's hips, Fanny worked up one side pinning the garment to a better fit, before moving to the other side. She stepped back and considered the garment again. "Thou does have a more womanly figure than suspected in thee tunic and breeches." She reached forward and pulled the garment up at the shoulder seams so the V-shaped accent at the waist would fall where it would flatter best and she secured the folds of fabric at her shoulders with more pins.

She reached under Aria's bosom and pushed up so Aria nearly spilled over the top. Fanny adjusted a few of the pins under her arms to support the weight and again stood back. "There, 'tis better. Now we shall remove it and I'll see to the sewing."

Aria put her hand over her exposed cleavage and cleared her throat. "Madam, might I ask—with great respect—for more to cover me, here?"

Fanny frowned and folded her arms under her nearly bare buxom chest.

"Please, madam. I have been dressed from the top of my head to the toes on my feet since I left home and I feel quite—exposed. I would nay wish any of King Edmund's lords to add wanton woman, to the thing they already call me."

"'Tis the height of Veronian fashion," Fanny huffed.

Aria dropped her head. "Please, Fanny, could you nay do me this great kindness? I doubt not your skill to masterfully modify the lovely garment without taking from its grandeur."

Fanny gave one final abrupt huff and searched her bag again. After a time, she drew out a short length of wide lace. She slid the stiff accent under the garment at one shoulder and pinned it to prevent it from moving. She worked to fold the strip in neat ruffles as she secured it around the neckline. She finished and considered the addition with skepticisms.

Aria sighed deeply. "Oh, thank you, dear friend. 'Tis perfect." Aria smiled and Fanny nodded her consent with a tight smirk.

"Now off with it. Thee will miss breaking the fast as it is, but if ol' Fanny hurries, mayhaps ye can eat in the hall for thy dinner." She moved to unlace the back.

"Madam," Aria yelped as she held the garment tight, getting poked with pins.

"Come now, m'lady. Thee can nay wear it with pins poking everywhere."

"You nay understand," Aria stammered.

"Ol' Fanny sees a garment in need of sewing and I can nay do it while 'tis upon thee."

Aria swallowed again as heat seared her cheeks. "Madam, I have dressed as a warrior since my arrival."

"Aye thus thee needs a gown," Fanny reached for her again.

"Naught but a man, Madam."

Fanny stopped and stared at her. Her eyes grew wide once more as Aria's true dilemma became clear.

"Thee has nay any intimate garments?" she whispered.

Aria felt her face flush hotter as she nodded.

Fanny stepped back and offered her a kind smile. "Ol' Fanny understands thee, m'lady. Child, take thee mistress into the inner chamber and help her—be mindful of the pins. Ol' Fanny will wait without."

Lindsay eased her out of the gown, helped her back into the nightrail and carried the garment back to Fanny.

"M'lady, I go with Fanny and will return soon with food," Lindsay yelled again from beyond the inner door.

Aria sighed and moved back to the warmth of the fire. She slid down onto the chair with care of her aching body. Though still stiff and tender in places, she felt better than she thought she would. She allowed her mind to wander, thinking of many things and naught at the same time.

Chapter 57

Lindsay returned some time later. The outer door opened and she spoke to someone in quiet whispers.

Aria stood stiffly as Lindsay slipped into the inner chamber and closed the door. Her movements were slow and her head hung low over the heap of fabric draped in her arms. What she held was uncolored except for a blood-red length of cloth lying over the top.

Lindsay's foot twisted nervously as she stared at the ground. "Forgive me, m'lady." Her small frame rose and fell with a deep sigh. "I only wished to help." The weight shifted to the other foot with an anxious twitch. "I didn't mean to cause trouble."

"Oh, by my sword, Lindsay, get about it. What have you done?" Aria tried to whisper but it came out as a harsh rasp.

"I went with Fanny and she provided the garments you lacked. Fanny said I could help you and you could wear a robe until she's done with the dress. I'm sorry, m'lady. I spoke without thinking and I told Fanny you had no robe. She sent me to one of the noblewomen." Lindsay's face rose. Her eyes filled with tears and her small lips— usually set in a perpetual smile—now drooped so low it broke Aria's heart. "I should've come directly back. I should've learned your wishes before … but I rushed to the lady." Her forlorn gaze returned to the floor. "I went and asked for a robe and she offered it readily, but she also—"

"She insisted on coming with you. That is who waits without,"

Aria groaned.

"Nay did I ask her to come. She is a noblewoman and I knew not what to say to stop her from coming with me."

"What is done is done. As you said, you meant only to assist." Aria sighed. "So friend, assist me into these many garments and let us go meet this noblewoman who demands an audience with me as I sit in her borrowed robe."

Lindsay did not move. "I am sorry—"

"Enough. Let us see to the matter at hand."

Lindsay helped Aria don the many items sent by Fanny. The braies covered from the waist almost to her knees. The stiff bodice, which sat below her breasts, though not laced over tight, gave support to her sore ribs and provided her more comfort. Hose to the knees went on next followed by a full underskirt and then a fine linen undertunic, which covered everything before it. Then Lindsay offered the brightly-colored robe. Aria secured it with the length of fabric around her waist and moved to the door.

"I do hope you did not overly chastise your poor girl, my lady. She could not deter me from coming to meet you—though she made a valiant attempt." The lady who had wielded the tray in battle sat reclined across Aria's divan. The skirt of her light green gown flowed over the foot of the seat like a great waterfall to pool on the floor. Her white hair was drawn up in another snood. This one was filled at all the crossing points with small emeralds. She smiled with a mischievous cock of her head as she drew a deep red grape into her mouth.

Something about the woman's playful banter put Aria at ease. "The girl could hardly be held responsible for the actions of a noblewoman."

A small tinkle of laughter escaped the lady's lips. "Oh indeed, noblewomen are oft times quite determined." She motioned to the chair across from her. "My lady, will you not sit and talk a spell?"

Aria moved to the chair and sat with a wince. "As you please, my lady."

The lady straightened, pushing her elbow deep into the cushion to right herself. "Oh, my dear, you are in pain. I have intruded on your convalescence."

"Not at all. I intended to go to the morning meal but there was a small difficultly with the gown provided me."

"You are quite sure you do not mind my intrusion?"

"Not in the least. As you were so generous as to come to my aid both that evening and now with the loan of your robe, I could nay refuse you."

She leaned back again and reached for another grape. "I was not a loan, my dear. It was a gift—a gift from a grateful friend."

Aria was confused, but thankfully the lady explained.

"I have not had such fun in years. Watching you spring across the king's boards and dispatch those vile heathens—oh, my heart thrilled like I was a girl again. The moment overtook me and I seized the tray and smacked that brute in the head before he could do you harm." Her palm tapped over her heart. "My heart is all a twitter recalling it again. Oh, to be a couple decades younger, I would demand the armorer provide me blades and insist you train me."

Aria could feel her grin grow. "You were more than capable the other night. We could still cross blades, if you wish, m'lady."

The lady covered her mouth and laughed demurely. "Oh, my son Lord Philip would be quite cross with me. But it would be ever so much fun." She sighed softly and her intense gaze captured Aria's. "You must call me Raven, for I have a feeling we are to be the best of friends."

Aria inclined her head. "'Tis a pleasure to make your acquaintance, Raven, I am Aria."

"Everyone knows who you are, Aria. The castle is abuzz with talk of you. Oh, do not frown so. The people love you. The novelty of both your beauty and your skill with the sword has all enthralled. 'Tis this reason I could not restrain myself when your girl came with her request. I wished to be the first to steal away a quiet moment to talk with you. I wished to know more of you—" she leaned forward and whispered with that mischievous grin "—and I shall be the envy of every woman, and man, in all land." She covered another small giggle.

Chapter 58

Aria settled as she talked with Lady Raven for several hours. They were only interrupted when Fanny returned with the finished gown.

As Fanny handed it to Aria, Raven reached out and rubbed the fabric between her fingers. "What a lovely gown. The blue will set off your beautiful hair well. I cannot wait to see you in it."

Aria thought Raven might leave and wait to admire the dress when they went at midday. But she remained seated as Aria moved to the inner chamber. Lindsay helped her into the garment and she returned. As she stepped back into the outer chamber for Fanny's and Raven's approval she caught her toe on the long hem and stumbled forward. Her hands landed on the table, preventing her from falling face-first into it. Air whistled through her teeth and pain-filled tears stung her eyes.

Raven sat upright and reached out a hand to steady her. "Oh, this confounded Veronian fashion. Our bosoms lay exposed before king and country, but heaven forbid the toes of our slippers be seen."

Aria righted herself, stuffing down the pain washing over her as Raven's tirade continued.

"Honestly Fanny, can naught be done about this? I know naught one noble-born woman and ought few men who favor this style. Why are we yet forced to endure it?"

"The traditions of dress are slow in changing. Especially when no queen sits beside thy king to bring attention to such matters."

Both women turned and stared at Aria. Sweat beaded under their silent gaze. She smoothed the skirt of the gown.

"Fanny!" Raven exclaimed as she rose to her feet with the grace of an elegant swan. "Oh Fanny, I love this neckline. You must do this to all my gowns before I leave. You must."

Aria watched Fanny's face twist in a scowl. "Of course, m'lady. I shall begin work as soon as thou has the garments to be altered."

Raven turned, took Aria by the wrists and spread her arms wide to admire her. Her smile grew as her appraising glance ran the length of Aria's body. "You are a vision, my dear. We but need a little covering of the wretched bruise marring your cheek, and you shall be ready to meet the rest of the nobility."

Aria's hand brushed her face. "I see naught why it matters—"

"Child, hurry back to my chambers and have my girl, Olivia, give you my small brown satchel. And when you return stop by the kitchen and ask Margaret for a bowl of lemon slices. Tell her they are for Lady Raven and she will give them to you."

Lindsay followed Fanny from the room.

"Raven, please—"

"Now, I will hear nay one word more on the matter. 'Tis one thing for the warrior woman Ari to wear a bruised badge of her bravery, but 'tis quite another for the Lady Aria to be so marked."

"Does not God tell us to avoid vanity?"

"'Tis not vanity to cover the evidence of wrongs done you." She moved Aria back to sit beside her on the divan and patted her hand. "This is the first time you go before the king and all his men as your true self. You should let naught mar your beauty."

Lindsay returned and as Raven set about covering her face with a white paste before brushing it with powder to return some of its color, Lindsay worked to free her hair of its many tangles.

"Lindsay, I wish it braided today."

"Oh," the girl moaned.

Aria looked at her. "What is the matter?"

"I wanted to do your hair like Momma always did hers."

Aria sighed.

"Momma pulled back this part here in the front," Lindsay took a small gathering of hair near Aria's temples. "And she pulled it back away from her face and fastened it in the back."

"Your girl is correct Aria, and 'tis more fitting for a maiden," Raven raised a brow, and Aria nodded. "I have a pearl clasp which will serve our purposes. Lindsay, go and fetch it, for the bell has now tolled calling us to the king's boards."

Lindsay dashed off as Aria turned to Raven. "The girl hopes to replace her dead mother, but I cannot stay with her. To so encourage her will only add to her pain."

Again Raven patted her hand. "You know naught of what the Lord has written for her future or yours. He will see to her care."

Aria forced a nod as Raven handed her the bowl of lemons.

"While we wait, rub these on your lips. They will make them red and full."

As the citrus's acid burned the tender skin, Aria understood. The poor skin could not help but revolt with pain, causing swelling, and turning them irate with color.

Lindsay returned. With her hair bound in the desired fashion, they rose to leave.

After Aria tripped twice before reaching the door she huffed her distain. "Fie! How is one expected to walk in such a garment?"

"You kick the hem as ya step." Lindsay modeled and Aria followed in the same exaggerated fashion to the landing.

By the time Aria reached the bottom of the stairs in her infernal long gown, muscles in her legs she never noticed before ached with the fierceness as if they had suffered blade strikes.

She stilled and glanced at the boards full of guests already into their meal. Raven looped her arm in Aria's and, with head held high, pulled Aria forward.

Lindsay joined a group of young maids at a table near the kitchen.

As Aria and Raven passed the first boards, a hush fell over all seated along their length.

Raven pulled her forward.

Aria clung to her, desperately hoping not to sprawl in the rushes.

They passed between another row and those gathered along their lengths also fell silent. The pattern continued. Once those seated saw them, all conversation ceased. About halfway into the room Raven motioned for young noble women to slide down a bench to make space for them. Raven released her to take the open seat.

As Aria took tiny sideways steps toward the bench, silence cascaded over each remaining table until it reached the front of the room. Everyone facing the high dais turned and stared. She glanced at the gown fearing something was dreadfully amiss, but she remained well covered.

As she bent to sit, the silence of the hall drew Edmund's attention from his conversation with Hawk. His jaw slacked and, with the speed of a slug, he rose.

Aria stopped and curtsied to the ground. She gritted her teeth against the pain extending the observance. Rising again, she looked to Edmund who appeared turned to stone. Did he yet breathe?

"Forgive me for coming late to boards, Your Majesty. I experience some unforeseen difficulties." She curtsied again.

Edmund still did not move or respond.

Both Eric and Hawk to either side of him gave him a nudge.

Edmund started, "Huh? Oh. Oh think naught of it, Lady Aria. We are honored and pleased you are recovered enough to join us."

Edmund remained standing.

Aria stood as well, though she shifted her weight between her feet.

Hawk stood and raised his cup high. "To the lady, Aria. May God bless her for the aid she has given Veronia and Balmore."

Every cup in the room sailed high. "Hazzah!" rang out as one voice causing her to startle.

Edmund reached for his cup late, and after nearly upsetting it, he joined the toast. He never took his eyes off her as he inclined his head. She responded with a dipped observance to all.

Aria slid in next to Raven, but all eyes rested on her. Several moments passed before the low buzz returned to the room and conversation resumed.

"Whatever was that about?" Aria asked Raven.

The pale drawn woman across the table from Aria answered. "They were taking note of their next—Ow!" The woman's words broke off with an abrupt jerk. She sat taller as her eyes turned toward Raven and narrowed in a fearsome glare.

"Think nothing of it, Aria dear. I told you everyone is quite enamored. 'Tis not oft such a renowned hero dines among us."

Raven passed her the tray, and they filled their plates. As they ate, Raven proceeded to introduce Aria to the women gathered the full length of their table. And as Wyatt had done on the tour of the castle, Raven expected her to remember every woman by name, as well as her father or husband and any children she might have borne—living or dead. Aria did her best to pay attention as she watched the delicate way the women ate and tried to model it. This was naught like eating with the knights.

The women bantered back and forth about needlepoint and

fashion, and passed along gossip of the court. At some point the conversation turned to her.

"Lady Aria, do you not find it dreadful to be in battle swinging swords?" one young woman asked, crinkling her nose.

Raven dropped her eating awl with a clang and huffed her objections. "Audrey, what a foolish question. War is dreadful for man or woman. If all but followed God Most High, we would live in peace. It might be odd to us, but we have a kingdom protected under God's care. Evil has near consumed poor Lady Aria's land." Raven's glance passed over the table. "I ask you true, if your men were cut down, who among you would not pick up whatever they found at hand to protect those left to them?"

They answered with a nod and mumbled assent.

The woman sitting across from Aria looked down her disapproving nose as she spoke. "But 'tis said the lady trains near every day with the king and his son."

Raven laughed. "If one must do battle, should not he—or she—be prepared to survive the fight?"

"But 'tis said she revels in the brute force of it."

"I feel God's pleasure upon me when I am fulfilling the will He has called me to," Aria said softly.

"God has called you to be a…a…"

"Warrior? Aye, truly. God's voice set my feet on this path."

"*Humph*! Indeed, the very thought God would want a woman to behave as man," the sour lady in front of her groaned.

"Lady Clovis, hold your tongue of any further disparaging of the king's own hero. If not for her warning, there would have been many blades hidden in this hall. You, your husband, or your daughter could have been cut down here in this room. You were granted yet another day on this earth. I do not think God intended you to use it to bear false witness against your sister." Raven held Clovis' gaze until the disapproving woman acquiesced and inclined her head.

"Lady Aria, may I ask when you first started training?"

The question pulled Aria's gaze from the king who still sat staring at her. She turned to the woman near her age on the other side of Raven. "The spring of my sixth year."

A murmur rushed around her table.

"So young?" one woman said with a shake of her head.

"The need is great in Wexxton." Aria said.

Another lady further down spoke. "Did you start with swords?"

Aria shifted on the end of the bench, uncomfortable under the interrogation and she caught sight of Edmund once again. Food lay mounded on his plate uneaten, and his glance brought unwelcome warmth to her cheeks. She turned back to the women. "No. We train our bodies and minds first, with running and physical agility. When these skills are well in hand we next pick up the bow. We learn to fire both from the ground and while charging on horseback. The final part of one's training is the swords. We start training in the blade between the ages of ten and twelve."

"Are you not frightened to hold such dangerous weapons?"

Aria fought to suppress a smile. *Are not all weapons by their nature—dangerous? Even knitting needles can serve as a powerful weapon in the right hands.* "We handle all manner of weapons from our earliest years. There is little rest from war in my homeland. Handling blades is no different than you handling an embroidery needle. Care must be taken and skill learned to avoid injury."

Edmund strolled past, a smile etched on his face.

"Have you suffered injury in battle?"

Aria groaned. "Many times."

All the women leaned over their trenchers to look upon her now and more than one asked her to tell of her worst injury.

A hand came to rest on her arm and Aria turned to see Hawk kneeling beside her table. She almost hugged him in her relief.

"Forgive me, Lady Aria, for intruding on a quiet moment with your fellow sisters. The council of lords is about to resume their afternoon assembly and King Edmund has requested your presence."

Aria came close to knocking him over as she sprang to her feet. "Gladly, sir."

He rose with a smile and held her cloak out for her. She turned as he placed it on her shoulders. "You left this behind the other night in your haste to join the fight. Though it is not far to the small hall, I thought you might welcome its warmth on such a brisk day."

She forced a slim smile as she fastened the cloak. She turned to the women and dipped a small curtsy. "Forgive me, ladies. The king has requested my presence." An odd mixture of emotions filled their faces. A couple of younger women covered their shy giggles, a few huffed and glared, and many smiled. Aria understood naught of what any of it meant and turned back to lay her hand over Hawk's upheld arm as he waited to escort her.

They jostled their way down the main aisle, as many were moving about. When they exited the doors, a cold blast of air hit them and blew Aria's hem under her raised toes, causing her to stumble.

Hawk grabbed her at the elbow and waist to keep her from falling flat in the mud of the ward.

She growled, took a handful of her skirt in her left hand and twisted it around until the toes of her boots could be seen. She straightened and raised her hand to place upon Hawk's once more.

He offered his arm and they proceeded.

"Forgive me for being so brash as to show my boot tips, but as you have seen the full length of my footwear many a time, I thought it preferable to arriving at council in a fine gown covered in mud."

Hawk laughed boisterously. "My wife, God rest her lovely soul, would have liked you indeed, my lady. She much hated this fashion though her illness took her before requiring her to endure it for long."

Aria's glance shifted toward him. 'My lady?' I change my attire and you feel you must address me with such formality?"

Hawk's face parted in a mischievous smirk as he leaned in close to whisper. "I revel in being able to speak the truth in the open for all to hear—my lady."

Chapter 59

Aria paused after entering the council meeting. The lords of the combined realms sat in tall-backed chairs in a ring around the central fire pit. Edmund sat in his grand carved throne, the great smile still upon his face as he turned to greet her.

Hawk covered her hand where it sat on his arm and pulled her further toward those gathered. A few more lords entered behind them and took their seats.

Aria stopped again a few steps from the nearest chair. Wexxton may permit its women on the battlefield, but even at home, women were not allowed to participate in council. She did recall one woman summoned to report on a recent battle as one of the few who survived. They escorted her in to give her report, and escorted her out as soon as she finished, allowing the men to discuss their next movements.

Edmund rose, his face still lit with a ridiculous grin, and waved her forward.

She stepped toward him as Hawk left her and moved to the chair on Edmund's far side.

Edmund reached out and captured her free hand, then pulled her within the ring.

The lords rose to their feet, and bowed in serene silence.

Aria dipped a respectful curtsy and waited to be given leave.

"Lady Aria, we welcome you to the high council of Veronia and Balmore." Edmund motioned for her to sit in the open seat to his left.

"I have informed my lords of the situation your people face in Wexxton and my desire to join you in the battle to come."

Aria still stood as discomfort at the thought of joining the men grew. The noblemen remained standing. Not a moment before she'd longed for the amiable company of the kingdom's hearty men, but now, presented with the opportunity clad in her elegant gown, it somehow felt wrong.

"Please, Lady Aria, sit. The lords have requested to hear of your need from your own lips."

Aria scanned the men circled about. They each inclined their head as her gaze passed.

"It is true, my lady. 'Tis unorthodox—we grant—but the need warrants your direct telling." A tall gray-haired man said. A grim expression marred his gentle face.

Edmund again waved for her to sit. She released the air she didn't realize she held and slipped into the seat.

As if one man, they all sat, and every eye rested on her until the heat of their collective gazes seared her face. She took a deep breath to steady her nerves. Staring at their somber expressions, the longing for the battlefield rose in her belly. She would welcome facing the entire horde over these few lords in this setting. She even thought she might welcome the chatter of the women's table over her current situation. Well, mayhaps 'twas not quite so desperate.

"Please, Lady Aria, you have told me of the dire need in your kingdom, those gathered would hear of it as well," Edmund coaxed.

Another breath and the words came haltingly across her lips.

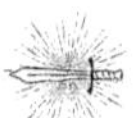

As the sun advanced the retelling of her people's fate came easier. She told the sorrowful truth in all its grim detail and the men nodded.

The lines of their mouths drew tight with concern.

Her report complete, she expected Edmund to release her.

Edmund looked to his men, his brows pinched together. "Men of Veronia and Balmore, you have now heard the situation direct from the lady's lips. What say you?"

"I pledge my men and myself to the battle," a lord said.

"Aye, I too pledge myself and my men,"

"Aye..."

"Aye..."

All around the circle one after another each man promised to come with all his fighting men to join Aria and her people on the battlefield in their last great conflict. Aria stared out at them. Words would not form on her tongue and grateful tears stung her eyes.

"On behalf of our honored guest, and your thankful king, I give you thanks. You are fine men of impeccable valor and I knew I could count on you," Edmund said.

As the talk turned to the timing of the gathering of the war host and the training they would need for this strange new enemy, Aria gulped down the lump in her throat and slipped away. She walked out into the gray chill winter afternoon on trembling legs. Swaying in her wonder, she wound her way to the chapel. As she pushed open the doors she found fellow worshipers. They sat in various pews bowed in silent solitary prayer. She turned toward the privacy of the gallery but as she reached for the door she realized she held no key. She made but a half turn to leave when the scraping of the key entering the lock tickled her ears.

Lindsay stood beside her, a great grin covering her face. "Here, m'lady." She waved her through the open door.

Aria brushed her hand down Lindsay's cheek. *What a precious child.* As she felt Lindsay lean in to her palm, she again regretted encouraging the girl's affections—and her own. She must always keep in mind the fragile state of Lindsay's emotions. Ari was destined to die and leave Lindsay alone once more.

Aria sighed and started up the stairs. She caught her toe on the hem of her skirt and fell forward. A curse tumbled out of her lips before she could contain it and she muttered her gratitude as the peeling bell drowned out the offensive expletive. A deep sigh tore through her, as those gathered in the pews rose to their feet.

"'Tis time for supper, m'lady."

"I suppose it would not be proper to arrive late twice in the same day," Aria groaned.

She carefully descended the stairs. The altar called to her soul. She wanted to meet with her Lord—to thank Him for the unimaginable gift of the aid for her people in the coming trouble. The cold air, from the open door Lindsay held, drew her outside and toward the incessant meaningless banter of the noblewomen.

Would King Edmund truly mark my absence if I chose to commune with the Lord? She groaned for she knew from the words of his greeting at midday, and the intensity of his stare, he would. She followed Lindsay to another meal of nonsense.

Chapter 60

The next few days became an unending succession of unimportant female banter and incessant battlefield questions from the men. Her heart drew her to the Lord's altar, but she never found a free moment. From the time she rose each morning, the Lady Raven accompanied her wherever she went until she retired to her each night. The woman was lovely and if Aria did not know her impending fate, she could have seen them being lasting friends.

The morning of the Christ Mass dawned bright and Aria rose before first light. She hoped to sneak out to the chapel before anyone else and seek a quiet moment with her God. She groaned for her stiff shoulder and aching ribs still required her to ask Lindsay's help to dress. She slipped from the chamber and tried to tip toe past the lesser nobility and honored knights now filling the upstairs chambers beside hers, but each step was accompanied by a groan, a creak, a squeak, or a pop of the timbered floor. She heard naught from the rooms she eased past and proceeded down the stairs and outside.

The ward lay deserted and she sped across it, hoping to make it through the inner gate and to the chapel unseen. She entered the bailey and looked toward the chapel entrance.

"Oh, Aria dear, there you are. I thought you might miss the dawn mass." Raven took several quick steps toward her as Aria stifled a growl. Raven looped her arm with Aria's and pulled her through the door and down the aisle.

Aria hoped to sit near the back, but Raven held her in her talons, and dragged Aria to the front pew. Before the considerate noblewoman could plop her in the pew reserved for the queen, Aria pushed her toward the third pew back.

Raven recovered with ease, gained her footing, and pulled Aria into the second pew.

Aria smoothed her skirt as the priest came down the aisle behind the swinging incense. The pungent spice filled Aria's nose, tickling her throat. She enjoyed the smell high up in the gallery, but here it threatened to prick tears and fits of coughing. Yet, standing with her sisters and brothers to celebrate the coming of the Christ child outweighed any momentary discomfort.

The joy of the service swept the congregants out into the bailey at its conclusion. Aria followed them with a heavy heart.

"Oh, what a glorious service. I know not whether it is the priest's words, the day, or the lingering joy of our salvation from that evil Sel, but I feel as though I could float all the way to the breaking of the fast." Raven twirled around as though she were Lindsay's age.

Aria forced a smile. "'Tis a glorious day. I will join you shortly."

Raven's face became marred by a deep pout.

"Please, go enjoy the festivities. I must...I need to collect something from the chapel. There is no need to wait."

Raven *humphed* her displeasure, but moved behind the others as they passed through the inner gate.

No one else stood about and Aria slipped back into the chapel. She scanned the quiet sanctuary and inched her way toward the high altar. At the bottom step she knelt and lay prostrate on the cold stones. Her right arm stretched out perpendicular to her body, while her injured left arm lay only a short distance from her side. The cold seeped from the floor through her clothes and added to the discomfort of her ribs.

Aria brushed all her feelings of cold, all her tenderness, all her frustration, and all her distractions aside and opened her soul to the One who created it. Her breathing slowed and a familiar warmth filled her.

Oh Father, how I thrill at Your sweet touch. That You would choose to come near to one such as I, is too much for me to bear. I fail You, break Your holy commandments, and do that which I should not. Still, You call me by name. What a precious sound Your voice is to my troubled spirit. I take breath, only because You give it. I move, only because You direct my steps. And I am blessed, only because You ordain it.

Thank You, Father, for the gift of Your only Son whose birth we mark this day. We are not worthy of such an excellent gift, yet You gave of Him freely for our sakes. Thank You, my King, for the guiding hand which led me here. Thank You, my Strong Tower, for saving this earthly king, Edmund, and his people from the hand of evil. Thank You, my Provider, for the men who have vowed to fight alongside my people. You have given more than I could have ever hoped or dreamed. You are too wonderful for me.

A radiating warmth spread from her core out to her fingertips and the tips of her toes. She reveled in it.

Ask daughter, for you have found favor in My sight. Ask and it shall be given you.

I dare not ask for more. I wish only to be in Your presence and to do Your will.

This humble request I will grant to the woman after My own heart.

The warmth consumed her—comforted her—and made her lighter than air. She lost all thought of the hard stones, the tall walls, and the sturdy beams. The Spirit within her took her to a place where she saw a vision of things to come.

As the dream faded and Aria became aware of her earthly surroundings once more, she dared ask, *What do You require of me, Lord?*

All of you, daughter.

The unyielding stone supported her once more. The cold bound her. But she would not rise to leave.

Chapter 61

A clicking noise lay on the edge of her awareness as Aria pushed to her knees, her eyes rising to the gold cross on the altar. *Thank you, Father.* She became more aware of the snapping vibration. *Praise, and honor, and glory, and power be unto Him, that sitteth upon the throne, and unto the Lamb forevermore.* A low rumble accompanied the clattering sound. Aria turned to see Lindsay seated where Aria and Raven had sat earlier on the end of the second pew. The girl's legs were hugged tight to her chest and her simple dress pulled over them. Her arms wrapped around and her entwined finger looked blue in the dim light.

Aria rose easily to her feet. "Where is your cloak, child?"

Lindsay shrugged, as her teeth clattered out a wild rhythm like some crazed woodpecker. She shimmied along the bench when Aria approached and snuggled under Aria's arm she she wrapped her own cloak around the child.

The frigid form of the affectionate girl, stirred Aria's aching heart as she laid her head on Aria's chest.

I must be Lord of all.

The words again echoed in Aria's thoughts. *Oh Lord, to have all of me, You must have all of my heart. There is naught I have to give Lindsay.* She attempted to swallow her heart, which felt firmly lodged in her throat. *It feels unfair to show me things, which I can never have, Lord. I am a woman and I want a family. To raise a daughter like*

Lindsay—or even to see Lindsay into womanhood would bring such joy.

She shook off the old longings and stuffed them back deep in her soul. *I give You all that I am, Lord. My hands are Yours to direct.*

She straightened to disentangle herself from the clinging child. "Lindsay, why are you here?"

"I wa—wa—was wa—wa—watchin' ovvvvver ya," she stammered.

"There is no danger to me now. I do not require a guardian."

Lindsay sniffled. Whether it was from the cold in the empty chapel or Aria's cold words was unclear. "Ya have an importtttanttt destiny. I thoughtttt it best to watttch."

Aria felt her lips twist in a smirk. "Lindsay, you do not know the complete truth of your words. It has been my destiny to come here. I have been with our Holy Father every year on this day since the winter of my sixth year."

Lindsay looked on Aria, eyes wide with excitement. "And God has met with you each time, like this year?"

Aria looked at the child, bewildered. "What makes you say God met with me?"

The smile on Lindsay's face grew until it filled the sweet oval feature. "You are like Moses whose face glowed after he met with God."

"My face glows?" Aria asked skeptically.

"A little, but more than that. You smile when God talks to you. Not the fake smile ya show everyone to make us feel better—but a real smile."

The innocent chastisement stung. She did not wish people to think her ungrateful or placating in her manner. Her prolonged sojourn in Veronia frustrated her, but it was not the fault of anyone around her.

She liked them.

I must be Lord of all.

She did not dare to become too friendly with them or she would fail her God.

"You smiled on the first Lord's day, when you said God wanted ya to train. And you were smiling when ya got up a moment ago. What did God tell ya, m'lady?" Here inconsistent speech patterns were endearing. She tried so hard to be a proper young girl.

Aria remembered her Lord's sweet touch and her fingers raised to brush her smile. She looked far past the altar and the gold cross, beyond the stained glass window and into the future the vision showed to her. "He told me the same thing He told me the first time."

Aria did not speak further and Lindsay slid close again. "Can ya tell me?"

Aria chuckled and started her tale with a sigh. "My mother had died in battle the previous summer, and I wanted to replace her. Father would not allow me to train. He said he had already lost his wife, and my brother trained and would enter the battlefield in another couple of seasons. He would not lose me too."

"Did ya get mad?"

Aria glanced at Lindsay who sat staring at her intently. "Oh, I became quite furious. I badgered him relentlessly for a month. Then I refused to speak a word to him from the harvest celebration up to the Christ Mass."

Lindsay laughed. "What'd your da do?"

"He tried to explain, he ordered, he made me gifts. I would not relent."

"How'd ya get him to change his mind?"

"I am not sure I did. I refused to eat the morning meal on the day of the Christ Mass. I came to the service but I would not look at him.

Then when everyone left, I snuck back into the sanctuary and came to the altar like I did today. I lay before the altar and cried bitter tears at my father's unfairness. At some point, when I was quiet, God showed me my first vision." Again Aria's gaze drifted far beyond the confines of the thick walls around her.

"I looked down on a battlefield between dense trees in a long, narrow valley. I saw a woman charge forward and cut down the Black Knight. Then she rode toward me and passed me her blades. When I looked up at her, I saw myself." Aria shook the vision from her thoughts. "The images startled and thrilled me all at the same time, and I wanted to run and tell my father. I tried to get up but I couldn't move. I struggled for some time, and cried in frustration. When I quieted again, I heard the still small whisper I have come to know well."

"What'd God say?"

"For these events to be true, daughter, you must follow Me. You must serve Me with your whole heart. And you must fight for My glory alone."

Lindsay shifted to sit on her knees. "What'd you say?"

"I said not a word. I—it was like I curled up in God's arms and accepted what He said with my whole being."

Lindsay's head tipped. "So how was your da convinced?"

"I did not realize how long I lay before the altar. But I became aware of movement and then shouting. I heard my father call my name and he sounded quite concerned. I remember the feeling of being in his arms, as he held me tight to his chest. His frightened heart pounded in my ear. Then I remember the priest stopping us. He laid his hand on my face and whispered to my father, 'she has seen God, sir. God has spoken to her.' I remember smiling and telling Father—though my voice sounded far away in my own ears, 'God has shown me I will strike down our enemy.'"

Aria tossed off the hold of the past and stood. Lindsay's stomach rumbled out once more and Aria motioned for her to follow as she made her way out of the chapel.

"And the vision was enough to convince your da?"

"Oh heavens no," Aria laughed. "But Father told me later I had lain there all through the cold night—in fact it was one of the coldest nights any could remember. Yet when they found me the next morn, the healer said I showed no signs of exposure. My skin felt cold but I was warm within. The priest insisted I did indeed receive a vision, and when I explained all I saw of the battlefield, Father said I could not know of the battle formation or describe the valley I never visited if I had not received a true vision."

"Then he relented and allowed ya to train?"

"Nay." Aria laughed as they stepped into the weak winter sun. "Then he lay before the altar every morning seeking to change God's mind for three full months. God would not be moved, and I was finally allowed to join the others my age in the daily training come spring."

"Do ya think your da is proud of ya now?"

Aria pulled up short to consider the query. "Nay, I fear he would still prefer me safe at his side, though the whole kingdom falls."

They started walking again. "I don't 'member me da. Do ya think he would be proud of me?"

Aria stroked the girl's wimple-covered head. "He would be prouder than a cock strutting about the henhouse, with his chest puffed out until it popped all the buttons off, Lindsay. Of this I have no doubt."

Lindsay slipped her frigid fingers into Aria's hand and looked up with a smile.

Chapter 62

Aria fought the need to tap her foot on the damp earth and fussed to smooth the pleats of her new pine-green gown as the wind tossed her still-unbound hair across her face. She scoured the ward, hoping to see Raven approach so she might bid her farewell.

At last Raven appeared from the tower entrance with Olivia struggling under the weight of many cloth satchels. "Aria, my dear. How I hate leaving you here with all these men—not a woman of your station within two dozen leagues to converse with, how ever will you survive?"

Aria forced a smile. "I have stayed in King Edmund's home for months Raven—"

"Aye, as a man. Now everyone knows you are no such thing." Raven looked about. "Where is your girl? You should never go about on your own, Aria dear."

"Do you think so little of Veronian men that one could consider doing me harm, and that such could happen within the king's own walls?"

"Oh, heavens no. But, dear, 'tis improper." Again Raven scanned the ward. "She is young but she should always be at your side or the tongues will go to wagging. It would soil your sterling reputation, dear. Now where is she?"

Aria placed a stilling hand on Raven's forearm. "Calm yourself, Raven. Lindsay is seeing to the moving of our meager belongings. The king insists I can nay remain in my chambers above the large hall."

"He has moved you to the castle?" A slim smirk grew.

"Aye. I am in the room next to Prince Wyatt—though the lad has not said more than two words to me since *that* night."

Raven patted Aria's hand where it rested on her arm. "The boy is young and still trying to make sense of his feelings. He will come to his conclusions soon and then, I am sure, you will remember fondly these quiet days."

Raven straightened with a deep breath. Her hand clasped over Aria's and held tight. "Now dear, I fear I must leave with my son. As it is, we have tarried far longer than is to his liking." She glanced around once more and leaned close. "He hates to be the last to leave. He fears it looks as though we need the king's care or that we prefer his home to our own." She smiled and straightened. Her gaze captured Aria. "I know you are of a mind to go to battle when the time comes and that your girl is precious to you. When Philip returns with his men to join the war band, I will return with him. I shall stay and see to Lindsay's care. You need not worry about more than returning to her."

Raven and Aria had never spoken of Lindsay. Aria continued to tell herself the sweet child meant naught. But at Raven's offer, Aria swallowed her choking tears. "I am more than grateful, Raven. 'Tis a huge burden off me to know Lindsay will not be left alone in her hour of need."

"Mother!" The sharp bark of Lord Philip caused them both to turn.

"Aye, I know, I know. You wished to be on the road directly following the breaking of the fast. Stop being so impatient, Philip. A few more minutes will matter little on a day spent in a rickety carriage."

"Now, Mother. I wish to beat the weather."

Aria watched as Raven's gaze scanned above the western wall at the far-flung gray skyline.

"You best be on your way, Raven." She forced another smile. "I look forward to your return."

Raven threw her arms around Aria, startling her. Aria struggled to return the tender embrace without stiffness and the reservation she felt in her heart.

"Mother, please."

"Oh, honestly, Philip." Raven scolded. She sat in the carriage and leaned out the opening waving until it was out of sight.

Aria released the remaining air in her lungs in a slow hiss. With the castle now empty of all the noble guests, she stood alone in the ward. She closed her eyes and enjoyed the stillness and quiet. A tapping on a window above her drew her gaze. Lindsay stood at the window waving with a bright smile. Aria moved toward the doorway and her dungeon—*my new chambers*.

Chapter 63

Aria reclined on the plush divan reading as the rain beat on the shuttered windowpanes behind her. Lindsay sat at the desk practicing her writing when the door burst open.

Wyatt marched in and stood in front of Aria. "She is to be educated with my tutor beginning tomorrow. You have done well to teach her to read the king's English, but 'tis time she receives instruction in arithmetic, Latin, philosophy and history."

Aria opened her mouth to respond but Wyatt whisked around and left the room as abruptly as he had arrived. The door banged closed behind him. Aria turned her gaze to Lindsay with a question wrapped tight about her tongue.

"He still hasn't said a word since that night you all fought in the hall. I think he hates me for lying to him. I can nay imagine he's pleased to be trapped in a room with me each morning."

"I could talk to the king if you wish?"

"No, I wanna—want to—learn. I couldn't hope for so much. I don't wish to threaten it."

"I will see what I can learn," Ari said, returning to her book.

The afternoon meal concluded and many pulled their cloaks tightly about themselves as they dashed from the hall into the heavy rain to continue their day's tasks. Edmund stopped between his chair and the quiet study and smiled at her. She rose from her seat and approached.

She dipped a deep curtsy. "I wished to thank you for seeing to Lindsay's formal education. It is exceedingly kind of you, Sire. Lindsay is ever grateful for your favor."

The corners of Edmund's mouth slid down and it appeared his cheeks pinked. "I regret to admit the idea was not mine—though it should have been. Wyatt came to me and demanded it." His mouth turned in a sideways half smile and he released a soft chuckle. "Though he never said her name and it took me the longest time to determine what exactly he desired to be done for whom."

"Lindsay and I both fear he is quite cross with us. When he entered to inform me of the lessons, it was the first time he spoke a full sentence to me."

"I have tried to talk with him about our need for secrecy. He has been in agreement that we did the right and proper thing to protect you. He is angry, yet he is behaving at odds within himself."

"I will continue to pray for him and hope he can find it in his heart to forgive us."

Edmund laid a warm hand on her shoulder, sending shivers through her entire body. "I do not believe he holds anything against you which needs forgiveness. Be at peace, my lady."

She curtsied again, relieving herself of his touch, then climbed the stairs to her chamber.

The following morning, their door burst open once more. Wyatt stood in the doorway, arms akimbo, and announced. "'Tis time for lessons." He did not wait for Lindsay and she had to run to catch up. He marched beside her, splashing droplets of mud on her boots and hem, but never uttered a word or even glanced her way. They went to the tower in the middle of the northern bailey wall behind the tavern and up to the second floor. Again, Wyatt burst into the room without knocking, startling the man inside.

"Prince Wyatt?" the slender man in a plain brown robe with the crown of his head shaved bald, looked down his long nose at the prince. "So what terrible thing has happened over the last most holy month that you enter my chambers without knocking?"

Wyatt froze and cast a glance over his shoulder though he never actually looked at Lindsay.

"Sit." Wyatt ordered her after a long pause, and pointed to a chair near the monk. "I believe you wished me to finish *The Iliad*, Brother Peter. I will begin over there." Wyatt moved to a window seat, snatched up a book and opened to where a bit of leather marked his place.

Brother Peter's long face turned to her with a single brow arched high over his dark eyes. "Do you intend to introduce your friend, Highness?"

Wyatt looked at him then his gaze finally moved to her. So many emotions played on his face that it made Lindsay feel as if he was looking at someone he had never seen before.

When Wyatt refused to speak, she curtsied low. "I'm Lindsay, sir. Lady Aria's servant."

Wyatt snorted his disproval. "No mere servant."

"*Lady* Aria," the monk said with great emphasis. "I had heard the great warrior who had saved the prince earlier was in fact a woman in disguise." Peter stood a little taller and folded his hands before him. A frown drew his face down, making it appear even longer. He reminded Lindsay of a stork she had seen painted in one of the king's books, and fought to suppress a bubble of laughter.

"*Lady* Aria saved me and my brother again at the harvest festival, do not forget, monk," Wyatt snapped the book closed and popped to his feet. "She also saved my father—the king—" he ground the reminder between his teeth. "—and his throne before the Christ Mass. If not for the *Lady* Aria and her great skill as a warrior, we would all be dead. And…Lin—dsay,"

The speaking of her name stuck in his throat and she feared he would gag on it.

Wyatt pointed at her. "She has been by her side protecting our great hero from the beginning. It is the king's order that you instruct her as one of his own."

"Yes, of course, Highness," Brother Peter inclined his head and waved his hand for Lindsay to sit in the chair that Wyatt had indicated earlier. She watched as the monk's eyes considered Wyatt with a slim smile, speaking of approval.

She curtsied again, "Thank you, sir. I'm eager to learn."

The monk's smile broadened and he bowed his head toward her. "Please call me Brother Peter, I am a humble monk. And I am eager to teach a ready student." His gaze shifted from her to the prince with a knowing look.

Wyatt snorted and plopped in the window seat. He said no more. The lesson concluded and they left. Nor he did speak to her for any of the days to follow. He marched her to Brother Peter's chambers and sat in the window seat while she received instruction, only to return her in silence.

As they left on the fourth day, the disquiet between them grew unbearable. She wanted to talk, but naught came to mind. She thought to turn off to the chapel as they passed, and pray on the matter— though she spent each day in fervent prayer with no results. But Wyatt never slowed his pace or gave her an opening to speak.

They tromped past the stables and two of the older boys stood in the doorway. They laughed and one elbowed the other. "Hey look, Damian, it's that girl who wants to be a boy."

The other laughed. "Aye, George, she does look quite brave and strong in her yellow dress."

"Well, I heard said she still wears boy's breeches under her skirts. Do you think she would still muck manure for us if we let her wear our clothes?"

They both laughed again.

Lindsay put her head down and felt heat sear her cheeks. She meant to keep walking and not look back.

Wyatt bolted from her side with a beastly roar and plowed into both boys. They stood near a head taller than him but both ended up on their backs under Wyatt's angry fist. He pummeled one on the face and followed with the other. The squires yelped and cried out until Olin pulled Wyatt off.

"What—by alls that is holys—is goin' on?"

Wyatt lunged at them again, straining against the man's hold. "Take it back! You apologize at once—or I will pound it out of you!" Wyatt growled and snarled at them as he fought to strike again.

The boys squirmed away as they still lay sprawled on the stable floor. They wiped the blood from their faces on their sleeves and muttered. "We're sorry."

"Apologize to her!" Wyatt spat, pointing back at Lindsay, who stood like a statue a short distance away. "You were crude and unkind to her. She did naught to you and she has the king's and his hero's favor. Apologize! Or I will see you regret it for weeks to come."

The boys crawled to their feet and inched past Wyatt. The first inclined his head, and his cheeks reddened. "Forgive me, Mistress Lindsay, for speaking so."

"Aye, we regret if we've done you injury," the other stammered as they side stepped around the stable, gave a quick bow and disappeared.

Wyatt jerked himself free from the stable master and stomped toward her. Anger flashing in his eyes, he shuddered and his breath came in quick gasps. "Are you well?" The words were sharp but burdened with concern.

She gave a swift nod and opened her mouth.

Wyatt snatched up her hand and pulled her toward the hall. His fingers intertwined with hers, gripping with a mighty force. "No one will ever hurt you! This I swear. As long as I draw breath you will be safe."

"Thank you, Highness," she whispered as she quickened her steps to keep up.

Wyatt jerked her to a halt and looked at her. Pain filled his eyes and she felt as though she had caused him some great hurt.

"Will you not call me Wyatt any longer?"

Lindsay smiled and released the air in her lungs. "If 'tis what you wish, I'd be honored, Wyatt."

For the first time in near a month Wyatt's shoulders rested in their proper place instead of being bound tight together near his ears. He breathed and—he smiled. He nodded once and, without releasing her hand, raced to the back of the hall and up the stairs. They were laughing and breathless by the time they reached Aria's door.

Chapter 64

The rain let up, the weather warmed, the snow line on the distant mountain ridge crept up. From her chamber window, Aria looked out across the castle grounds as the first of the traveling merchants rolled into the ward below. Winter faded and spring would arrive, bringing with it the final battle and her end. She closed her eyes as air slid from her lungs. *I am Yours, Father. Your humble, flawed servant is ready to serve.*

The old order to train stirred her heart. Lindsay entered as Aria finished binding her blades to her leg.

"My lady?" Lindsay pulled up short, causing Wyatt to smash into her as he followed her inside.

"Are you finally feeling well enough to train again?" Wyatt's smile sparkled. "Eric and Pres have been saying how they have missed crossing swords."

"In truth, Wyatt, since the Christ Mass when I met at the altar with the Lord, I have been healed."

Both children gasped. "God healed you, my lady?" Lindsay whispered. Her time studying with the monk was washing away the last of her peasant tongue. Aria missed it.

"He did indeed. Now who wants to go and fetch those two fine warriors? I am in the mood for a good workout.

"I will go!" Both children shouted as one and sped from the room.

Aria smiled, quickly plaited her hair, and folded its length over itself binding it with a bit of leather. It hung down her neck like a man's warrior knot.

Stepping into the fresh warm air, she walked quickly to the training area behind the stables and commenced with her forms. Near three months had passed since she had stood there doing this. At first her muscles tightened and fought her controlled precise movements, but in time they remembered the routine and flowed with ease.

Faint steps tickled her ears. Her eyes remained closed. Near silent *shh*-ing danced around her. The scent of fresh leather kissed her nose —Eric had sported new boots a few days ago. He stood to her left.

She turned slowly, straining to find Preston. A moment later, the whisper of his sword drawing from its home revealed him before her. A rock scraped under a boot behind her. Three challengers. She smiled. Drawing up to her full height, she pulled her blades in tight until they lay on her shoulders and spun like a twisting wind ravaging the valley floor. Her swords flew out and clanged against three long swords in rapid succession. She laughed as they staggered back, muttering under their breath.

"Fie! I will never learn how you do that." Eric grumbled and she took the opportunity to press the man behind the voice she would still not open her eyes to see. Their weapons crossed and he gave ground to her for several steps before he collected himself again and challenged her to defend her position.

He spun away and another took his place. The grunt accompanying his heavy blows told her that Edmund stood before her, and he was not pulling his efforts to favor her. Soon Edmund stepped aside and another came forward. The tang of fern-ash and vines told her that Hawk now crossed blades with her. He had allowed his beard to grow out over the winter and had taken to cleaning it with the fragrant herbs.

Preston was next as each man took a turn to face her. She spun and stood between two, caught their blades with the tips of her own and swung her arms in big circles. She almost succeeded in relieving them of their weapons, but they stepped back, pulling free first. The mock battle continued for a time, filling their practice area with the ringing of steel. At last she laughed and opened her eyes.

Even in her breeches, armor and tunic, she dipped them a grateful curtsy. "I thank you, gentlemen." She sighed as she sheathed her weapons. "That felt exceedingly good. The first good sparring after the confinement of winter is always a great joy, and you have not disappointed."

Though she held no weapons and prepared to exit the space, Eric smirked, nodded at Preston on her other side and they lunged at her with their blades.

Aria crouched under the glistening steel between them. She balanced on her left toes and the fingertips as her right leg shot out. She spun and swept both men's feet out from under them, dropping them to their backs beside her.

She laughed, brushed the dust from her hands, and offered them to the men who sat laughing on the ground.

Aria returned to her chambers and donned the blue gown once more before entering the hall sup in.

Chapter 65

Hawk strolled from the stables as a squire came running toward him.

"Sir, sir," he panted. "We have visitors. Men who say they have come a long way and are dressed in white tunics and breeches—like the Lady Aria when she arrived. It's them, sir. The rest of Lady Aria's companions. I'm sure of it."

Hawk put a hand on the excited lad's shoulder. "It does sound like they have finally arrived. Now, go inform the king and then find a kitchen maid to alert the lady as well."

"Aye, sir." The boy sped away.

Hawk straightened his jerkin as he moved to the outer gate. A gathering of knights and men at arms stood a half a pace from the visitors and more hung over the battlement from above to get a look at Aria's friends.

They stood beside their horses, who had not seen a good brushing probably since they left Wexxton. The one in the center stood a step forward of the other two, his large gloved hand resting on the hilt of his sword, which hung at his side.

Hawk smiled to himself, for he would not actually agree with the squire's assessment that the men were dressed in white. Their garments might have been white when they left home, but clearly their half a year was not spent within shelter. Surely they had not wandered the back woods of Veronia all this time. But their clothes were stained, well-worn and sported a few small holes. Hawk was eager to hear of their last months.

The men looked ill at ease with so many staring at them. The man in the center was tall with dark hair. Each man sported an overgrown beard, attesting to the many days of their journey. Hawk approached, waving the crowd to their work.

"Good day to you, sirs. I am Hawkins, King Edmund's thane. Glad we are of your long-anticipated arrival." Hawk extended his hand to the first man then to each of his companions.

"Thank you, and good day to you as well. I am Prince Raleigh, these are my men, Weldon and Cenward. We have come on urgent business from—" The prince inclined his head by his eyes never left Hawk.

"From our dear brothers and sisters in Wexxton. Aye, we are well aware of your need. Please come. All is in preparation for you." Hawk waved them to follow. "The Lady Aria will be most pleased to see you again."

Prince Raleigh stumbled and stopped abruptly. He grabbed Hawk's forearm. "Aria—she is here? She is safe?"

Hawk smiled and motioned for them to start moving again. "Aye, she arrived before the harvest six months back. We have heard of your need and everything is in preparation as I have said."

They stopped before the stables and Hawk called several squires. "Lads, take our honored guests' mounts. See they get a good brushing and plenty of food and water." The wide-eyed squires nodded with slack jaws and muttered acknowledgment.

"This way to the hall and King Edmund, friends."

Raleigh stopped him again. "Dunham—is he here as well?"

Hawk turned back to him and shook his head. "I regret to say no, Highness. He has been laid to rest in consecrated ground at the church in the town below."

"How did he die?"

"His body and that of his horse were found by our people about a month after the Lady arrived. It appeared that his horse had stepped into a snake's den and been badly bitten. The beast must have thrown Dunham for he appeared to have suffered a broken neck."

"But Aria is well?"

"Aye, quite well." He started walking again, forcing Raleigh and his men to follow. "In fact we are all quite well because of the lady. The day she arrived she saved the life of the king's young son. She later saved the lives of both his boys and even King Edmund himself. If she had not arrived when she did, the kingdom you came to seek aid from would no longer exist. She has been a gift from the hand of God Himself."

Hawk pushed open the doors and allowed the men to enter first.

Edmund sat in his tall wooden throne near the central fire, awaiting his guests. Aria had yet to arrive, but he knew she had been informed. The servants had pushed two of the long boards aside and brought five chairs to the fire so they could sit in comfort and talk. Winslow entered behind two maids. One carried a pitcher of wine and the other goblets. Others in the kitchen were preparing a quick meal and the noise rattled his anxious nerves. His heart thrilled to know how happy Aria would be to see her friends all well once more. The girls left their items on a small table and returned to the kitchen, and Winslow waited to pour the refreshment.

At last the door swung open and three well-worn travelers entered. His heart pounded. *Where is Aria? Whatever takes women so long to prepare?*

The men stood near the door blinking. The sun was bright outside and the hall lay beset with heavy shadows. After a moment their gazes fixed on him and they bowed deep at the waist.

Hawk coaxed them forward, walking a few steps in front of them.

They took a few more steps, stopped, and bowed again. They had bowed low four times before Hawk was close enough to introduce the men without shouting across the hall.

"King Edmund of Veronia and Balmore, may I introduce to you the honored Prince of Wexxton, His Highness—"

"Ri!" A woman's squeal erupted and all eyes turned to Aria. She held her hated skirt high, revealing much of the length of her tall boots as she raced full speed across the room toward the prince, rushes covering the floor fluttering in her wake. Her face lit with a radiant smile. Steps from the tall newcomer, she released her gown and threw out her arms. Her toe caught and she launched into his embrace like a great stone from a trebuchet.

The man encircled her slender waist as they dropped to their knees to keep from falling.

Aria held him tight and Edmund's heart stuttered.

She pulled from him. Tears glistened on her cheeks in the torchlight as she cradled his face between her hands. She drew near him and kissed his right cheek, his right temple, his right brow, his forehead, left brow, left temple, left cheek. She giggled as she kissed his hair-covered chin and then his nose. She fell into his embrace once more and her head rested on his shaking shoulder. "Oh, how I have missed you, Ri," she sighed.

Edmund's heart shattered like fine glass, tearing his insides to shreds. Pain consumed him. "See they are made comfortable," he moaned and staggered to his study.

Chapter 66

Aria pulled from Ri's firm hold though his arms still encircled her and reached with each hand to grasp the men who stood behind Ri. "Weldon, Cenward. It is so good to see you both. Are you well?"

"Aye, my lady. Now that we have found you whole and hale, all is well."

Ri pushed to his feet and pulled her up to stand beside him. "She appears far more than hale." His eyes scanned her from head to hidden toe. "See our fair lady is now dressed in a grand gown and eats at the king's boards. She has not suffered under the hardships of a winter in the wild."

Aria felt the heat rise to her cheeks. How could she be so quick to forget his sharp tongue? He never failed to put her in her place each time she did something he disapproved of—which occurred all too often.

"I dressed in the breeches I left in for much of the time I have been here. Since my true identity was discovered, I have been obliged to dress as is appropriate for the women of Edmund's land."

"Edmund?"

Aria sighed. "Oh, do not scowl at me so."

"You hid your identity and slinked about as a rogue spy?"

"Oh, by my sword Ri! I came as ordered—to secure the weapon we need—"

"You have the weapon?"

"Nay, not as yet, I have secured aid of a different fashion from King Edmund. His majesty has been more than kind in his care of me in my sojourn here. He feels indebted to me and has enlisted the aid of his entire standing army to fight beside us." She turned to introduce Ri and his men to the king before he scolded her further. The hall lay empty except for Winslow who stood with a scowl that mirrored Ri's.

At her silent confusion, the steward who always treated her with such kindness stepped forward. "King Edmund asked me to see to the care of your guests, my lady." He bowed with an odd stiffness and when he straightened his hard gaze would not leave hers.

"Thank you, sir," she muttered under his unaccustomed harshness.

"Do your men require a meal or drink?" Winslow's hand swept to indicate the cups behind him.

"We are not *her* men, sir," Ri snorted.

"Of course, forgive me, *Highness*."

Winslow's gaze never moved from hers. She turned to Ri. "Mayhaps you would like to clean and rest? I am sure the tunics and breeches, provided me upon my arrival, will fit you."

"As you stole my extra set it would appear so," Ri said dryly.

Aria felt like a child under his hawk-like stare. She bowed her head and stepped aside, allowing them to follow Winslow.

The steward did not move for a moment, and a last he jutted his chin in the air and spun toward the back of the hall. They ascended in silence and as they came to the first door on the left Winslow swung it open. He inclined his head toward Cenward with a gentle smile. "You may have this room, sir. These rooms are small but there is a warm room off the back of the old kitchen where you can bathe. Servants stand available to attend you if you so wish it."

Cenward bowed and offered a sigh of thanks as he entered.

A maid scurried up the stairs with a flickering candle in one hand as she shielded the flame with the other.

"Light the lamps in these two rooms, Nell," Winslow said as he threw open the next door. "Sir, your room," Winslow said with a smile to Weldon.

As both men disappeared within their chambers, Winslow turned to address Ri. No smile accompanied his words and a tremor of anger colored his tone. "Do you wish to bed with the lady, or do you wish a chamber of your own, Highness?"

"If the king of all Veronia and Balmore can nay spare a room, I can sleep with one of my men," Ri quipped.

Again Winslow's chin sailed into the air and his shoulders squared. He stepped to the opposite side of the wide hall and threw the door open next to Aria's. "A bath can be drawn for you in the inner chamber if you so wish."

Ri nodded.

"Nell," Winslow called as the girl darted between the other two rooms. "Light these lamps as well and tell all the servants who are available to heat water for baths for Lady Aria's guests."

She inclined her head and proceeded with her current task.

Winslow glared again at Aria. "If there is naught further, my lady, I have other tasks to attend with these arrivals."

"Thank you, sir. We can manage."

Winslow left with his newfound haughtiness as a soft giggle bubbled behind her. Lindsay stood in her doorway. She stepped out into the hall with a bright smile. "Is there anything you require, my lady?"

Ri's fists clenched. "You have a servant waiting on you?"

Aria felt her shoulders sag lower under the continuing disapproval. "Ri, you do not understand—"

"Nay I do not. You know of the crisis of our home. You know

naught of the fate of those we left behind months ago. You ran off and left me to worry, only to sit pampered in a fine castle, draped in fancy frippery with servants waiting on your every childish whim."

Tears stung her eyes. Her voice—little above a whisper—trembled as she spoke. "I see the extended journey has done naught to dull your sharp tongue or to soften your displeasure of me. I did as God led me, and I have found favor here for our people. They have never left my thoughts for a single moment, and I have prayed for them without end —as I have prayed for your safe arrival as well." She turned to move away. "I will leave you to bathe and rest. Mayhaps it will wash away some of your fowl temper."

Ri seized her by the arm and spun her around. His grip bore into her arm as his stare rooted her to the stone floor. He raised his hand and she half believed he aimed to strike her. She made no move to prevent it.

Much to her relief, he laid his cold hand on her hot cheek. He brushed away the tear tumbling over her lashes and drew her closer. His voice whispered across her face, husky and full of emotion. "Oh Aria, my heart. I knew naught of what became of you when you charged off in the night. Willful to a fault." A slim smile turned one corner of his mouth. "I mean not to be at odds with you. I have been near driven mad from fear." He pulled her close, draped his arms over her shoulders, and tightened his embrace.

She eased into him, wrapping her arms around his waist as he sat his chin on her head. "I have worried over you too, Ri. Forgive me for not remaining with you. I did not mean to be disobedient. I love you so."

Lindsay gasped behind her and Aria heard her run into their chambers and slam the door.

Aria looked at the door, which still reverberated in the dark hallway. She turned back to Ri, who stared with his brows arched high.

"This is a strange land you speak so fondly of. My men and I received a hearty greeting at the gate, but the king vanished before he shared a cup of welcome with us. His servant appeared surly and disapproving of making accommodations for us, and now your own servant slams the door on you."

Aria shook her head. "Lindsay is not my servant. She is an orphan who has accompanied me. She has been my aide as both my page and now a lady-in-waiting. She is young and prone to swings in emotion. I know not what troubles her now. Mayhaps she has sparred with the young prince again."

Ri's brows rose all the more.

"It matters not the infatuations of children. Go you now. Rest and bathe—for you stink, Ri." She managed a tight smile and a small chuckle. "I am sure the king will be pleased to meet you when you do not make his eyes water so."

He cupped her chin in his palm. "You are sure you are well?"

She rested her hand on his wrist. "Worry naught over me. I have been well cared for. I have found favor with the king."

"You keep saying such." He turned her face from side to side, his eyes narrowing in close inspection of her. "What manner of care has this king offered? You have a strange light about you, Ari. I think you have been changed?"

She pulled from his grasp. "Fie, you are ever infuriating. I am no more than well rested, for the quietness of this peaceful kingdom. It has naught to do with King Edmund. Now, go you."

"I know you well, Aria, I will uncover the truth of the color in your cheeks and the lilt in your voice as his name lights upon your lips."

She spun away, her skirt whirling with a swish. "I have told you all, though I have no doubt you will find a way to invent some manner of thing with which you may continue to make sport of me." She pushed through her door.

"Oh, have I missed you, little one."

She shut the door with a small thud and fell back into it as she trembled. "What manner of humiliation awaits me with you here?" Her gaze rose to Lindsay who glowered at her. *Ri appears and the whole castle goes mad.*

Chapter 67

Ari stood at Ri's open doorway and leaned on the frame. He sat on the divan lacing his boots. His men stood nearby, all now dressed in her old simple tunics and breeches—each man donned in a different color. With the sun flooding the ornately decorated room through the un-shuttered window, they reminded her of a rainbow. They were clean-shaven and their hair brushed and bound in tight warriors knots.

Ri continued to thread the second boot without looking up. "A plump old woman bustled about my room insisting on measuring my person to fit me with 'proper' attire. These are not our ways, Aria. Have you taught them naught of your people?"

"You are crown prince, Ri. King Edmund, I am sure, only wishes to make you comfortable."

"The old woman came to us as well, Aria." Weldon grinned.

She sighed as Ri rose and continued to frown. Without the heavy beard, the depth of his disapproval became all the more clear. "I know naught why the king wishes to provide you with fine clothes. Mayhaps he wishes to present you with a gift?"

"Is such how you gained his kindness, by announcing you are princess and begging favors?" His snide sneer heated her cheeks again.

"I have said naught as to my title, sir. Any favor I have garnered is from my work with the blade and my help to thwart a challenge to King Edmund's throne."

"The king cannot defend himself. He must look to you?"

"Why must you take every opportunity to cut me low? I have worked hard here. And while the threat smoldered here long before I arrived, when the challenger discovered my true identity he used it as a final challenge against the king. So if you must know, I have brought the king as much trouble as I have brought aid—as I always have you." She moved toward the stairs.

Hot, painful tears stung her eyes and fear fouled her belly. Living within the same walls, Ri would make sure everyone knew her lack. He would use her weaknesses, that he knew so well, to bring her low. At the first step her legs trembled so she reached for the wall to steady herself, and laid her other hand over her churning stomach. Lindsay had left their chambers hours ago, Aria could return and lie down.

His strong hand gripped hers and pulled it from her middle to rest entwined on his solid forearm. "There is little need to work yourself into such a state, my sweet." His words were soft and kind. But as she glanced up, worry mixed with some emotion she could not identify in his eyes. "I meant naught against you in my retort. I thought to cast a light on your beloved king. But once again you have come to his defense—this time at a cost to your own pride."

"As you have assured, sir. I have no pride. Naught in my life have I to be proud of." Her voice trembled and she swiped at another uncontained tear. She made to pull from him but he held her firm.

Pressed against the wall he lifted her face. "I … Aria …" He stared at her, confusion drawing his brows tight together.

The final bell signaling the beginning of supper rang in the distance and she shook herself free. "The meal begins, sir. Let us see you fed with good company." She hastened down the stairs and entered the near-silent hall.

A few heads rose as she approached but they sat wide apart, not allowing room for her or Ri and his men to join them. Their stares were hard and cold. They bent in hushed conversation, never looking her way again. Perched off to the side, a new long board lay set for four. She motioned for the men to take a seat on the benches and slid into place beside Ri. A serving girl appeared and dropped a tray between them with a thud and a snort.

"Friendly bunch," Cenward muttered, snatching a hunk of meat.

Aria glanced at the high table. Edmund did not join them. Hawk looked at her with such sadness she thought her heart would break. "I do not understand. Never in even their darkest hours have they behaved so. They welcomed me readily."

"It would appear clear they prefer the company of women to fellow knights."

Aria frowned at Ri. "I came as a knight. They did not know me as a woman until the Christ Mass."

Ri patted her hand. "All will become clear when I have opportunity to meet with your King Edmund. Mayhaps they have changed their minds about aid in the coming battle."

"Stop calling him *my* king. Nay do I belong here. I return home to fight."

Ri bit off a mouthful of dark bread and mumbled around it. "Aye, so you say but what of after the battle?"

Aria lowered her head and swallowed the lump choking her. She had yet to take a bite and now she knew she would not eat this night. She rose and returned to her chambers.

Edmund knelt before the altar, pain wrenching his body. Aria's love had arrived over two days ago and Edmund still did not have enough courage to face the man.

Aria's love. Oh, Lord, what am I to do? Without knowing it I have given my heart to this woman. I asked not of You or Your will on the matter. Now I suffer as when You took my beloved Jocelyn to Your side. No answer came—no warmth or comfort. A tear tumbled and splashed on his clasped hands.

Hawk had reported that the entire castle went about scowling and shunning Aria and her men. She was a beautiful woman. Edmund should have known her hand would be claimed. She rebuffed him enough times to alert him to the state of things. She did not love him. The thought seized his heart and another tear fell.

I cannot continue to mope about and hide from my people.

Edmund felt a tender familiar stirring in his spirit.

I need to meet with the prince and affirm that we will fight with Wexxton. I will not abandon them over my own foolish heart.

Another wave of God's pleasure washed over him. He lumbered up, looked to the cross. "Give me strength, Father."

Outside the chapel, the sun splashed the bailey with joyful waves, mocking his pain. Hawk approached, concern contorting his face. Edmund raised a hand to silence him before he spoke. "Inform the prince I will meet with him in my study when supper has concluded." Edmund trudged off before Hawk could respond.

Chapter 68

A single thump sounded on his door. Edmund steeled himself. "Enter."

Hawk pushed opened it and motioned Prince Raliegh to the far chair.

Edmund rose and shook the man's hand before they all sat. "Glad we are you have arrived safe to our door."

Edmund noted that the prince did his best to suppress a snort. "Aye, the welcome has been unlike any I have ever experienced."

"We have left you alone to allow time to reunite. But I wished to assure you my kingdom will honor our promise to your Lady Aria. We will soon call the war host together and prepare to accompany you back to your homeland."

"Ari has spoken of you these last days with great fondness and regard, so I did not fear you would turn back on your vow. Though I wondered if you avoiding being alone with me for some reason."

Edmund cleared his throat and tried to force a smile to his tight lips. "Nay, Highness. As I said, we wished only to allow you time alone. I remember well the pain of leaving a wife behind."

"Wife?" The prince startled. He looked from Edmund to Hawk and back again. His gaze moved toward the door. After a long moment, an abrupt snort-half chuckle burst from the man. He turned back to Edmund, unable to contain his mirth. "Wife? You think Aria is my wife?"

"Aye?"

The man fell into fits of uncontrolled laughter. The boisterous noise rattled the windowpanes in their frames. "Aria?—stubborn, willful Aria consent to submit to a husband?" the man muttered around his great guffaws. He wiped tears with the back of his hand. "Oh, forgive me, Majesty. I mean not to make sport of you. Oh," he sighed again as chuckles continued to rattle in his chest. "I have known the girl since she drew her first breath, Sire, and know well her revulsion to such entanglements of the heart—though many have tried. You see, Sire, I am her brother."

"Brother," Edmund said with such a powerful sigh, he slumped back in his chair.

The last of the laughter died as Raleigh wiped the remaining tear. "Aye, and I take it by the return of color to your face you are much relieved her hand might still be for the winning."

Edmund could not keep a true smile from turning his lips.

"I can give no consent but only warning. Her heart is not a prize easily won, Sire. She claims a higher calling, and Father will not force her to take a husband."

Edmund nodded. "Nor would I."

"If she is your sister …" Hawk stammered. "She is the king's daughter?"

"Aye?" Raliegh said with obvious confusion.

"Of course it would follow so, forgive me, but a conversation with the princess came to mind, from not long after her arrival. She promised any of our unlanded knights, who fought for Wexxton, and professed a saving knowledge of the Christ, would be granted a fief by King Maddix. I thought it presumptuous of a knight in the king's service—but as his daughter …"

"Oh aye, if Aria promised it, Father will grant it. He would never refuse her the smallest to the grandest of requests. Though I will admit, I would have offered likewise. It is sound strategy to assure more hands on the battlefield and the repopulation of our decimated people and lands—should we be granted victory."

Raleigh leaned back in his chair and considered Edmund. "So you are smitten with her?"

"I fear it is well beyond such simple emotions, sir. If the last two days are any testament, I am besotted, enchanted, and well bewitched."

"She has a pleasant enough face," Raliegh said with a wave of his hand.

"The woman is a vision," Hawk blurted.

"Truly, she is lovely, but she has a strength of both body and spirit I … love … as well. I have never seen another warrior with her skill."

"She is touched with a gift from God's own hand."

"The lady led us to believe she is not remarkable among her peers in Wexxton." Hawk leaned on his forearms propped on his thighs.

The prince glanced from one to the other. "Truly?"

"Aye. More than once she has spoken of being among the least skilled," Edmund said.

Raleigh's gaze shifted toward the door though Edmund thought he did not truly see it. "I may have some work to do with her." He did not speak more, lost in his own musing.

His gaze returned to Edmund. He sighed with a small smile. "It is good we have cleared the air between us, Majesty, for I fear our misunderstanding has set your home a kilter."

"The fault does nay lay with you, Highness, but my own ill behavior. Please forgive me."

"A heart in love is want to do any number of unwise things and we men fall prey to the foolishness of it more so, I believe."

Edmund returned his smile. "Let us put it behind us with a hunt in the morn. You, your men—"

"And the Lady Aria, of course." Ri chuckled.

"Oh aye. We could nay forget her." Heat warmed Edmund's cheeks.

Raleigh stood and offered his hand. "I will see she is ready before first light. And I wish you well, Sire. From what I have seen and heard I would welcome you as a brother. If any has a chance at her heart, I think it might be you."

Edmund would not release his grasp. "Truly, Highness?"

Raleigh rumbled with laughter once more. "Hear me clear, my friend, I make you nay assurances, she is a woman of her own mind. But there is something in the way she talks of you and the glint in her eyes I have never seen of another. You must pray God tempers her willful heart to accept such an offer."

"Thank you, Highness. I will do so and see you on the morrow."

"Please, call me Ri, I am only a friend here."

"And hopefully a brother."

"Aye, God willing."

Chapter 69

Aria stood in the failing light on the battlements looking out to the great ridge to the north. Snow, kissed pink and gold by the setting sun, lay draped like a woman's mantle atop the peaks. Heavy footsteps thumped the stones, drawing her from her wandering thoughts.

"There you are, sister." Ri kissed her temple as Lindsay, who sat huddled nearby, gasped.

"What did the king say?"

Ri laughed and her stomach flipped. *What horrid thing did Ri do to bring shame on her?*

"Once I corrected the king of his misunderstanding, we continued in an amiable conversation. He has again promised his support."

"What misunderstanding?" She hated the tremor in her voice.

"A common confusion has beset the entire castle."

His wide smirk only served to make it harder for her to breathe. But she would not beg him.

He leaned in to her and feigned a whisper. "They have all believed I am your husband."

Confusion swirled her thoughts. "What would it matter?"

Ri turned and leaned back, his elbows rested on the crenel behind him. "It matters a great deal if the king is in love with you."

Aria smacked his arm. "There is no kindness in making sport of me so. Truly, what did you and the king speak of, my lord?"

Drawing himself up, he rubbed his arm without concern and his brow rose. "I tell you truly, sister, we spoke of the king's love for you and his desire for your hand in marriage."

"Do not be so foolish—"

"But we all love you, m'lady," Lindsay offered with a tender smile.

Aria no longer possessed the patience to contend with Ri's skimming and the child's worship. She thrust her finger at the girl's nose. "I have warned you about such things, child. I will not allow it."

Lindsay lowered her head but would not be silent. "You can nay order someone not to love you. 'Tis something born in our own hearts."

"I can and I will. You will stop this instant and speak no more on the matter." She whirled back on Ri with the same wagging finger. "And you sir, can take your smug notions and your fanciful ideas and choke on them. I will not give my hand to any. There is a battle to be fought and I will not be distracted from it by you or the king—if in fact he ever said such a thing."

Ri placed his hand over hers to lower her finger. "I do not take kindly to being called a liar—even by you, dear sister. Now, you can take up your thoughts with the king himself on the morrow. We have been invited to join him in a hunt."

"Nay!"

"Aria, I have already promised your presence."

"You should know well not to speak for me. I will not be made your sport." She stomped her foot like a petulant child. "I will not accompany you and watch as you make me the fool before a king who at present holds me in favor. I will not go." She turned to leave and Ri growled at her.

"You will attend of your own or I shall throw you over my horse and take you nevertheless."

She turned to him and curtsied as she ground her teeth together. "Regretfully, I must decline your kind offer, my lord. As you and your men have all my breeches. I can nay think of soiling so fine a 'frippery' gown by crashing through the woods with you men."

As she came to the first step of the tower which lay less than a pace away, Ri called out to her. "Then you will be relieved to know, I have your own clothes in my chamber."

She stopped and glared at him. "I am not a mouse to be batted about in your paws, sir. I will not attend to watch any man fawn over me true or no." She made it down the three steps to the door before she heard Lindsay's words.

"She hates the thought of anyone loving her, Your Highness, because …"

No, Lindsay, do not speak the words.

Lindsay huffed. "Because she believes she will die in the battle. She hopes to spare us the pain of her loss."

Aria flew up the steps and seized Lindsay by the front of her garment. "How dare you reveal such a confidence, you wretched child. I have long tolerated your sniveling and your clinging, but no more. I am done with you. Find another to pester." Aria threw her down in a heap of tears as Ri seized her own arm.

"Is what she speaks true?" He shook her, his fingers boring holes in her flesh. "How long have you thought such a thing?"

She would not look at him and would not speak. Fury like a spewing volcano and guilt deeper than any bottomless pit consumed her in equally intolerable waves.

"Fie, woman. Tell me!"

Her voice low, she snarled her words. "It matters not what I say or what you hear. I will be on that battlefield and none can stop me save God's hand alone."

Ri released her and stepped from her. Aria fled down the stairs and to her chambers. Anger flamed through her blood so she thought she would be consumed from within. Remorse forced hot tears to her eyes and great rivers ran down her cheeks. Ri knew, but it mattered not—he would not stop her—she vowed. Lindsay would forgive her too, she hoped.

A small tap sounded at Aria's door well before the sun dared raise its head. The door inched open. "My lady?" Lindsay's voice trembled and guilt seized Aria's heart afresh. "Lord Raleigh has brought your clothes."

"I care not, child. Leave me." The words were not harsh but firm.

"My lady? He feared you would protest and urged me to relay his message. He says you can either dress yourself or he will do it for you."

Aria flew from her bed and rushed past Lindsay, who cowered out of her way. She flung open the door to find Ri standing without, arms crossed and his feet set well apart. "What game are you about, sir?"

He smirked. "The finest game to be found in the king's forest, dear sister. I aim to bring down a boar. And you?"

"What must I do to get through your thick head?"

He sprang forward. wrapped his arms under her backside and lifted her into the air.

She squealed in surprise.

"Fuss and fume all you wish, little one. Your hair may be flowing fire itself and your eyes flaming darts, but you will come on this hunt. I have dressed you before—and I wager even after all these years, I can still do so again. Now stop fighting what you can nay win and dress yourself."

She squirmed in his arms, but he held her tighter.

"Do you yield, knight?" he demanded.

She kicked at him and pounded on his shoulders, but it only served to tighten his grip on her.

"Yield, fair knight."

Her toes tingled as he tightened his grip all the more, like a great snake wound around her—he would crush her if she did not relent.

Wyatt stepped from his chamber into the hallway, bouncing with excitement. "Lady Aria, Lord Raliegh, how can you waste time at play? We have a hunt to attend. Come, come." He raced down the stairs.

"The lad expects you. Now yield, knight, and come."

She stopped all her thrashing and lowered her head until it rested only an inch from his. "I yield, sir."

He slid her to the ground and wrapped her in a tender hug.

As feeling returned to her legs, she pushed away from him. "It matters not the timing of it. You are bent on once again bringing me low. Let us attend the hunt, brother, and be done with it." She noted a wash of pain cross his face as she slammed the door. She snatched up the clothes from Lindsay and entered her inner chamber.

All stood about the small hall snacking on cheese and warm bread, washing it down with a bit of ale as they waited Aria's arrival.

"If she does not appear soon, I will be forced to go and fetch her, Edmund," Ri said with a mischievous grin as the man again glanced back toward the stairs.

"She is a woman, we must allow her a few more minutes at least."

Wyatt bounded around him.

"Son, please go and see if the horses are ready. Your excitement is wearing on me."

The lad dashed off without comment.

Ri raised his head with a smile and Edmund turned to see Aria approach.

"Good day, my lady."

"Good day to you as well, Majesty," she said, but worry marred her features. Her gaze shifted to her brother and she trembled.

Edmund watched as she closed her eyes, drew in a tremulous breath, and squared her shoulders. "Are you well, my lady?"

She looked on him with such pleading. "Aye Majesty. All is well." A slim smile graced her lips that were pulled tight with an inward strain. "Shall we be about the hunt?" She glanced around them. "I fear the young prince may have left without us."

"The stable master will not allow him to leave us behind," Edmund laughed. "But do you not wish to break the fast before our adventure?"

She glanced at Ri, to the food, and back to her brother once more. Edmund was sure he saw a flush of green race over her face, and she placed a trembling hand on her stomach as she shook her head. She moved toward the doors and Edmund fell into step on one side while Ri walked on the other.

"You wear an interesting garment today, my lady."

She glanced down for a moment as they stepped into the cool pre-dawn morn. "'Tis a simple fighting skirt, Sire. They are quite common in Wexxton." She strolled off ahead of him as Winslow approached for a quick word before they departed. Edmund watched her go. She wore a long sleeved chemise with an embroidered doublet over it, and while it looked like many Jocelyn had worn, Edmund noted the laces down each slim side, which were drawn snug to accentuate her narrow waist. The thought occurred to him that the laces could be loosed so the garment could still be worn over her armor into battle. But the skirt drew his attention. It lay about her sumptuous, swinging hips in long overlapping panels. When she stood still it appeared a common pleated skirt. But when she walked it revealed the dark breeches beneath which were tucked into her high boots. Feminine as it swished about her, but it would be highly functional in a battle. His heart fluttered to watch her move. Her long red braid caressed her back and it occurred to him how he wished he were that length of hair.

Winslow placed a hand on his arm to pull his attention from her. "She is a vision, Sire."

"Aye," Edmund sighed.

Chapter 70

Aria approached the gray horse she had ridden when she saved Wyatt, and swung into the saddle with ease.

"I want to be able to mount like Lady Aria," Wyatt groaned.

Ri ruffled his hair. "I am afraid but a few are so nimble and yet strong enough to manage it. I never have. Only the lady is so gifted." He smiled up at her as he passed and mounted as all the others, with his stirrups.

Wyatt groaned as Olin boosted him up.

Aria fidgeted. Her stomach rumbled as fear rent her insides. Ri never allowed her a moment of success growing up. He would feign praise in private only to thrust her down on her backside in front of others. She served as his best sport and he took every opportunity to bring her shame at her own hand.

As the thought of what awaited her nearly doubled her in pain, she feared she might wretch. Edmund and his people held her in esteem. Everything would change this day. She turned to Ri and glared at him. *Have your way, brother. I will not cower before you any longer.* Her contemplations were bold, but she trembled all the same.

"Where is Lindsay? She is not coming?" Wyatt asked as he directed his horse beside her.

Aria tried to shake free of her fear. "I asked but she mumbled something about falling off the horse. I am afraid I did not ask further." She took the quiver and bow Hawk handed her and watched as Wyatt stared at her action with keen interest to do as she did.

The party, now mounted and armed with bows and arrows, proceeded out of the inner gate two-by-two. Edmund passed the pens of the hounds and looked back to those riding behind him. "I do not wish to hunt par force, or even by bow and stable today. Let us test our mettle and run the game to ground by our skill alone."

A 'huzzah' rang as they exited the outer gate to wind down the narrow path into the valley below. Nearing the bottom, Ri called from behind her to Wyatt who rode to her right.

"Highness, did the lady tell you of the time she brought down a bear with a single arrow?"

The barb of his familiar chide pierced her flesh and she closed her eyes for the mocking she knew would follow.

Wyatt twisted in his saddle, "Nay, sir. Was it a big bear?"

"No," Aria quipped, saving Ri the trouble.

"Oh, he was enormous. Three times her height, I would wager, and she could not have been much older than you at the time."

Wyatt gawked at her in awe. The words were kind but the rub lay on his next breath. She steeled herself and waited.

They left the path and entered the valley. Edmund fell back to hear the tale better. Aria shuddered as she noted they all rode in a tight huddle to be sure not miss a word. As Ri came even with Wyatt on his far side, she turned and glared at him. Pain she did not understand again filled Ri's face.

Ri's voice rang out clear in the early morning air, and she feared the whole town could hear. "Aria had only begun her training with the bow, you see, Highness. Not more than a month passed in her efforts, truly. We train in a large field a league from Father's castle near the edge of a huge forest. There is a small rise there where we can prop up the targets and a river nearby to refresh ourselves after our hard labors.

All the youths my age were up the road a short distance where we trained with the sword." He raised his eyes and smiled at her.

She turned away from him and hefted her chin high. His favorite part yet waited.

"What happened next?" Wyatt said.

"The young archers took a break and walked toward the stream. At the same moment the bear left the trees on the far side. He too wanted a drink. The others screamed and fell away. When my group arrived moments later, I saw Aria—bow drawn and ready in her hand. She was the only one standing, mind you. The others all lay cowering on the ground or running toward us. Though we carried blades, we were too far away to lend her aid. She stood against the bear alone."

Ri glanced off in the distance as if seeing the event afresh. "The bear roared and even the youths nearest me stepped away, but Aria never flinched. He charged toward the water and hit at it splashing a great wave near her feet and still she did not move. He bounded across the shallow water and ran at her. I tell you, I sore feared the great beast would devour her whole, it looked so large next to her. Still, Aria did not move. The bear then made his fatal mistake."

"Yes, yes, go on," several others voiced their encouragement.

"The foolish bear reared up on its back legs, pawing the air. In doing so, he exposed his weakness. He showed the huntress his heart. She loosed the arrow, piercing his tough hide clean into the thumping organ. His roar cut short. He wavered there in the air and tried to bat at her, but he fell dead, his nose touching her boot."

As awe murmured through his audience, Ri again looked to Aria. She would not allow him to so shame her again. "'Twas an easy thing when the creature is ancient and frail."

Ri frowned at her, and again the unknown emotion washed over his features. "We ate that bear all winter. He was young and hale or he would have been too tough to stomach. It was an amazing feat."

Ri said no more for some time, and Aria's gut churned.

At Wyatt's prodding, Ri regaled them with more of her prowess and wondrous accomplishments. Each time she tried to voice the barb he loved to use to put her in her place, but he would correct her and sing her praises all the more.

As they neared the entrance to the royal hunting grounds and repositioned themselves in neat pairs for the narrow trail, Aria waited and pulled beside Ri. "I ask you again, brother, what game are you about?"

"I do not understand?"

She seized his horse's bridle and pulled him to a stop. Glaring, she hissed. "Know I well your ways, Raleigh of Wexxton. Never have so many kind words for me crossed your lips at one time when you have not turned them on me and humiliated me. I told you at my door, do what your heart is set to do and be done with it. But stop lifting me to such great heights for no other purpose than to make the fall all the more painful."

He laid his hand over hers and his face filled with the unnamed emotion. Did guilt or regret show there? "Forgive me, sister, for my childish behavior. I never knew the damage I wrought on your tender heart."

"Lady Aria, are you coming?" Wyatt called.

She pulled from Ri and started her horse forward again. "Fear not, brother, my heart is now well calloused by your frequent sport. Do your worst. You can nay hurt me more." She spurred her horse to greater speed and left Ri without further thought, though she continued to tremble.

The large group separated, Hawk, Eric, and Preston leading Ri and Cenward off to the north while Edmund and his guards led her, Wyatt and Weldon to the south of the spacious grounds.

Edmund dropped back to ride beside her, opposite Wyatt. "My Lady, you do not look well. Are you ill?"

She turned to him and saw it. Love softened his gaze upon her. It threw back his shoulders, curled the corner of his lips, and cocked his head. The tilt and the tremor in his lips told her clear, if she but leaned toward him, his lips would caress hers. She swallowed the sudden lump of her heart in her throat, but choked on it instead and broke into a small fit of coughing.

Wyatt *shhh*-ed her.

Oh, Lord, help me. It lies within the son as well. I cannot bear the love of these good people. You ask too much of me, Father.

Edmund's hand came to rest on her arm, sending bolts of fire through her entire body. Though she tried to hide it, her alert horse pranced with nervous energy. Breaking the king's hold, she shuddered and shook from her growing dread.

"Please, worry nay over me, Sire. I am in good health, but sibling angst has set my mind to trembling. I am the younger and my brother excels at assuring I know my place beneath him."

Edmund frowned—concern washed his face like the sunlight between the leafy branches above. She could not bear to look on him.

"Would you wish me to speak to him on your behalf, my lady?"

She shook her head and urged her horse to catch up with Wyatt. "It would only worsen his treatment of me. Fear not, I am well accustomed to his behavior."

Once beside the young prince, she pointed down a narrow trail and he led the way, forcing Edmund and the others to file behind her. They rode some distance in silence as Aria struggled to gather her scattered thoughts like sticks from the forest floor to be piled and burned. She fought to cage her emotions, while those around her were bent on releasing those same sentiments to a mighty storm which now threatened to consume her.

Wyatt stopped at a junction of several trails and turned for direction.

Aria closed her eyes and forced a slow breath through her lungs. *Lord, I yearn for Your perfect peace.* A gentle whisper of a movement caught her attention and she looked up to see a small hart with eight points. Though not a hart of ten—an animal worthy of hunting—he would be a good first kill for the young prince and she offered a wordless pointed finger.

Wyatt turned as if to lead his horse in the direction but stopped when he saw her remove her bow from her shoulder and draw an arrow from the quiver. Wyatt did the same.

Aria eased her horse beside his at the moment he spotted the hart.

Wyatt fumbled to notch his arrow and drew back.

Aria placed a stilling hand on his straight arm. "Patience, Highness," she whispered in his ear.

He smiled, "Like with the bear?"

She managed a slim nod as she straightened and removed her hand to handle her own bow. The hart bent his head to eat, unconcerned by the four-legged creatures walking at the end of his small clearing.

Wyatt waited.

Weldon's horse huffed at the delay. The hart's head rose and it turned, ears alert.

Wyatt fired, and Aria did the same a heartbeat behind. Wyatt's arrow went wide and pierced only the bit of skin at the front of the neck. Startled and in pain, the hart bent to leap away but Aria's arrow drove home and he fell dead.

"You killed him," Wyatt groaned.

"Nay, Highness. Your arrow struck first. He is your kill." Wyatt looked at her, his brows high. "I speak the truth, Highness, my release came late. "'Tis yours."

"Aye, I saw it myself, son, the lady's arrow struck after yours. The honor of your first kill awaits." Edmund waved out his hand, urging him forward.

Wyatt whooped his excitement, sending the birds above them to flight.

"Come, young prince, let us prepare your mighty kill to take home," Weldon said with a smile and a wink to Aria as he passed.

Once his son moved out of earshot, Edmund spoke. "Thank you, Lady Aria."

She turned to him though she would not meet his eyes. "I know naught of what you speak, Majesty."

Edmund's smile grew. "You know well Wyatt's arrow did no serious harm and if not for your quick action the poor creature would have been lost to suffer in the forest with an arrow through a bit of his neck. Thank you for your kindness to both the hart and my son."

Aria turned her horse back up the trail they had traversed moments before. "None shall ever hear from my lips that any but Prince Wyatt took down the animal."

Edmund's smile grew and he nodded as she passed.

She came to the wide trail where they had left the others and reined her horse as Edmund drew alongside. His guards continued along the trail for more game and Weldon still remained in the clearing with Wyatt. To her shock, Aria realized she sat alone with the besotted king. She dared not look at him.

"I know the time is not yet, Lady Aria, but I hope you will

consider—"

She raised her hand to hold his next words. "As you say, the time is not yet, Majesty."

He nodded and they fell into an uncomfortable silence. As she sat fighting for an even breath with her heart fluttering against her ribs, again a rustle drew her attention. She closed her eyes and tilted her head to find its source. Her bow with another arrow notched rested on her thigh and she raised it again.

Edmund grunted and she opened her eyes to see him backing away from her line of fire.

She felt the heat in her cheeks, but he turned toward the noise he now heard too, and raised his bow. Aria released before anything came into view and a boar slid from the forest brush on his belly—dead, her arrow buried between its shoulders. She fired again as the thrashing through the underbrush grew. Another boar lay lifeless at their horses' hooves. She let loose a third arrow and dropped a third hairy beast, but laid a stilling hand on Edmund's unfired arrow as Eric burst through the trees. The group veered off in every direction to keep from colliding with the crown prince and a small herd of squealing shotes fled between the horses' legs, startling them and setting the lot of them to neighing their disapproval and stomping their hooves.

Calm restored as Ri eyed the three fallen prey and looked back to her. "I might have guessed we would do all the work, for you to garner all the glory." He smiled, his tone light and playful, but Aria heard only the barb.

"Have no fear, brother. Prince Wyatt brought down his first hart. The glory will not be visited on me this day."

Ri frowned and opened his mouth, but Wyatt joined them with great shouts of triumph and all attention turned from her. She turned and rode back alone.

Chapter 71

Again Ri found Aria atop the battlements. She could find little peace from him. He stood beside her for some time, charging the air with his tension.

"So, brother, what shame did you rent of my honor on your way back?"

A heavy sigh tore through him and his head hung low. "I swear, by all that is holy, Ari, I did naught but praise you."

She snorted and turned to look out on the mountains again.

He grabbed her hand drawing her back. "Can you ever forgive me, Aria?" His eyes pleaded—clearly filled with the guilt drowning him.

Wild emotions of fear and hate warred within her, like giant dragons vying for the territory of her heart. "Why? What evil have you done me lately?"

"All your life I have played the role of the jealous brother. I have caused you such pain and not until this day have I known the damage I wrought on your dear spirit. Forgive me."

She jerked free and stepped back. "What are you planning?" She trembled as terror consumed her. "Never have you treated me with such kindness without next smashing me on the rocks of my pride."

"Oh, Ari, we have not fought side by side for near eight years …"

"Aye, you refused to fight beside such an unskilled warrior as I."

"This is what you think? You believe yourself so unskilled I did not want you with me?" He groaned and drew near again, pain pooling tears in his eyes. "Nay, dear sister, I did not fear your lack of skill but my own. This is what I wished to hide."

She snorted again. "You possessed enough skill to knock me flat before our people more than once."

"Only out of fear of you doing the same. Aria, from the day you picked up the bow and I saw you fight that bear, I knew you were far beyond my skill." A wry smile lay on his face, twisted by his guilt. "Five years your senior and your skill dwarfed mine by such a wide berth I could not contain my resentment of what God so clearly gave to you. In only a matter of weeks after taking up the blades, you surpassed all our warriors. I feared you would see my lack and look with disdain on me—that everyone would. Forgive me."

She stared at him and waited.

A huff roared through him as he straightened his shoulders, and anger colored his tone when he spoke again. "Tell me how you suffered the wound which left your thigh with such a hideous scar?"

There lay the barb. "Well I know the story, brother. I went off without your permission. I charged headlong and willfully into battle and suffered for my own stupidity."

He shook his head and barked, his finger pointing at the hidden disfigurement. "No, I did that! My jealousy all but got you killed."

She could not believe him.

"You offered a good and sound plan, but I could not hear it because it came from your lips. From any other I would have welcomed it, but I could not accept it from my little sister. You charged into battle sure of it nonetheless and our battalion rushed to join you. I hated knowing they wanted to follow you into battle over me. I pulled in front of them and halted their advance with the threat of charging them with mutiny. Like King David, I pulled them back from aiding you. I left you unprotected to be crushed by the horde.

What kind of brother does such an evil thing?"

He spun from her, raking his hands through his hair and mussing his knot. He turned back, his voice low and burdened. "Even without us you cut down more that day than I did all season. Your blades flew and near shimmered with an inner light of God's own pleasure. A mounted enemy charged at you from the side—but I did naught. He raised his blade to kill you—and I stood silent. You cut him down but not before he laid your leg open. It did naught to stop your forward progress—not until you lost enough blood. I watched you slide from your saddle and as I rode out to find you, I believed you dead."

A single tear rolled down his cheek and Aria's heart wanted to believe his plea.

"Do you remember what you said to me when I came to you?"

She shook her head.

"You begged me to forgive you. You told me how much you loved me and how you only wanted to make me proud. You asked for so little and I gave you naught but pain. That same day I told Father, when you were healed, you should lead your own force. I did not want to fight beside you again for fear I would again put your life in danger out of my pettiness. I swore I would never seek your harm again."

A smile filled his face. "Oh, but dear sister, I came each night to the campfires with eagerness to hear of your victories and your amazing skill. I took great joy in your success and I said with all pride those things were done by *my* sister. You are the best of us, and I know it will only be by your hand any victory for our people is ever won."

She swayed under his words, her thoughts conflicted within her. "No, God alone will save."

"But He will use your hand."

She shook her head.

Ri stepped forward and snatched up her hand once more. "You

must believe. If you do not accept as true your own destiny, you will fall, and I will not lose you, Aria."

She pulled free. "I am one among many, naught special—"

"You are God's chosen deliverer," he announced, grabbing her above the elbow. "I will show you. You must believe."

He pulled her to the nearby tower and down the stairs. She struggled against him. "What are you doing? Ri stop, you are hurting me."

"I will not see you die for my sins. You will know who you are!"

He pulled her into a large expanse in the ward between the halls and the inner wall. A violent quake raged through her as she remained held fast in his firm grasp. Scanning the open space, he spotted Lindsay going to the well. "Lindsay, fetch your lady's blades at once."

Terror seized her as his loud shout turned all the heads in the ward. "Please, brother," she said in a near whisper. "I beg you, whatever you aim to do to me, do not. I am sorry for speaking so to you, my lord. Please do not shame me in front of all."

He turned on her, fresh pain etching his face to a harshness she did not recognize. "You are our deliverer, Athaleyah. I will prove it to you —and all here."

Her knees threatened to collapse and she grabbed in desperation at his tunic. Her heart thundered in her ears so loud she could scarce hear her own words. "Please, Ri, please do not do this to me."

He took her blades from Lindsay with a tight smile and thrust them at her. "Prepare!"

She held up her quaking hands in surrender and would not take them, "Please, Ri." Tears burned her throat and wet her cheeks.

He handed her swords back to Lindsay. "Prepare the lady." When she hesitated, Ri placed a hand on the girl's shoulder. "If she does not believe she is who God has called her to be, we will lose her in the battle, child. If you love her, do as I ask and put her swords on her. She must believe."

Lindsay did as he bid her, though Aria cried and begged all the more.

The sound of shouting in the ward outside his study window drew Edmund from his work. He brushed the vellum aside and stepped to the glass to see what caused the commotion. Seeing Raleigh holding Aria as she cried, Edmund moved outside with quick strides.

Aria stood between Weldon and Cenward their blades drawn and ready to strike as Lindsay knelt to finish securing the chape around her leg. Aria trembled and her face lay drenched with tears. Edmund made to move towards her as she pleaded with her brother.

"Ri, please, no."

Ri raised his hand toward Edmund and shook his head, preventing him from coming to her aid. To Aria he said, "You will train and you will be prepared and you will acknowledge who you are, Athaleyah. Now begin." Ri released his grip on Aria's arm.

Both men raised their swords and waited. Aria did not move. Her head dropped low.

"Athaleyah! Train!"

She cringed at his sharp bark, but inched her swords from their home. Her hands shook so it looked as though she would drop them in the dust. Edmund had never seen the lady show the least amount of fear, and here she quaked like an inexperienced child."

Lindsay came to stand by him and slipped her hand in his. It trembled and she too bore the wet trails of her fear on her face.

"Athaleyah! Begin now!"

"Why does he keep calling Lady Aria that name?" Lindsay asked without taking her eyes from her lady. Wyatt came and joined them as all in the castle gathered around to watch.

Ri did not turn, but called back over his shoulder. "Mother named her Aria—'Gentle Music,' but after her vision and when Father saw her skill for battle, he took to calling her Athaleyah—it is Hebrew for 'Lioness of God.'"

Edmund watched as Aria took her position of her first form—something he had observed her do without understanding many times. Now with her opponents in place all became clear.

Eyes closed, she and bent reached for the ground. Her blades hovered over the dust as her right foot rose in the air. As she swiveled back—with slow purpose—to an upright position, her blades stretched out and came a hair from severing the flesh behind Cenwards calves. She slashed near the muscles above his knees, ruffling the fabric of his breeches but not cutting it. She sliced at his gut and feigned the cut, which would have robbed an enemy of his head.

At the same time she offered offense before her, her defense kicked out her leg on its descent, targeting her rear opponent in the head, stomach, groin, side of the knee and shin. With the other two men there to receive her mock blows, her movements made perfect sense.

"Oh," both Wyatt and Lindsay said, as they too understood her odd formation for the first time.

Aria straightened and moved to the next of her forms. Weldon lashed out and hit the blade in her left hand. In her trembling, she lost her hold on the weapon and it flipped over the back of her hand. Her wrist whirled and she snatched the blade before it hit the ground—her eyes remained closed.

Edmund felt Lindsay tighten her fearsome grip on his hand.

Ri stood with his arms crossed and barked orders. "You are better than this, Athaleyah! Control. Purpose. Target. Attack. Get it right!"

Soon Aria grew comfortable with the two combatants, so Ri looked away from them to the crowd. He spotted Hawk nearby, pointed at him and motioned for him to join the fight.

Hawk looked to Edmund who gave a weak nod.

Soon Ri waved Eric into the effort with the others.

Aria struggled to tamp down her fear over Ri's true motives in order to still her mind to focus on those assembled against her. Four circled her. Now another joined. Five. He'd never made her face so many alone before. Her heart stuttered in her aching chest. Block, thrust, swing, duck, kick. All became a blur of known movements. Another opponent came and another.

She dared open her eyes for a moment in her shock of Ri's challenge. Honed steel glinted all around her and her heart froze in her chest.

Seven—Lord, help me.

Ri delivered a kick to her backside, shoving her forward into the points of the blade before her.

She snapped her eyes shut as she spun and blocked the weapons, saving herself serious injury. Her composure would not return. The flat of a blade slapped her right arm and another her left thigh. *Lord, help me,* she cried in a panic. *Save Your willing servant to defeat Your enemy.* She forced a deep steadying breath into her lungs. *My blades are wholly Yours, Father. I trust in Your promise.*

Warmth tingled in her core and grew in power. It filled her chest as new strength came to her arms. The warmth ran down their length and flooded her hands. Her blades flew of their own with no conscious thought from her.

A collective gasp surrounded her like a rushing wind and the seven stepped away. No one moved or even breathed. She could have heard a feather light on the ground. A span of many frantic heartbeats passed—nothing. She feared they had all vanished.

She opened her eyes to awe-filled faces and slack jaws, but their gazes all rested on the sword held far above her head or the one poised to swing from behind her back. She brought them before her and saw that they glowed with a fierce holy brilliance. She almost dropped them in her amazement.

Edmund's voice came breathy and soft. "You have done it, my lady. You have found the weapon—God's light."

Ri stepped before her, a smile parting his sweat-drenched lips. "You are Athaleyah, our warrior leader. There is no doubt to any here —but do *you* now believe?"

Her breath raced about her lungs in quick gasps, but after a moment she nodded her head.

"Huzzah!" The shout rang out so loud and sudden she jumped. It echoed in a growing chant, until all broke to ask her how she called forth the light.

She raised her hand. When quiet descended once more, she explained her prayer. All who held a sword closed their eyes and soon holy light surrounded her.

Aria dropped to her knees, exhausted and elated, and raised her empty hands to the heavens. "Thank You, Lord God Almighty, for the favor You have shown Your humble servants this day. May we only ever fight in Your name."

Chapter 72

Lindsay stood in front of Aria as she sat on the edge of her bed. She placed her hands on Aria's shoulders and tried to keep her within its folds. "My lady, you can nay go today. You must rest."

"I need my armor and my clothes."

"Nay. I'll not help you."

"Lindsay, I have not the energy to fight you."

"Thus ya nay have the strength to train the men." The more frustrated Lindsay became the more her proper speech slipped.

"Lindsay …" she sighed and her head hung. "We leave for Wexxton in less than a fortnight. I must train them so they are ready and will not die."

"Ya've been training with the men near a month. Ya rise before the sun, travel down to the camp behind the town and not return till well after the sun sets. Ya sleep little and eat less. Ya're exhausted. Ya can barely hold yar own swords and stand upright. Ya must take a respite. At least one day."

Aria pushed to her feet with some effort. "If you will not help me, I will go without the armor today."

"Fie, ya are a stubborn fool."

"Lindsay!"

"See what yar willfulness is doin'? I never curse. My lady—"

Aria put her hand up. "I will train the men today, and tomorrow. I will rest on the Lord's Day and I will return to train the men again. It must be done. Now, help me or remove yourself from my path."

"There're others to train them—a castle full in fact," Lindsay grumbled as she helped Aria dress.

Lindsay followed her down the stairs and through the deserted hall where they parted ways. Lindsay ran to the kitchen. She snatched up a hunk of cheese and a warm loaf of bread and raced to meet Aria before she rode out. She stood in front of the tall gray horse, fighting her own fear, and handed the food to Aria.

Aria took it and waited for Lindsay to move.

"I'm comin' today," She fought to keep the tremor out of her voice.

"It is a long walk down the hill. The wagon will come down after the others have broken the fast."

"Nay, I go with you." Lindsay struggled with which she feared more—Aria's safety or riding a horse. She took a deep breath and raised a hand to have Aria pull her up into the saddle. Aria did not. "I'm goin' with ya, my lady, so if ya wish to move forward, ya must help me up."

Soon she sat behind her lady, clinging to Aria's waist. Their progress was slow, and Lindsay wondered if Aria slept for short spells as the horse trudged down the well-known path to the army's camp.

By midmorning, Lindsay stood on the bottom rail of a simple enclosure were Aria trained each man one-on-one. Her arms lay crossed on the top rail and she set her chin on top of them, watching Aria with a growing fear. Knights and men-at-arms milled around but they took no notice of a small maid. The last of the warriors had arrived earlier in the week and as with all the others, once their tents were set, they trained, honing their old skills into battle readiness. Each new group started with Prince Eric and Sir Preston, moved to

King Edmund and Sir Hawkins and on to Prince Raleigh and Sirs Cenward and Weldon. When the men finished there, they came to Aria and she completed their training.

A hand pressed to the small of her back and Lindsay looked up to see Prince Raleigh standing beside her. She tried to step down to curtsy, but the prince held her still. He leaned down, resting his arm on the rail on her other side trapping her.

"How is she this morn?"

"Exhausted, Highness. She cannot even hold her blades. Can you not speak to her?"

His frown deepened. "Oh aye, I can talk, but I can nay make her listen. I have succeeded in making her believe she is God's instrument only to also convince her she is His *only* warrior." He shook his head and looked to Lindsay. "You are down here early this morning, little one."

"I made her bring me. I worry, sir."

He smiled. "When I first learned a girl attended Aria, I was upset. We do not have such luxuries at home, but my misgivings were unfounded, Mistress Lindsay. You care for her in a way she has allowed few others ever to do. She is better for having you in her life." He kissed the top of her head. "You were brave to overcome your fear to be with her. Stay close, for you may be the only one to save her from herself." Raleigh walked off to see to his own trainees.

Lindsay stayed on the railing, cajoling Aria to eat and drink any time she did not face another sparring opponent. By midday, as others took a break for a meal, Aria swayed on her feet.

"Please, my lady, come sit, eat and rest."

Aria waved her off. "You have made sure I ate all day, child. I have too many to train."

"Ya've but nibbled. Everyone else is taking a rest—"

"Everyone else does not have the fate of these men's lives on their shoulders. I must see they are well prepared so they will not die."

Lindsay huffed and muttered under her breath, "Their fate is in God's hands no matter what ya do. And ya are bent on dying before ya even get to the battlefield."

Aria turned and looked at her, puzzlement twisting her features, "What did you—?"

"Greetings," a lanky youth stumbled into the training ring.

Lindsay could not see what he tripped over, and after a few more awkward steps she realized he struggled with his own gangly limbs. Her stomach knotted and she gripped the railing harder.

Aria sighed, "Greetings, young knight."

"Oh, I am not a knight yet, my lady, but I hope to be one by the end of the season." His eagerness made him pace eradically around the ring and a huge smile filled his face.

Aria raised a hand at him as his sword waved unsteadily before her. "I think it wisest …"

"Brandon, my lady."

"Aye, I think it wisest, Brandon, for us to work with the wasters first. No need to suffer injury before we even leave camp." She handed him the practice weapon and he circled her, holding it with both hands.

Lindsay's heart pounded.

Aria ducked a few wild swings. "Brandon, have you spent time with his Highness Eric and Sir Preston?"

"Nay, everyone says you're the best, and I want to be trained by none other."

Aria lowered her sword and Lindsay's heart stopped. "Brandon, there is a proper—"

THWACK!

The hollow sound of the wooden sword making contact with Aria's head was deafening. "Aria!" Linday scrambled over the railing.

Aria dropped to her knees.

"Aria!" Lindsay jumped into the corral and pushed Brandon out of her way.

Aria fell to her side, angry red blood streaming from her left temple.

"Aria! My lady!" Lindsay cried, pulling Aria's head into her lap. She pressed a wad of her kirtle's hem to the spot.

"I…I'm so sorry," Brandon stammered.

Men gathered at Lindsay's cries. The training area came to life with their shouted orders and Raleigh knelt beside her. Lindsay started to move away but he held her hand firm to Aria's head, "Nay Lindsay, you are doing what she needs. Continue to staunch the flow. It will help." He looked to the man trembling in the corner and back to Lindsay. "What happened?"

"He wants to be a knight. In his eagerness, he came to the lady first." She leaned over Aria and whispered. "He is not the least bit skilled. The lady made him use a waster—thank the Lord above. But she dropped her sword to instruct him back to Prince Eric and Sir Preston. He swung and she was too tired to react fast enough." She looked down at Aria's still, pale face. "Will she be all right, sir?"

He brushed her arm. "She will recover. She is strong and stubborn, remember." He stood and moved toward Brandon, who cowered from him.

"I am sorry, sir, I—"

"Your only fault is in your eagerness. But she is too exhausted to be here. She will bear the burden of the injury, not you. Now, go get something to eat and meet with Prince Eric and Sir Preston to proceed as all the others in a proper order."

"Yes, sir. Thank you, sir." Brandon bowed and hurried off.

Tinsley arrived in the small wagon from the castle. Aria did not wake or make a sound as they moved her, but the blood had slowed.

Lindsay rode cradling her head all the way to the healer's home.

Chapter 73

Edmund entered Tinsley's healing room and found Lindsay kneeling next to Aria's cot, her head resting on her arms near Aria's side. Lindsay's hand held Aria's in a tight embrace. He brushed her head and the girl looked up at him. Her eyes, red and puffy, held his gaze with a silent plea. Edmund sat on the stool beside the bed and reached out his arms.

Lindsay stood and fell into his embrace, wrapping her trembling arms around his neck, burying her face in his shoulder. She stood between his knees, as he pulled her close and kissed the side of her head.

"Shh, daughter, our lady will recover."

"But Sir Tinsley says she should've awakened long ago. A concussion should nay be so deep unless there is a more serious injury like softening of the brain."

Edmund stroked her hair and marveled at how grown up she sounded. "Do not worry, Lindsay. You said yourself, the lady has not slept of late. God has seen to it she gets the rest required, so she can fight in the coming battle." Lindsay trembled more. "Aria will be fine. We will pray, but the doctor is sure she will be awake by morn." Edmund pulled her away and held her hands. "Why not go and get some rest yourself? She will need you in the days to come."

Lindsay shook her head. "I'll nay leave her, Majesty."

"You are dear, Lindsay." He smiled and brushed her tear away with his thumb. "I planned to tell you this before we left, when Aria would hear, but I think you need to know now."

She looked into his eyes and her lower lip disappeared between her teeth.

"Oh, do not fret, 'tis good news. At least, I hope you will think 'tis good." He allowed his glance to wash over her sweet face for a moment longer. "Lindsay, I want you always here with me. I have come to love you as a daughter. It is not permissible by Veronian law to make you an heir to the king." He sighed with a slim grin. "After my father's father took in a wild child and he almost became king, the lords of the land made King Edgar write a law declaring only blood could be heirs. But I can make you my ward, daughter."

Lindsay tipped her head and her brows drew together.

"You will live in the castle, in your own room with your own servants and ladies-in-waiting to attend you. You will receive the finest education and be raised like Wyatt as his near-sister. When the time comes, I will find a good match for you among the noblemen of the land."

Her head dropped.

"Lindsay, you will live like a princess and never want for anything."

"I only want to be with Lady Aria," she whimpered.

Edmund chuckled and pulled her back into a hug, again kissing her head. "If our Lord answers my prayers, she will be here too. I will seek her hand from her father King Maddix after the battle. Lord willing, she will return and be your mother by my side."

Lindsay relaxed into his embrace and soon she grew heavy with sleep. Careful not to wake her, he pulled her into his arms and cradled her to his chest. Her head rested on his shoulder and he kissed her forehead. "Rest, daughter of my heart. I will watch over our lady for a time. The rising sun will see a new day with new promise—Lord, I pray these words hold true."

Throbbing, unrelenting pain assaulted Aria's muddled awareness. She moaned and it thundered in her own ears, adding to her pain. The small hand holding hers tightened.

"My lady?"

The words burst in Aria's skull like a battle-ax. She groaned again and her stomach revolted. Turning away from Lindsay on the small pallet, Aria wretched.

A hand rested on her shoulder, "My lady?"

The violent action and cacophony of noise rent her stomach once more. It held little to expel, but the traitorous organ within would not be still. She heaved in quick succession over the side of her slender bed. Hot tears burned her eyes. Lindsay withdrew her hands.

Footfalls stomped from the room only to return moments later. A torrent of rushing water assaulted her ears and a cool cloth wiped at her mouth. Lindsay rinsed the bit of fabric in a bucket and caressed it over Aria's entire face.

The cool cloth soothed, caused her stomach to relent, and she lay back again. She took a few slow breaths, fighting to think, but new heavy steps thundered into the room and the resulting pain threatened to reignite her stomach.

"Lady Aria, can you open your eyes?" The voice boomed, causing her to grip her head and whimper. "Please, my lady," Tinsley whined softer.

She dared crack one clenched eyelid, only to be assaulted by light from a nearby window. Turning from it in pain, her gaze landed on a candle burning with the intensity of the sun. She covered her eyes with her hands and moaned. Aria heard Lindsay moving around and Tinsley pulled her hands from her face.

"We have covered the light, my lady."

She managed to half open her eyes. Tinsley opened each further and stared into them. He patted her on the shoulder, and stood, turning to the shelf filled with corked jars behind him. He took several down and placed them on a table at the foot of her bed, and waved Lindsay to come to him.

"Here child, have the lady chew these juniper seeds and drink a little of this wine." He handed her the ingredients. "It will help with the pain while I mix a tonic made of ginger and mint—to sooth her stomach, great mullein and lovage—to help with the pain, and a little papaver rhoeas to help her sleep. I will also make her a new ointment of marigold for her wound."

Aria knew Tinsley recited the list of ingredients for her benefit, and not Lindsay's. She might have protested if she possessed the strength to draw the complaint into her lungs. Instead, she lay like a helpless child and allowed Lindsay to raise her head. She chewed a few of the hard, light-colored seeds, their strong taste stirring her stomach once again. The thin white wine trickled over her lips and added to the tumult of her belly.

Tinsley came to her with a small brown earthenware jar and raised it to her lips. He mixed the concoction of herbs with honey water to help it go down but Aria still coughed and sputtered at the horrid mix of tastes. The reaction renewed the agony of her head and she pushed him out of the way to wretch in the bucket Lindsay had placed beside her cot.

Lindsay wiped her mouth and Tinsley tried again. "Take slow sips, my lady, a drop at a time. It will help."

Aria struggled to get the vile potion down and keep it there. Soon the blessed oblivion of dark and nothingness engulfed her again.

Four days passed as Aria drifted in and out of her fitful pain-filled sleep under Lindsay's steadfast watch. Lindsay now slept on a cot of her own by Aria's side in the healer's room. Aria needed constant monitoring for anytime she woke, she tried to rise and return to her self-assigned duties. Lord Raleigh looked in on her and assured her all the army's needs were being seen to in adequate measure. When she continued to fuss, Lord Raleigh picked Lindsay up and set her on Aria's chest.

"Do whatever you must, Mistress Lindsay, to keep our lady on her cot," he told her with a wagging finger.

When Aria relented, she slid off. As the lord left, Aria stared at her. "Mistress Lindsay?" she whispered.

"Aye, my lady." Lindsay lowered her head and would not meet the lady's eyes. "King Edmund has made me his ward."

Aria sighed and her body sank back into her cot. She reached for Lindsay's hand. "Thank the Lord above for the favor you have found with a man after God's own heart, child. I could not do better for you. God Himself rewards you for the kindnesses you have shown me."

"I wish to be with you," Lindsay choked on the words as they burned her throat.

Aria turned her gaze. Lindsay found herself caught in it. "Do not wish the hell of battle and death upon yourself when God has chosen to bless you richly, Lindsay. It makes you ungrateful to both your kings."

Lindsay attempted a nod and curled beside Aria on her cot. She felt Aria's body become stiff but Lindsay would not be parted from her—not until God tore Aria from her arms.

Aria stood in the ward. As she watched servants, men-at-arms and knights move about, it stirred the dizziness again.

"My lady, how fare you this day?" Edmund asked as he dropped from his saddle a pace away.

She struggled to curtsy on unsteady legs and looked out the open inner gate as she answered. "Fine, Majesty."

"Lindsay says you still fight the dizziness, sour stomach, and headaches."

"Lindsay speaks too much, Sire. I am fine."

He laid his hand on her arm. "Lindsay is intelligent beyond her years and she would nay lie." His face lay marred by a deep scowl.

"In truth it matters nay how I feel, Sire, for I will be on a horse with your army on the morrow as we begin our journey back to my homeland."

"As you have said for the near two weeks since your injury. Are you sure you are ready to fight?"

"The march to the heart of Wexxton should take about a fortnight. I will continue to heal on the way."

"Lord willing," Edmund muttered.

Aria nodded and walked with him into the hall for the evening meal. She sat beside Lady Raven, who had returned days after her accident. But even her friend could not comfort her. Aria ate little as her stomach would not contend to hold anything within it. When she retired early, Lindsay followed her and helped her undress.

"Tomorrow these chambers will be yours and Zanna will move to the pallet in the outer chamber to attend you, Mistress Lindsay." Aria tried to sound cheerful. "Lady Raven will also see to your welfare until King Edmund returns."

Lindsay did not speak. Her mouth lay set in a hard line, her eyes clouded by a steeled determination.

"I will pray for your best and your happiness as long as I take breath," Aria offered.

Lindsay picked up the hairbrush and stroked it through Aria's hair with great care.

"Will you not speak to me, Lindsay?"

"You know my heart, my lady, and care nay for what will make me happy."

Aria swung the girl in front of her, aggravating both her headache and the incessant dizziness. "It will not make you happy to watch me die, Lindsay. I know. I saw my mother cut down in battle and I do not wish you to remember me the same way. And you know too the pain of watching your own mother die."

Lindsay remained stiff and stoic before her.

Aria fought a tear, stirred by the frailty of her injured body. "You therefore intend to punish me by leaving me with a final memory of you like this—angry with me. Where is the girl who has filled my sojourn here in a foreign land with wonder and joy? Can you not do me this last kindness, Lindsay?"

Lindsay's expression did not change, but a lone tear trickled down her cheek. "You have all my love. My heart will never be the same. I can nay do more." She set the brush on the bedside table and fled the room.

Chapter 74

Unable to find Lindsay the next morn, Aria dressed alone. She now waited beside her horse as the final matters were seen to.

"I thought Wyatt and Lindsay would be here to bid us farewell," Edmund said as he led his horse beside hers.

"They are furious with me, and will not do me the honor." The words caught in her throat and stung her eyes.

"Lord willing, we will return victorious before the summer solstice. They can make amends upon our return."

Aria turned from him and hid on the far side of her mount. She fought the welling tears, knowing if they started she would never be able to contain them. Her heart called to the absent girl. *My heart will never be the same either, child. How I have loved you when I never wished to, and how you have added to my pain now.*

"Shall we mount and join the troops?" Ri called as he walked past.

"Aye," several around her answered. She stuffed her threatening emotions down and struggled into her saddle. As her horse shifted under her weight, queasiness gripped her stomach. *This is going to be an arduous journey, Lord.*

The first week passed accompanied by fair weather. It surrounded the war host in warmth but not undue heat. They made good time traveling near thirty miles each day without over stressing the animals or the men. They lodged with a few lords as they journeyed and collected another one hundred and fifty fighting men, swelling their ranks to over fifteen thousand.

Now two days into Wexxton, the terrain bore the evidence of God's missing presence. The hills were brown from years absent of rain, and the riverbeds lay cracked and desolate. Not a bird could be heard and not a green thing grew in her land. The progress slowed as their mood darkened with the surrounding terrain. Amiable chatter dried up like the parched dirt.

As she plodded along in near silence, Aria again set her heart to prayer. *Lord God, I have come home to again see a land without Your favor. I have journeyed far and I have trained as You directed. I discovered the weapon of Your own presence in our weapons and I have taught all who carry You in their heart to wield it. Yet still I suffer with the pain in my head and constant dizziness. How can I hope to win the victory in Your name when the least movement threatens to make me wretch?*

As with every day on her journey, no answer came. The sweet warmth of her Father's presence did not fill her. She fell deeper into her despondency and cried out, *Father, will You not help me?*

Silence answered.

"A large pass through a dark valley lies ahead. We should make camp here for the night." Ri said.

Drawn from her painful thoughts, she turned to her brother on her right.

She looked ahead. "Aye, the Valley of Woe is no place to be caught at night."

"Valley of Woe?" several voices behind her questioned.

"It served as the first foothold and the favored place of the horde to attack travelers, seeing as it is the only pass to escape to the eastern lands," she said.

"There are too many niches and holes for them to hide in," Ri added.

"Sounds dangerous even in the light," Edmund countered as he gave his captain the signal to sound the call to camp.

"It is," Ri consented as Aria cringe at the trumpet blast.

She waved off his concern, stepped her horse a little away from the rest, dropped to the ground, and wretched.

She joined Edmund, Eric, Hawk, Preston, Ri, Cenward and Weldon as they sat around a fire and ate. Father James left earlier to cover all in prayers. The captain, commanders and lords sat round fires, encircling them and the body of the troops camped beyond the reach of their fire's light. Somewhere among those gathered were wagons full of provisions for both man and beast in this barren land.

Aria sipped sweet mead and nibbled a small biscuit. She thought to retire to her tent early this evening and hoped with a bit of Tinsley's tonic to see a better morrow. A movement caught her attention first and she looked past the fire to the priest's return. He stood tall and rigid, arms behind his back and a scowl deep on his face.

"Your Majesty, I have something of great concern to report." The words ground through his teeth.

Edmund sat straighter. "Aye, Father?"

"I have discovered some who have snuck into the wagons to accompany us on this dangerous venture."

Aria's heart stopped and she felt she would wretch again.

Father James drew out his arms to either side, an offender's ear held tight in each hand.

"Fie! Wyatt, Lindsay, what—by all that is holy—are you doing here?" Edmund sputtered as he leapt to his feet.

Lindsay pulled from the father's punishing hold and dropped to her knees. "Forgive me, Majesty, I could not bear to be parted from my lady. It proved too much for me and I came to see her through. The fault does not lie with your son, Sire, Prince Wyatt only came to see to my safety. The blame is mine and mine alone." She drew in a stuttered breath. "If ya no longer want me as part of yar household, I understand, Majesty."

Edmund raked his hand through his hair and worked at the knot in his neck as he paced. "If Wyatt were truly concerned for your welfare, daughter, he would have prevented you from coming at all."

"He could not, for my heart was set."

"We will have to send them home, it is too dangerous—"

"Nay, Edmund." Ri interrupted.

"Nay, we are all in danger even in this large number. We would too greatly deplete our forces in seeing them well guarded and it would still be unlikely they would reach Veronia alive," Aria groaned. "As much as I abhor the thought," she glared at them both, "they will be safer with us."

"And what are we to do with two children in a military campaign?"

"Majesty, there is good news. Both children have been assisting the women seeing to the supplies and the preparation of food. They have been naught but helpful, I am told," Father James conceded.

Edmund looked to Aria and she nodded. "You will continue to work and help wherever you are needed."

"Yes, Your Majesty."

"Aye, Father. We will nay be in your way and we will cause no further trouble." Wyatt glanced up at his father, brows raised. "We left a note on the altar so everyone in the castle knows where we have gone. I made sure we did not cause any worry, but I would not allow Lindsay to travel alone."

"I did not find any such note on the altar before I left," Father James said. "And as Father Peter was not due to arrive until the Lord's Day for services, he would not have seen it until a few days ago."

Wyatt's head dropped. "Forgive me."

"Wyatt, you have acted with childish rashness and caused a great deal of worry to both those left behind, and those gathered around this fire. I pray you are both ready to face the consequences your action will wreak on your tender hearts in the days to come." He groaned and waved out a hand to his son. "Come, Wyatt, you will sleep in my tent tonight, where we can discuss the matter further."

Wyatt walked behind Father James and Lindsay, squeezing her shoulder with tenderness as he passed. She remained on her knees and slipped her head up only enough to glimpse Aria.

Aria waved her over as well, stood and led the way into her tent.

Inside, Lindsay again fell to her knees and she cried in her distress. "I know ya're angry, but I could nay stay. If ya have but days to live I want to spend them with ya. I love you, Aria—no matter how you hate it—I love you with all my heart."

Aria sat on her cot and pulled the child up into her arms. "I do not hate your love, Lindsay. I wished only to save you the pain of losing another to whom you were so attached. I am grateful to you in so many ways, but you have now added to my pain as well. My thoughts, already impaired by the throbbing still ravaging my mind, will now be further distracted by worries of your safety and the horrors you will soon be forced to bear witness to."

"I would endure any pain to be with you even one more hour."

Lindsay cried for a time before she helped Aria out of her armor. She lay in only her chemise and battle skirt, listening until Lindsay's breath became slow and steady. Aria rose and slipped from the tent. She walked to the outer ring, stopped between two sentries and knelt in the dirt to pray.

Father it is me, Your daughter. I do not understand Your ways and come seeking Your guidance."

Silence louder than a twisting wind assaulted her.

Will You not help me, Father?

A breeze stirred the dust and she sneezed. It brushed her cheek and she felt the familiar warmth. *I did not think you wanted My assistance, child.*

Aria's heart seized. Of course she needed the Lord's assistance. It would be foolish to move without Him. A torrent of thoughts assailed her. She fell prostrate, resting her aching head on the back of her hands. *Oh, Father, forgive me. How many times must I learn this lesson? I am only Your instrument and I can do naught without You. I have been striving in my own strength, but victory will be found in You alone. I did not find the weapon—You gave it to me. I have not trained the men—You have prepared them. I worked until I made myself sick and still would not trust You to handle Your own affairs. You caused me to be injured to get me out of Your way. Oh, Father, I am a fool, so full of pride I could not hear the plan You wanted.*

Tears wet her hand as she released the emotions she could no longer contain. Sobs consumed her and much time passed before she could form a coherent thought again.

"I am Yours to wield, if I can still be of any use to You, Father. I am Yours."

You are ready to give me everything you are, daughter?

"Speak, Father, for Your servant is finally listening."

Chapter 75

Edmund glanced around at the nearly dismantled camp. Aria could not be found all morning and Edmund had sent Hawk to look for her. His thane returned a short time ago without her. He finished overseeing the saddling of the horses as Ri approached, pointing over his shoulder.

"Brother, call your commanders and lords, our lady has received a vision from God."

Edmund turned to see Aria approaching. The pain which had consumed her was now replaced by a visible peace. Her steps, confident and controlled, were highlighted by a contented smile. Her red unbound hair blew in the wind of her movement, framing her like a radiant halo. As she drew nearer, Edmund saw that her eyes danced with a glow similar to the light that filled their blades with the Spirit's presence.

She knelt in the dust and picked up a stick as the men circled around her. "The battle will begin in two morns in Rising Meadow."

"Rising Meadow is a three days march away," Weldon countered.

"The Lord has told us we must hurry, but He will sustain us on our journey. This is how the Lord says we will find our victory in Him."

She scribbled out her instructions, the the large war host made haste to divide into three parts and they were on the road within a quarter hour.

Atop the hill at one end of Rising Meadow, King Maddix looked down on the gathered horde below. The evil-infested bodies, shriveled and blackened, formed lose ranks of naked men. The sun had been risen for more than an hour, yet they made no advance. They waited for something.

Maddix stood apart from his small remaining band of warriors. Today would see the end, he knew. Either God Almighty would grant them some unlikely miracle or their blood would fill the soil of the only patch of green still left in the land. At least if they died they would find themselves free of the pain of this life and in the Almighty's presence.

"Maddix, what are you doing sulking over here? Your warriors need your words of encouragement and hope," his brother scolded.

"I have no such word today, Firth."

Firth punched him in the arm. "Trust in the Lord."

"Have you seen what lies below us, brother? We are outnumbered near ten to one."

"God gave Gideon and Jonathan victory when greatly outnumbered. Take heart."

"Our best warrior ran off to find a fabled weapon, and my strong right arm with her. My heart left with them and I have no words to offer. The only one left to me is my daughter-in-law and she is holed up in the castle with her young son. A child Raleigh never met. You see to the warriors' needs. I cannot."

"Your children are in God's hands as they always have been, Maddix." Firth's words were becoming more pleading.

Maddix gripped his hands behind his back. "A scout arrived yesterday to report enemy warriors in equal number coming from behind to encircle us. I have no hope of walking off this field today."

"Fie, Maddix. I expected more from a man of God."

"God has abandoned—"

A flash of light passed between the two men. Maddix followed it and found a glowing arrow imbedded in the chest of one of the horde as he stood with his blade raised. The arrow shimmered bright and the creature howled and evaporated in a puff of dust. A second glowing arrow sailed into another approaching blackened creature and it too vanished with naught more than a fallen blade to mark its passing.

Maddix scanned the surrounding hillside and, seeing no others creeping near, turned to the source of the arrows. He saw a young boy standing with an arrow notched and drawn. He couldn't have been more than eleven or twelve and his curly blond locks looked like writhing snakes in the sun. Beside him stood another youth in similar plain tunic and breeches but the hair hung longer and the face held a softness about it—a girl. Her wide, horror-filled eyes stared back at him as she worried her bottom lip.

A moment later, a brown-robed priest stepped behind the children, huffing for breath. When was the last time Maddix had seen a holy man dressed in proper robes? It made them a target for the horde and the few men among his people who still possessed a little knowledge of Scripture dressed like everyone else for their own safety.

As Maddix considered the strangers, Weldon rode over the rise. He leapt from his horse and took a knee before his king. "King Maddix, I have returned to you. Where may I be of service?"

"Weldon? Where did you—How did you get through the approaching horde behind us? Where have you come from?" A myriad of questions assaulted Maddix's tongue all at once.

Weldon stood, a smile nearly splitting his face in two. "Nay, Sire, those who approached from the west are not the horde, but the mighty war host of all Veronia and Balmore under the banner of our Athaleyah."

Maddix grabbed for his brother's arm to steady himself. "Aria still lives?"

"She is well, we all are—save Dunham, the Lord bless him." Weldon turned and spoke, pointing to the battlefield below. Lady Aria with Cenward and Sir Hawkins, the king's elder son Prince Eric, and their warriors are in the trees to the north, all the way to the far end near the great Merciful River. In the tree line to the south, assembles Prince Raleigh, King Edmund, and Sir Preston with their warriors. The enemy thinks we are outnumbered, but they are surrounded with no hope of escape. The Lord Himself gave our Athaleyah a vision of the victory, Sire. It is all in God's hands now."

"If Aria and Raleigh returned with a war host could they not find the weapon?"

It looked as though Weldon's smile grew. "Nay, our Lioness of God found the weapon and we all wield it now."

"All?" Maddix struggled to comprehend the wonder of the report.

"Aye," Weldon turned and led the king over to the children and the priest. "It is a power borne of God, Sire and even the surrendered heart of a child can wield it. My lord king, this is Prince Wyatt, King Edmund's younger son." He turned to the girl. "The king's ward and dear friend of Lady Aria, Mistress Lindsay, and the king's personal priest, Father James."

Each gave him a deep observance. "You can all brandish this weapon of God?" he asked again.

Weldon spoke. "It is God's own light, Sire. Here, let us move from the sight of our enemy gathered below and I will demonstrate."

Weldon led the king away and Lindsay fought to breathe as she tugged on the priest's robe. "Father?" she stammered.

Father James stood with his hand clasped over the large carved cross hanging around his neck, his lips moving without sound.

Lindsay pulled harder. "Father? Father?"

"Shush, child, I am praying."

Lindsay grew desperate and yanked with all her might on the priest and screamed his name. "Father James!"

He scowled on her.

"Father, it is not true, is it?"

"What, child?"

"Lady Aria is not below ready to charge into battle? She is coming here first. Tell me, Father, she is not down there." Lindsay pointed and shuddered at the creatures gnarling below.

The priest rested a hand on her shoulder. "You knew she came to join the battle, child. Where else did you think she would be now?"

Lindsay dropped to her knees. "You do not understand, Father. Aria left the tent two nights ago and did not return. I was ordered to pack her belongings in a wagon and was told she would come for them soon. She has not. Father, I have her armor and her blades. She goes into battle with naught to protect her." Lindsay let the tears come.

"Child, she travels with many warriors. They have provided for her need, I am sure."

Wyatt pulled her to her feet and held her tight. "God will protect her as He always has, sister." He brushed away her tears. "Now, let us find a place out of the way to see what God is going to do." He took her hand and led her to a flat rock jutting out from the top of the hill. They perched on it and Wyatt put his arm around her. "Trust in the Lord, Lindsay. He will save our lady."

Chapter 76

Aria sat mounted in the shadows of the tall trees that surrounded Edmund's men. The mounted warriors were ahead of those on foot. They would lead the quick and deadly advance when the time came, followed close behind by the men on foot. The Black Knight lay in her sights, framed between two large elms in the center of the field. Today it would all end. Her people would be free and praise God for His hand on them. She knew what it would cost her, but it was a small price to pay for the many she loved.

She again gripped the borrowed long sword as it rested across her lap. After the vision, she'd become so captivated by the Lord's message, she had never claimed her own blades. She also wore no armor, but it did not matter. Her Savior already claimed the victory, now only the battle remained.

The horde shimmered as they moved into tight ranks. Soon—it would begin in a matter of moments. She looked to those around her and raised the heavy blade. They prepared.

A sound grew—only a rumble at first—but it congealed into a wicked laugh. The Black Knight raised a black gauntlet-covered hand over his black helmet, adorned with a long black plum. "Today it ends, king of the Light. Your God has forsaken you, and I will have all."

"'Never will I leave thee nor forsake thee,' declares the Lord God Almighty," Father yelled from far up the hill.

Aria smiled.

Their enemy laughed only a moment more before he roared so the trees around her shuddered. A battle cry rose from the horde and they moved forward as one.

No one around her stirred.

The enemy advanced one foot—two—three. Their leader howled with laughter.

Not a defender breathed.

The horde formations dissolved into a disorganized charge.

Aria leveled her sword on her target and called forth the Spirit to fight through her. When her blade glowed bright, she spurred her horse to speed. She burst from the trees onto the field a heartbeat before those around her. Seconds later, from the far side and back of the field, Edmund's troops emerged and Wexxton's army on the hill descended. None of those with Aria made a sound as they rushed forward and cut down enemy after enemy with the mere touch of their God-filled blades.

Those of the horde in the middle continued forward, momentarily unaware that the defenders were sinking so far into their ranks with their silent attack. Their numbers dwindled in puffs of dust without a cry to warn them.

Aria dispatched any who stood in her path, but she never took her eyes off her prey.

The Black Knight turned to her and roared with the fierceness of the dark beast within him, and the horses shied.

Aria held tight to her mount and set it to charge again. But the enspelled black soldiers were aware of the defenders now. They swiveled their attack on those charging their lines.

The enemy raged.

Men now cried out a battle cry.

Screams of pain. Bellows of anger. Clashing swords and loosed arrows.

Aria's mount, unfamiliar with the horde, jerked and reared. It bucked out, kicking away at those clawing at his flanks.

Arms grabbed at her. With only a single long, heavy blade and no shield, her left side was near defenseless. Her target slipped from her gaze as she fell. A roll and she was on her feet, thrashing out at the shriveled masses clawing at her. A back pressed to hers.

"Oh, but these are vile vermin, m'lady." Hawk gulped air.

"Quickest path to success—dispatch them to hell with all due haste."

"Aye. God be with us."

Ari echoed his quick prayer, as they circled, guarding one another's flank. A slash of a black sword opened her left arm. Hawk bellowed a curse. But the enemies they cut down were replaced by others of their bothers in unending waves.

Claws tore her thigh, and she went down on one knee.

Hawk whirled in front of her, dispatching five before they could lop off her head. "Think you can still flip?" He cut down several others as she rose to her feet. Before she could question, he whirled, clearing a wide circle around him, crouched with his hands cupped together between his knees and nodded over his shoulder with a wink. A small gap free of the horde lay several feet behind him. The Black Knight fought on the other side.

She ran the three steps to Hawk, planted her foot in his palms and he launched her over the tight knot, dispatching many as she flipped and twisted over them. She landed facing her foe in a crouch, took only a blink to gather her energy and launched spinning, kicking, and slashing through the last twenty-five enspelled creatures between her and the Knight.

But her adversary turned from her. The Black Knight would not face her head on. He spurred his enormous black horse away and drew his huge curved and serrated black sword. Not at her. No, he glanced at her for only a moment and aimed it at Edmund.

Aria's heart convulsed. She'd spent her entire life preparing for her own death. But the enemy denied her. She could not bear to watch Edmund fall. Her borrowed sword lost its glow and fell from her hand. The horde surrounded her and she lost sight of Edmund as the Knight swung. He fought unaware of the danger. She tried to yell, but her voice was swallowed in the din of battle.

I must have all of you, daughter. God's whisper touched her above the noise.

You can have every bit of me, but spare him. Please Lord, save Edmund.

Edmund holds your heart and not Me. Am I your only Lord?

She was slammed into the ground.

Lindsay ... Aria's heart moaned. She inhaled her last breath.

All of you. I must be Lord, of all.

The horde fell upon her—teeth and claws bared. Skin tore. Bones broke.

"I am Yours and Yours alone, Lord of Heaven and Earth. 'The LORD is my light and my salvation; whom shall I fear?" Her voice rose as the words fortified her. "The LORD is the strength of my life; of whom shall I be afraid?'"

The horde shrieked at the holy words and fell away.

Warmth filled her body and she rose to her feet. From her fingers sprang the light of God. It forced her mouth open and filled her gaze. She turned on the Black Knight and the light fell on him.

He squirmed and roared, bellowed and moaned. Smoke came from under his black armor and it sagged from his emaciated and ancient horse. The horse's flesh turned to dust and the bones dropped to the ground. They were caught in the breeze and vanished. Only the knight's armor remained. It lay broken and rusted on the soft grass.

Light filled the entire clearing as others abandoned their swords and allowed God to fill them.

The light vanished. Aria's arms dropped to her sides and her head hung as she fought for a deep breath.

A breath.

She still lived.

She scanned the clearing, only Edmund's people and her own remained. The battle was over—the victory complete. And she still drew breath—though now she couldn't breathe. She mounted the nearest horse and fled back into the forest.

Raleigh stood on the rise with his father, as Edmund and Preston joined Hawk and Eric in the center of the field. They greeted one another with a firm hand and turned toward Raleigh who waved them to come.

"As far as any of us can tell, Father, none of our people have fallen," Raleigh was saying as they dismounted.

Edmund and his men bowed and extended a hand of friendship. "'Tis the same among my men, King Maddix. None have fallen. Even the wounds we sustained in the fight vanished with the holy light. The Lord granted you a miraculous victory."

"All praise to our Mighty God!" Maddix raised his fist.

"All praise!" those around answered in return.

Maddix scanned the warriors. "Where is Aria?"

Edmund turned and examined the field, but he could not see her with so many milling about.

"Father." Wyatt's hand filled his.

"Not now Wyatt, we are looking for the Lady Aria. Can you see her?"

"Father, Lindsay knows." Edmund looked down and followed Wyatt's gaze. Lindsay stood at the crest of the rise, tears glistening on her cheeks, pointing into the distance. As he approached, she stood still—as if she were turned to stone.

"Lindsay, did our lady disappear through there?"

She gave a single nod.

Edmund knelt behind her, wrapped his arm around her waist and looked over her shoulder. "There between the crooked oak and the white elm?"

Her head bobbed.

Edmund kissed her. "I will get her and bring her back, daughter. Take heart."

He stood, waved to his men, and mounted.

As they sped away, dodging warriors collecting weapons of the enemy, Maddix moved to follow. Raleigh put a hand on his father's arm.

"Leave them to it. Edmund will nay return till he's found her."

Maddix's brow rose.

"He is in love." Ri pointed at the two children clinging to one another as they watched the men disappear into the trees. "They all are."

"And Aria? How does she feel?"

Raleigh smiled, shaking his head with a shrug. "I think she is now off alone trying to figure the matter out for herself." He draped his arm over his father's shoulders and turned him back to the warriors. "Now, come and meet some of Edmund's men, and tell me do I have another daughter or son?"

Aria broke into a clearing surrounded by thick brush. She dropped from her horse and staggered to a ray of light. She fell to her knees in the glow and raised her hands to the heavens.

"Father, have I displeased You?"

Well done, good and faithful servant.

"But I do not understand. I thought you called me to be a deliverer for my people, like Deborah and Samson.

Your people are free, daughter. They celebrate but a little way off. Can you not hear them sing My praises.

"But Father, I thought …"

Oh, daughter, I need all of who you are. I alone must be Lord in your heart. Your life is My gift to you.

She sat silent and still trying to comprehend.

… Aria? …

How long did Deborah serve Me after I used her to deliver My people?

"Forty years," Aria stammered.

And Samson? How long did he serve Me?

… Aria? …

She dropped back on her heels, her hands falling to her lap. "Twenty, Father."

Yes, daughter.

"Lord what am I to do now? I know only battle."

Do not wish the hell of battle and death upon yourself when I have chosen to bless you richly. It makes you ungrateful to your King.

… Aria? …

Her own words slapped her.

Perhaps now, My child you will accept the blessings I have given you and not push them away in wrath.

"Blessings, Father?"

"Aria!" Edmund's call broke through to her conscious thoughts.

She turned in its direction. He's alive?

Yes, daughter, he is but one of My many blessings.

Edmund broke into the clearing as Aria popped to her feet. Her eyes were as wide as a startled hart's and she trembled. He leapt down and walked toward her.

She did not move but stared as though seeing him for the first time. Her shirt and battle skirt where torn and bloody.

A tear shown on her face, and he could not hold back his hand. He brushed it, expecting her to slap his hand away.

She didn't.

Her breaths where quick and shallow, and her heartbeat pulsed in the curve of her neck. Her lips lay so close. He longed to kiss them. She would not approve, but he eased nearer. Slowly, so she could pull away, he lowered his head.

Still she did not move.

His lips brushed hers.

She raised her hand to his chest, and thinking she would push him away, he straightened.

But her hand filled with his overtunic as her nails and knuckles bumped over the rough mail beneath the cloth. She pulled him closer and kissed him with a hunger.

… Aria? …

He slid his hand from her cheek to the back of her head and her lips opened to him. His other arm encircled her waist.

She pressed close and warmed his flesh even through the cold mail.

… Aria? …

… Aria? …

She wrapped her arms around his neck as she pulled him closer still.

"Aria?"

Edmund pulled from her, gasping for breath, and rested his forehead against hers.

Still they called. Edmund hated to answer, but Hawk and Eric were close. "Here," he gasped.

Aria's cheeks were flushed and tenderness swam in her eyes, but she still did not speak or move.

They called out again. Preston's voice now ringing loud.

Edmund let his hand run along her neck, over her shoulder, and down her arm. He interlaced his fingers in hers and stood beside her. "Here! Hawk, Eric, Pres, we are here."

Brush crashed and soon all three men looked down from atop their horses. Their collective glaze fell to his and Aria's bound hands.

Hawk raised a brow.

"All is well," Edmund breathed deep. "We have found the lady. Let us see her returned."

The men nodded with a growing smirk.

"Are you well, my lady?" Hawk said.

She only nodded.

Edmund looked for her horse and, not seeing it, mounted his own, and reached for her. She gripped his arm and swung up behind him. As they left the clearing, her arms wound around him. She pressed against him and laid her head on his shoulder. He rested one hand over hers and locked their fingers once more.

As they came into the open field, Aria tried to sit up and pull from Edmund, but he held her hand fast. Heat warmed her cheeks at the bemused smiles of those gathered around.

Edmund eased his horse to the middle of the field, turned it to the side so she could see her father, and stopped.

"King Maddix, I have found your precious daughter, but I fear I cannot return her to you."

Father crossed his arms.

"You see, honored King Maddix, Lady Aria has captured my heart, and I beg you for her hand in marriage."

Every voice in the field fell silent. Their mail and armor rattled as they, in unison, turned toward her father.

"If you speak true of loving my beautiful girl, you know well she is firmly possessed of her own mind. I can nay speak for her." He paused and his gaze shifted to her. "What say you, my heart? Do you love this man and accept his claim on your hand?"

Every head swirled back and gazes captured her. They stole the air. She pulled from Edmund to drop on shaking legs. She leaned against the horse and tried to capture her erratic thoughts. *Did she love him?* She remembered the fear as the Black Knight charged toward him—and the despair at thinking him dead. But her heart thundered when she'd heard him call moments ago. *He is for you,* the Lord said. She brushed her trembling fingers over her lips. She could still taste him and feel the warmth of his kiss. Her heart pounded and she dared look up at him.

Locking her in his adoring gaze, he reached out his hand.

She took it and called out, "Yes, Father. I love him. I will accept."

"HAZZAH!"

The sudden, loud shout caused her to fall against his horse.

Edmund dismounted and pulled her into a tight embrace and his lips once again claimed hers.

Their people cheered. "Long live King Edmund. Long live Queen Aria."

She pulled from him and rested her forehead against his, as he had done. "Queen?"

Edmund smiled. "The title comes with the marriage, my love." He kissed her cheek and took her arm to lead her through the throng of well-wishers to her father.

Something collided with her and engulfed her waist in a fearsome embrace. Only Hawk's steadying hand at her back kept her on her feet. The top Lindsay's head alone was visible as she clung to her. Aria pried the child loose and knelt before her.

Lindsay wrapped her arms around Aria's neck. Lindsay buried her face and Aria felt the dampness of her tears on her shoulder. "I am sorry, my lady."

"Whatever for?"

Lindsay pulled away enough to meet Aria's gaze. "I prayed everyday God wouldn't let you die. I didn't want to loose you."

Aria smiled and kissed the precious child's cheek. "And I thank you for it, my dear girl. I am ever grateful our Father listened to your prayers, for in truth, I did not wish to be parted from you either."

Another arm seized her neck covering them both as Wyatt came to her side. "Now we both have a mother," he said squeezing them tight.

"She is a mother for all of us," Eric said as he stepped from behind her and inclined his head. "Welcome to the family, Aria."

Glossary of Terms

Bow and stable – though less noble, was a medieval hunting style, which could produce greater results. The quarry, often a whole herd, would be driven by hounds to a predetermined place, where archers would ready to kill the animals with bow and arrow.

Braies – underpants, fairly loose drawers

Chape - the lowermost terminal mount of a scabbard.

Crenel – any of the open spaces between the merlons of a battlement

Divan – a long, cushioned seat, usually without arms or back, placed against a wall

Fief – a piece of land, formerly granted by a feudal lord to somebody in return of service

Fremd – Old English for alien or strange

Hart – an adult male red deer

Hart of ten – a ten point red deer. Only ten point and higher were considered worthy to hunt.

Kirtle – a woman's loose gown, worn in the Middle Ages.

League – a unit of distance, in English-speaking countries usually estimated roughly at 3 miles

Merlon – (in a battlement) the solid part between the two crenels

Nightrail – a woman's loose garment

Pace – 5 feet

Par fore (or *par force de chiens*) – by 'force of the dogs' or 'by strength': The noblest of hunting styles in the middle ages where the game was run down and exhausted by the dogs before the kill was made in a manner of five set stages.

Rod – Measurement of land, 16.5 feet after 1066.

Shote – young boar

Snood – a netlike hat or part of a hat or fabric that holds or covers the back of a woman's hair.

Soapwort – a plant, of the pink family, whose leaves are used for cleansing.

Steward – the man responsible for running the day-to-day affairs of the castle with the lord was absent

Thane – originally meaning a military companion to the king, a thane was a man holding administrative office

Vellum – calfskin, lambskin, kidskin, etc., treated for use as a writing surface.

About the Author

Michelle Janene (Murray) the office manager/secretary/go-to-gal her her church by day
and writes Christian fantasy and historical fiction in all her free time.
She lives in Northern California with two crazy dogs and the characters of her imagination.

If you enjoyed *Hidden Rebel* please review it on your favorite site.

Join Michelle's email list and get a free novelette at
MichelleJanene.com
You can also connect with Michelle:
Facebook: Michelle Janene-Author or Strong Tower Press
Twitter: @MichelleJaneneM
Instagram: michellejanene_author
Pinterest: www.pinterest.com/michellejanene
Goodreads: Michelle Janene
StrongTowerPress.com

Other Books

Check out these books also by Michelle

Mission: Mistaken Identity

The Changed Heart Series:
God's Rebel
Rebel's Son
<u>*Hidden Rebel*</u>

Seer of Windmere

Barbarian Hero

Guardians of Truth

Culling a Miracle

Lost Stones

The Last Good King

The King's Vengeance

Thice a Bride

Dragon Fire